AN UNCOMFORTABLE TÊTE-À-TÊTE

"Mr. Valentine North, I presume."

"Your servant, Miss Sparrow," he said, not quite looking at her. "Now that you've satisfied your curiosity, you can take yourself off to whatever sinkhole you sprang from. I have serious business which you rudely interrupted, and have no desire to indulge hysterical females succumbing to fits of self-serving rodomontade."

"Ah, I see," she said. Dear heaven, what a paradigm of the worst of the *ton,* the arrogant, puffed-up, self-consequential, heedless toad. "Informing you that last night I was drugged and your wards abducted is hysterical rodomontade. How fascinating. That's an application of the term I'd never envisaged when I had to write out sentences employing it correctly for my governess."

Silence greeted her bitter words. She pulled several pounds from her reticule and tossed them on the floor. "Consider this my notice, effective immediately."

"Where are your glasses?"

She glanced across the room to find North scowling into the middle distance.

"I found I needed them less and less and discarded them, Mr. North. Why? Was it on the basis of my wearing spectacles that you determined I was worthy to have charge of your wards? Inadequate vision appears to be a characteristic you insist your hirelings share with you, as clear vision would lead to their quitting your service on the instant."

"My God, but you've got a waspish tongue."

"Only when addressing those who deserve nothing better."

"Who *are* you, Miss Sparrow," he said, eyes narrowing. . . .

BOOK YOUR PLACE ON OUR WEBSITE
AND MAKE THE
READING CONNECTION!

We've created a customized website just for our very
special readers, where you can get the inside scoop on
everything that's going on with Zebra, Pinnacle and
Kensington books.

When you come online, you'll have the exciting
opportunity to:

- View covers of upcoming books
- Read sample chapters
- Learn about our future publishing schedule
  (listed by publication month *and author*)
- Find out when your favorite authors will be visiting
  a city near you
- Search for and order backlist books from our
  online catalog
- Check out author bios and background information
- Send e-mail to your favorite authors
- Meet the Kensington staff online
- Join us in weekly chats with authors, readers and
  other guests
- Get writing guidelines
- AND MUCH MORE!

**Visit our website at
http://www.zebrabooks.com**

AN
UNCOMMON
GOVERNESS

Monique Ellis

Zebra Books
Kensington Publishing Corp.

http://www.zebrabooks.com

ZEBRA BOOKS are published by

Kensington Publishing Corp.
850 Third Avenue
New York, NY 10022

First Printing: September, 1998
10 9 8 7 6 5 4 3 2 1

Printed in the United States of America

For Jim and Raquel; and Ember, Rain, and River—
With all my love . . .

Chapter One

"Freddy Tyne's gone and done it, by damn!" Valentine North stared in disbelief at the letter in his hand. "Took him donkey's years, but his sticky fingers'll be lightening my purse from now till lilies bloom in hell."

Across the breakfast table, Dabney St. Maure lifted clear gray eyes from the *Morning Post*. "That's a clever trick. Who's Freddy Tyne?"

"The bane of my existence since we were boys. Avoided him as much as possible, but there were times when it wasn't— possible, that is."

North pushed his half-emptied plate away, appetite lost. Around them the breakfast parlor of his London town house gleamed amber and rust in the lemony sunlight of a late winter morning in 1813. On the floor above, the other Irregulars, an informal band devoted to enjoying life's pleasures while avoiding the altar, still snored away their indulgences of the previous evening, too sodden to stagger to their own lodgings, and grateful for his customary hospitality and the tolerance of his elderly staff.

"Well, who is this Tyne?" St. Maure repeated.

"Fearless Freddy? Distant cousin on my mother's side—the

feckless type one keeps out of sight except at weddings and funerals. My father paid for his schooling and bought him his colors.'' North set the letter aside as he stared at his friend in mock despair. ''Expert at guiding one up a tree, then leaving one to extricate oneself as best one can. A few years my senior. Charming, of course. His sort has to be, or starves.''

St. Maure's frown, his glance at old Jitters hovering by the hunt table, were a recommendation for discretion. North shrugged.

''Knew Freddy when we were lads, didn't you, Jitters,'' he said.

''That I did, sir, and a rapscallion he was then too. Sorry to learn of his death.''

''So am I. Freddy's an old military type,'' North explained, turning back to St. Maure. ''Tried to lighten my pockets for the millionth time after he landed in parson's mousetrap about eight years ago. Wife wanted gowns and a carriage and a London establishment. I showed him the door. Not my fault he'd gotten a country girl with child, or that her father cut her off without a *sou*. Heard via the family news service Freddy was posted to Canada soon after. Now he's dead, and Fanny right along with him.''

''Poor fellow.'' St. Maure set his journal aside as a lost cause and helped himself to another muffin. ''Indian raid, I presume? Horrible way to die, especially for a lady.''

''Indian raid?'' North chuckled. ''Not Freddy. Winter storm. They were traveling to a Christmas entertainment by sled, got lost in the snow, and froze. Horses too, from what his colonel says. Fanny loved parties.''

''Dreadful. You shouldn't laugh, Val. Not proper.''

''Freezing's not so bad, they say. Y'simply go to sleep. Freddy probably got the easiest death he could hope for.''

''There's that, of course.''

''Of course there is. I'm not totally heartless.''

''Still don't see what the death of a distant cousin can have to do with you.'' St. Maure's gaze sank back to the journal. ''Doesn't he have any other family?''

''Not to speak of. Told you Fanny was with child when they

wed. Now there're two—Robert, who's seven, and a five-year-old named Tabitha—and I'm to be saddled with 'em as soon as passage can be arranged. Should be here in a month or two.''

"They will? Interesting,'' St. Maure murmured, then let out a low whistle. "Good Lord—Caro Lamb and that Byron idiot've had another public spat. At least I think that's who's meant, or is she still in Ireland? If she is, then it must be someone else. Saddled with both what?''

"Children, blast it. Aren't you listening? Freddy's left them to me—memory of happier days, according to this thing.'' He waved at the close-written pages lying by his plate. "Actually, to slip his fingers in my purse—if only by proxy—for the rest of my natural life. Cleverest trick I've encountered in twenty-nine years of giving as good as I get, but then, Freddy always was clever except when he got Fanny with child. That didn't turn out the way he planned it. Come to think of it, traveling to a ball in a storm wasn't all that intelligent either.''

"You? Oversee a pair of the infantry?''

"For my sins.''

"Well, there's always your mother. She'll know—''

"Afraid not. Hasn't been herself this winter. Rheumatics, according to her abigail, for all Mama doesn't mention it in her letters. I'll be damned if I'll burden her with Freddy's tadpoles, no matter what it takes.''

"You don't burden her, and it'll take quite a bit.''

"I'll manage. Well, I will,'' North insisted at St. Maure's skeptical glance. "I have you fellows, after all. Shouldn't be impossible—settling a pair of brats and paying someone to see to 'em. No need to tell my mother.''

It was late afternoon by the time the remaining Irregulars appeared in North's book room, more or less themselves thanks to Jitters, and calling for flagons of the restorative for which North's antiquated valet and general factotum was famous.

News of North's change in circumstances, once heads cleared and spirits mellowed, had the band chortling.

One of their sort, cursed with a pair of rug-crawlers? No

matter how great the depths of irresponsibility to which North claimed his cousin had previously sunk, this, they declared to a man, surpassed them all. North would fail. His wards would become cutpurses or worse. As for setting up a reputable establishment for them given he had no intention of taking them into his home, the notion was ludicrous. That he refused to involve even Aaron Burridge, his canny man of business, called forth sad shakings of the head and much casting of pained glances at the ceiling.

"Y'might at least consult your mother," Stephen Clough—accurately dubbed Stubby—suggested, shoving short, muscular fingers through his taffy-colored locks as the amused protests subsided. "Or mine, given Lady Kathryn's at Hillcrest."

"My mother hasn't been well," North returned with fading patience.

"One of your sisters, then."

"Impossible. Christina's just been brought to bed of another boy, and Georgiana's expecting her first in March. Besides, Freddy left 'em to me, blast it. It's up to me to see to them."

"Best way t'do that is turn all over to someone who knows something about it."

"Fustian. Plenty of agencies for servants and such. That's how my mother did it when she was in Town."

"But they've got to live somewhere. Y'know—a roof over their heads."

"Places're always being advertised. 'Superior gentleman's residence available to discriminating tenant,' that sort of thing. Make 'em come to me with the particulars. Set up the downstairs reception room as an office, give a false name, and pretend to be my own secretary."

"Y'said Freddy Tyne was a fool. No reason for you to copy him," Clough pressed. "I know y'think I've not that much in my brainbox, but I'm beginning to believe you've got even less. How about my great-aunt Augusta if you won't consult your mother or mine? Always had a fondness for you, and she's in Town. She'd have all organized on the instant."

"No." Visions of the superannuated grande dame had North

shuddering. "Not that I'm not fond of the old dragon, but I'll muddle through on my own, thank you."

"And make a mull of it," Clough muttered, subsiding with a sigh.

They sprawled on sofas and chairs covered in buttery maroon leather, the draperies drawn, a brisk fire on the grate, saying little but looking much once all seconded Clough's opinions.

Nothing North said in support of his capabilities made an impression. Quite the contrary: He would come a cropper. He'd take a house with inadequate drains, smoking chimneys, and a leaking roof. He'd hire a governess with more in her past than a Borgia and less in her attic than a sparrow, or he'd fall into any of a dozen other traps. In the end, he'd be forced to consult those wiser heads he claimed were superfluous.

"Over my dead body," North protested, now with an edge to his voice. "See to Hillcrest well enough, blast it. A major estate's considerably more complicated than a pair of bib-droolers. Has to be a simple matter, when all's said and done. Nothing to it."

"How much?" Quintus Dauntry rumbled from where he lolled slightly apart from the others, leg propped on a stool to ease the ache of a wound incurred at Salamanca in July of '12.

"How much what, Quint?"

Knowing black eyes taunted North from beneath lowered lids. "I presume you're going to make this interesting for the rest of us?" Dauntry drawled.

"You've my leave to watch if you wish. Won't have much opportunity for amusement, though, and you'll be forced to apologize when I've proved every last one of you wrong."

"Dull, dear fellow—dull."

"Not our place t'do more'n that," St. Maure protested from the table, where he was avidly devouring a volume of the pseudonymous Isaac Stowaker's famous—or infamous—and chatty *Origins of the Great Families of England, Ireland, and Wales,* several sets of which North had both in Town and at Hillcrest, along with stacks of the equally scandalous—if much shorter—*Extracts,* a legacy from North's grandfather none of the Irregulars questioned too closely.

"Going to play conscience, Dab?" Dauntry's tone barely avoided the caustic. "Of course consciences have their uses, what with goading and barring, and occasionally stinging some poor fellow's soul to remind him what's done and what isn't. No need to keep us on the straight and narrow in this instance, however. A small wager'd do no harm and liven things up considerably, don't you think?"

"It's tedious as turnips now that Boxing Day's past and the weather's too inclement for racing," Tony Sinclair chimed in, green eyes brightening. "Might even tempt Val to pinnacles of effort he's yet to scale, Dab. A highly moral wager with the weight of good intentions behind it. Surprised you didn't suggest the notion yourself."

"Be a sport, Dab," Clough pleaded. "Haven't had a chance at a good wager since Quint drew Chuffy Binkerton's cork for importuning a nursemaid in the Park."

"Y'won't want me wagering on the same side as the rest of you," sighed Pugs Harnette, North's country neighbor and handy with his fives for all he was the least pugnacious of fellows. "I lose every time."

"Not this one." Dauntry grinned. "It'll break the streak. I say we make it fifty pounds each. You'll cover that, won't you, Val?"

"With ease, and double the odds. I'll win too."

"This isn't for the betting book at White's," St. Maure cautioned, "not with children involved. We won't want it public, Quint. No others joining in, and then encouraging disaster. Val's new pets'll be confused enough after such a voyage, and having lost their parents into the bargain."

"We do need a few rules." Dauntry shifted his leg and winced. "Private wager, and Robert and Tabitha aren't to be put at risk, are we agreed? Nor anyone Val employs to see to 'em, nor whatever place he hires for his irregular nursery. We can play adjunct uncles, keep an eye on things, but nothing more. That suit your sensibilities, Dab?"

"If we keep to the rules," St. Maure said as he rose and stretched.

"Since when have we ever—"

"It's not the rules, but the interpretation of them has me a trace concerned. Just so we all understand one another?"

"I'd never put children at risk."

"Not knowingly," St. Maure conceded. "It's just—well, what with one thing and another, matters never seem to go quite as one would expect when you propose a wager."

St. Maure and Dauntry exchanged an understanding look as North watched with a wry grin. Clever, that pair. Ever playing off each other. Their little band might be known as North's Irregulars and he as their leader, but the real heads belonged to Dauntry and St. Maure, and long heads they were.

"We'll guard 'em as if they were Val's own—which in a sense they are," Dauntry assured St. Maure, and by inference commanded the others given his voice carried like a bell on a still night—a vestige of his years under Wellington. "This way all's aboveboard. Otherwise?" His shrug was expressive. "Anything could happen."

That evening North begged off joining the rest at White's for dinner and later at a cockfight, claiming business on behalf of his soon-to-arrive wards.

Instead, after telling Jitters to serve him in his book room, he scanned recent journals and wrote a note requesting particulars regarding a town house on the fringes of Mayfair that came staffed, and was cheap enough. Next he composed the notice to be placed in the morning papers: "Superior governess sought. Dry sticks need not apply. Tolerance of frogs essential." After a moment's consideration he added, "and other wild creatures" after "frogs" to make it clear he wasn't referring to the French. When that didn't do the trick, he changed it to "frogs and mice."

Between bites of roast duck he made lists of essentials: miniature soldiers, a rocking horse, a hoop, balls to throw, kites to fly, a toy sailboat, then—reluctantly—wrote "books" as a general item with attendant question mark. Any governess worth her hire would probably insist on a few. There wasn't much he could do beyond limiting their number. Plenty of time for books when one went away to school—another thing he'd probably have to consider. That, or a tutor for the boy. Blast, but it was getting complicated.

Under the encouragement of a modest glass of brandy he waxed enthusiastic over ponies, tack, and a groom experienced in teaching bib-droolers to ride.

A second more generous glass and a cigarillo brought to mind a carriage to take them to places of educational value such as Astley's Amphitheater, and inspired a hack for the governess as well as the requirement that whoever sought the position be able to ride, and to drive a dogcart. A passing acquaintance with the arts of fencing and cricket wouldn't be amiss either.

He frowned as he considered assorted livestock under the encouragement of what was either a fourth or fifth portion of brandy, finally determined a puppy would suit best by requiring healthful walks in the park, and added one to his list.

Duty done, he leaned back and pondered how best to handle the situation on a personal level. He had no desire to see the children. Certain to make 'em cry, all else aside. What could he say to them, after all? "I'm sorry your mother was so foolish as to freeze to death?" "I'm devastated your father hadn't the sense to remain safely by his fire?" Good Lord, no! Unthinkable. Besides, with the exception of Christina's brood, children terrified him. He'd be good for little more than pats on the head and chuckings under the chin, and he remembered those with loathing. Better to stay out of their lives until they reached an age when he could awe the girl with trinkets and the boy with a round at Gentleman Jackson's.

He didn't want to deal with the governess either, except to hand all over to her and leave it at that. No entrapments for him. He'd learned to be wary during the past few Seasons. The strategies of marriage-minded mamas were as ingenious as they were underhanded. It wouldn't surprise him for one to pass her daughter off as the latest thing in governesses, then scream rape and demand a swift trip to the altar.

His first notion—turning an unused reception room into an office and pretending to be his own secretary—had more than a little to recommend it. The name was easy: Tidmarsh. It possessed a convincing ring of persnicketiness. Pericles Tidmarsh—that's who he'd be in honor of a long-ago Latin tutor with a predilection for tortuous phrases and an unlikely passion for Ovid.

The trouble was, even he realized his close to six feet of dark-haired, dark-blue-eyed, athletically inclined, elegant gentleman-about-Town in no way resembled the usual secretary. Especially not one calling himself Pericles Tidmarsh. There was no need to consult the pier glass in his dressing room to determine that. His height was against him. His shoulders were against him. His toggery was against him. His very tone and bearing were against him. He needed help. Since it didn't have to do with Freddy's tadpoles directly, assistance in becoming Tidmarsh wouldn't lose him the wager.

North tugged on the bell rope, shrugged on his coat, then folded his lists and tucked them in a pocket.

"Have this placed where it'll do the most good," he said when Jitters appeared, handing him the notice for a governess able to stare down a popeyed frog without having the vapors. "This other one's about a house, and needs to be carried 'round. I'm going out. Not certain when I'll return, but it won't be early unless it's early tomorrow."

"Going to visit Mrs. Sherbrough, sir?" Jitters said with a resigned look.

"I've a need of a woman's touch to sort out this mess."

"Captain Tyne's offspring, I presume."

"And attendant problems. If any of the lads happen by in need of a bed, help them to their usual rooms."

"Naturally," Jitters murmured, shuffling toward the fireplace. "I always do, sir, if Mr. Bassett and Webster are otherwise occupied. Beds're made up and waiting."

North paused by the door. "Would you ask Pickles what's required for little girls? I've a notion I've left something out."

"Mrs. Pickles, sir? What would a housekeeper know of girls?"

"She was one once, wasn't she?"

"A long time ago, sir. Not much use now."

"Maybe I'll ask Chloe," North murmured.

"An excellent notion, sir. Better yet, you might write Lady Kathryn."

"I'll not have my mother's peace cut up," North repeated for what felt like the hundredth time that day, and fled his book room.

Chloe Sherbrough, customarily up to anything, proved unequal to the task of advising North where five-year-old girls were concerned.

Her playthings, she informed him once she'd stifled her laughter at the notion of his being anyone's guardian, had been her mother's paint pots and her father's shaved decks of cards—surely not what he had in mind. Moppets were reported to delight in dolls. Beyond that, who knew? He'd do best to consult his mother, or some other respectable female accustomed to the foibles of gently born children.

North rolled his eyes, stalked to the drinks table, and poured himself a glass of the excellent brandy with which he kept Chloe's cellar stocked, then paced the elegant little drawing room. He was accustomed to being regarded with indulgent amusement by his current mistress. Normally he liked it, believing it proved him a dashing fellow. Attracting a woman a few years one's senior was quite the thing. Tonight her twinkling violet eyes rankled.

Why did everyone assume he was an idiot, blast it! He could be as sober and responsible as any man when the occasion demanded. It was just that he customarily organized his life so such occasions didn't arise beyond seeing to Hillcrest and the welfare of its people with a devotion he knew bordered on the fanatic.

He felched up at the Adam chimney surround, stared absently into the fire, then glanced up, lips twisting at the hazy reflection of Chloe's figure superimposed on the floral watercolor above him. That such an earthy female could present such an appearance of delicacy and refinement always intrigued him. One tended to forget what she was most of the time. At least he did.

"What about a place for them to live?" he pleaded, turning and propping an elbow on the mantel. "You'll help me there at least, won't you? Go with me to see it?"

"My dear Val, were I to appear on the scene, it would be assumed you were hiring a residence for a very different purpose—hardly the end you desire."

"Nonsense. It's well known I've got this little pied-à-terre. Have for eons."

"Indeed it is—in certain circles. Unfortunately, even among those we've entertained, it might be believed you were only seeking a more convenient location in which to keep me. The appearance of children soon after would lead to highly logical— if incorrect—conclusions. I doubt you'd want that."

"We've been together only six months," he protested, tugging at a neckcloth that was suddenly far too tight. "Hardly time enough for that, even if either of us were so careless as to permit it to happen."

He had the notion she was biting her lips not to make them swell and pout as she usually did, but to keep from indulging in the countrified guffaws that escaped her in unguarded moments.

"Val, be serious," she managed to say at last. "No matter what you think, even my most restrained pelisse and bonnet proclaim my calling. Too many feathers and ribbons, too daring a cut, and far too spectacular hues. No, unless you want your wards to become an instant scandal, you'd best leave me out of your arrangements."

"B-but what about finding a governess?" With a sigh he came and sat across from her, forearms on his knees, cradling his glass to warm the brandy. He thought of running his fingers through her jet curls, decided against it. He didn't need distractions at the moment. Incomprehensibly, even her lush lips didn't appeal. "I'd counted on you for that. You could play the part of my spinster cousin."

"I, a spinster cousin? Ridiculous. Don't come the helpless schoolboy with me, Val. I know you too well. Besides, what acquaintance do I have with governesses other than the ones I've played on the stage? No, my dear—you're on your own in this."

"It's not fair," North grumbled.

"Very little in life is. Seek your mother's guidance. She'll know what to do, and be delighted by a little activity. The winter months are so dreary in the country."

"I will not importune my mother," North snapped. "Hasn't been quite up to snuff, according to her abigail's interminable reports. Besides, I'll be damned if I'll have her coming to Town and shoving every milk-and-water miss of her acquaintance under my nose in hopes of a grandchild."

"Turn the matter over to Mr. Burridge, then. He's sure to be capable of arranging everything."

"Old Burridge wouldn't know any more about children than I do. Doubt he even understands how they're gotten. Besides, I made a wager. With the fellows," he added at Chloe's inquiring glance. "Got to organize it all myself. They say I'll make a mull of it. Well, I won't. You're certain you don't know what a little girl'd need?"

"Other than pretty clothes, I'm afraid not."

"Blast! I suppose my only recourse is to find a toy shop and order one of everything."

"Heavens, no." Chloe stretched catlike, running dimpled fingers through her tousled curls. "Such riches would confuse the poor mite, arriving from some snowbound forest primeval as she will be. Why—Tabitha, isn't it—may not even know how to eat at table, let alone play with anything but sticks and dried leaves. Lord knows I didn't at that age, and I was born in England. Chances are she'll arrive garbed like a red Indian, smear herself with bear grease, and bolt her food like a piglet."

"Never thought of that. Be just like Freddy to raise 'em as savages. He'd think it a glorious prank."

"Why not leave all to the governess? She'll be certain to know what's best."

"A governess know what's best? Dull books and duller

sermons, and constant moralizing—which happens to be their preferred activity—best? At least that's what my sisters' was like during the period I was cursed with her. School was a welcome release. Wouldn't even let me keep a frog in the nursery. I won't have Freddy's posterity stifled in that manner. No, whatever harpy I hire, she's going to receive strict orders as to what she's permitted and what she's not.''

Chloe gave vent to a sigh that would've set ships careening across the ocean. ''What'll you do, then? You must have some plan or other.''

''Pretend to be my own secretary, I'd thought. That should assure I'm not overcharged. Even have a name for him: Pericles Tidmarsh. Really why I came to see you. I need to become an oldish fellow like Burridge—the sort who shuffles and dithers, and peers at one over his spectacles.''

''Mr. Burridge does none of those things when he delivers my allowance, and he certainly doesn't require spectacles. He's a fine figure of a man.''

''No need to fly into a pet.'' Her eyes fell before his. Odd, that. ''If I wanted old Burridge,'' he sighed, ''I'd *get* old Burridge. Thing is, he'd notify my mother—aside from which I lose the wager if I turn the problem over to anyone. No, I want to be a horror no governess'll find attractive. I'm familiar with those roles you've played, and I haven't the slightest intention of being caught in parson's mousetrap by a female cleverer and more determined than I.''

Chapter Two

Lady Amelia Peasebottom shivered, poring over the morning papers in the faint light filtering through the lodging house's attic window. Rain mixed with sleet slashed the panes, streaking the grime without washing it away.

She'd been in London for three discouraging weeks, each day seeing her precious horde of pounds and shillings dwindle. Even exchanging a bedchamber for this arctic hell hadn't helped much. She should, she realized now, have taken the first position she happened on, and be damned to the roving eye of the widowed master of the house. His pretensions would have been easy enough to depress.

Nothing had offered since, for no reputable agency would represent her. A governess without references? Without experience? Without so much as a list of the schools she'd attended or letters containing the panegyrics of teachers and headmistress?

She shivered again in the stubborn draft, sneezed, and pulled her cloak more tightly about her, huddling on the trunk she'd dragged by the window to serve as a chair, and ignoring the nearby scrabblings that betrayed a foraging mouse.

It was discouraging. Eyes that kept young cousins in check under the most trying circumstances while still permitting one to be a favorite among the nursery set counted for nothing. As for an unmistakable air of elegance no matter how one was garbed, that was a detriment of the worst sort. The narrowed looks, the stern injunction that earning one's bread wasn't for those who found their personal circumstances temporarily less than appealing, had been all too knowing.

She had those essential documents now—or at least Miss Abigail Sparrow did—one written in a hand that mimicked the Countess of Pease's arrogantly illegible penmanship to perfection, and proclaimed Miss Sparrow a paragon. All added five years to her own twenty-two, as twenty-seven seemed a far more reasonable age for an experienced, if youthful, governess. It had been purest luck she'd slipped several sheets of vellum bearing the family crest in her reticule, intending to use them for a diary.

The worst was that she couldn't apply where she might be recognized. Caps, dowdy gowns, spectacles perched on the tip of one's nose, and a muddy caste to one's golden curls could disguise one only so far. While generally no more attention was paid to servants than to a stick of wood, it would be just her luck to have some acquaintance pause, brows rising— or, more likely, a hireling whose position demanded superior powers of observation. Given she didn't want to pass herself off as her father's by-blow, that eliminated nine tenths of the private notices.

It was, she admitted with a sigh as she set one journal aside and picked up the next, a problem whose magnitude she hadn't realized when fleeing Bottomsley Court. Then she'd believed her greatest challenge would be selecting among droves of offers. Precisely those traits that made a disaster of her come-out four years previously, and placed her firmly on the shelf ever since, should've assured that if only logic were considered.

Unfortunately, the ladies of the *ton* managed their affairs on premises that had little to do with logic. She was, she'd been informed until she was forced to believe it, far too young to be a governess, and far too pretty, even if she'd failed at Almack's.

She scanned the next group of notices. One requested the

services of a nurse-companion for Lady Augusta C—. Impossible. The old lady had apartments in her nephew's house, and was received everywhere. If Amelia remembered the autocratic dragon so clearly, she was sure to remember Amelia.

The next almost set her to laughing. A professional duenna was required for the two younger daughters of the Earl and Countess of P—, who would be making their country come-outs in York that May. So the earl had refused to spring for a London Season, just as he'd threatened when she failed to take. What would her parents do if she turned up on their doorstep requesting the post? Dear heaven, they'd kill her, though perhaps they'd permit her a final meal first. She could do with one.

Her eyes strayed to an article containing the latest *ton* tattle. Heart in mouth, she devoured it. Either God or Fate was kind: There was no mention of a Sir Reginald W— or a Mrs. Alfreda W— of Chilcomb Manor somewhat to the south of Manchester.

But, he'd come. No question. London drew Reginald Whifler like a bone drew a dog. No, make that a cur. A foul-breathed, sly-eyed cur who had unaccountably become one of the earl's favorite companions during one of his forays to Brighton. They drank together. They ate together. They wagered together. She assumed they whored together. They were such bosom bows that the earl had purchased Sir Reginald as her future husband.

Her shudder this time had nothing to do with drafts. Only that term fit. Sir Reginald, ever garbed in black in imitation of the famous Brummell, had been purchased at debilitating expense so her younger sisters could make their come-outs and marry well, rescuing the family fortunes. Retirement to Bath had been forbidden. No matter that Bath would have been far less costly than Sir Reginald. The eldest daughters of earls weren't permitted the humiliation of spinsterhood. They married no matter what the expense or how insufferable the bridegroom with whom they were cursed. At least the eldest daughter of the Earl and Countess of Pease did.

Only, she didn't—not the real Lady Amelia. Instead, she rejected martyrdom and planned carefully, fluttering her lashes at Sir Reginald while secretly acquiring ready-made garments in York when seeing to bride clothes. A sudden "sick head-ache," a bedchamber in which to recover at one of York's better inns, the dismissal of her abigail, and a crown changing hands so she could slip out the back way had ensured the essential liberty.

She'd packed her purchases in a cheap portmanteau, and left it at an undistinguished inn to be collected by "Sophronia Wilde" the following week.

She'd determined a mixture of watercolor pigment, coal dust, and coffee worked into a paste and permitted to coat the hair for ten minutes yielded the desired muddiness.

She'd traveled more or less openly to Bristol, wasting precious pounds to lay a false trail ending at the docks, then used her own name and created a fuss when making inquiries regarding passage to the American Colonies so she'd be remembered. There was no way the earl could trace her from there even if he tried, but he was more likely to have shrugged and claimed her forever beyond reach, especially as she'd left her jewelry—the legacy of her mother's childless aunt, of whom she'd been a favorite—at the court. He'd consider the valuable pieces adequate recompense for the loss of a daughter.

Amelia sighed, wondering if she dared sneak down the back stairs and beg a scrap of yesterday's bread and a cheese rind from the cook. Her purse extended to only a single meal a day now, and it was hours until evening.

Her landlady's harsh voice floated up the stairwell.

No, it wouldn't do. Ignoring the grumbling of her stomach, she continued to search the journals for the sort of employer her situation demanded.

"Miss Abigail Sparrow," Jitters said, closing the door of the converted reception room behind him, "concerning the matter of the governess who will have charge of Mr. North's wards, sir."

"Oh, very well," North grumbled with a peevishness befitting Pericles Tidmarsh, overburdened secretary, sweeping the dice with which he'd been amusing himself into a drawer.

He drained the last of his claret and handed Jitters the glass. "Might as well get it over with. Show the woman in. Probably as unsuitable as all the rest. I'd've thought mentioning a partiality to frogs was clear enough, but apparently not."

He sat at the writing table and shuffled some papers, his back to the windows down which sleet mixed with rain slid like oil. The coal fire in the chimney hissed, casting a warm glow over the litter he'd spread as what Chloe termed "stage dressing."

He'd proved an apt pupil. Shawls swathed his shoulders and torso. Mitts with the tips cut off masked strong hands Chloe had taught to mimic an occasional palsied tremor. Ink stains further confused the issue. Gray wig, spectacles, rusty coat, hump, severe black cravat, and a querulous voice more high-pitched than his customary velvet baritone completed a disguise good enough to have fooled even St. Maure, who'd stopped by earlier and been witness to one fruitless—and hilarious—interview.

The door opened again. Light steps crossed the floor, stopped. North playacted, peering at scraps of paper on which he scribbled in an illegible hand.

Then, without lifting his eyes, he barked, "Sit. I ain't partial to hovering females, and my notes're in code so y'won't be able to make sense of 'em. My master's business ain't your business, not any of it."

There was a rustle—not the soft sibilance of silk, but the dull whisper of shoddy goods. Well, what had he expected, a Paris confection?

The chair facing him across the table shifted. The sudden whiff of lilacs, given earlier experience, was anachronous. Eau de peppermint or essence de camphor were more usual. There might be hope for this one.

He peered over his spectacles. Dear Lord—another Medusa, complete with what little hair peeped from beneath cap and bonnet writhing in snakelike bands, and a complexion washed of color. A miracle he hadn't been turned to stone the instant he glimpsed the dried-up stick facing him.

"Should've kept a burnished shield by me, or a silver platter at the least, way this day's gone," he muttered.

The twitch at the corner of the fright's lips proved his voice had the carrying power he'd intended. It also proved the current Medusa—against all expectations—had a sense of humor despite the spectacles perched on the tip of what might have been an elegant nose if framed by more prepossessing features.

"Abigail Sparrow, is it?" he growled to cover his embarrassment. It wasn't the poor soul's fault she was a torment to the eyes. "Well, what're you here for? Position as governess, I'll warrant, hey-hey? You've the name for it, at least."

The woman flushed and nodded, clutching her cloak about her, rusty coal-scuttle bonnet wobbling.

"Well, ain't you going to give me my name?" he said in another attempt to unsettle her.

As with referring to the most famous of the Gorgons, the question had worked with the others. This one merely shook her head.

"I can't, sir. The notice gave only an address," she said.

The voice didn't fit, thank the Lord. He'd expected nails on a slate as well as a lecture. Instead, he was being treated to a mellow viola.

"Pericles Tidmarsh, secretary," he said more mildly. "Acting for Mr. Valentine North in the matter of his wards. Infantry, both of 'em: Robert Tyne, seven, and Tabitha, five. Distant connections of Mr. North's. Been living in the Colonies. Probably little better'n heathens. Not due for a few weeks, but if you're hired you'll be paid and housed from today. Lot t'do preparing for 'em. Y'got a firm hand?"

"I believe so."

"Believe! Don't you know?" North demanded, tone wavering between his own and Tidmarsh's. "I should think any governess worthy of the designation would know whether her hand was firm or light."

"I don't approve of striking children, if that's what you mean by a heavy hand."

"Even when they deserve it?"

"There usually are other methods of handling childish infractions,'' the stick proclaimed with pursed lips, heightened color, and elevated chin, ''just as there are skittish mounts.''

Well, he'd grant she had the right of that. At least in his case there always had been, worse luck. A birching was swiftly over. Translating unending pages of Ovid for penance took considerably longer.

''Or impertinent gentlemen,'' she added as if in afterthought, giving him a narrowed glance.

He felt the flush reach his ears at that thrust. ''Up to running a household?''

Miss Sparrow raised her brows. Odd. This query had set the others first to bristling, and then falling into raptures. He waited.

''You're seeking a combination housekeeper and govern-ess?'' she finally responded, doubt rather than outrage in her tone. ''How unusual.''

''Lord, no. Place's already got one, but a housekeeper's only as good as the mistress who oversees her. Not a grand establishment like this, mind you. Not needed for the infantry, but Mr. North wants it run properly.''

''The children won't be residing with their guardian, then?''

''Trim his sails too close, having bib-droolers about.''

''I see,'' the woman murmured.

How he wished the rest of her fit that voice. If it had, Freddy's tadpoles would've taken to her on the instant. Unfortunately, from the top of her clumsy bonnet to the tips of her thick boots, this pathetic, faded instructress was a caricature of the type, even if she couldn't have more than twenty-some summers to her credit.

''House is already hired,'' he continued. ''Furnishings ain't new, but it's clean and has a decent address. Staffed, so y'won't be having to worry yourself about that.''

''I see.''

Didn't she know any other phrase? Blast, but she was inscru-table. It'd never occurred to him a female might prefer selecting those over whom she had authority. Certainly the others had raised no objection. Besides, what would a governess know about staffing a house in Town, even a small one?

''All concerning the household'd be left to you. There'd best be no problems. And no, Mr. North don't want to see his wards. You either. Why should he?''

"What a cold, unfeeling monster he must be," Miss Sparrow murmured. "The perfect gentleman of the *ton.*''

"What would one of his sort know about the infantry, for pity's sake? Or want to do with them? Rug-crawlers're best left to females, who have an affinity for 'em given they're both feather-brained.''

The jaw firmed. The gloved hands clenched in the lap, fingers twisting. The chin lifted again. So—at least one barb had sunk home. A stinging one, from the look of her.

"Y'know globes?'' he snapped, turning the subject.

"And literature, watercolors, how to play on the pianoforte and harp, history, mathematics, philosophy, Latin, French, a little Gr—''

"Ain't asked you about any of that. Brats probably haven't had any schooling to speak of. If they can count to ten when prompted, know half their alphabet, and use a spoon when eating rather than their fingers, that's the most you can expect.''

"Dear me.''

Well, at least it wasn't another "I see.''

"The position ain't a sinecure, if that's what you were hoping.'' He leaned back and rested his elbows on the chair arms, steepling his fingers and continuing to regard her over the gold rims of his fake spectacles. "What's your opinion of Astley's? Ever hear of it?''

"An excellent reward for excellent behavior.''

"Madame Tussaud's?''

"A venue for those who can, according to age, recite the kings of England in chronological order or, by visiting there and having their curiosity sparked by judiciously lurid tales, be encouraged to learn the same.''

"The Royal Menagerie?''

"A living text from which to instruct children regarding the wonders of God's world.''

"Vauxhall? Sadler's Wells? Brighton in the summer?''

"Not for children.''

"Walks in Hyde Park?''

"Lessons in natural history and botany, and the sailing of toy boats and flying of kites with attendant instruction on the power of the wind. The exuberance of the young must be dissipated in healthful and instructive fashion, or one risks losing one's mind in attempts to curb their innate proclivity for mischief."

Stuffy. Pedantic. Almost a parody of the type except for the glorious sense of the ridiculous. And the voice. It beckoned and soothed, inviting one to drown in the billows of a tropic ocean or soar like an eagle above magical mountains. He'd be comparing every other female's to it unfavorably until the day he died. That such a voice could issue from such a faded slip of a thing was incongruous. "Frogs?"

"In the garden. *Strictly* in the garden, but worthy of observation. More interesting than worms or snails, but only marginally. Not to be teased."

"Dear Lord, I wish you'd been *my* governess," he murmured. "Wasn't even permitted to watch 'em playing. 'Course, they weren't exactly playing, doubled up like that." She blushed, but she didn't attempt to strike him with her umbrella as two others had. Not missish, then. "Visits to the London docks?"

"Impossible unless accompanied by their guardian."

"Afraid you'd say that. Possibly one of their courtesy uncles'll stand buff. North won't—you can count on that."

"Courtesy uncles?"

"There'll be some fellows stopping by, friends of North's," he explained, manner and tone continuing to waver between his own and the one he'd assigned Tidmarsh. "He's charged 'em with overseeing the brats, and making sure you do your job properly."

"I see."

There it was again—the damned "I see."

"Y'got references, I presume, hey-hey," he said, coming erect as he donned the mantle of Pericles Tidmarsh with more assurance.

Indeed she did. The letter, what little he could decipher of it, was complimentary. She'd been employed in an earl's household? And given what the countess considered satisfactory—even praiseworthy—service? Not bad. He scowled at the signature, then shrugged, folded the letter, and returned it to her after pretending to examine the contents in more detail than was possible given the execrable penmanship. The letters from former headmistresses were the usual puffery. He barely glanced at those before returning them as well.

"Seems in order. The position's yours if you want it. You ride, I presume?"

"Actually, I do."

"Excellent. Not a one of the others did. Seemed incensed by the notion. Mr. North's already acquired ponies for the pair, set up a stable in the mews behind the house—no expense spared. What d'you want in the way of a mount for yourself?"

He could tell she was struggling with the answer. Finally she said, "Whatever Mr. North considers suitable," she said. "Perhaps something already in his stable."

"In North's stable?" he snorted. "Nothing for a lady there, believe me. How d'you feel about puppies and kittens?"

"Unfortunately, they have a nasty habit of turning into dogs and cats. Children lose interest rapidly."

"Nonsense. Having pets teaches 'em responsibility."

"And here I'd always believed pets taught servants responsibility," she murmured. "Goodness, to think I've been so deep in error all these years."

North felt his ears grow warm, as well as his face.

"Yes, well," he choked.

Sense of humor? A keen one. Highly out of keeping with employment in the home of a gentleman, even if that gentleman was somewhat removed. Indeed, the more he thought of it, the more he realized Miss Sparrow had a manner unlike that of every other female who'd sought the post. The household in which she'd previously earned her keep must have been more than a trifle eccentric.

Peasebottom. Bottomsley Court. He had a notion he'd encountered the Earl of Pease once or twice. The name was paired in his mind with unsound wagers and a pudgy wagerer often in his cups. Beyond that, he had no idea who they might be. Country sorts, he supposed. That, or unusually high in the instep—though that didn't seem probable given their former employee.

"Regarding the matter of remuneration," she suggested.

"Ah, that. Yes. You'll be housed and fed, of course. There'll be funds for purchasing clothing, toys, and educational materials for the children, and for taking them on junkets. And there'll be a household account. The housekeeper—that's Hortense Grimble, motherly sort, completely trustworthy; her husband's the butler—will see to that, but you're to check her figures weekly as a matter of form, just as any mistress does." North opened the center drawer, retrieved a fistful of banknotes, and dealt a hundred pounds. "As to your remuneration for services rendered, will this be adequate as a deposit?" He placed the stack in the center of the writing table.

"More than adequate," she said, eyes widening.

The eyes didn't fit the usual image either, he noted with approval. The rest had peered at him through thick spectacles, their expressions vague, or else possessed a sharp and knowing squint. Above spectacles apparently intended only for reading, hers were a clear, intriguingly changeable hazel that appeared green or amber or gold according to how she turned her head. He was beginning to wonder if the very best governesses responded to advertisements. It was entirely possible they were passed from family to family, just as his sisters' had been. He was fortunate this one had shown up.

"It's in the nature of a deposit," he explained, "not your actual salary. For each week that passes during which you find it unnecessary to consult me, you'll receive an additional five pounds. However, you'll forfeit ten pounds each time you seek advice or instructions. What remains at the end of the year is yours to keep, and we'll start the next year with another hundred pounds. I assume that's agreeable."

"I demand to see Mr. North," she snapped, drawing herself up. "Immediately!"

"Not agreeable, then." That was interesting. The others had leapt at the chance. His estimation of Miss Sparrow rose another notch. This one was passing every test he and Chloe had devised. "All right, we'll reduce your forfeit to a pound per consultation rather than ten. Better?"

"I wish to see Mr. North."

"I'm afraid that's impossible, Miss Sparrow."

Her brows soared.

"He is, ah, otherwise occupied."

"At Gentleman Jackson's, no doubt, or one of the less salubrious hells. Very well, I'll wait."

"Actually"—North grinned—"he's tending to important business in a most responsible manner. You'd be amazed were I to explain the extent of his charitable instincts and sense of duty."

"Wagering on a mill, then," she muttered.

"In this season? With the weather we've been having? Oh, come now!"

She blushed again. Rosily. He liked that.

"Well," he said, "will you accept the post?"

She nodded. "Certainly those poor children will need someone who views them as more than an inconvenience," she said.

He shoved the hundred pounds toward her.

"They will indeed. Take it. Word of warning: I'm serious about neither Mr. North nor I being troubled with his wards and their concerns. You come complaining and you'll be charged a pound each time, just as I said. Naturally you'll be rewarded for each week that passes during which you don't seek advice. You'll learn to make decisions quickly enough under those circumstances. Consider yourself their mother. Lord knows, you can't help but make a better job of it than their own did."

Amelia opened her umbrella against the chilling wet and scurried along the pavement, waving off the jarvey trailing her in hope of a fare. She had no intention of squandering a small fortune on a hackney—not even if she did have Mr. North's hundred pounds hidden where no cutpurse could find it without causing a scandal. No, not even though Mr. Tidmarsh had provided her with additional funds from his own purse to defray the expense of removal to the house hired for her future charges.

Additional funds? He'd tossed the five-pound note at her as if it were a spill for lighting tapers.

What an oddity he was. One would expect a certain starchiness of the secretary to a *tonnish* gentleman in comfortable circumstances—and certainly the appointments of both entry and office had proclaimed Mr. North at least modestly comfortable. All had been modern, simple, and in the best of taste, if somewhat stark. No feminine touch allowed on Wilton Street, that was certain.

As for Mr. Tidmarsh, he'd been more schoolboy plotting pranks than secretary seeing to a pair of orphans. As they said: Like master, like servant. She'd obtained a good notion of her employer's character during those minutes in the comfortably heated and well-appointed office. It was no wonder the secretary's tone wavered between courteous and testy. While Mr. Tidmarsh hadn't put such a name to it, the terms he'd stipulated had all the earmarks of a wager inscribed in the betting book of a gentleman's club: her wits against Mr. North's, and winner take all.

Well, Mr. North would learn he'd met his match. At the end of a year she'd have those hundred pounds intact, plus the additional two hundred and sixty. Three hundred and sixty pounds for a gentleman's wager was a paltry sum, given what she knew of her father's indulgence in the impoverishing amusement. But, as a year's salary for a governess? Unheard-of riches. Mr. North had best look to his pockets, for she intended to lighten them considerably.

Amelia rounded the corner, skirting puddles and praying her good fortune would hold. To think she almost hadn't answered the odd advertisement. Tabitha Tyne was only five. That meant years of employment. Twelve at the least, by which time she'd be in her mid-thirties, and have saved over—she did the calculation in her head, and almost laughed—three thousand pounds!

She'd consider then what came next, a matter she hadn't thought of when planning her flight from the court—or else hadn't dared for fear she'd find the future beyond reaching London too daunting, and so lose courage. God bless Captain Tyne for appointing Valentine North the guardian of his children, and Mr. North for being a bachelor disposed to thrust his responsibilities on others.

The important thing now was that by that night she'd be comfortably domiciled. No more counting pennies in the hope counted pennies would stretch vanishing pounds farther than pounds had ever stretched before. No more burned potatoes or watery stews. No more being looked at askance by her landlady, whom she had taken to paying by the day rather than the week. No more frigid attic or thin straw pallet and ragged quilt. No more fear an elevated guest would pass her in the entry of some modestly respectable household, recognize her, and summon the hounds of hell.

Umbrella low against the stinging sleet, she dodged a clump of refuse, then a solitary pedestrian scurrying in the opposite direction. It was coming on to the frigid dusk of a day that had almost ended in despair.

Fearing a foray so deep in Mayfair despite the season and the inclement weather, she'd responded to the unsigned notice only when all the other posts about which she inquired proved filled. Luck had been with her: Not a soul she recognized anywhere. More to the point, not a soul who recognized her.

Better yet, once she'd found Wilton Street, a few questions of a delivery boy had revealed the advertiser to be an untitled gentleman unknown to her. His predicament was, the boy had said, grinning, all the talk belowstairs, with wagers being laid as to this event forcing him to succumb to parson's mousetrap at last. Best of all, given her fear of being unmasked, Mr. North's mother resided in the country, and rarely darkened his door.

Mr. North had ought to've summoned his mam was the general opinion, the lad had said before descending the area steps two houses away—not that belowstairs opinions counted for much in the great world, which was a good thing by his lights. He'd laid two coppers on Mr. North coming a cropper.

Amelia chuckled at the thought, gaze directed at the slippery, uneven pavement. The reclusive Mr. North, forced to a step he had no desire to take? From Mr. Tidmarsh's few comments about their employer, she feared the delivery boy had made a poor investment. Mr. North knew precisely what he wanted, and even more precisely how to get it: The continuation of a hedonistic life unfettered by the responsibility of a pair of unwanted wards, his soul untrammeled, his pleasures uninterrupted, and a governess bribed to see they remained so. He'd have her full cooperation.

There was no way to be certain how it happened.

One moment she was battling the wind-driven mixture of sleet and rain, head lowered, thoughts abstracted, boots and ankles sodden. The next she was skidding into a spongy mountain that emitted an incensed "Oof," or else it skidded into her. She landed in a puddle, icy water soaking through cloak and gown, her bonnet crushed, her face splattered with mud, her umbrella collapsing over broken spokes.

She shook her head to clear it.

The gathering crowd shouted of magistrates and thieves and females who were no better than they should be, hands tearing at her cloak. Above the cacophony soared the voice of a gentleman demanding a constable be summoned, and raining imprecations on her head for marring his favorite boots.

Chapter Three

"What d'you want, Jitters? And why bring my coat and boots here? I'll be up in a bit to dress. Won't be meeting the fellows until nine. Plenty of time yet."

The entryway brouhaha that had begun with businesslike pounding on his front door a few minutes earlier had North indolently curious, though not curious enough to investigate. It had been a long and arduous day. Interviewing addlepated harpies was not his notion of the manner in which a gentleman should pass his time. Freddy must be splitting his sides, wherever he found himself.

"You're needed, sir."

"Really?" he demanded, cocking a brow. "What's to do?"

"It's Miss Sparrow."

"Already? How lowering. Assumed she was more resourceful than that."

"In the custody of a constable, sir."

Jitters's tone had North swinging his morocco-slippered feet from the fender, brandy set aside, letters from Hillcrest abandoned. "What the devil?" he said.

"Accompanied by a Mr. Binkerton."

"Chuffy Binkerton? Why does that scoundrel forever insist on cutting up my peace?"

"It's rather Miss Sparrow's he's cut up, sir. Apparently she ran into him, or he ran into her—there's some confusion on that point—in the wet. Miss Sparrow ended on the pavement, sodden as a newborn chick. He's charging assault and battery, theft of a hundred pounds, and demanding Newgate at the least and transportation by preference. Seems she damaged his boots."

"Good Lord."

"Precisely, sir. Contrariwise, she claimed she is in your employ, and that your secretary had paid her the hundred pounds as an advance on her salary as governess to your wards. Mr. Binkerton is insisting you have neither wards nor secretary, that no one would pay a governess half so much, and it's all a Banbury tale she's invented to explain her possession of the hundred pounds that are actually his. She's crying slander."

"Guess I'd best sort things out," North sighed, heading for the door, the skirts of his fur-trimmed dressing gown flapping about his ankles.

"Not like that, sir."

"Whyever not?"

"Ladies present," Jitters muttered, flushing.

"Y'can't mean Miss Sparrow?"

"Mrs. Pickles has made herself part of it. You don't want to appear like that in front of her, sir. Your mother's sure to hear of it, and she won't like it a bit."

"Pickles's seen me in deshabille a thousand times and more."

"But not Miss Sparrow, sir, and Mrs. Pickles has taken one of her likings to the young lady."

"Young lady? Pickles calls her that? Oh, drat!"

"Exactly, sir." Jitters held out the corbeau coat. "If you'll just remove your dressing gown, we'll have you regularized in a trice."

Moments later North stood in the shadows at the head of the stairs, as yet unobserved by the combatants below. Binkerton was swatting at his boots, whining like the pusillanimous nonentity he was. The constable, gripping a drenched Miss Sparrow who appeared every bit the derelict Binkerton claimed she was, commiserated with the bully and promised swift justice. Passersby who'd made themselves important by claiming to witness the supposed assault milled about, muddying the marble tiles and knocking into things as if they owned the place. One fellow was actually slipping a Meissen figurine into a capacious pocket. Lord knew what else'd found its way in there.

"Here, you—stop that!" North roared from the shadows. "Constable, that fellow's helping himself to my property."

"Ain't in no way. Just protecting it, your honor," the light-fingered miscreant protested, returning the piece to the chest from which he'd filched it. "I'm a honest man, I am. Always have been. Ask anybody, sir."

"Naturally you are—so long as there's someone watching you every second." North stayed at the head of the stairs, the light streaming from the book room well to his left. "Go down, Jitters," he hissed. "I'll want you to get the first of those forfeits from Miss Sparrow."

"You'd never, sir!"

"I certainly would. Make her more independent in the future. That's what I require of her: Independence."

The putty-colored faces were turning toward him now, eyes like dirty puddles, as Jitters descended the stairs. Miss Sparrow, shivering under a blanket provided by Pickles, was a pathetic sight—bonnet crumpled, cap awry, hair straggling in lank tangles around her drawn features, the water dripping from her cloak puddling at her feet. He felt a twinge he insisted was irritation, not sympathy.

"Well, Miss Sparrow, what d'you have to say for yourself?" he barked.

"You know this female?" Binkerton squeaked.

"My secretary retained her services as governess to my wards just this afternoon," North said more calmly, then chuckled at Chuffy Binkerton's dismay. "She should have the hundred pounds Tidmarsh advanced her somewhere."

"You ain't got a secretary," Binkerton protested, "and you ain't got any wards. This is all a hum, Constable. Aaron Burridge sees to North's affairs—everybody knows that—same as his father did for North's father.''

"I don't know about my father's arrangements," North retorted, "but old Burridge definitely does not see to *all* my affairs.''

"She's probably his convenient," Binkerton spluttered over the gasps.

"Her? You're blind as well as a fool, Binkerton.'' Bad to worse. Nothing he was saying came out right. Good Lord, what ailed him? "Constable, this young woman was hired not an hour ago by my secretary, who—''

"Where is he, then? Show us this Tidmarsh.''

"It may be your custom to keep those in your employ at your constant beck, Binkerton," North snapped. "It's not mine. He's gone out.''

"I insist you produce this secretary called Tidmarsh. Can't, can you," Binkerton sneered. "Constable, I'll be taking my leave—once you turn my hundred pounds over to me. In it together, that's what they are, trying to rob an honest man.''

"Pockets to let, eh, Binkerton? Just returning from Watier's, I suppose, or some hell," North said, each word dripping like acid on marble. "Once we question those with whom you spent your time, I wonder what they'll say regarding those hundred pounds you're so eager to claim.''

"Now, see here, North—''

"I believe you'd find it wisest to make yourself notable by your absence, Binkerton," North snapped. "Immediately. Once you admit this young lady's in my employ, the hundred pounds are hers, and far from her robbing you, it's you who've been attempting to rob her. Now, Binkerton. Don't be all day about it.''

"What about my boots? She ruined 'em.''

North descended a single step, still keeping to the shadows. He almost laughed as Binkerton, ever true to his nickname, chuffed, then quickly made his departure to cries of "shame" and "scoundrel" and "varlet.''

"Please see the, ah, 'witnesses,' out, Jitters," North said once the door closed on the bounder. "Oh, Constable, check that fellow's pockets before you leave. I believe some belongings of mine may've accidentally fallen into 'em.''

"Ain't never nothing accidental about what's in Dick Toper's pockets," the constable said. "Entirely purposeful, he is."

"This time, however, I do believe it was an accident, as I've neither time nor patience for it to've been anything else."

An enameled snuff box, a small silver vase, and what appeared to be the leather-bound volume of Shakespeare's sonnets North had misplaced some days before appeared as if by magic, neatly aligned on the chest beside the figurine. Then constable, witnesses, and light-fingered opportunist made their departure.

"Pickles, please see to our sodden guest." North eased deeper in the shadows as the woman gazed up at him. "She's making a mess of my entry, and is like to catch her death. That wouldn't suit my convenience. I—ah, old Tidmarsh didn't enjoy having to interview a procession of crows to find one sensible sparrow. He mustn't be forced to repeat the experience.

"Jitters, have one of the carriages brought 'round once Miss Sparrow's been made presentable. Then collect her belongings and escort her to Milbury Place. I'll give you a note for Mrs. Grimble, else she'll be turned from the door, given the way her luck's running. Oh, and collect Miss Sparrow's forfeit."

"Here, you may have it now," came the lovely violalike voice so at variance with the young woman's appearance. "If you'll take Mr. North his pound—of flesh, as it happens—I'll be on my way. No need to summon a carriage."

North turned back, brows soaring.

"You are in my employ, Miss Sparrow," he said with a sweetness more threatening than the loudest roar. "It's best you accustom yourself to following my instructions, just as I'm certain you accustomed yourself to following the instructions of your previous employers. I'm no more in the habit of having my decisions questioned by underlings than they will have been. Now, give Jitters the pound that's owed me. Then go to the housekeeper's parlor and regularize yourself. I'm sure dry clothing of some sort can be found for you."

* * *

"He's truly that kind of a gentleman, just as his father was before him," Esmerelda Pickles rattled as she tucked another coverlet around Amelia after introducing herself formally. "Can't think what came over him, miss. Most unlike Master Val, that was—to call you to book as he did. And in front of others? Why, he hasn't done that in his life. No, not even the time he caught Jem Pflager—what was a stable boy then and not a groom at all, and'd been training for a cutpurse afore that, which is how we come to have him, for he wasn't very good at it—helping himself to the brandy, and Jem reeling like a trooper who'd happened on the officers' store of spirits.

"Entirely private he kept it, except for asking me to nurse the lad through the sorest head you've ever seen or will see. Not so much as a cold look did he give Jem. Lad's that devoted to Master Val in consequence. Couldn't've been more'n eighteen himself. Just after Mr. North died, it was, which is why I remember it so clear. Always a long head from the day he was born, Master Val's had, and always a merry smile."

"How wonderful for you," the newly hired—and even more recently chastised—governess murmured, shivering by the fire and curling her bare toes on the soft carpet as she sipped the tea to which Mrs. Pickles had added a generous dollop of brandy on instructions from Mount Olympus.

"And his mother's that sweet of a lady as well," the housekeeper continued as she spread Amelia's gown before the fire now that it had been given a thorough sponging, "just as you'd expect from knowing Master Val even as little as you do—not that you're likely to meet the poor dear. Terrible rheumatics she has in this season. Keeps her confined to the country. She'll be feeling more herself come spring, but she suffers fierce wintertimes, for all she never complains. Often thought she ought to try Italy, if only that dreadful Corsican could be brought to heel.

"No, you're that fortunate to've been given a position by Master Val—well, by Mr. Tidmarsh—as you'll come to appreciate."

"I'm certain I will." Perhaps. In some land as yet undiscovered in a time yet to be. But not here, Amelia fumed, and not now. Arrogant, insufferable commoner! "Certainly Mr. North is all consideration," she agreed, knowing any attempt on her part to acquaint an aged retainer with facts contrary to her high opinion of her employer would fail before they began. She'd never considered herself particularly conscious of position, but to be spoken to as if hen-witted? It wasn't to be borne—except it must.

She choked down the last of the brandy-laced tea, set the cup down, and gazed around the housekeeper's parlor.

As with the office employed by Mr. Tidmarsh, it was all restrained elegance, even to the Sèvres cup she'd just emptied and what she assumed was the second-best silver pot cooling on the second-best silver tray. A small Constable flanked by a pair of modern lamps graced the mantel. The furnishings would've done the young ladies' parlor at the court honor. In fact, such comfort would've sent her sisters into raptures.

She sighed and closed her eyes against the room, which seemed to be approaching and receding at an alarming rate. Apparently the brandy was going to her head. Well, and no wonder. She'd had nothing to eat since the night before, and wasn't likely to remedy the problem soon, given she'd missed the lodging-house dinner for which she'd paid that morning. Perhaps when she arrived at the house on Milbury Place she'd be able to cajole some cold meat or a slice of cheese from the housekeeper.

"What does he look like?" she said in an effort to remain awake. "Mr. North, I mean. He kept so deep in the shadows that I wondered if he was deformed."

"Deformed?" The housekeeper's peal of laughter was too merry not to be genuine. "Oh, my dear, he's that handsome of a gentleman. Everything that's elegant and proper, and with a kind heart and a generous spirit into the bargain. Often such a face and figure don't offer any good but what's on the surface. Master Val's as bonny within as he is without. Last Season he had half the young ladies of the *ton* fainting at his feet in hopes he'd notice 'em, and the other half twisting their ankles on his doorstep—with their mamas' assistance, I might add. Too clever to be trapped, thank goodness."

The housekeeper prattled on about the glories of Mr. Valentine North, Esquire, as Amelia's lids sank. Her last thought brought a smile to her lips. What in heaven's name would the earl and countess say could they see her now, garbed only in her chemise and a borrowed dressing gown, wrapped in coverlets, dozing unchaperoned by the housekeeper's fire in the residence of an unattached gentleman? Even one in comfortable circumstances at whom diamonds of the *ton* cast their handkerchiefs?

Amelia had no notion how much time passed, though she retained a notion Mrs. Pickles absented herself for some reason. Then a hand was shaking her shoulder, a voice making encouraging noises regarding chicken with wine sauce, mashed peas dusted with mint, and potatoes roasted on the spit.

"Dear me, I must've been wearier than I thought," Amelia murmured, forcing her eyes open. "Do forgive me. How long have I been like this? I had no intention of inconveniencing you."

A small table had been pulled before her. On it were all the riches she thought she'd merely imagined, plus countless more.

"Long enough to recover yourself, but not near long enough to be an inconvenience. 'Tisn't much tonight, Master Val dining out with friends as he is—just a pickup supper for ourselves," Mrs. Pickles apologized, placing a bowl of amber consommé in front of Amelia, then handing her a spoon as if she were a child. "Nothing grand at all. François is almost pining away. Day can't come soon enough when Master Val finds himself a young lady worthy of François's sauces.

"You look that famished, so you'd best have this soup he made up special for you when I told him about that dreadful Binkerton person knocking you into what was little better than a kennel. It's in the way of a restorative. Then we'll see about the rest."

Amelia saw about the consommé. Then she saw about everything else before her, barely restraining herself from giving an impression of a starving savage. It'd been barely a month since she fled the court, but apparently she'd forgotten how decently prepared food tasted and smelled. This was far beyond decent. It was ambrosia fit for the gods. Yes, even the god who resided on his own private Olympus at the head of the stairs, and wouldn't deign to descend a few steps when attending to the affairs of common mortals.

At last she pushed the tray away and leaned back, smiling at Mrs. Pickles.

"Please inform François I'm his slave for life," she sighed. "That was the most perfect, magnificently prepared meal I've ever had the honor of consuming."

"Hunger's the best sauce, but François is a wizard in the kitchen," Mrs. Pickles said as she retrieved the tray. "Well, it's getting on to seven of the evening. Now that we've restored you as Master Val wanted, Mr. Jitters'll be sending to the stables for a carriage to take you to Milbury Place before it gets too late and you're forced to spend another night in whatever unsuitable lodgings you managed to find for yourself."

"They're not that unsuitable, merely a tad chilly, and of course the cook doesn't deserve the sobriquet."

"Cheapest you could find, I'll warrant," Mrs. Pickles scolded, "and you Quality from the tip of your dainty toes to the top of your pretty golden head—and yes, your hair's guinea-gold where it got wet, so there's no sense pretending it isn't. Don't know who or what's responsible for your fleeing your natural protectors, but they deserve a whipping.

"Oh, no, I'm not asking," she forged on, bustling to the door and ignoring Amelia's protest that she was no more than she appeared. "Wouldn't dream of it. Who and what you are is no business of mine, nor ever will be other than perhaps to lend a hand if you need it. Will you be wanting the traveling carriage?"

"No, whatever is smallest will do. I've only a single portmanteau."

"Traveling light, then." The housekeeper paused at the door, propping the tray on one broad hip. Amelia discovered her eyes were stinging. Dear heaven, she'd reached this moment without longing for a friend—if one didn't count when Mr. Binkerton insisted thievery had been committed upon his pockets as well as assault upon his boots. Did a kind word, a sympathetic glance mean so much?

"Thank you," she murmured, wishing she were no more than

she claimed, and could form part of this welcoming downstairs world for the rest of her life.

"You find Milbury Place less than it should be," Mrs. Pickles cautioned, shifting the tray, "there's no need to trouble Master Val. No, nor Mr. Tidmarsh either. I'll stand your friend as long as you need one, and so will the rest of us. Poor Master Val's that put out over his cousin's orphans, seeing them as a curse one minute and a joke the next, and with no more idea how to see to them than if he were a newborn babe himself. Children aren't the rightful province of gentlemen."

"I see."

"Thought you would. Freddy Tyne was an irresponsible scamp from the day he was born, for all he was that engaging of a one. Master Val, now, he's not like the captain. Responsible as the day is long. It's just that he doesn't know how to go about being responsible in this case."

"I understand."

"I hope you do," she said, groping for the door handle with her free hand. "Reason I've run on in a manner I don't hold with is it's best you have a notion of who employed you. There's problems, don't you be blaming Master Val. His inten-tions're all that's honorable, no matter what you think. Pro-tecting his mother, you see. She hasn't been well, and he'll not have her troubled, nor his sisters either.

"Your gown's over on the settee, freshly sponged and pressed, and I've set you out a cloak of my own, as yours is past praying for. I'll leave you to it, then. Down the stairs and across the hall is where you'll find the rest of us when you're ready to leave."

Amelia squinted, then scrubbed at the damp clouding the window. The carriage lurched to a halt on broken cobbles.

So this was Milbury Place. The fringes of Mayfair, indeed. The far and tattered fringes, its few lamps unlit, its areaways clogged with refuse. The dwellings crouched, dark and forbid-ding, each on its narrow lot, smoke twining from crooked chimneys. Curtains were drawn, scattered windows shuttered.

What she hoped was a cat slunk along the railings, a scrap that squeaked and writhed dangling from its jaws.

She shuddered.

The central gated garden was empty at this hour, the branches of city-stunted trees groping toward a cloud-covered sky from which a dispirited drizzle still fell, though the worst of that day's storm had passed. Those gaps might be paths along which children could run and laugh. That lump might be a fountain in which to sail a miniature boat. At night there was no way to tell.

The house before which they'd stopped appeared deserted. Even the knocker was missing.

Jem jumped down from behind, opened the carriage door and let down the steps, then took her portmanteau to the entry and assaulted the door.

"Well, Miss Sparrow?" Jitters said.

"Well, Mr. Jitters," she returned brightly. "So this is my new home."

"So it would appear. Good thing Jem knew the way. Couldn't've found it on my own if my life depended on it. No, don't get out just yet. I'm not all that certain I should be leaving you here. Don't like the look of the place."

"If this is the home Mr. North has selected for his orphaned wards, I'm certain it can't help but be suitable for one such as I."

"Then you're certain of more than I am, and I've known him, man and boy, since before he was born."

"It's just the hour that makes it seem odd," she said, willing herself to believe it. "I'm sure even Grosvenor Square presents a forbidding appearance on toward ten of a winter night."

"If you think that, you've never seen Grosvenor Square. I'm of half a mind to take you back. Mr. North'll be returning early, and—"

"And he'll demand another pound's forfeit if you do," she sighed. "No, leave well enough alone. I'll manage."

"I don't in any way approve of those forfeits, you know. None of us do."

"Elevated eccentricity must be allowed its amusements. I'm not complaining. It's just that I'd rather retain as much of my wages as possible. If the price is living in this house, I'll pay it gladly. Shall we go?''

A light came on in a front room of the house next to the one Mr. North had hired. Draperies were being parted. Light streamed across the sill and plunged to the pavement, where it widened and vanished. Jem continued his fruitless pounding.

''It would seem our arrival is causing a certain amount of curiosity,'' Jitters complained.

''It's ever thus.'' Amelia shrugged. ''You don't expect human nature to suffer a sea change merely for your peace of mind, do you?''

''No, I suppose not. Well, if you're determined to remain, I suppose we'd best get on with it.''

More lights were coming on in the houses surrounding the iron-fenced garden. More draperies were being parted. Head high, Amelia accepted Jitters's assistance from the carriage, then swept across the pavement and up the steps.

''There must be someone here,'' she murmured. ''There simply must.''

''Not meaning to disoblige, miss,'' Jem said, ''but it isn't as if they was expecting us as Mr.—ah—Tidmarsh forgot to send word we was coming. That's why you've got that note for Mrs. Grimble from himself, don't you see? Didn't want you to suffer from Mr. Tidmarsh's lapses, Mr. North didn't, nor yet call the old fellow to account. Getting on in years, Mr. Tidmarsh is, and that forgetful. Why, I mind the time he—''

Jitters's sharp cough cut the young groom off. Two burly footmen came charging up the area stairs of a house two doors down, brandishing cudgels.

''Whatcher think you're doing,'' one shouted. ''Master says to get gone.''

''We'll fetch the Watch, you don't go peaceable,'' the other threatened as they skidded to a halt, livery awry, wigs askew. ''Mistress is having the vapors, all the noise you're making. Can't have that, the master says. Has the right of it too. Cause all sorts of discommodations, the mistress's vapors do.''

The knockerless front door opened at last, revealing a thick-necked lout in shirt-sleeves and a greasy leather apron silhouetted against the dim interior.

"Yar?" He gave Amelia a quick glance, then belched. "Get along with you. No more noise, understand? An' no protests neither. Gone respectable, we has."

"I know you have, Mr. Grimble." Jem thrust himself beneath the man's bulbous nose as Jitters descended the steps to deal with the footmen. "I was here a week ago, remember? With Mr. Tidmarsh, what went over the place and paid your wife a year's rent in advance. This is the governess Mr. Tidmarsh hired for Mr. North's wards."

"Governess?" a female voice shrilled from another area way. "And I'm queen of the May, that's who I am!"

"Old fellow's doxy, that's what," another incensed female voice called, "arriving in the middle of the night in hopes no one'd notice. Well, we noticed. Setting up his convenient and pretending it's something else—that's what's happening. Well, we don't want no more of that."

At those words Amelia, who'd been wishing she could vanish in a puff of smoke, drew herself up.

"I beg your pardon?" she snapped, every inch the daughter of an earl, turning to face the street. "Watch your tongues, or you'll find yourselves in Newgate for slander or Bedlam for lack of wits, whichever the magistrate finds preferable. I've no intention of indulging your apparent taste for low-bred farce."

The tone and diction only generations of breeding and years of training could yield silenced the babble. Amelia turned back to the lumpish fellow in the doorway.

"If you'll be so good as to fetch the housekeeper," she said, voice carrying clearly to the nearer houses, "I'm unutterably wearied by the behavior exhibited by those inhabiting these less than elegant environs, and would appreciate being shown to my quarters, a bath prepared, my bed turned down, and a cold collation provided."

There was a moment's shocked silence. Then the footmen slunk away. Doors closed. Draperies fell. The little drama was over.

Chapter Four

Nothing Jitters had said, no matter how true, had served to induce Amelia to quit Milbury Place. She'd insisted all was as it should be, then strode past the growling latter-day Cerberus and into the darkness, instructing the churl to close the door rather than stand there gape-mouthed.

Now, a week later, she wondered.

Hades had yet to make his appearance, but in every other way she felt a Persephone who'd unwittingly consumed a pomegranate seed. That it was the tag end of winter strengthened the illusion, for it seemed spring would never put in an appearance.

Oh, the superficials had been seen to. Furnishings now shone from applications of beeswax. Draperies had been brushed and rehung, carpets lifted and beaten. Thin sunlight streamed through panes so clean, they might not exist. The highly improper paintings that had graced the public rooms—goodness, but Zeus had been a busy fellow—were packed away, as well as the odd china. The substitutes she'd purchased were more in keeping with a gentleman's residence. Narrow cots for the children and nursemaid and a modern bed for herself would be delivered that day, replacing the monstrosities with mirrored canopies and oddly shaped posts that previously dominated the bedchambers. The funds provided by Mr. Tidmarsh to outfit the nursery and the children had been barely sufficient for these essential alterations.

Unfortunately there was a lingering stench of cigarillos and cheap perfume no amount of vinegar or beeswax could banish. As for the library—what library there was—the lot had been removed to the farthest attic cranny, where not even children exploring on a rainy afternoon would discover the shocking volumes.

Amelia sighed as she descended the main staircase, spectacles perched on the tip of her nose, cap covering her dulled hair.

With those hired to give the house a thorough cleaning paid and gone, the first hints of renewed neglect were appearing: a smudge on the banister, a drift of dust at the base of one of the spindles, flowers decorating the entry dropping their petals on a chest that no longer gleamed. She'd have to speak with Mrs. Grimble—again.

A giggle from the front drawing room had Amelia hesitating at the foot of the stairs. The giggle was followed by a shriek. Jaws clenched, hands balled into fists, Amelia strode across the entry. It was the Scrudge girl—this time with a bandy-legged fellow Amelia didn't recognize rather than one of the insolent footmen. The ruffian's face was buried in the hussy's bosom, his fingers fondling her posterior.

"Bessie!" she snapped. "Report to Mrs. Grimble. At once."

The girl paused in her good-natured tussle, still giggling. Then she pulled away, not bothering to cover herself. Amelia flushed and turned her back.

"Report to Mrs. Grimble," she repeated. "If there's a recurrence, you'll be given the sack. Is that understood?"

"I was here afore you, and I'll be here long after you're gone, ducks," Bessie retorted. "It's Hortie Grimble what owns this house, as she ought to've told you long afore this, and told that Mr. Tidmarsh into the bargain—which she ain't done, not wanting to queer things. It's her says who goes an' who stays. Since she ain't told you what's what, I am."

A bucket of water emptied over her head would've been

preferable. Amelia turned, strangling on words better left unspoken.

"That's trimmed your sails right enough, ain't it, Miss High-and-Mighty," the housemaid continued with a toss of her dusky curls. "Watch your step, or it's you'll be given the sack, and Hortie'll be the one as does it."

The city-bred girl brushed past Amelia with a twitch of her hips, pointed nose in the air, and strode across the entry as if she owned the place.

"Get out," Amelia shot at the stranger who'd been indulging himself moments before. "If I find you here again, I'll summon a constable."

He turned to face her, grinning, and performed a deep bow. She stared at him in horror as she crumpled on a chair.

"Can't do that, Lady Amelia," he said. " 'Course, we threw that race just outside York last summer on his lordship's say-so, and he won a pretty packet betting against himself secretlike. Paid us off just as he promised, your pa did, but he put the word out against us all the same after we left as agreed, and we landed here. Wanted something more certain, you see. Working for gentry's chancy. Lords is chancier still."

"I always wondered why his lordship seemed so pleased with himself after his horse lost." Her eyes widened as she shuddered. "Mick, isn't it? Mick Grady? You were an undergroom."

"Dead to rights. Might want to think hard, my lady, afore you summon a constable. You do that, I'd have to tell him who you be, and your pa into the bargain. The earl'd pay a pretty penny to know your direction, I'm thinking."

"I doubt it." She stumbled to her feet and paced the little drawing room. "I'm of no interest to him, but you're correct: I have no desire to have him apprised of my whereabouts."

"Didn't think you would."

She shuddered at the sensation of knowing eyes following her.

" 'Course, it'd take a clever sort to recognize you," Mick chuckled. "Changed yourself more'n a bit, and not just your name neither. Couldn't stomach the notion of being tupped by that Whifler fellow was always hanging about the place is my guess, if he come up to scratch and you was about to say your vows.''

"No," she murmured absently, "I couldn't.''

"Nasty type. Handy with his crop, whether it was his mounts or the stable lads. They learned pretty quick belowstairs 'twas best if a footman brought him his eye-opener in the morning and his composer at night. Must've caused a deal of satisfaction when you bolted, for you was that well liked. No hard feelings, my lady? You keep your mummer shut, and I'll do the same. Not healthy for any of us to be thinking too hard about the past, Miss Sparrow, nor yet remembering things best forgot.''

"You're absolutely correct, Mick.''

"That's the ticket. We've put it about me'n Mike spent a bit o'time in Portugal afore hiring on as grooms here. S'the truth, though not all of it.'' He gave her a saucy grin. "If y'got to lie, stick as close to the truth as you can, miss. I'll do my best to see Bessie don't bother you. She's a lively girl, but there ain't no need for her to be lively when you're about. Been taunting you, thinking you too full of yourself for one what works for her bread same as she does, even if y'does it on your feet.''

"But they're neither of them available, Miss Sparrow," Bassett protested, forcing the door closed against the gusting rain a week later. "Mr. Tidmarsh is, ah, out on the master's business, and Mr. North has yet to ring.''

"At this hour? What a slug-a-bed.''

Amelia handed Bassett her dripping umbrella and unlatched the clasps of her cloak as she swept past him. She could feel the disapproving frown drilling between her shoulder blades.

Poor Bassett. She was causing him no end of problems. Ladies didn't call at the residences of single gentlemen demanding to see said single gentlemen without delay —above all, not ladies in the employ of said gentlemen. Well, that's what butlers were paid for: to deal with problems. She suspected that in her Bassett realized he'd met an insoluble one unless it was solved to her liking.

She handed him the cloak and sat on a tapestried chair, arranged her skirts, folded her hands in her lap, and gave every indication of taking root. "Certainly Mr. North doesn't intend to sleep the entire day, does he? That would imply a very sore head indeed. Unfortunately for Mr. North, I have business with one or the other of them, and it won't keep."

"But—but—" Bassett glanced up the staircase that swept to the floor above, chewing his lower lip in a manner inconsistent with his position as the front rank of defense in North's household, her sodden cloak dangling from one hand, her cheap umbrella from the other, then returned his attention to Amelia. "There're other gentlemen here as well, miss."

"That's no concern of mine."

"Who're out of sorts, and would find the presence of a lady inconvenient."

"Suffering the aftereffects of their debaucheries, are they? Well, that's no concern of mine either."

"No, miss, it isn't." Bassett drew himself up, chest to the fore, nose quivering. Neither butler nor governess noticed Jitters by the door leading to the service stairs at the rear of the house, or the pair of gentlemen easing back from the head of the front stairs a floor above them. "Which is why you must return to Milbury Place and send a note requesting an appointment."

"I have. Three times, as you know perfectly well. Neither Mr. Tidmarsh nor Mr. North saw fit to reply to my request for a meeting yesterday, the day before yesterday, or the day before that. Surely you're aware of that as well."

"They were otherwise occupied, Miss Sparrow."

"Mr. North no doubt in amusing himself with his cronies, and Mr. Tidmarsh in ensuring no one disturbed him while he did it. I begin to suspect neither gentleman has been given my notes, as no true gentleman would ignore a lady's request in such a manner, so I decided to come in person. Certain things can wait. Others cannot."

"I'm afraid, Miss Sparrow," Bassett said with an apologetic

cough, "that it's not the province of an employee to dictate to her employer, nor yet criticize his actions."

Amelia blushed, knowing the truth of that. "Nevertheless," she insisted, "I must see one or the other. Since Mr. Tidmarsh is unavailable, I suppose it must be Mr. North, no matter how inconvenient he may find the interview."

"Perhaps if you were to explain your concerns to Mr. Jitters or Mrs. Pickles?"

"What good would that do? They're as powerless to remedy matters as I am."

"Might have a notion as how best to proceed, miss, or bear a message."

"Not in this instance," she sighed. "Mrs. Pickles hasn't seen Milbury Place, and Mr. Jitters was only in the entry. They've neither of them any notion of conditions there. I've already spent most of the sum provided to outfit the children rendering it habitable. You wouldn't believe the filth, Bassett, and many of the furnishings required replacement." She lowered her eyes at his questioning look. "The owner had odd tastes. I'm in need of additional funds. It's that, or Mr. North's wards will be reduced to going about in whatever they have on their backs when they arrive, and playing with sticks and stones and reading dried leaves."

"Mrs. Pickles," Bassett insisted as Jitters, still unobserved, slipped through the service door. "She's the one to see to this. If you won't come to her, then I suppose I'd best fetch her to you."

"Oh, no—I couldn't put her to such trouble." And so much for being a problem with which Bassett couldn't deal. "Can't you ask Mr. North to give me a few moments of his time when he rises? I won't insist on a perfectly tied neckcloth or Hessians polished until I can see my face in them. A banyan and slippers will do."

"Mr. North doesn't wish to be troubled with his wards. That's why you were hired."

"Then I'll be perfectly happy to wait for Mr. Tidmarsh— in his office, perhaps?"

The sudden hammering on the front door caused both to jump, then glance at each other guiltily.

"Hadn't you best see who that is, Bassett?" Amelia said when the elderly butler appeared frozen in place.

"But there's no one with business here at this hour."

"Perhaps not customarily, but clearly someone feels they have a right to some attention, even if not that of Mr. North. Or perhaps," she concluded on a hopeful note, "it's Mr. Tidmarsh, and you relocked the door and he's forgotten his key."

"Mr. Tidmarsh would have come through the mews or the areaway. Uses a service entry, just as any hireling who knows his place does." Bassett set her cloak and umbrella on a bench, straightened his shoulders, and opened the door.

"This be North's place?" a deep voice growled. "The North what was cousin to Captain Tyne what got hisself froze, and left a pair o' brats to be seen to by others?"

The butler's shoulders went rigid, his jowls quivering. Amelia peeked around his considerable bulk. A wagon containing several shapeless bundles was drawn up before the areaway. On the stoop a ruddy-faced fellow attired in the coarse garments of a seafarer scowled as if the town house were a prize to be boarded.

"Open you budget," the fellow barked. "This the place?"

Bassett gasped, "Deliveries below," and struggled to close the door in the man's face.

"Not this delivery." The man stuck his foot in the opening. "This be it," he called over his shoulder. "Move your stumps afore I give you a taste of me fist."

"Oh, dear heaven," Amelia murmured as two of the bundles proved ambulatory once the carter set them on the pavement, "it's them already, and not the slightest attempt at sending word they'd docked, poor mites."

"Poor mites? Pair of walking disasters more like, as you'll learn to your sorrow." The sailor gave Amelia's person a sympathetic inspection. "You Mrs. North?"

"No, their governess."

"Well, they ain't governable. Y'ain't being paid enough by half, miss, no matter what your wages. Run you ragged, slip of a thing that you are, when they're not puking on your skirts. My woman's worn to the bone seeing to 'em, and the captain's lady into the bargain. Ended up having to put Mr. North's precious wards in the brig for the sake of us all, and their own into the bargain. Othergates they'd've been swept over the side, running away from us as they did every chance they got, and hiding in any cranny they could find.''

Amelia stared from one dirty, innocent face to the other as Bassett backed across the entry, stumbled, and sank onto the chair she'd lately quitted. The children were gagged, their wrists bound, their ankles fettered with ropes so short they could take only a single step at a time. Matted hair, layers of filthy clothes—she could well believe they'd spent the rough winter passage in chains belowdecks.

''You and your captain should rot in Newgate for this,'' she managed to get out through clenched teeth as she knelt.

''Bedlam, mayhap,'' he retorted.

''Oh, you poor things.'' Why, they were no older than her favorite cousin's pair. Torn from the only home they'd known? Incarcerated in the hold of a frail, creaking vessel? Rattled about like dice in a cup during a tempest-tossed crossing? Provided heaven alone knew what filth in the guise of food? No wonder they'd attempted escape. ''I'm Miss Sparrow. Come here and let me loosen those dreadful ropes,'' she pleaded, tears welling in her eyes. ''There's nothing for you to fear now, I promise.''

''Fear? It's you should be quaking,'' the sailor snorted, lifting them over the sill and setting them before Amelia. ''Newgate's where them changelings belongs, not the captain or me, nor any other honest man what's been imposed upon by his betters to rid themselves of something they don't like nor yet can't manage. 'No trouble,' the colonel said when he brung 'em to us. 'Innocent orphans deprived of mother and father in one cruel blow,' he said. 'Liven up the voyage for Mrs. Morton,' he said.

''Had the right of that, though not in the way we understood. Innocent? Captain Tyne could make port in hell better berthed than he was alive cursed with this pair. Worst crossing the *Linnet's* ever had."

The man's laugh was loud and bitter, masking the rheumatic shuffle in the corridor and the clatter of boot heels on the stairs.

"Here now." The sailor pulled the children from Amelia as she fumbled with the ropes, retaining a firm grip on the backs of their necks as they attempted to kick him in the shins. "None of that afore you gets the doors locked and barred, if you please, miss. You let 'em loose now, and they'll be down the street and around the corner afore y'know it. Took half the crew to catch 'em when they bolted on the docks." Still gripping the waifs, he kicked the door shut, then turned to Bassett. "I'd be grateful if you'd send someone for their bundles," he said with surprising mildness given his earlier words. "I ain't got all day."

"What's this, hey-hey?" Mr. Tidmarsh croaked, scuttling up like the wizened crab he was, Jitters hard on his heels. "Mr. North won't in no way be pleased at this racket."

The scowl he bent on Bassett had the poor butler stammering.

"What d'you mean, coming here without being sent for? Saying your prayers, are you?" he snapped at Amelia, who still knelt in the center of the entry. "Not a bad notion, that. Told you not to bother us. Well, didn't I, hey-hey? Told you Mr. North wouldn't have it. Told you not bothering us was what you were being paid for. Told you you'd forfeit a pound each time you came round, and so you shall!" Then the old man's eyes widened as he took in the sailor and the waifs. "What're these beggars doing muddying up m-Mr. North's entry? Y'didn't mention them, Jitters," he roared. "Who the devil are they? Bassett, you've a deal to answer for!"

Amelia considered retrieving her umbrella and assaulting Mr. Tidmarsh across the shoulders. She considered fainting, or indulging in a fit of the vapors. She considered tears, screams, drumming her heels on the floor or her head against the door. She considered pelting from North's town house, and a swift return to Bottomsley Court and the repulsive arms of Sir Reginald Whifler. She considered them all in less time than it takes to draw a single breath, head bowed, fists clenched.

"See here, Tidmarsh," a light voice reproved, "that's no way to speak to a lady. North'd have your liver and lights if he heard you carrying on so. I've a good mind to report your behavior to him."

Firm steps trod across the entry to the tune of Tidmarsh's incensed splutters. Gleaming Hessians stopped just before Amelia, reflecting her downcast face. Strong hands seized her elbows, lifting her to her feet.

"Anthony Sinclair, at your service." The ginger-haired stranger gave her an assessing look, bowed, then nodded in the direction of a handsome young man with golden curls and a devil-may-care grin. "That pretty colt over there is Ollie Threadwhistle. Friends of North's. Now, ma'am, what's to do? Poor old Bassett seems indisposed, and Tidmarsh's understanding's never been of the best."

Mr. Tidmarsh's wordless roar drew a reproving glance from Mr. Sinclair. Mr. Threadwhistle whooped like a schoolboy. Poor old Bassett didn't seem just indisposed. He appeared as if he might go off in the faint Amelia'd been considering for herself only moments before.

"I'm Miss Sparrow," Amelia explained when neither Mr. Tidmarsh nor Bassett appeared up to the task of making her identity known. "Mr. Tidmarsh hired me as governess for Mr. North's wards, who've just this moment arrived. This man"— she gestured at the sailor—"is from the *Linnet,* which brought the children back to England, and these"—she pulled the bound and gagged children forward—"are Mr. North's wards."

"North's wards?" Mr. Tidmarsh squeaked. *"Here?* Get 'em out! Don't want 'em here. Not today. Not tomorrow. Not ever! Why, they're crawling with vermin."

"Just as you would be had you been treated as they have."

Amelia knelt before the children, making quick work of their bonds now that a semblance of peace had fallen over the entry. In recompense she received a swift kick to her stomach, the lightning wrench of a stray curl peeping from beneath her bonnet, and pinches in abundance about the neck and shoulders. She gasped, hunching over.

"Warned you," the sailor said. "Well, as you've things

firmly in hand now, miss, I'll be taking my leave. You'll find their bundles in the areaway, for not no one nor not anything will induce me to come back. I know what happens next.'' He shook his head at the crown being held out by Mr. Sinclair. "It's I should be paying you,'' he muttered, and was on the stoop with the door closed before any could stop him.

Mr. Tidmarsh sidled forward, eyeing the children with foreboding as he kept a safe distance. Amelia took a deep breath, then untied the gags with which the pair had been struggling. Howls filled the entry, causing even Mr. Sinclair, who appeared an intrepid soul, to blanch. Mrs. Pickles surfaced at the end of the hall, brandishing a rolling pin, François hot on her heels with carving knife the *en forte*, Webster toting a poker, behind them what appeared to be every servant on the premises.

"Cease that this instant,'' Mr. Sinclair ground out, somehow making himself heard above the children.

They stared at him in shock. The bigger one poked the smaller one in the ribs. The smaller one—who had to be five-year-old Tabitha, given her height—cast up her accounts, baptizing Amelia, the entry floor, and Messrs. Sinclair and Threadwhistle with impartiality and thoroughness as the bigger one—clearly Robert, at age seven the leader—looked on.

"I can do that whenever I want,'' the moppet lisped when she was done. "It's a trick. Mama always said it was a clever one. When I did it, Papa gave me anything I wanted to make me stop.''

"It worked better'n tears,'' the boy explained. "Papa'd just walk out of the room if one of us cried, but he'd rush to help if Tibbie was sick. O'course, Mama insisted Tibbie never do it on the carpets.''

"Good God!'' Mr. Tidmarsh managed to get out on a strangled note as he beat a hasty retreat up the stairs. "Freddy Tyne,'' his voice floated to them, "I'd kill you if you weren't already dead!''

Chapter Five

With a "Here now, we'll be having no more of that, missy!" and a "Master Robert, keep your hands to yourself, if you please," Pickles herded the filthy children and mortified Miss Sparrow toward the rear of the house, speaking sternly of laundry rooms and strong soap and scrub brushes and lard to suffocate the head lice, and calling for the largest washtubs to be filled and the laundress summoned from her starching.

Valentine North sagged against the wall, watching as Jitters trailed Ollie Threadwhistle and Tony Sinclair up the main stairs. Below, Webster was holding a tumbler of brandy to Bassett's lips.

"Bassett won't survive this," North muttered. "Always been fond of old Bassett. Perpetual source of clandestine horehound drops and Turkish delight when I was a boy." Then, "They're monsters," he moaned, rolling his eyes as he removed his spectacles, crammed his gray wig in a pocket, and led the way up the next flight of stairs. "Veritable minions of hell."

"And you're a veritable scarecrow, Val," Threadwhistle chuckled, for all he was a tad green about the gills. "Hair on end, and more tatters to you than a Haymarket bawd. Not the

sort of example y'ought to be setting those wards of yours.
Your cousin must be rolling in his grave.''

"Hush! Don't want Miss Sparrow hearing you, blast it. When
she's here I'm Tidmarsh—not North.''

"Just how're you going to proceed now?'' Sinclair said.

Footmen and maids toting cans of steaming water were
already chaining down the hall like ants, disappearing into
Sinclair's and Threadwhistle's bedchambers.

"Get 'em all out of my house soonest possible, and hide
under my bed until they're gone,'' North replied as he headed
for his own quarters.

"What? The intrepid Valentine North, routed by a pair of
bib-droolers?''

"Thoroughly and completely. They're *puking* bib-droolers,
you'll remember.''

"How could we forget,'' Threadwhistle sighed, glancing at
his ruined leathers.

"And pluck to the backbone, unlike their guardian,'' Sinclair
murmured.

"We're going to visit Chloe, gentlemen, and hold a council
of war,'' North tossed over his shoulder, then turned to face
the pair with a grim look. "Nothing's changed merely because
Freddy's brats're on English soil, and better prepared to cause
me misery than I dreamed they might be in my worst nightmares.''

"And soiled into the bargain,'' Sinclair forged on with a
devilish glint in his green eyes, "as well as intent on bringing
their betters to their condition, though I suspect Mrs. Pickles
intends to do something about the surface soil. Their minds
and souls're another matter. Past praying for, is my guess. How
that poor governess is going to survive is more than I can
imagine. They need an animal keeper.''

"Don't know what you're paying Miss Sparrow,'' Threadwhistle threw in, "but it's not near enough. Best have her lay
in a year's supply of birch rods. Stout ones.''

"No, I won't have them struck,'' North said, dropping his
half-bantering tone. "Whatever their faults—and those cursed
tadpoles have 'em in plenty—it's none of their doing. Look to

Freddy and Fanny for the cause. That's why I want Chloe. Sure to have a notion as to how best to proceed. Clever woman, seen a deal more of the world than the rest of us."

"She'll tell you to seek your mother's counsel, being she knows her limitations."

"No! I won't burden her with those hell-born babes—especially not after seeing 'em. She'd never survive the encounter."

"Actually," Threadwhistle grinned, "she might find it invigorating."

"Don't be more of an idiot than you already are, friend. Sorry about your leathers. I'll pay for their replacement, of course."

North slipped into his bedchamber, shedding shawls and scarves like the layers of a chrysalis as Jitters trailed him, gathering up the bits and pieces of his disguise.

"Why was Miss Sparrow here, Jitters?" the beleaguered gentleman demanded, giving birth to a hump formed of straps and a pair of pillows, then shifting his shoulders and sighing with relief. The thing was damnably uncomfortable, and forced him into the shuffle that was becoming Tidmarsh's hallmark—a mixed blessing.

"I couldn't say, sir."

"Y'knew enough to come wake me and cram me into this damned contraption."

"Naturally, sir."

North stripped to his smalls and sat at the lady's dressing table brought down from the attics when the farce began, opened the pot of cream Chloe had given him, and spread a layer of the gunk over the stage paint that helped transform him from vigorous Corinthian to doddering antique. Lord, but the stuff was cold and slimy—like a trail left by a garden slug. How actors bore such foolishness on a daily basis he'd never understand.

"Case of 'won't say,' isn't it, Jitters? I still pay your wages, y'know." He watched his man's reflection in the triple mirror as he worked the stuff. Gradually it turned a noxious putty color streaked gray and brown with touches of pink.

"It was Bassett with whom Miss Sparrow conferred, sir."

"I'm not accusing you of listening at doors, blast it." North cocked his head, studying his reflection. A blasted clown, that's what he'd become thanks to Freddy Tyne. "But you have to've heard something." He picked up a rag and began to swipe at his face. The silence grew as Jitters laid out fresh clothes and a stack of neckcloths. "Well," North sighed, "if you won't tell me, then I suppose Bassett must come up, poor fellow. A pity, that. He's been through enough this morning to lay a far younger man low, but then, I suppose that doesn't matter to you."

"Funds, sir," Jitters replied on cue. "Miss Sparrow finds herself in need of additional funds."

"She does, does she?" North hid his smile under the rag, then scowled as the import of Jitters's words sank in. "Damned expensive female, if that's so. Whatever for? Chloe doesn't cost half so much."

"Mrs. Sherbrough doesn't have a house full of children, sir."

"There's that, but the place came furnished and staffed, and staff's being paid separately."

Jitters's eyes met his in the mirror. Then he glanced away, chin firming.

"How carefully did you go over the house, sir?"

"Drains didn't stink, which is the main thing in that part of Town. Rooms were a decent size, what I saw of 'em. There was a garden in back, and another in the square."

"Take note of the way the place was furbished, sir?"

"Not particularly. Draperies were drawn and the shutters up. Why?"

"Perhaps you should've, sir." Jitters's back was to him now, though his voice was clear enough. "The previous tenant had an odd taste from what little I saw of it. That, or the owners do."

After his council of war with Chloe Sherbrough and his Irregulars, Valentine North—in his guise of Pericles Tidmarsh—sent a note to Miss Sparrow stipulating all decisions were in her capable hands, and cautioning that any more trips to Mr. North's residence would see the deposit on her wages dwindling with a rapidity that would horrify her. If she had need of more funds, she need only send an accounting—complete with receipts—to Mr. Tidmarsh for his approval. The funds would be forthcoming. He and the fellows had agreed permitting the woman a free hand would be far less fatiguing than going on a tour of inspection.

A few days later, counter to Chloe's repeated cautions, North went on a shopping spree that included most of the best toy shops in London. Then, considerably lighter in the pocket and infinitely satisfied with himself, he joined the fellows at White's for dinner and an evening of cards.

"Imagine yourselves treated to a Christmas such as no child ever dared dream of," he gloated when well in his cups, "and it's not even Christmas. Little Miss Sparrow'll be hard pressed to control the monsters. Such a clash of wills that'll produce! Wish I were a mouse peeking past the wainscoting. Should prove deuced amusing."

"Why d'you persist in tormenting the poor woman?" Dabney St. Maure protested, himself fairly well to pass. "Not her fault they're monsters."

"Not tormenting her in the least," North hiccoughed. "Presenting her with a challenge. Every woman needs a challenge once in a while."

St. Maure shook his head. "Don't understand what you're about. Don't understand in the least," he muttered.

Dauntry chuckled while Threadwhistle, with the look of an innocent cherub, piously folded his hands and recited, "Here's the church and here's the steeple; open the doors and see all the people." Then he peered toward the nave of the church he'd formed with palms and fingers. "That you, Val?" he said incredulously. "What the devil're you doing in there? And who's that with you? By damn, I do believe it's Miss—"

"Not likely," North snorted, knocking Threadwhistle's hands apart. "You've seen her. Pathetic. Fine eyes, though, and a voice to set the heart singing—I'll grant you that. Good nose too. Elegant. Unfortunate the rest of her falls short of that sample.''

''Don't think she really needs spectacles,'' Threadwhistle murmured, ''and when she opens her budget she don't sound the least like any of the governesses m'sisters an' cousins were cursed with,'' but the others ignored him.

One bottle of excellent brandy led to another, and then another. Miss Sparrow and North's wards were forgotten.

That night, as North and his Irregulars strode along Bond Street warbling a ditty that wouldn't've passed muster in even Chloe Sherbrough's drawing room, he hit on the notion of stopping by Marie Duclos's shop and ordering several ensembles for the put-upon Miss Sparrow. If Freddy's horrors were to be treated to a few luxuries, it wouldn't be fair to leave their fierce little governess out.

Nothing would do but that they traipse halfway across London and rouse the demimonde's prime modiste. The sleepy seamstress who answered their knocks and shouts proved incapable of understanding that the governess North had hired for his wards needed shaking up a bit. Even informing her that the bookish female had far too few gowns, and that two of those few had been ruined thanks to him, did not the least good. Gentlemen did not buy gowns for governesses—certainly not at three in the morning, and not at this shop.

It took some doing, but at last Marie Duclos appeared, yawning, but eager to please such a generous patron despite the hour. Yes, she had items that hadn't been called for as yet. Precisely what did *les messieurs* desire?

''Not sure.'' North grinned, pushing his hat back and lounging on the blue velvet settee on which he'd spent so many hours he felt he owned the thing, as the others hovered by the door. ''I'll know it when I see it.''

''For Madame Sherbrough, *n'est-ce pas?* A gift to smooth your path after a *bêtise?* We will want, then, items of the most vivid and the most expensive.'' The modiste waved her hands at the seamstress waiting at the back of the showroom. ''The red gown trimmed with the black lace originally intended for

Hetty Muggins, who has *rompu* with her *cher ami,*" she ordered, "and the black *châle* embroidered in gold, Suzette."

"No, that wouldn't do at all. Not intended for Chloe," North broke in, flushing. "Here, you, Suzette, wait a moment. Someone else entirely. Little. Not much to her. Same height as Chloe, but the rest's lacking. Name's Sparrow, and it fits."

"The hair?" Marie Duclos said, considering.

"Dull."

"The eyes, they are how?"

"Changeable."

"And her air? Her style? The bosoms?"

"Has none," North mumbled, wondering if this was such a grand idea after all as the fellows grinned. "She's a governess."

"Une gouvernante? Ah, mon dieu! I have nothing for such a one," Duclos protested, drawing herself up. "Nothing! Absolutely. You are, as they say, making sport of a poor innocent who must work for her bread. You could cost her her position. This I will not have. *Non, non,* return to your home and seek your bed, Monsieur North. That is where you belong. Clearly you have indulged yourself to excess this evening."

"But I'm the one who hired her, blast it! I won't discharge her because I take it into my head to see her garbed decently."

"Décemment is precisely that of which I have nothing. And what need do you have of a governess?" the modiste snorted, ignoring good business in her outrage. "A governess, indeed! Two ladies at once? Your pockets may be deep and you may be vigorous, monsieur, but you are not that vigorous. Neither are your pockets so deep."

"No, it's true," Threadwhistle broke in. "North's been saddled with a pair of orphans. Parents died in the Colonies. Froze to death. Doesn't want anything to do with 'em, and so he's hired a female to see to 'em."

Mademoiselle Duclos peered narrowly from one to the next, gaze finally coming to rest on Dabney St. Maure. *"Eh bien,"* she said, "you have a reasonable air. This *tra-la-la*—it is true?"

"They exist, all right." St. Maure grinned. "Woke me out of a sound sleep. Younger one deposited breakfast, lunch, and

dinner on the poor woman. On purpose. Clothes're ruined.
Baptized Sinclair and Threadwhistle here as well.''

Mademoiselle Duclos stood in the middle of her showroom,
arms crossed, foot tapping. Then, with the air of one conferring
a great favor, she nodded. "Fetch the periwinkle wool rejected
this morning because of the neckline that could not be adjusted,
Suzette, and the entirely-too-tight rose merino. Two gowns
have been ruined. Two gowns will be replaced. But no more,
do you comprehend me, Monsieur North? More would be
improper. This may be something you do not understand, but
you must believe me when I tell you this Miss Sparrow would
feel it like a knife in the bosom. Is that what you wish? To
plunge a knife in her bosom?"

The gowns, while not precisely what Abigail Sparrow
might've selected for herself, North decided, were of far better
quality than the shapeless black things in which she'd been
appearing. After some cajoling, he convinced Duclos a pair of
contrasting shawls wouldn't be excessive, and a jade pelisse
was mandatory given the weather. Christmas would be arriving
out of season for little Miss Sparrow as well.

The results of those sprees, when delivered to Milbury Place,
had Tibbie and Robby Tyne alternately shrieking with delight
and battling like Saracens and Christians.

Not only were there enough playthings for an army of children. Not only did their arrival destroy the first traces of routine
Amelia had managed to establish during the past week. Worse
yet, by eight in the morning the schoolroom was cursed with
an untrained spaniel puppy, a white ball of fluff whose pink
tongue protruded whenever a saucer of cream was offered, and
a glass globe in which golden fish wandered. The combination
held the children's interest for all of five minutes.

At nine a canary in a gilded cage arrived, and at nine-thirty
a family of white mice. Ten o'clock produced a parrot whose
vocabulary was unsuited to tender ears—all these in addition
to a stream of deliveries that included, among other improbable
items, a rug fashioned from the skin of a bear, complete with

head. The note accompanying it explained this was, of all luxuries the world contained, the one Mr. North most coveted as a boy. Tibbie screamed. Robby, after a single gasp of disbelief, dove upon the thing and attempted to thrust his head between the fang-rimmed jaws.

Amelia confessed—if only to herself—that her laughter upon reading North's words had verged on the hysterical. The bear rug, while totally inappropriate to a seven-year-old boy, was precisely the sort of thing a seven-year-old boy would treasure, and revealed an uncanny perspicacity on Mr. North's part.

But that wasn't the worst. Oh, no, indeed. Either Mr. North or his henchmen had been creative, and equally busy. At ten-thirty, just as one spate of deliveries ended and another was about to begin, Jitters appeared on the stoop. She should have recognized something was wrong given the blankness in eyes that never quite met hers. Jem Pflager lurked on the step below, toting a pair of boxes. Another in the endless procession of wagons drew up behind the carriage from Wilton Street, bearing a magnificently caparisoned rocking horse that sparkled in the sun.

"Oh, dear heaven," she murmured. "Will it never end?"

"Mr. North instructed these be brought 'round." Jitters took the boxes and thrust them at her. "With Mr. North's compliments. For you, not the children."

Then, imitating Mr. Tidmarsh's custom, he turned tail and scuttled down the steps, Jem close behind. They jumped into the carriage that had conveyed Amelia to Milbury Place what seemed a lifetime ago, and clattered out of the little square.

"Hush, Robby," Amelia pleaded as the boy jumped to the pavement with a whoop he boasted of having learned in the Americas. "Gently." She handed the boxes to the footman and seized Tibbie's shoulder before the moppet could follow her brother. "Take those to my sitting room, William. Some decorum, Robby, if you please," she called, knowing it a lost cause.

"Isn't fair," Tibbie whined around her thumb, already-broken doll dangling from her chubby fist. "I want a horse, too."

"I'm sure there's something far more interesting than a rocking horse in the wagon for you, Tibbie dear."

"Wanna *horse.*"

The lower lip managed to protrude in warning of what was to come despite the interfering thumb.

"No, Tabitha," Amelia cautioned as her grip on the child tightened. "Take a deep breath, remember you're a little lady, and be still."

"*Want a horse,*" Tibbie howled in the same wail that so shocked North's household the week before. "*Want a horse— want a horse—want a horse!*"

And if there was a soul still asleep in the houses rimming Milbury Place after that, only God Himself had managed the miracle.

"Of course you do at the moment, dear, but I'm certain you'll be far better pleased with what your kind guardian selected for you at this particular shop once you see it than you would by a silly horse. Horses are so, ah, pedestrian."

Still pouting, Tibbie gave a fair imitation of a scowl. "'Destrian?"

"No, that's not precisely accurate. Common, then. Rocking horses are common."

"Oh." Tibbie took a deep breath. "*Common,*" she shrieked in perfect galloping rhythm. "*Horses're common—common— common! Horses're common!*"

At North's, none had realized words lay embedded in the ear-splitting sound. That discovery had taken time, but it helped matters a bit. At least Tibbie merely shrieked now when she wanted something rather than getting the determined expression that presaged a deposit on the floor. When life settled, Amelia had every intention of replacing the carpets. Once the puppy and kitten provided by Mr. North in contravention of her wise counsel learned control. Once Robby no longer hurled food across the room. Once Tibbie relinquished blackmail. Once the millennium arrived, and angels ruled on earth.

Mick and Mike were already by the wagon, helping the carter unload the rocking horse and what appeared to be a doll's house large enough for Tibbie to enter.

"See?" Amelia declared, pointing. "Now, that's better than a horse, isn't it? How elegant. How fitting. How positively, ah, sybaritic."

"Sibbie?"

"Luxurious. And costly. Far more costly than the rocking horse."

Robby's ears were as acute as Tibbie's understanding once the words "luxurious" and "costly" were uttered. With a precision that mocked nature, he became a destructive devil. Within seconds the doll's house lay in splinters, cupola crushed, roof shattered, furniture scattered.

"Not a word, Tabitha," Amelia murmured. "Not a word, do you hear? Pretend you notice nothing. That will bring your brother low as nothing else could."

Futile injunction. And, Amelia would've admitted in a saner moment, far from befitting a proper governess.

That assaulting a sturdy rocking horse with an already destroyed doll could cause no harm to the rocking horse clearly mattered not to Tibbie. Doll's bonnet went this way, wig that. Still, Tibbie flailed. The doll's head parted company with its torso, flew onto the cobbles, and shattered. The rocking horse, aside from rocking, remained intact. Robby—naturally, given what Amelia had learned of his character during the past days—jeered.

"Oh, heavens," Amelia whimpered. She collapsed on the stoop and buried her face in her hands. "Perhaps Sir Reginald wasn't so dreadful after all."

It took an eternity to separate the warring pair, another to settle them in their bedchambers and make the girl she'd assigned nursemaid duties understand both children were to remain where Amelia placed them for a full hour. By the time they were released, the carter would have deposited the rocking horse at Mr. North's house. Amelia didn't care what that *tonnish* gentleman did with it so long as she never saw the cursed thing again. This time the neighbors' servants had appeared in force. Her ears and cheeks still burned.

More weary than she would have believed possible given the clocks had yet to strike noon, temples throbbing, once the children were settled and Florrie Whissett on guard, Amelia opened the door to her sitting room, fully intending a brief nap to restore her. Her eyes widened. Her hands balled into fists— an almost hourly occurrence in this house from hell since the night of her arrival.

"And precisely *what* do you two think you're doing?" she snapped over William's cheerful whistling of a jig.

Bessie Scrudge stopped in mid-caper, back to the door, skirts of periwinkle blue swirling around her ankles.

"Brung up your parcels just like you said." William unfolded his gangly length from the lady's chair by the fireplace and pulled down his rumpled livery jacket. "Bessie unpacked 'em so's you wouldn't be put to the trouble. Real kind of her, 'specially since you ain't been treating her respectfullike."

Bessie's clothes and cap lay beside the open boxes. Silver tissue drifted against a candlestick table on which a note had been tossed. Another gown, a pair of shawls, and a pelisse lay on the narrow window seat overlooking the rear garden. Bessie turned, bosom about to explode from its scanty restraint.

"I like this one." She grinned. "Looks better on me than it ever could on you. I'm going to keep it. Ain't suited to a governess anyways. Pink one'll do fine for Florrie, and Hortie Grimble'll be having the pelisse and the shawls."

"Remove that gown, Bessie. Now!" Amelia ground out, what had been the beginnings of a headache moments before now making her suspect a blacksmith had set up shop inside her skull.

"With Willie here?"

"He was here when you donned it, wasn't he?" Amelia snapped, hardly able to believe she was uttering such words. "What difference does it make? I'm certain he's seen you in far less than your shift."

She stalked across the sitting room, retrieved the note, and opened it.

To brighten your day, it said in a strongly sloping hand, *two to replace the ones that were ruined. Other things are because it's still winter. Think you'll agree Mary Duclos's styles're more fetching than those horrors you hide in.*

At the bottom was scrawled "North" in letters so bold, they were like a gauntlet flung in her face.

Dear heaven, the impropriety of it! And of him. And of the message. Any gentleman acquainted with a modiste about whom even Amelia had heard scandalous whispers during her single Season could be nothing but a rake. Next he'd be demanding her services in boudoir and bedchamber for himself rather than schoolroom and nursery for his wards, holding out some naughty concoction of feathers and lace designed to titillate rather than cover as inducement. Sir Reginald's appeal was growing fast, his faults fading to phantoms of a too-squeamish imagination.

She crumpled the note and turned to face the others.

"Pack them up," she snapped.

"Whatever for?" William said. "I'm just taking 'em to Bessie's room."

"No, you're not. You'll be returning them to Mr. North. Immediately."

"Told you she wouldn't want 'em," Bessie crowed. "Knew it the second I saw Duclos's name on the boxes. Cost a mint too. Fellow give me a petticoat from Duclos once. Has her new girls make those up on the cheap t'train 'em. But a gown? Never dreamed I'd have one. Prime articles, these two are."

"And *for* 'prime articles,' " Amelia managed to say, shocking herself once more. Living beyond the conventions surrounding an earl's daughter was certainly enlightening. "Such are never to be found in a house pretending to respectability. Do I make myself clear? Fasten your bodice, Bessie. Now! Then you'll pack it all up for William to deliver to Mr. North."

Amelia waited, cheeks flaming, arms crossed. Lips in a pout Tabitha would've envied had she seen it, Bessie fastened her dress tabs. Then, under Amelia's unwavering gaze, she packed away the gowns, the shawls, and the pelisse, all the while muttering of dogs in the manger too stubborn for their continued good health.

Chapter Six

The next week passed no more peaceably. The house remained as unkempt and unruly as its inhabitants, barely short of a state that would've forced Amelia to lodge a protest with Mr. Tidmarsh or, preferably, her actual employer. Only Florrie made the least effort to please, and then only when none of the others was about to sneer. Worst of all, the drizzle continued, the sort of wearying wet that accomplished only disharmony, fraying tempers and making a mockery of any attempt at good humor.

At least that's how Amelia saw it, and as far as she was concerned, she was being charitable.

The puppy continued to piddle on carpets, floors, feet, and laps, and destroyed any footwear that came within its reach. The parrot was banished to the servants' hall—actually a cramped nook in the kitchen—where the footmen taught it thieves' cant. The goldfish gave up their souls to the great beyond, their bodies to the kitten's clever paws, and their bowl was placed on a high shelf to gather dust. The rocking horse, thankfully, didn't reappear.

The gowns, shawls, and pelisse, however, did. Repeatedly. Amelia would have them returned to Wilton Street. Within hours they would be back at Milbury Place. Inevitably a new item would've been added: a bonnet, gloves, silk stockings, in the end even a watch intended to be pinned to a lady's corsage. It was, Amelia decided, a duel of sorts. She sent the bonnet back crushed, the gloves stained, the stockings shredded, deploring each act of destruction but unable to devise a clearer message regarding the impropriety of the gifts.

When faced with the watch—an exquisite thing whose gold case held a miniature of a lad with laughing eyes of a blue so dark as to be almost black—she sighed and hid it at the rear of her night table, placed the contested clothing, still in its boxes, on top of an armoire in her bedchamber, and admitted defeat. Even she had her price. The watch had been some lady's treasure, however little her employer valued it. Perhaps the time would come when she could return it to its rightful owner.

As for the neighbors, she'd lost count of the sodden strangers who pounded on the door in the middle of the night, demanding the services of Bessie or Florrie at full voice in such explicit terms that any doubts regarding the girls' former employment and the house's nature before its owners decided to turn respectable vanished. Worse yet, the place had clearly been one of the lower sort, catering to a clientele without concern for its own reputation or the house's anonymity. No wonder the other denizens of Milbury Place regarded them all askance.

North's wards continued impossible. Robby's snort when Amelia, driven beyond endurance following the canary's demise from a surfeit of Tibbie's teasing, finally demanded, "Haven't either of you so much as opened a book and looked at the pictures? Or sat at a table to do more than eat?" explained a great deal.

"Hadn't no books. Didn't need any, 'cause we didn't have a governess," Tibbie said around her thumb. "Mama said Papa's eyes didn't stay where they belonged if there was pretty ladies about, an' so we couldn't have one. Didn't want one anyways. Books either."

"Papa liked pretty ladies." Robby shrugged at Amelia's shocked look. "Had a squaw woman mended our clothes an' fed us when we was hungry. Squaw was ugly and smelled, so

Mama didn't mind her. Didn't need nobody else, 'cause when squaw'd help herself at Papa's drinks table, his batman'd see to us.''

Tibbie pulled her thumb from her mouth. "You'd've been all right though. Papa wouldn't've liked you, so Mama wouldn't't've taken a switch to you the way she did the others afore she chased 'em off.''

With a long-suffering sigh, Amelia set about teaching the waifs to remain seated for fifteen minutes at a time, bribing them with treats to accomplish even that much. She began reading them tales while they played, stopping at the most interesting parts and leaving the simple books lying about, insisting her eyes were tired. Robby at least knew his alphabet, and could spell out words of one syllable.

Something, she decided as she paced her sitting room that night, had to be done—not only for her sake, but for Tibbie's and Robby's as well. If nothing else, humanity and her own sense of duty required it. What, however, was the question. Any attempt at a hug or a kiss or a kindness was rebuffed. The Tyne orphans had no ''better nature''—only stingers and prickles, and redoubled misbehavior for which they had no remorse if she showed them the slightest leniency.

She sank on the window seat overlooking the back garden and pulled the draperies aside to lay her aching head against a cool pane.

The cinder-clogged plot belonging to the little town house was dark. Lights from the servants' quarters shone on puddles twinkling with rain pocks. A stunted tree reached bare branches above the wall, silhouetted against the mews behind. Roses that would never bloom again cowered at the back gate, all twisted branches and iron thorns.

It was, she sighed, the most dispiriting view in the world— unkempt and unloved, just like Tibbie and Robby. For this she'd cast off the court's generous grounds, and the luxury of flowers in every room? As her lids drifted closed, Sir Reginald's sneering face superimposed itself on a vision of trellised roses and a hill covered with wild lavender. She shuddered, letting the drapery drop as she stood. It was time for bed. Tomorrow would yield up its problems soon enough.

That night she dreamed of a young devil who pursued her from attics to cellars and out onto Milbury Place, shouting forfeits were due him. Clad only in feathers and spangles, she stumbled through the garden gates, tripped on a root, and sprawled on the sodden path to the tune of the neighbors' catcalls. She woke shivering, then lay rigid for hours, waiting for sleep to return. It was long in coming. The young devil lurked behind her lids whenever she lowered them, jeering as only such young devils can.

The next morning she roused to Florrie's shrieks. Tibbie and Robby had gone missing. A quick search yielded no trace of the pair. Amelia and the staff gathered in the entry once they'd poked into every cranny and explored every nook, and uncovered only cobwebs and mouse droppings and a quizzing glass with an improper handle.

"No, Mrs. Grimble, no Bow Street Runners," Amelia repeated over Florrie's hysterical sobs, squaring her shoulders as she pulled her dressing gown more tightly about her. "No notification of Mr. North either. He's not needed. Neither is Mr. Tidmarsh, who's more trouble than he's worth. And be still, Florrie. Such noise is more likely than not music to those imps' ears. They're enjoying this. Else why play such a prank?"

"Imps? Beasts, they be! Satan-born, both on 'em," Florrie gulped, dabbing at eyes and nose with her apron.

"It's Mr. North what pays our keep," Hortense Grimble insisted as she crammed straggling hennaed curls under her nightcap, "and yours into the bargain, Miss Know-Everything. I've a sight of years on you, and a deal of experience, and I say one or t'other's to be fetched instanter. Doesn't do to play at knowing what's what when one's betters're mixed up in it, for what one thinks is ever different from their notions."

"I'm in charge," Amelia reminded the woman, overriding the others' mumbled support of the blowzy housekeeper. "While your experience may be extensive with gentlemen of the *ton,* your knowledge of their offspring is limited. Mine, however, is not. This is a commonplace game given children're involved.''

''On your head be it then, for I won't take no blame. It ain't my lookout what happens to them monsters. Ain't any of the others' here either.''

''It's not Florrie's, who is their nursemaid? Dear me—and I always understood a nursemaid was responsible for her charges.''

Amelia cursed her intemperate words at Florrie's renewed wails. With a long-suffering sigh she put an arm around the girl's shoulders. ''Hush,'' she murmured. ''With children such as these, no one's to blame. Heaven knows at what hour they disappeared, but it was probably when we were all asleep.''

Then, as Florrie's tears—which she'd begun to suspect weren't all that genuine—subsided, she turned back to Mrs. Grimble.

''Charles and William have already confirmed all the doors and windows remain locked,'' she said, ''and Mrs. Chiddy that nothing's missing from her larder—though something may be now, more's the pity, for I didn't think to set a watch before we began our search. That's enough to settle the matter.''

''What has doors to do with anything? You're just afraid o' being given the sack, that's what, and don't care for what may've happened to 'em, poor sweet innocents that they be.''

''That's not what you called 'em yesterday when they turned over a barrel o' flour in my kitchen,'' Mrs. Chiddy snapped. ''And it certain ain't what you called 'em when Robby got into your paint pots an' tarted hisself up like a red Indian. Not what you called 'em a few minutes ago either.''

''Well, it's what I'm calling 'em now.''

''There ain't no way the beggars can've got out lessen it were up a chimney, lovey,'' Pimplow Grimble rumbled beside his wife. ''They're here, don't y'see? Just don't know where exactlike, for they've hidden 'emselves away good an' proper.''

''And don't you think Mr. North an' Mr. Tidmarsh'd like to know how that one,'' Mrs. Grimble fulminated, pointing at Amelia, ''don't see to 'em as she ought, nor yet teach 'em proper manners, having which they wouldn't plague us so? Being paid a good wage, an' she ain't earnin' it. Better the money should come to us. Needs to be chased from the place, she does."

Grimble shrugged. "Nothin' she could've done to stop 'em. Ferrets, both on 'em. An' if they're here, ain't no reason to inform those as we'd rather not tell that they've gone missing, m'love. Y'know how gentry-coves go blaming the wrong folk ever' time something goes amiss. Like as not, it'd be us or Florrie'd get the sack, an' not her nibs what thinks she's so much better'n we are, and with the rent sued for an' us left to find another tenant. Seen it happen afore, both on us have, an' paid for it. 'At's why we bought this house. That North fellow might even cry Newgate an' the Antipodes."

Mrs. Grimble subsided when reminded of the less pleasant characteristics of gentry-coves, though not until she'd given Amelia a look that promised retribution should aught go amiss. Amelia's answering smile was all that was superior.

She gestured for the others to gather more closely, then whispered, "Mrs. Chiddy, they're bound to be hungry. Nothing of substance since last night, even if they've snuck a crust or two. Children of this age are full of grandiose plans, but most improvident when it comes to carrying them out. I want you to prepare a breakfast for the rest of us that'd delight the hungriest man: muffins, and sizzled gammon and roasted apples and grilled kidneys, and anything else you can think of that smells heavenly. Robby's quite the trencherman, and Tibbie's not far behind him."

"Why not set the pup to finding 'em," Mrs. Grimble nattered. "Should be able to sniff 'em out. You don't do that, it's acause you know they ain't here."

"Point one: Their scent is all over the house, which would confuse the poor animal. Point two: I will not have them hunted down like criminals. They're merely children trying to devil us. The pup will remain tied up in the nursery. Point three: The goal is to encourage Tibbie and Robby to reappear of their own volition. If we can't manage that, they win and we lose. I'm not about to lose.

"Then, Mrs. Chiddy," she said, turning her back on the housekeeper, "I want you to begin work on a dinner fit for a king. The kitchen doors open, our lives to continue as usual, and not a scrap of effort wasted on searching for Tibbie and Robby."

A look of grudging respect came over Mrs. Grimble's features. "Don't like to admit it," she muttered, "but it ain't a bad notion. Where'd you happen on it? So clever, I should've thought of it m'self."

"Some children visiting my previous employer once took French leave. While I didn't have official charge of them, I didn't want the family bothered. I conferred with the staff, and we hit on a similar solution."

"Didn't think you'd come up with it yerself," Mrs. Grimble muttered. "Like as not it were the potboy."

"They weren't as stubborn as Tibbie and Robby," Amelia continued, ignoring the interruption, "so they appeared when my breakfast was served. I suspect we won't see this pair until dinner. I want watches posted at the outer doors. As you go about your work, I want every one of you to exclaim over the aromas from the kitchen. When they do appear, I want them very hungry and very contrite."

"The watch worked," Valentine North informed his cronies later that same day, stretching his legs to the generous fire in his book room and stifling a sneeze. "Excellent notion, that was. Glad I thought of it. She's kept the blasted gowns as well."

"Wonder what your mother'll think when she learns what you've done with the thing rather than having it repaired as she requested," Ollie Threadwhistle said.

"I'll get her another. A better one that actually keeps time."

"Won't be the same. Might well irk her, y'know. Females set store by such things. Your father gave it to her to mark your fourteenth birthday."

"And made me sit for hours for the miniaturist when I'd rather've been anywhere than a stuffy garret." North repressed a shiver, then rose to add more sea coal to the fire. "Deplorable fashion in which to spend so much of one's holidays. Mawkish thing anyway. She's better off without it."

"Doubt she'll agree." Threadwhistle ducked his head at North's sardonic grin. "Well, she won't," he muttered, "as you'll learn to your sorrow. Just you wait."

"He's right, you know," Quint Dauntry drawled. "If your mother favors the thing to the point where she sent it to you by messenger, you'll be front and center when she learns you've given it away. Cup-shot wisdom, that was, and sure to bring you grief."

"Then I'll buy it back from Miss Sparrow." North shrugged. "Find something even more to the lady's taste, and of considerably more value." He gestured impatiently as Threadwhistle's mouth opened once more. "Have done," he growled. "You're worse than my sisters' old governess. What a moralizer that one was."

"Could be Miss Sparrow places the same store on it your mother does, as she hasn't returned it in pieces," Dauntry suggested with a wink to the others. "Portrait's very like, if I remember correctly."

"Female's never seen me so far as she knows. Isn't going to either. Told Chloe I wouldn't be the butt of some low-bred farce, and I meant it. Besides, I doubt my youthful lineaments would thrill Miss Sparrow. Now, have done for pity's sake. Day's cheerless enough without flogging such a dreary topic to death. You must be bored to tears, the lot of you."

Their derisive looks had North gripping the arms of his chair until his knuckles turned white. The fellows'd been far too interested in Miss Sparrow of late, and far too interested in his wards. At least they'd indulged in none of the mischief he'd anticipated, but even so, he was beginning to regret the wager. Winning it was proving deuced expensive, and not a little troublesome.

With apparent lack of intent, Dauntry rose from his chair across the fire from North and wandered the room, exchanging banter with Pugs Harnette and Stubby Clough regarding the speed with which a particular lump of coal would disintegrate to ashes, pausing by the drinks table to refill his glass, then fetching up at the table where St. Maure was conspicuously ignoring the rest of them as he devoured another volume of Stowaker's gabble-mongering *Origins of the Great Families,* and from which he'd been reading them scraps regarding a low sort named Bottom who'd had the good fortune to pimp a yellow-haired doxy who caught the eye of Henry the VIII.

North's eyes narrowed as Dauntry leaned over St. Maure's shoulder and murmured a comment regarding a handsome hand-colored illustration, supposedly the delectable Griselda. St. Maure nodded and turned the page. Dauntry's lips continued to move well after his voice faded. St. Maure nodded again.

North grinned and started to count. By the time he'd reached twenty, Harnette and Clough had returned to tossing dice and Dauntry was across the room, sipping his Madeira and studying the raindrops greasing a window overlooking the garden.

"Have you been to see how Tyne's progeny go on now that they've had a bit of civilizing at Miss Sparrow's hands?" St. Maure inquired without raising his head.

"What, surfacing, O indefatigable scholar of moldy tittle-tattle? No, I haven't," North chuckled. "Lord, but you fellows've become bores since Freddy saddled me with his tadpoles. They go on well or they go on poorly. Doesn't matter to me in the least."

St. Maure lifted his head as the others turned to watch North. "Perhaps it should."

"Whatever for? They're housed, they're fed, and they're seen to. Properly, I might add, by a proper governess who's more mouse than sparrow, if you want to know."

"Then maybe the rest of us should go to Milbury Place," Harnette chimed in, "see how they get on. Y'did say as how we might play adjunct uncles, and if you're not going to see to 'em, then somebody must."

"Miss Sparrow's no looker, if that's your interest. Prunes-and-prisms, and that's on a good day. As for the brats, they're terrors, both of 'em. That's why I'm cursed with that blasted thing." He pointed to the rocking horse in the farthest and darkest corner of the book room. "The girl was intent on destroying it—after the boy destroyed her playhouse. Jitters learned that much from the groom who bought it here.''

"Has nothing to say with how this Miss Sparrow treats 'em, or whether she's suited to having charge of a pair of children. Jitters hasn't stepped foot inside the place since they arrived, I'd wager, any more than you have.''

"What, Pugs—you're going to accuse Miss Sparrow of taking a whip to them? It'd be out of character, believe me. She's punctilious with her accounts too—hoards every seed she happens on now that she's made her nest, good little mouse that she is. Most females given a free hand'll go their length, even Chloe. Not Miss Sparrow. References said she was a treasure, and she is. Besides, Pickles approves of her as much as she disapproves of me these days. So do Jitters and Bassett.''

"Still and all, it's a dreary day,'' St. Maure said, closing his book and rising from the table. "Think I'll go and have a look if you don't mind, Val. Any of the rest of you care to join me?''

There was a general shifting as heads turned and eyes widened.

"Didn't know you'd such an interest in petticoats, Dab,'' Sinclair chuckled.

"Especially petticoats that tend to prunes and prisms,'' Pugs Harnette threw in, "and'll rap your fingers each time you set a foot awry.''

"Or the infantry,'' Stubby Clough added. "I'd swear your own nieces and nevies haven't the slightest notion what you look like.''

St. Maure merely smiled and cocked a brow.

North insisted there wasn't the slightest need to go as himself, and even less to rig himself as Pericles Tidmarsh—especially to appear in a setting he couldn't control. The fellows' knowing grins at his disenchantment with playing antiquated secretary had him grinding his teeth.

Dauntry, who'd instigated the transformation of a desultory interest in Milbury Place to a keen desire to see what went on there, played punctilious guest, insisting North mustn't be left to his own devices on such a cheerless afternoon, especially after losing a rain-slashed curricle race around Hyde Park to Tony Sinclair the night before. The rest decided the adventure of visiting Milbury Place was preferable to making up the fire and watching it die down again. North shrugged and summoned one of his carriages.

Thus it was that at four in the afternoon, just when the aromas of roasting turkey, apple tarts laced with cinnamon, and a pudding rich with plums, raisins, and citron were reaching their peak, knocking echoed through the house on Milbury Place. Amelia—who'd been treating herself to Childe Harold's adventures—shuddered. Just so did the miscreants who'd previously patronized Milbury Place assault the door, howling for Bessie or Florrie.

Grimble, assigned picket duty, could be heard grumbling as he clumped across the entry in the stout boots he insisted on wearing instead of the more customary, and definitely quieter, felt-soled pumps she'd provided.

Sighing, Amelia set Byron's work aside and dragged herself back to London. It was too much to hope for an entire afternoon of freedom, especially one without sirens and alarms. She cracked the drawing room door, on the alert should Grimble prove unequal to the task of defending them against the latest band of inebriated bucks.

After a glance behind him to make sure neither Tibbie nor Robby lurked in the shadows, Grimble was unbarring the door and removing a huge key from the waistband of his stained yellow livery. Amelia inched the door a little wider, trying to catch sight of the stoop as a gust of rain blew into the entry.

"Here now, on your way." Grimble yawned, tucking the key back in his waistband like a pistol. "We ain't in the business no more. Sophy Minch's got a place two streets over. Red door. Knocker's a bare-arsed lovely."

"Miss Sparrow, if you please," she heard to her horror.

Dear heaven, how had such louts come by her name, even her assumed one?

"Y'don't want her," Grimble insisted. "Wouldn't be no

good to you a'tall. It's Minch's place y'wants," he continued more loudly as Amelia sped across the entryway, shoving Bessie—who had appeared from the nether regions—to the side. "Get on with you, or I'll call a constable."

"I'm afraid you don't understand," one of the louts said as another chuckled. "We ain't here about entertainment."

"Grimble, step aside, please. Bessie, return belowstairs. Now!" Amelia shoved the girl in the direction of the service stairs, ignoring the strangers in favor of more immediate mortifications. "I'll deal with this."

"Y'aint got no business with these here fellows," Bessie snapped, doing her best to thrust herself between Amelia and the open doorway. "Found the right place, even if they got the name they was to ask for wrong. I'm Bessie," the trollop said with a bold smile and a toss of her dark curls. "Florrie's that busy, but I'll be glad to show you a bit o' fun. Herself can go for a walk if she don't like the notion."

"I, ah, believe there's been a misunderstanding," a mediumish young man with light brown hair and gray eyes choked out. Good heavens—was that Mr. Sinclair just behind him? And Mr. Threadwhistle? "Is this where the wards of Valentine North reside with their governess? Because if it is, we're here to pay a call on them."

"You ain't never," Bessie giggled. "For real, y'want the Sparrow? That why y'got them flowers? Well, there she is. Sure y'wouldn't rather 'confer' with me? Deal more fun, that I promise."

A young man with a neck like a bull's and a chest like a barrel was muttering in the ear of another with the look of a country squire. Then he bowed, doffing his hat.

"Name's Stephen Clough," he said, taffy-colored hair glistening in the rain. "Friend of North's, don't you see? North said he'd told you—ah—told old Tidmarsh to inform you we'd be stopping by. You are Miss Sparrow, aren't you? Ollie, you've seen her. Is that Miss Sparrow?"

Amelia nodded, heart sinking. "It's inconvenient," she managed to say, trying to close the door. "The children are upstairs, taking naps. They, ah, have colds. You'd best return another day. Good afternoon, Mr. Sinclair, Mr. Threadwhistle, gentle-men.''

''What a clanker,'' Bessie spat out loudly enough to be heard by those on the stoop. ''Gone missing, them poor innocents has, and herself at fault from start to finish.''

Clough shoved his foot between jamb and door. ''Gone missing?''

What had appeared to Amelia to be rather vacant, almost colorless eyes were suddenly boring into hers with acute interest.

''Not precisely missing,'' she protested. ''They're some-where about the house.''

''Don't you believe a word on it,'' Bessie snapped. ''Gone missing permanent, and herself not letting us tell Mr. North, nor even Mr. Tidmarsh, for fear of being sacked.''

''I suppose you'd best come in,'' Amelia sighed, opening the door wider and stepping aside as the brows of those on the stoop rose. ''Grimble, see to these gentlemen's coats and hats, and then show them into the drawing room—but lock and bar the door first. I don't want Tibbie or Robby sneaking out in the confusion, and proving Bessie right.''

Then she squared her shoulders and shoved her spectacles back up her nose.

''Gentlemen, thank you for the flowers. Infinitely thoughtful. I'll join you in a moment. Bessie, please ask Mrs. Chiddy to prepare tea for our guests. Then you may arrange the flowers and have them brought to the drawing room.''

Turning on her heel, Amelia fled toward the stairs and the temporary haven of the upper regions of the house.

Chapter Seven

"That Miss Sparrow you hired?"

Stubby Clough stretched short legs to the book room fire and wiggled his stocking toes, cradling a glass of brandy in his palms to warm it, a smile flitting over his lips. The sodden Hessians in which he'd arrived at Wilton Street now steamed by the kitchen hearth under Jitters's supervision, their shape and size preserved by a pair of adjustable forms.

North groaned, stifling a sneeze.

With the exception of Dauntry, who'd parted the draperies to stare at the sodden gardens and lowering skies behind North's town house, the fellows sprawled on chairs and divans scattered about the book room, puffing on cigarillos and sipping claret or port or brandy as they struggled to keep heads from nodding and lids from sinking—when they weren't chattering like magpies about the superior Miss Sparrow, that was.

"Yes, well?" North snapped when Clough forgot what he was about to say. "Come on, man—what of Miss Sparrow this time?"

"She's well, very well indeed," Clough replied. "Charming in an elder-sister sort of way, and not that repulsive to look at. Had us eating out of her hand, and our first welcome wasn't what one would have expected at the home of a friend's wards. Not a one of us didn't regard her with a skeptical eye in the beginning. Stayed to dinner. She offered when it was ready, and there was little we could do but agree. One doesn't refuse one's betters. Passable dinner too.''

"You've told me that before. More than once.''

"And elegant in spite of the bombazine,'' Clough continued as if North hadn't spoken. "Not certain I'd describe her voice as a viola though. More like an oboe. Restful, but haunting.''

From the divan on which he sprawled, Tony Sinclair emitted a sound halfway between a chuckle and a snore. "Poured out as if she were serving the queen rather than a pack of ne'er-do-wells. Like taking tea with one's maiden aunt. We watched ourselves, that I can tell you. Not a foot set awry or an improper oath uttered.''

North buried his head in his hands. "You sound like moon-calves,'' he muttered. "If I must listen to this nonsense yet again—''

"Not moon-calves at all,'' Ollie Threadwhistle protested. "You're all about in your head if you think that, Val. Not a one of us willingly does the pretty, but we danced to her tune, and were glad to do it too. That's the sort she is.''

"Good Lord, deliver me!'' North growled.

"And when those scapegraces of yours finally turned up demanding their fair share just after we sat down to dinner,'' Threadwhistle went on, "she treated their tangled hair and dirty faces as natural.''

"Didn't say a word about their clothes, which were past praying for,'' Clough overrode the genial Threadwhistle. "Just insisted Florrie—who's the best of a bad lot, which isn't saying much, but she's country bred and doesn't seem as hard as the others—make 'em presentable before they joined us. You'd've thought Miss Sparrow'd known where those little rotters were all along—though she didn't, that I'll swear—and had been humoring 'em.''

"Yes, I know.'' North sighed, closing his eyes in resignation. " 'Not one word of recrimination,' '' he quoted, mimicking

Clough's slightly slurred diction. " 'Not even the hint of a scold.' "

"Not one," Clough agreed, "nor any evidence they feared the switch later rather than sooner. You've found a jewel. I'd've killed for such a governess when I was a lad."

" 'Just a smile, and a sunny "Good evening, Robert and Tabitha." ' ' "

"Doesn't call 'em that. Calls 'em Tibbie and Robby."

"At least you're not claiming she's a diamond."

"Oh, no." Clough grinned. "Diamonds don't sport spectacles or drape themselves in bombazine. Certainly they don't skin their hair back so tight, they give a fair imitation of a plucked chicken, or powder it with coal dust to dull the luster. All that aside, who knows? What one sees ain't necessarily what's really there."

"Fustian! Y'still haven't explained how you came to have what appeared to be the entire contents of the Thames in your boots when the lot of you arrived on my doorstep," North said to turn the subject from one with which he had become heartily irritated three minutes after his friends returned from Milbury Place. They had no need to puff up Abigail Sparrow. He'd been uncomfortably aware of her good points within minutes of her entering the reception room that first day. Why did they think he'd hired the woman, blast them?

"Attention was what they wanted, you see," Clough forged on, ignoring the question for all he colored up nicely, "and that was what she refused to give 'em. Clever woman—infinitely clever. Y'ain't paying her half enough, no matter how much it is."

"It's a small fortune to one of her sort, believe me. Now, what happened to your boots—not that I won't countenance a friend taking his ease in his stocking feet, or appropriating my man's services to salvage his footwear."

"Stepped in a puddle," Clough muttered.

"The size of an ocean?" North snorted. "Give over—what happened?"

"Children got out while we were leaving, if you must know."

"They are devils! And?"

"Got across the street and into the garden, locked gate or no. Slipped through the railings."

"Which still explains nothing."

"Leave be, Val," Sinclair said without bothering to open his eyes. " 'Twas only because that pup you gave 'em escaped, since Florrie hadn't tied it up as Miss Sparrow told her to. Tibbie and Robby wanted only to get it back, as even Miss Sparrow admitted once it was over."

"Ah—a slight crack in the mirror of perfection." North chuckled, choking back another sneeze. "Berated the lot of you before she regained her equanimity, hmm?"

"Not at all. Pup got in the fountain, the children followed, and Miss Sparrow followed them. Stubby waded in and handed 'em over to us one by one, and we carried 'em back to the house while the neighbors gawked. Over and under the gates, though in the end we had the key. A regular Charon, he was. Just too modest to admit it."

"Now, *that's* something I would've dearly loved to see."

"No, y'wouldn't," Clough said. "Wasn't only water got in my boots. Blasted pup's a fountain when it wants to be. Mortified poor Miss Sparrow no end. You ain't paying her enough by half," he insisted over North's laughter.

"No—Val's being generous enough they could be taking orders from Satan and she'd have no complaint," St. Maure said from his place across the fire from Clough as the others protested Miss Sparrow's superior merits. Then, voice suddenly sobering, he said, "Well, perhaps she should at that. Complain to you, that is, Val, if you'd only give her the opportunity. Not fair to her, you know—the way you're keeping yourself aloof."

"What has she to complain of? She's housed, fed, clothed— or would be if she'd make use of those gowns I sent her— provided with a mount for when it's clement and a carriage when it's not, and I'm paying her a hundred pounds a year, and an additional five pounds for each week she doesn't come importuning me. All this for overseeing a pair of the infantry? For pity's sake, what more can she possibly want?"

The others shifted about, looking anywhere but at him.

"Perhaps," St. Maure said at last, rising and joining Dauntry at the windows when it became obvious the others wouldn't inform North what was lacking in his employee's life, "she'd prefer a home that didn't give every indication of having so recently been a house. D'you know, Quint," he added, "I do believe it's coming on to clear. Clouds seem to be dispersing, and I swear that's a star up there."

"They claim it's a brothel," North grumbled once he'd convinced the others to go on to White's without him, and then scurried to his mistress's as rapidly as his town carriage could take him, shivering all the way, "or as near as makes no difference."

"Now?" the raven-haired pocket Venus demanded incredulously.

"Well, no, but that it was until just before I leased the place."

"Ah," Chloe Sherbrough murmured, "I couldn't believe I'd been so seriously misinformed." She sighed, shaking her head. "You've had a tendency to leap before you look for weeks now, just as with the matter of the gowns and pelisse for Miss Sparrow and the superabundance of toys for the children. Such leaping causes everyone no end of trouble, including yourself. I'm afraid this is another instance."

North filled his glass with brandy. As ever when he called on her these days, there was a disjointedness to their conversation, an air more of fondly scrapping siblings than welcoming mistress and ardent protector. They'd always been friends, of course, but there'd been a certain spark, a fire, if you will. Now the fire appeared to have sunk to ashes amid which only a dull glow lingered. Strange.

"Dammit, Chloe, what they claim's impossible. I inspected the place myself," he said as he sipped the brandy, praying it would warm him. The chill of last night's race remained with him, a reminder that winning a wager could sometimes be more costly than losing it. "It was no such thing. A bit down at the heels, just as any property for lease is bound to be, but perfectly respectable."

He flushed as she paused in her pacing to glance at him over her shoulder, her brows rising. Dammit, but he felt odd. It wasn't just that he was out of sorts. The cold seemed to start at the very core of his being, running along each artery and vein like mice with icy feet. He hoped to hell he wasn't sickening for something.

"The maids may've been bolder than my mother'd countenance," he admitted, "and the housekeeper had a come-hither air to her, but she thought I was someone else, and this is London, not the back of beyond."

"Ah, this is London. I hadn't realized."

"One must expect that sort of thing if one has more than two pennies to rub together and isn't well known to the individuals involved," he insisted, absently noting he sounded more like a pompous idiot than the rational man he'd always considered himself. "The fellows're bamming me, that's what. Not sure I like it."

"Poor lamb."

Chloe continued to pace, repositioning bibelots and straightening chairs as North watched her with growing irritation from his customary seat by the fire.

"For pity's sake, leave that to your maid," he snapped. "I didn't come here to watch you play housewife. The room's fine as it is."

She continued setting things to rights, glancing at him over her shoulder as she rattled a chair. "You haven't had a moment's peace since that letter arrived from the Colonies, have you," she said.

"No, I haven't. Makes one wonder why fellows marry, for that must be ten times the inconvenience."

"Yes, I imagine it must, from all I've been told," she returned, now twitching the draperies at the windows facing the street, "for all there are those who prize the estate, even long to enter it." From below came what might have been the sound of the front door closing. She peeped out, then turned back to him with an air of relief. "I gather your friends have been combing your hair?"

"You'd think it was their favorite pastime," he moaned, refilling his glass from the decanter on the table at his side.

"Really, Chloe, the whole mess has long passed beyond the mildly amusing and entered the realm of the unendurable. If Freddy weren't already dead, I'd murder him."

He took a swallow, then set his glass aside, scowling.

"Even Pickles has been stiff-rumped," he complained, "and I was always a favorite with her until Freddy's waifs appeared. As for Jitters, he's barely speaking to me. I've had enough. Half a mind to move in here and let them all go hang."

"That wouldn't do at all."

"Why not?"

"You'd lose your wager."

He opened his mouth, but she shook her head, then sank onto her chaise longue and picked up a piece of embroidery—something he'd never seen her do before. She frowned, setting stitches as awkwardly as a girl working her first piece.

"What are you going to do?" she said.

"Damned if I know. The only thing that comes to mind is a bolt for the Continent, and that's as out of the question as the other."

"I gather playing septuagenarian secretary has palled."

"Totally. A game for an idiot. Problem is, now that I've begun, there's no way to stop. Miss Sparrow is all that stands between me and disaster, and she'd vanish the minute she learned the truth. Frankly, I wouldn't blame her."

"Have you considered calling on your mother for advice? It would seem the situation has deteriorated to the point where that may become necessary."

The look he sent her caused her rosy cheeks to pale. "All right, then," she sighed, "why not consult Mr. Burridge? I know you'd lose the wager, but if it really is a house, or even if it was one only recently, you've lost it in any case. Aaron— Mr. Burridge has stood buff in the past, no matter how many scrapes you've tumbled into. He's always been rather good at straightening things out too."

"I do not tumble into scrapes."

"No? Adventures, then. I suppose that's what gentlemen call them once they've achieved their majorities. Goodness, but you're sour this evening."

He shrugged—a favorite habit these days when no cogent response came to mind. "Old Burridge lectures with his eyes now as effectively as he used to with his mouth in the past," North muttered, "and as often."

"Mr. Burridge isn't old. Well, he's not," Chloe insisted, coloring at North's narrow glance.

"He's forty."

"Thirty-eight, actually."

"And that's such a difference? Either way, he's old."

"Only because you're twenty-nine."

" 'A man in his prime'? Don't be an idiot. He's old. Wears flannel waistcoats, for God's sake."

Damn, but he sounded sour-stomached and sick-livered. Still, he was glad to see she subsided after that bit of reality. Well, what could she say? It was the truth. Burridge had been born old, a ledger in one hand, a pen in the other, and an abacus in his cradle instead of a teething coral or a rattle.

The silence grew. It wasn't the companionable one that placed no demands on either and stressed the perfect accord in which they generally found themselves. This was a new thing he couldn't put a name to, and just as intolerable as the too-many-words his cronies were spewing these days.

To have something to do, he rebuilt the fire. Damn, but it was cold. Or he was. Or something. He sat. He shivered, hunching his shoulders and insisting it was the situation that galled, and not that he was feeling helpless and inadequate.

"I'm sorry, Chloe," he murmured after a bit, drained his glass, and refilled it.

"As well you might be," she returned, "insulting Mr. Burridge—who's never shown you anything but a respect you've done little to earn, and has given you devoted service."

"Enough. If you'll have it old Burridge is a cockerel hatched this spring, then he's a cockerel hatched this spring. Who gives a damn when he pecked his way out of the shell? Certainly not I—especially when confronted with female irrationality."

Somehow that wasn't the right thing to say either. The silence grew again, strained by retorts he could tell Chloe was choking back in the interest of an illusion of harmony.

North twisted and turned the situation, trying to find some way out of the trap that had eluded him. Short of appealing to Burridge or his mother, as Chloe suggested, he could find none. It wasn't so much he minded paying up. It was that the fellows would be proved right. Freddy, in saddling him with the brats, had performed the single most irresponsible act of his irresponsible life. That rankled. That roiled. And there was no escaping it.

"Shouldn't've inflicted my presence on you tonight," North muttered after the clock on the mantel had twice struck the quarter hour and was stubbornly making its way toward midnight. He'd managed to down three glasses of brandy in that interminable half hour. Instead of creating a glow, the last swallows hung on the back of his tongue like bile. He staggered to his feet and stumbled toward the door. "No' decent company for anyone."

"Perhaps you should take advantage of the guest bed chamber. We can discuss this in the morning," Chloe said.

He glanced at her. She was haloed, as if she stood before a mirror with another at her back, endlessly repeating until the reflections slanted into nothingness, each repetition less distinct than the one before. An infinity of raven-haired Chloes.

"Want my own bed," North said, attempting to regulate his slurred speech. This wasn't like him—not like him at all. He enjoyed being slightly above par. Most fellows did. But sodden? And the dear Lord knew he was sodden in addition to whatever else he might be. "No good t'stay. Better call Jem," he gulped, staggering against a table and overturning it, then collapsing on a bench by the door. "Not myself. Truth. Did not drink tha' much."

It took some doing, but between Jem and Chloe's footman, they got him down the stairs and stuffed him into his greatcoat. They managed to cram his hat on his head no matter how many times he batted their hands. Chloe even saw to gloves that balked at sliding up uncooperative fingers, clucking all the while about the head he was sure to have in the morning.

She was right, he mumbled. It was going to be the head to end all heads.

"Once you've recovered," she murmured after Joseph had put him in a chair and Jem had gone to signal the carriage on its next circle of the street, "you might consider discussing matters with Miss Sparrow. From what you haven't said as much as from what you have, she has a sound head on her shoulders."

"Have t'rig as Tim-Tam-Ti'marsh," North complained between hiccoughs and sneezes. "Uncomfortable—rigging as Ti'marsh—best times. Tomorrow worst."

"It might be more uncomfortable in the end if you don't make the effort," she cautioned. "As she's your wards' governess, no one can claim you're seeking advice in any corner but the proper one. If she advises you well, it proves you showed superior judgment in hiring her and so are fit to have charge of a pair of innocent babes."

"Not in'cent babes," he insisted. "Hellcats."

Then Jem was at the door, and they were getting him down the steps and into the carriage. The world, after a single gut-wrenching lurch, faded to nothingness.

"We's cold. Inside an' out."

Amelia twisted away from the insistent voices and tiny clutching fingers.

The dream had been a pleasant one for once, filled with the scent of spring and the lilt of birdsong. A high hill, an ancient chestnut, a rivulet that twined past hamlet and farm like a satin ribbon, a field carpeted with dandelions and daisies. There had been no hint of the devil with the laughing eyes, no neighbors peering down their noses as she danced in spangles. She'd been garbed in sprigged muslin, gathering wildflowers like any proper young lady. She had no desire to abandon the dream for the house on Milbury Place, but she knew once she opened her eyes that was where she'd find herself.

"And—and we're sorry."

Robby's muffled apology that encompassed so much more than yesterday's mischief convinced her. She knew the tone. Her youthful cousins had used it often enough when, desperate to shelter them from the attention their peccadilloes elicited, she assumed blame for broken vase or shattered cup, earning a reputation for clumsiness. With a sigh Amelia relinquished the dream of a place where her only responsibility had been finding perfect blossoms, opened her eyes, and blinked.

They huddled in the light of her veilleuse, cheeks tearstained, curling their toes against the icy floorboards like a pair of ghosts in their white nightgowns.

"Nightmares," Robby said. "Coal chutes—only they went to hell 'stead of the cellars, an' there was coal pouring on us. There was devils with pitchforks in Tibbie's. Mine didn't have pitchforks. I told Tibbie all'd be right come morning, but she wouldn't listen."

Amelia didn't bother to speak. She merely lifted the covers. The children scrambled in and tucked themselves against her, Tibbie on one side, Robby on the other.

In the morning they were gone. At first Amelia thought their appearance had been an extension of the tree on the windswept hill. It hadn't. When she entered the nursery to see if Florrie needed assistance getting them dressed—generally a battle that left Florrie in tears and Amelia wondering if the saw of spare the rod and spoil the child might not have something to it after all—they were sitting at their table consuming porridge as Florrie bustled about the room, confusion in every glance.

Of course it might be thanks to the sun streaming through the nursery windows. That in itself was enough to soothe the most savage breast. But no, it wasn't just the sun. The eyes that lifted to hers lacked cunning. The smiles, though they were wary, were genuine. Best of all, there was no sign Florrie'd wiped up clots of porridge flung at walls or floor.

Amelia beamed while sending providence heartfelt thanks. She'd been close to despairing of ever being more than a jailer.

"What shall we do today?" she said, sitting on a child-sized chair and tucking her legs behind her so her knees wouldn't rise above her ears. "I think we should declare a holiday in honor of the sunshine, once you've had your nuncheon."

"Outdoors," Robby said. "Anywheres, just so's it ain't in here no more."

" 'Isn't.' Outdoors sounds perfect to me too. Where shall we go?''

''Not where people're buried, like that big church you took us to. Is there some place there's trees? Not like that.'' He nodded at the windows beyond which the garden intended to brighten Milbury Place languished. ''Those aren't *real* trees. No bigger'n bushes. Someplace where there's no people or carriages so Beezle can run.''

''Beezle?''

''Him.'' Tibbie pointed her spoon at the button-nosed dust mop wagging its tail in hope of a beggar's portion. ''Robby gived him a name.'' A glop of porridge fell to the floor. In a flash it was gone.

" 'Gave; Robby *gave* him a name.' You did?'' Amelia turned to Robby. ''That's a rather unusual one—Beeezle.''

''Well, he's always getting into mischief. When we got into mischief, Papa used to call us Ponds of Beezlepup, an' so I figured that'd be a good name for him. Tibbie shortened it to Beezle 'cause Ponds of Beezlepup's too long for something that puny.''

Amelia stared blankly from one child to the other.

''You know,'' Robby explained, ''like in *Pilgrim's Progress*. Papa's batman used to read that to us if we were good. You oughta know it. It's about morals and things.''

''Oh, dear heaven,'' she said, brow clearing. ''Did your papa by any chance actually call you spawn of Beelzebub?''

''That's what I said, isn't it?'' Robby snapped. ''Ponds of Beezlepup.'' Then he reddened. ''Sorry,'' he mumbled. ''Didn't mean to be rude. I know that was, even if I don't know much.''

''We'll ignore it this time. Do you know who Beezle-ah-Beelzebub was?''

''A devil, just like us.''

It crashed about her then: the vision of a mother pouting because she was forced to dress in last year's styles, of a father who ''liked pretty ladies'' calling his children spawn of the devil, and a grizzled batman reading to them from a book, parts of which could give even the least suggestive nightmares.

Unfortunately, given the children's descriptions of their father's batman, those were precisely the portions he would've favored.

And wherever they looked, the forest, soaring so high it seemed to trap the clouds in its branches, the only sound the soughing of the wind.

"I believe you're right, Robby," she gulped. "Beezle could do with some exercise. There's a place called Hyde Park. In the early afternoon there aren't many people about. The fashionable hour isn't until much later. We'd need to take the carriage, but that's what your kind guardian provided it for."

Chapter Eight

The morning wasn't without its troubles. Angels, Amelia knew, weren't created from Ponds of Beezlepup in a single night. Robby overturned his inkwell when faced with a page of subtraction that included borrowing across zeroes and ones. His apology was forced at best, and had more to do with fear the promised treat might be withheld than remorse.

Then Tibbie decided copying her alphabet was too tedious. Slate and chalk went flying as feet drummed on floor, and face turned so purple from held breath, Amelia feared a form of infant apoplexy. Only Beezle's whimpers and cowering accident, sternly pointed out by Robby, ended that contretemps. Unfortunately, Tibbie's tearful regrets were all for terrifying the pup rather than her tantrum or the shattered slate.

Still, it was a beginning. Compunction was unnatural to either. As for behavior expected of children in a well-regulated household, that couldn't be dreamed of as yet. The main point on this first day of sunshine was to teach them adults could be counted on to keep their word.

In the early afternoon, Beezle on an improvised leash and the children bundled in warm coats, they entered Hyde Park. Florrie Whissett trailed after them, brassy curls peeping from a flowered confection that was not what one would expect of a proper nursemaid. Hidden beneath her hooded cloak and coal-scuttle bonnet, Amelia kept a nervous watch for previous acquaintances.

Paths were clogged with last year's leaves. The lawns were brown stubble. Branches had yet to swell with buds. There wasn't a flower in evidence. With the exception of a few children in the distance and a handful of saunterers trying out their newest garb, the park was deserted.

It was, Robby declared with a joyous whoop, heaven.

He released Beezle from his leash and took off down the nearest side path, the pup bumbling at his heels on churning legs. Tibbie wrenched her hand from Amelia's and stumbled after them, crying, "Wait for me! Wait for me!" The moppet tripped, fell, picked herself up, and took off once more, unconcerned that her knees were muddy and bruised, her stockings torn.

"No wonder I haven't been able to make the least impression on them," Amelia murmured. The contrast between Tibbie and Robby and the children mincing at the side of governesses or nurses couldn't't've been greater. "We'd best follow them, or heaven knows what may happen."

"I ain't walkin' that far," Florrie protested.

"And you a fine country girl? Come along."

"I don't hold with walking no more. In Lunnon they look at you like you're a rooster with teats if you walks about too much."

"Then crawl."

"I'd never." Florrie stood in mid-path, arms akimbo. "My boots pinch. I walk that far, I'll be crippled, an' then what'll you do? Not a moment's peace, and that'll be on the good days."

Florrie limped to a bench at the side of the path, hips swaying. Just beyond them a pair of young bucks on the strut paused to observe the dispute between servant and mistress.

"Best look lively, Miss Sparrow," the girl said. "They're gettin' away, and I ain't certain they don't mean to do it permanentlike."

Amelia glanced to where Tibbie and Robby had been, then beyond. Far beyond. Robby had taken off across a field, Tibbie in hot pursuit, Beezle cutting circles around them. Amelia followed, squelching along the hypotenuse of a triangle only the most liberal would have termed "right," dodging the worst of the puddles and mud. Fortunately within moments Robby had found a stick and was attempting to teach Beezle to fetch—a far better place for the exercise than the halls of Milbury Place.

They didn't notice as she strode up, so intent were they on making the most of their freedom. A million reproofs died on her lips. If one considered how they'd lived, this race across Hyde Park was proper conduct. They'd bothered no one. They'd remained in view. One might almost say they'd waited for her.

"Feeling better?" she said.

"This is something like," Robby crowed as Tibbie nodded. " 'Course, there's all that." His finger encompassed London. "Isn't there someplace with just trees, and maybe a lake or a hill, and a fox or two?"

"Your guardian wants you in London," Amelia replied, avoiding the main issue.

"Why? He don't come to see us—just those friends of his, and they've been only once. If we could live in a place like that, we'd be good for a month of Sundays."

"One day perhaps you may discuss it with him. For now, I'm afraid you'll have to make do with parks and gardens, but think of all the exploring you can do."

"In places where people dress like him?" Robby pointed in the distance at a boy garbed in velvet and lace, and gave one of his better snorts. "Couldn't you say something? He'd have to listen to you, wouldn't he?"

"I'm afraid I've never met your guardian, though I did catch a glimpse of him once." Amelia flushed at Robby's skeptical glance. "It's true," she said. "I've met only Mr. Tidmarsh, who is his secretary. Mr. North is rather reclusive, and finds matters of business fatiguing. Perhaps he's not in the best of health."

"Or maybe he's a cripple. Papa's batman didn't like to go out, though I think that must've been because it hurt him to walk. Having a stump or a limp isn't odd if one's been in the army long enough. Nobody stared. Maybe we should write him a letter.''

"Your papa's batman? What a kind thought."

"No, clunch—our guardian."

"An excellent idea," she agreed, ignoring his slip in favor of a golden opportunity. "Of course Mr. North would expect perfect penmanship, and a felicity of expression without which your request would fall on deaf ears."

"Don't you mean lie before blind eyes?"

"I do indeed," she chuckled.

"You could write it for us." Tibbie slipped her hand in Amelia's and gazed up with her most winsome expression.

"It wouldn't be the same," Amelia and Robby chorused, for once in agreement.

"And you must each write him," Amelia hurried on as Tibbie tugged on her hand, "or he'll believe it's only one of you would rather live in the country, and so keep you both in London for his convenience."

"Couldn't you speak to Mr. Tidmarsh?" Robby said.

"I'm afraid such decisions aren't part of his duties. It would be like asking a sergeant when one requires a colonel's permission."

Robby nodded. He might not understand *tonnish* gentlemen, but he understood chains of command.

"What about those men came yesterday, and ate everything up?"

"They're only Mr. North's friends. While I'm certain they'll report to him on your behavior and welfare, no recommendation of theirs would carry more weight than that of a stranger. Mr. North is a gentleman given to seeking his own counsel."

"I guess we'll have to learn to write," Robby sighed.

"I suppose you will—if you would prefer to live in the country, that is," Amelia said with an equally somber expression. Then, at Tibbie's repeated tugs on her hand, she smiled at the mite. "What is it, dear? And don't point. It's not ladylike."

"Is that them now, talking to Florrie?"

"Is who what?" Amelia turned, following the direction of

Tibbie's offending finger. "Oh, dear. No, those aren't Mr. North's friends. Even Mr. Harnette had an elegance to him despite his country air, and all five were gentlemen. Those are *not* gentlemen. Best learn the difference immediately."

The bucks had joined Florrie. As Amelia watched, the nursemaid accepted their arms and sauntered up the path without a trace of a limp, duties forgotten.

"Is it right for her to go off like that?" Robby said.

"It's equally improper for you to notice it."

"Can't help it. I got eyes, don't I?"

"Well, then, to mention it."

"She going to come back?"

"I don't know," Amelia sighed. "I don't believe she enjoys being a nursemaid. Who could in such a household."

"But I didn't kick her shins today," Tibbie protested. "Who'll feed us our supper and put us to bed?"

"Perhaps you should think of that the next time you find Florrie's shins a tempting target."

Florrie returned that evening in time to put her charges to bed, full of tales of her grand outing. Nothing Amelia could say once the children had been seen to served to convince the girl that accepting a grand tea from a pair of strangers was out of the way.

The weather held. Tree buds burst, painting London's parks green. Gleaming knockers blossomed throughout Mayfair. The first carriages arrived from the country, depositing hopeful misses at modiste and bazaar to acquire the trappings of desirability. A fortnight later, Amelia watched the children and Beezle from a bench overlooking the Serpentine, face averted from the graveled path, where Florrie flirted with any male who happened by. At least a severe scold—and the bribe of a new bonnet in a month's time—now kept the girl from wandering off with the best of whatever offered.

"No wading, Robby," Amelia called, "and watch your sister, please. If Beezle takes a swim, I don't want her tumbling in after him, as she did yesterday."

Robby waved and pulled his sister back. Then he knelt to reset the sails of his boat. They'd already been around the ornamental water three times to retrieve it. With the wind off the *Jolly Wench*'s beam, if Robby had his way, there'd be a fourth.

Beezle strained forward, pink tongue lolling, and helped himself to a drink.

"Back from the edge, Tibbie," Amelia called.

The moppet made a face, but she scrambled up the bank, plopped on her rump, and began examining the carpet of flowers. Beezle whimpered, looking from brother to sister, then followed Tibbie away from the water's edge, leash dragging behind him.

Amelia smiled. If one made allowances for the nature of the house on Milbury Place, things could hardly be better. Determined to escape London, Tibbie and Robby were demonstrating the same tenacity in mastering lessons they had previously devoted to driving anyone in their company mad. Improvement, slow at first, had begun to exceed even Amelia's fondest hopes.

No, they hadn't undergone an instant transformation into pattern cards of infantine virtue. There were still tantrums. Food continued to find its way to wall and floor. Tibbie held her breath when crossed, and Robby's tongue remained as undisciplined as his mind. No school would have considered them model students, no tutor or governess endured their mischief. Still, she forged on, heartened by each scrap of progress and refusing to be dismayed by backslidings. Of course things were always easier out of doors. There the children thrived, and the few disputes were easily settled.

Amelia smiled as moppet and spaniel toddled up, Tibbie holding out a mangled dandelion and crowing she'd found the first flower that resembled those she'd known in the Colonies.

"But Robby don't want it, 'cause he says boats don't have dainty-lion-captins, an' asides, he's the captin," she mourned.

"How sweet of you to offer it to him though. That was infinitely kind. Would you like it in your hatband?"

Tibbie shook her head. "Yours," she said. "I already got silk flowers."

"So you do, and very pretty ones." Amelia slipped the tattered bloom in the ribbon gracing her bonnet. "Is that better?"

Tibbie shook her head. "Isn't nothing going to make that bonnet passable," she said in a fair imitation of Florrie.

"Ah, but governesses aren't supposed to be as fetching as their charges. Silk flowers wouldn't do for me."

"Florrie's got flowers in her bonnet. Got feathers an' ribbon knots too, and it ain't black."

"But then, I'm not Florrie."

"No, you're not," Tibbie said after a moment spent studying her governess that had Amelia trembling for fear of what might next tumble from those youthful lips, "but Mama was a lady an' she had flowers on her bonnets, even if they were dreadful old an' she complained about 'em to Papa. An' they weren't black."

"There's a deal of difference between what's permitted mamas and what's permitted governesses," Amelia countered with a sigh of relief.

"Do governesses got to wear spectacles, same as ugly bonnets?"

"Why do you ask?"

"You always look over the tops. Doesn't matter whether you're reading or looking way off. I don't think you really use 'em. I think you wear 'em to look ugly."

Amelia knew it wasn't just the sun warming her face as she shoved the offending spectacles up her nose. "Perhaps I don't need them as much as I did," she temporized.

"Then you ought t'stop wearing 'em. An' you ought t'start wearing those dresses Mr. North gave you, an' buy a pretty bonnet."

" 'Gave you.' I can't. They're winter gowns."

"Isn't summer yet. You aren't ugly, you know. You just try to be. That's silly. Mama always said a lady should make the most of her 'tributes."

" 'Attributes,' " Amelia murmured as Tibbie, with a saucily

warmhearted smile, tore back to the lake's edge to join her brother, Beezle bounding behind.

Then she sighed once more. Certain things, such as meeting with her employer, remained past praying for. She'd given up all hope after Bassett, apologizing a trifle more than the case warranted, had again showed her to Mrs. Pickles's parlor when she called at Wilton Street two afternoons before, demanding to see Mr. Tidmarsh, or, preferably, Mr. North.

Amelia squinted into the sun, almost blinded by its reflection on the water. "Not so close to the edge, Tibbie," she called again. "Perhaps you'd best bring Beezle to stay with me."

Mr. North was recovering from a case of the French grippe that had descended briefly to his lungs, his temper shortened or, as Mrs. Pickles put it more delicately, his sense of infallibility strengthened, by his illness. No wonder her notes regarding the house on Milbury Place had gone unanswered beyond a single scrawled "Do as you will, dammit, and leave me in peace. That's what I pay you for." Unfortunately, Mr. Tidmarsh had chosen just this time to be away on Mr. North's business. Heaven knew when he would return, or if he would grant her an interview when he did.

"Not that I hold with Mr. Tidmarsh. Never have, nor ever will," Mrs. Pickles had continued, back turned as she fussed with teapot and biscuits. "It was an unhappy day Master Val happened on the notion that fellow'd be the solution to his problems, and so we've all told him. But will he listen? Ah, no—not until enough milk's been spilt to fill the Channel, with considerable left over should the North Sea have need of it."

Then the housekeeper had turned the subject to Robby's latest pranks and the first signs Tibbie might be bribed with the occasional hair ribbon, and refused to return to that of Pericles Tidmarsh and his apparently recent arrival at Wilton Street.

Amelia roused from her abstraction at the tug on her skirts. Tibbie and Robby were still by the water, bedraggled and flushed from the sun. Beezle gazed at her, tail wagging, a stick in his mouth. He dropped it at her feet and barked.

"What's the matter, pup, no one to play with?"

She gave him a pat, tossed the stick, then glanced back toward the path. Florrie had acquired a new beau, whose golden unmentionables and wasp-waisted purple coat assaulted the eye even at such a distance. The fool struck a pose, beaver of improbable lavender pulled low over his eyes, golden-tasseled Hessians gleaming like mirrors, shirt points soaring above his ears. As Amelia watched, he turned to gaze first at her, then at the children, his face hidden by a quizzing glass of mammoth proportions.

"Dear heaven," she giggled, "Florrie'll never be able to resist this one. If we ever see her again, it'll only be after she's cast off."

Realizing the walks were more populated than usual, she glanced at the watch she'd taken to wearing to keep it safe from the light-fingered footmen after having it repaired. Blanching, she rose and called Tibbie and Robby. London was safe only if she exercised care. Today the children had behaved so well she'd been lulled into dangerous laxity.

Obviously aware they'd overstayed their time, Robby retrieved his boat without complaint, pulled Tibbie to her feet, and whistled for Beezle. The pup bounded up, yipping and holding out his stick. Robby shook his head, seized the leash and handed it to Tibbie, then took the stick and tossed it aside with a stern "Heel!"

For a miracle, the pup obeyed. Looking the veriest urchins but behaving like angels, the children beamed at her as they came up.

"That was something like," Robby exclaimed. "Won't be no time for sums and globes today, not if we're to have our riding lesson."

"'Any time,'" Amelia said, softening the correction with a smile of her own. "We'll see. I suspect we'll find a spare moment for sums and alphabets."

"Slave master," Robby retorted, but he was grinning as well. "I hope you'll find time for us to eat too. I'm so gut-foundered, I'm about to stick me spoon in the wall—as Papa's batman was used to say."

Amelia let the cant pass in favor of harmony as they climbed to where Florrie bantered with her latest swain, Beezle sniffing each shrub along the way.

"La, you do joke so, Reggie," Florrie was giggling as they came up, "but then, you was always a great one for bamming. An' banging."

"And I do miss the banging, my dear, perhaps even more than the bamming," the fop leered, chucking her under the chin with his quizzing glass.

Amelia stumbled, the world swimming about her.

"Won't be spending all m'time hunting a bride—not that I want one, except for the pounds she'll bring me," he continued. "Mama's orders, y'understand. Told her this time I'd choose for m'self though. She made a mull of it. No notion what a man needs if his stomach's not to turn at the prospect of getting himself an heir."

Only one man could possess such a noisomely insinuating tone or that ass's bray of laughter. But the clothes! No wonder she hadn't recognized him. Alfreda Whifler must be at Chilcomb, for she'd never have permitted her son to appear in public garbed as a figure of fun.

Amelia pulled the deep brim of her bonnet forward and ducked her head. Just when things were beginning to go well!

Sir Reginald Whifler was turning, Florrie on his arm. Sir Reginald was raising his quizzing glass, the sun reflecting from its lens. Sir Reginald was looking her up and down as if she were a scrap ready for the dustbin and he the prince regent.

"Demme, this the fright y'work for?" he sneered as if Amelia were deaf. "Amazing she don't give you nightmares just to look at her."

The growl at her side should've been warning to step back, taking children and pup with her. But, as it was Robby who did the growling rather than Beezle, Amelia merely lifted her head, the sun at her back, looked at her would-have-been husband, and swore that come what might, she'd never return to the parental fold.

"Won't listen to Hortie Grimble no matter what she tells 'er about dressing proper," Florrie giggled. "Himself sent her a coupla gowns from Mary Duclos's shop, but she won't wear 'em. Won't let Bessie or me wear 'em either.''

"A dried-up stick—y'had that right. No wonder the brats can't stand her.''

Robby attacked with an aboriginal howl reminiscent of his first days on Milbury Place, kicking and stomping and hitting. Within seconds Sir Reginald's Hessians no longer gleamed. It might have been loyalty. It might have been because they dangled enticingly. Beezle leapt, teeth bared, and the golden tassels lay on the path. Then Beezle used the Hessians as a tree trunk—Sir Reginald's signal to howl and prance in earnest. And then it was over, Beezle whimpering after a swift kick to his ribs, Robby on his back, where Sir Reginald had sent him flying, the boat with mast snapped and hull splintered lying just beyond.

"Robby—oh, thank goodness.'' Amelia knelt beside the boy as his lids flickered.

They were gathering a considerable crowd—park saunterers, children with governesses and nursemaids, and a gaggle of officers accompanied by a tallish gentleman with dark hair. Florrie eased behind the curiosity-seekers and took to her heels.

"There's been an accident?'' a deep voice drawled.

"Wasn't an accident. That little devil ruined m'boots and broke every bone in m'feet a'purpose, and *then* his dog pissed on me!''

" 'Made water,' sir. Ladies present. Having your boots baptized is no excuse for laying the dog's owner flat—especially when that owner's a child and the dog a pup.''

"Shame!'' a woman in a vivid cherry gown and indigo spencer shrilled, snapped her sunshade closed, and rapped Sir Reginald smartly across the shoulders.

"I'll have you transported for assault,'' Sir Reginald yelped.

"Transport a duchess?'' the gentleman snorted. "I'd dearly love to see you try.''

The woman looked at the tall stranger, giggled, and winked.

"Please, could someone help us to our carriage?'' Amelia pleaded. "It's waiting just beyond the gate.''

"I'm goin' to cast up me accounts,'' Robby muttered, rolled

over, and deposited what remained of his breakfast on the path. It wasn't from lack of trying that no splatters landed on Sir Reginald's boots.

"I demand satisfaction," Sir Reginald roared.

"He insulted our Miss Sparrow," Robby gasped. "It's him someone should call out, the shit-mouthed, belly-crawling tit-sucker."

"Well said, sprout. Intend to cross swords with an infant?" the stranger said after looking first at Tibbie and Robby, then at Amelia, as his brows rose. He waved his military companions away.

"I'll see that female chased from her position," Sir Reginald snarled. "I'll see she's never hired by a respectable family again. I'll see her on the high road begging. And when she tries to steal her bread, I'll see her branded and transported!"

"Excessive," the stranger laughed. "Have you been threatened with just such a fate? You do seem to dwell on it."

Sir Reginald thrust out his chin, pulled off his glove, seemed to think better of it at the stranger's cold look, and instead ground the ruined boat into the gravel with the heel of his dripping boot. Then he turned on Amelia and attempted to jerk her to her feet. She shrank away, ducking her head. Then his hand was gone.

"It's ridiculous, of course," the stranger said, helping Amelia to rise. "That fool's creating a fuss over nothing, but it might be wisest to give him your direction and permit the children's father to handle the matter, Miss Sparrow."

"They have no father," Amelia whispered as she buried her face in her hands and peeped between her fingers at first Sir Reginald and then her champion. The others, satisfied the drama was over, drifted away. "They're Robert and Tabitha Tyne, the orphaned wards of Mr. Valentine North, whose residence is on Wilton Street in Mayfair."

"There, are you satisfied?" the stranger said, turning to Sir Reginald.

"Never heard of him."

"Ah, but then, I doubt he's ever heard of you either. Knowing

Val, he'd probably prefer to keep it that way. Doesn't hold with encouraging mushrooms.''

"I'm no Cit, you ass," Sir Reginald fumed, complexion purpling to match his gaudy garb. "I'm Sir Reginald Whifler of Chilcomb Manor just south of Manchester.''

"Can't say I'm overawed by the knowledge. Well, now you have the information you wanted. I wouldn't be too eager to seek out Mr. North though. I doubt he'll be pleased when he learns you assaulted his ward, and when Mr. North isn't pleased, those who cause him displeasure tend to suffer for their transgressions.''

The stranger turned to Robby and helped the boy up. "Can you make it on your own, sprout?''

Robby gulped and nodded. "Takes more'n casting up me accounts to lay me low," he said. "Did that all the way to England, so I've a deal of practice. Beezle's the one we should be worrying about. Will he be all right?''

The gentleman knelt by the pup, who'd crawled to Tibbie's side, removed his gloves, and ran his hands expertly over the cowering scrap of fur. "Nothing but bruises so far as I can tell, Robby. There, little fellow, easy now," he murmured. "I'm not your enemy.''

He pulled off his coat, cradled Beezle in it, and rose.

"I'd offer you my arm," he said to Amelia, "but this chap seems to have a greater need. He's going to be sore for a few days. Shall we?'' He nodded in the direction of the gate, ignoring Sir Reginald, who still watched them through narrowed eyes.

Amelia nodded, not daring to look at Sir Reginald. Robby picked up what was left of his boat.

"Don't worry, Robby, I'll see that's replaced," the stranger said.

And then they were walking toward the gate, Tibbie round-eyed and clinging to Amelia's hand, Robby striding beside the stranger and clutching the ruined toy, the stranger limping slightly. Robby looked up at him.

"Was that lady really a duchess?" he said.

"No, but it amused me to claim she was. That shit-mouthed,

belly-crawling tit-sucker needed putting in his place—my apologies, Miss Sparrow, but the boy's description is apt—though this Whifler's such a flat, I doubt he understood my intention.''

Robby nodded. ''She smelled like Florrie and Bessie,'' he said, ''so I didn't think she could be.''

''Ah, yes,'' the man choked out with a glance at Amelia. ''You're not to use such language in front of a lady again, however, Robby. No gentleman would. The name's Dauntry, by the bye, Quintus Dauntry.''

Chapter Nine

White's was crowded even this early in the Season, though the more serious wagering wouldn't begin until the moon was close to setting and eyes were bleary from the late hour and the consumption of the best the cellars had to offer. For now it was a light-hearted assemblage, noisy with spicy *on-dits* and the latest tattle regarding the Prince Regent's current *inamorata*.

Valentine North sprawled at a table set slightly apart from the others, tossing a pair of dice without apparent interest in the sum of their spots, but nevertheless sweeping up the bank-notes and vowels wagered by his opponents with the efficiency of a shepherd gathering his flock.

"Damnable string of luck." Pugs Harnette sighed and stood, yielding his place to one of the crowd watching the proceedings.

"Mine, or yours?" North grinned.

"Mine, of course. Yours is always excellent. One of these days I suppose I'll give it up, but that seems such a paltry thing to do."

"Ah, but unlucky at the tables, lucky in the boudoir."

"Not much luck either place, if you want the truth. You have it all."

The others chuckled at Harnette's good-natured lament.

Of the Irregulars, only ginger-haired Tony Sinclair now remained seated, doggedly wagering against North and muttering that such a streak of good fortune couldn't last forever. Quint Dauntry, who'd positioned himself where he could watch the doors, coughed. North nodded, then knocked over the half-filled glass of brandy at his elbow. In the ensuing confusion he shifted his chair to examine the newcomer.

Nugee—there was no other candidate for the tailor who'd contrived that coat of changeable peacock satin straining across buckrammed shoulders so exaggerated not even Tom Crib could have boasted their equal. The scarlet waistcoat embroidered in gold and emerald had whelped. The litter of fobs dangling below trembled with each breath, suckling at a rainbow of ribbons.

"Good God," North mouthed as Whifler stifled a yawn, gaze roving the room, "you should've warned me."

Dauntry shrugged as others turned to see what had caught their interest.

"He did," Sinclair murmured, "but you wouldn't listen. Have a care. I suspect he's well above par and oozing cupcourage. Dangerous combination, given this is only your second night out since rising from your sickbed."

Laughter rippled across the high-ceilinged room, meeting a backwash of comment that lapped at Whifler's heavy-lobed ears like a sulfurous ocean. Only his darkening complexion betrayed he wasn't pleased by the reaction to his magnificence.

North turned back to the table.

"Wagers, gentlemen?" he said, scooping the dice into their leather cup and rattling them. Banknotes and vowels fluttered to the center of the table.

A hand reeking of attar of roses pulled the cup from North's fingers before he could toss the dice. North froze. Quint *had* warned him, and Tony was right: He hadn't believed the half of it. The fellow wasn't a mushroom. He was an out-and-out toadstool.

"Valentine North, I'm informed," a voice with the nasal rasp of steel on stone slurred behind him loudly enough to be heard by the room at large, its accents not quite those of a

gentleman, possessing, instead, a certain something of the manufactory in the near past, and a hint of the farmyard more
deeply buried. "Took me a deal of effort to find you, you
unregenerate wastrel."

"I suggest," Dauntry said, easing from the wall against
which he'd been leaning, "that you return those dice to Mr.
North and apologize, sir. You mightn't like the consequences
otherwise."

North shook his head, the slightest of smiles curling his lips.
He'd anticipated difficulties with the fellow, what with Miss
Sparrow's almost incoherent note and Quint's more rational
description of the encounter in Hyde Park. He shouldn't've
worried. Any man who'd made a fool of himself in the morning
could be counted on to be a jackass by evening. This one had
started braying the moment he entered the room.

"I don't believe I've had the pleasure," North said in a
tone devoid of expression, turned, and looked the fellow over.
"Amazing," he murmured so low, only Whifler could hear
him. "You must give me the direction of your, ah, costumer."
Then, before the idiot could strike him, he grasped Whifler's
wrist and rose. "This is a gathering place for gentlemen," he
said in the manner of a tutor explaining the gerundive to a
lackluster student. "Have a seat if you feel you belong here,
though how you gained entry is a mystery. Perhaps your toggery
blinded the porter?"

North spun Whifler into the seat he'd just quit. With the
exception of Sinclair, the others rose, backing away as North
took a seat that put him beyond Whifler's reach, then pointedly
shifted his winnings to his new place. Dauntry gave a nod to the
footmen flanking the entry. They eased forward, arms hanging
loosely at their sides.

"Tony, some brandy for Mr.—ah—I don't believe you
favored us with your name?" North said.

"I," Whifler said, drawing himself up, "am Sir Reginald
Whifler of Chilcomb Manor just to the south of Manchester,
as you know perfectly well, given *that* cur is here." He pointed
at Dauntry.

"My goodness—I'd no idea we were in such distinguished

company. Do pour this person a glass of brandy, Tony. I believe he's sick-livered, given his high color.''

"I don't want brandy," Whifler snapped. "I'm here on business."

"Business? At this hour? *Here?* You must be mad. Where did you say Coldbrush Manor is?''

"Chilcomb Manor. Personal business.''

With an air North could've sworn the man had practiced before a mirror, Whifler helped himself to a pinch of snuff. There was a slight pause, then an explosive sneeze that turned Whifler's snowy handkerchief umber.

"You have business with me?'' North said, eyes wide, as Whifler pointedly returned his snuffbox to his waistcoat without offering it around.

"A matter of honor. You've a pair of wards want correction, North. And you *are* Valentine North, so don't bother denying it. Had you pointed out to me.''

"How clever of you. Why should I deny it? Most everyone here knows me—at least by reputation, which you clearly do not—though I doubt a one of us has a notion who you might be. Your name and style are hardly famous, for all they might become infamous if you continue as you've begun.''

"That whelp of Satan in your charge insulted me in public and ruined my boots!''

"For which heinous transgression I understand you sent the lad flying and kicked a helpless pup.''

Murmurs of ''shame'' traveled up and down the company as it drew closer, better to inspect this latest enlistee in the legion of the gossip-worthy.

"I want 'em whipped, and I want their bird-witted governess discharged.''

"You do?''

"The incident was intolerable. Far beyond what a gentleman should be expected to endure.''

"Dear me," North said, shaking his head, "and here I thought you'd come to apologize for assaulting a child of seven and abusing his pet after the boy but remonstrated with you regarding an insult offered his governess. How odd.''

"Me, apologize to you? You're the one who owes me an apology. I'm giving you the chance. Ought to thank me for it."

"And to this end you come troubling me at this hour on a minor domestic matter? My dear man, where *is* Icefork Manor—the Antipodes? Who let this buffoon in?" North demanded of the room. "I can't believe he's a member. We have certain standards."

"I demand satisfaction!" Whifler roared.

"A duel?" North asked in the sudden silence. "You can't be serious. Fobs at twenty paces? Quizzing glasses at dawn? Will someone kindly rid me of this popinjay?" he pleaded. "Wriggler positively terrifies me."

"*Whifler!* They ruined my new boots. The boy belongs in Newgate."

North pulled a pair of bills from the mountain before him and tossed them at Whifler. "That should see to their replacement. Can't've been prime ones, if your current rig-out is anything to judge by."

"Green Park, tomorrow morning, dawn! Name your seconds."

"But hadn't you heard? No, I suppose not, living at—what was it now? Ah, yes, Frozenspade Manor. Dueling's been against the law for eons, Wimpler—especially dueling with one's inferiors. In fact, that's always been against the code. Besides, there's such a disparity in our ages—if you haven't yet seen the shady side of forty, you aren't missing it by much— any contest between us would be patently unfair."

"You're a bleater and a man-milliner if y'won't meet me!"

"And you, sir, are a shit-mouthed, belly-crawling tit-sucker—I believe that's the phrase my ward used, and most apt it was—not worth my trouble. However, I do suggest you avoid encounters with my wards and their governess in the future. If you don't, I fear I'll be forced to administer the correction you so justly deserve."

At North's signal, the pair of footmen hovering behind Whifler seized the man by his fleshy upper arms, pulled him from the chair, and encouraged him toward the door. Whifler tore free and stormed back, towering over North.

"I won't be ignored!" the man spluttered.

North sighed and rose. "You won't?" he said. "You're certain of that, Sir Ratling Whiner of Coxcomb Manor? I've shown considerable forbearance."

"You're bloody well right, I won't! Was betrothed to an earl's daughter until a bit ago. That should tell you something."

"But no longer betrothed, I take it? Apparently the girl had some sense, or else her connections did."

"I broke it off. Perfectly proper. No announcement'd been made. Left the jaw-me-dead bluestocking heartbroken," Whifler boasted.

The murmurs redoubled as those present attempted to determine which earl's daughter Whifler had all but jilted. The consensus was the windbag had never set eyes on an earl's daughter, let alone been on the verge of betrothal to one.

"Ah, well—I regret this, but you leave me little choice. Don't want to do more than's necessary, you understand." North pulled out his handkerchief and handed it to Whifler. "Have a care. You'll need this if you're not to ruin your linen."

Then he planted a set of fives on the knight's nose.

"Now you may escort Sir Ringworm from the premises," North said as that worthy crumpled to the floor like a paper fan over which a bucket of water is tossed. "Summon a hackney. His sort never has its own carriage. And do make use of my handkerchief to stem the ruby flood. I shouldn't care to see such splendor blood-spattered. If someone would bring me a basin of water and a towel, please? It seems I've soiled my hands."

The applause had North bowing. "All in an evening's play, gentlemen," he said before returning to his seat and picking up the dice cup. "I doubt that clod will be troubling us again."

"Unwise, Val," Tony Sinclair murmured under cover of the continuing applause and laughter as Sir Reginald Whifler was carted from the room and the others returned to their tables. "That fellow's not the sort to understand he's been bested. If he can't avenge what he considers his honor in one manner, he'll find another. Someone got him in here.''

''Don't be ridiculous.'' North grinned. ''We've seen the end of that gilded jackdaw.''

''When're you going to meet with Miss Sparrow?'' Dauntry prodded.

The Irregulars had just quitted White's, North considerably plumper in the pocket. The horizon, what they could see of it at the end of the street, held a rosy glow, the last of the stars winking out like sleepy carousers intent on seeking their beds.

''Concerning Whifler? No need.'' North yawned, strolling arm in arm with Dauntry and Sinclair as the others ambled ahead, footsteps a trifle unsteady, not caring what route they followed so long as it led to Wilton Street. ''I'll send her a note telling her the matter's been seen to. You've promised the lad a new boat, so that's no problem. Least said, soonest mended.''

''Their nursemaid was hanging all over Whifler just before they came up.''

''And you think I should concern myself with a nursemaid's poor taste?''

''Nursemaid?'' Sinclair snorted. ''Perhaps she is now, but I'll wager that wasn't her profession until recently.''

North felt their eyes on him. It didn't take much to sense the pair's accusing expressions. He made a show of stifling another yawn.

''I've encountered Florrie as well, you'll remember,'' Sinclair nattered. ''Treated me to a private viewing that would've turned an abbess pale. Ran for my life.''

''That again? You fellows're becoming bores on the subject.''

''Robby and Tibbie are a rather engaging pair of imps,'' Dauntry scolded, a touch of acid to his voice. ''A pity you've decided to ignore 'em. If you won't confer with Miss Sparrow, you should at least make an effort to figure in their lives.''

"And what would I do with a pair of rug-crawlers other than terrify them?"

"Y'might try teaching the lad to throw a ball properly."

North's muttered curse expressed his opinion of such a pastime to perfection.

"I remember visits to Astley's with considerable fondness," Sinclair threw in. "Father took me, generally in company that would've sent my mother into spasms had she known. Females in spangled tights atop a horse's back? Pure magic to a lad of nine. Not the slightest trouble to my father. Wasn't until I was considerably older that I realized he'd conducted his amours beneath my innocent nose."

"Then take 'em to Astley's, but don't expect me to form one of the party."

"They need a father."

"They need a steadying influence," North countered. "I'm paying Miss Sparrow to provide that. God knows, I can't. Given what *little* you've said of the tadpoles in the last few days, she hasn't done badly with them."

"She's faced with a problem only the most selfless of females would endure."

"Then marry the woman if she's such a paragon," North snapped, pulling away from Dauntry and Sinclair. "That's what her sort always wants. Now, stubble it. I've more than done my duty by Freddy Tyne's leavings."

He stalked down the center of the pavement, cognizant that, as was their custom when he quit one of London's clubs considerably richer, he was being guarded by his friends. One didn't saunter about alone with full pockets—certainly not at this hour—if one was wise. Well, as was his custom, he'd deposit all but the vowels in the nearest poor box, and then the nagging gadflies could take themselves off.

"Summer's coming," Dauntry murmured behind him. "Not particularly healthy in Town. Always went to the country when we were children. Mother insisted."

"Mine did the same," Sinclair said, voice carrying clearly. "Amazed Val hasn't thought of it. I know his never countenanced Town in the summer months either. Far too much disease. Brighton might be a notion, or one of the lesser seaside places. Lyme even, or a watering spot such as Tunbridge Wells.''

''In another hired house such as the one he's gotten 'em here?''

''No, I suppose that wouldn't do.''

''No,'' Dauntry agreed, ''it damn well wouldn't.''

North was thankful when they fell silent. They were hinting he take the far-from-birdwitted Miss Sparrow and Freddy's tadpoles to join his mother at Hillcrest, even stay there himself. Well, they could hint all they wished. Self-immolation held no attraction. Brighton to see if his luck at the tables held there, a month or so touring the Lake District with Chloe, and a week at the Willing Wench, a secluded inn to the south and east of London that was a particular favorite of hers—that's how he'd planned his summer, and that's how he'd pass it. He'd stop by Hillcrest to see his mother on his way to join the Quorn in the fall. Freddy's tadpoles would fare perfectly well in London. Thousands did. Plenty of parks.

A thud made him glance over his shoulder in time to glimpse Tony Sinclair's eyes rolling as he joined Dauntry on the pavement. The band of toughs charged, brandishing cudgels—a squat one, a burly one, and two skinnier ones garbed in castoffs that reeked of the stews and blue ruin, scarves wound high to hide their faces. Two more sporting masks lurked at the mouth of a narrow passage, knives glinting.

With a roar to alert the others, North lowered his head and let loose with his fists. The next time he had a chance to look, the knife-toting lurkers had vanished and the other four taken to their heels as swiftly and silently as they'd appeared. St. Maure was kneeling by Sinclair, holding out a flask of brandy.

''Good God,'' North muttered, nursing bruised knuckles, ''how long d'you think they were following us?''

''Since White's, I suspect,'' St. Maure said. ''That organized sort don't attack unless they're certain of the rewards.''

''Warned you,'' Sinclair mumbled. ''So did Quint.''

''Ridiculous.'' North glanced at the others in the growing light. ''No way that was Whifler. No time to set it up.'' St.

Maure's eye was swelling fast. Threadwhistle's nose streamed as red as Whifler's had earlier. Harnette was limping. Clough nursed his arm as if it might be broken. "I'm sorry about this, fellows."

"We'll survive." Dauntry wiggled his jaw, then took a pull from St. Maure's flask. "Just tell us one thing: Did they get all of it?"

"My winnings? Of course not. Chased 'em off before they could."

"Make sure."

North felt for the fine steel mesh he always inserted in the reinforced pockets his tailor constructed in the linings of his evening coats.

"What the deuce?" he muttered as his fingers slipped inside his coat from the outside. The linings were gone, along with the hundreds of pounds they'd held.

"Thought so," Dauntry said. "One or more of 'em were cutpurses."

"Still doesn't mean it had anything to do with our Manchester toadstool. Some lackey at White's paid to pass information as to who's departing heavy in the pocket and who's departing light. It's happened, though not at White's, but that doesn't mean it couldn't. A man might be tempted, seeing all those lovely pounds lying about."

"He might indeed. Whifler's rig-outs may be atrocious, but they didn't come cheap. Neither did his Hessians, which were definitely Hobby's work. His sort always outruns the constable when it bolts. My guess is Whifler's chewed his tether, and is running as wild as an unbroken colt for all he's more of an age to be sold to the knackers. Like as not, there was an earl's daughter, platter-faced and on the shelf, whose parents were eager to sell her off so they could drive a better bargain with her younger sisters, and he's celebrating his escape."

"D'you think you could delay this argument until later?" Stubby Clough pleaded. "My arm's paining me something fierce. I'd like to have it seen to while there's still hope of retaining the use of it."

* * *

Dust motes danced on bands of light filtering past draperies still drawn for the night when Amelia Peasebottom descended to the breakfast parlor at her usual hour of six that morning. The covers had yet to be set. Neither did the customary boiled eggs, rack of toast, or pot of tea wait at her place.

She didn't notice at first, so deeply was she preoccupied with the events of the previous day. Sleep had come to her late, fitfully, and only with reluctance. More than once she'd risen to pull her portmanteau from its dusty home atop an armoire in her bedchamber, convinced she must flee London or be unmasked. Only thoughts of Tibbie and Robby immured in this household from hell, their invisible guardian so lacking in compunction that he must be the king of knaves, had held her back. She would have to give notice, though how she'd manage it with Mr. Tidmarsh gone and Mr. North on his sickbed, she had no notion. Another conference with Mrs. Pickles was called for, though of late she'd been of less than no assistance. Once a replacement was hired, she'd flee—to Wales, perhaps, or Cornwall. Attempting to hide in London had been the act of an idiot.

Then she glanced about, brows rising. Looping the draperies aside was a simple matter, but no matter how she tugged the bell rope, it was as if there was not so much as a mouse to keep her company on Milbury Place. A survey of the downstairs rooms took moments. No footmen. No Bessie. Work candles had guttered where she'd left them in the back parlor the night before. Footprints she hadn't noticed mired the entryway.

Seething, she descended the service stairs. Murmurs proved the kitchen, at least, was inhabited. The impulse to learn what she could before she announced her presence was overwhelming. Ignoring a twinge of guilt, she eased forward in the murk. She needn't've bothered. Only the occasional hiss reached her.

With a sigh she entered the kitchen. "Good morning," she said.

Mrs. Chiddy jumped as if she'd been prodded by one of

her own knives. Three heads swung to face her, expressions guarded.

"What're you doing here?" Hortense Grimble demanded from where the trio huddled around the kitchen table.

"Ain't never come down afore," Grimble complained, watching her from beneath lowered brows.

"This morning I have. Why are you lurking in the dark like a pack of wolves? More to the point, where are Bessie, Charles, and William?"

"I sent 'em on errands," Mrs. Grimble said after a moment.

"At this hour? All three? What errands?"

"Don't see as that's no lookout of yours," Grimble said. "Hortie knows how to run a house without no help from you, nor any questions or comments either."

Amelia crossed her arms, eyes hard, and waited.

"Wanted the papers," Grimble said, shifting in his chair.

"And I had no eggs, nor yet any gammon," Mrs. Chiddy chimed in. "Didn't realize that until just a bit ago. Been distracted, don't you see. That dreadful business with the little lad yesterday put going to market clear out of my head."

Amelia looked from one to the other. "All right, that accounts for two. Where's the third? My breakfast has yet to be prepared, let alone served. The entry is filthy. The draperies would still be drawn if I hadn't opened them. The only person in this house other than myself who has so much as lifted a finger to perform her customary duties is Florrie, and she's acting as if she's dancing on broken crockery."

"No need to fly into the boughs, Miss I-expect-to-be-treated-like-the-queen-of-the-May," Mrs. Grimble snapped. "There's bread and cheese in the larder. Some of us have more on our minds than bowing and scraping."

Amelia neither gasped nor censured. She merely continued to wait.

"Bessie's visiting a old friend," Mrs. Chiddy finally admitted, flushing.

"A sick one, I presume?"

"Very sick. Like to die, as a matter of fact."

"Poor soul. And Charles and William—do they also have bosom bows about to expire?"

"Got 'emselves into a tavern brawl last night. Staggered back a bit ago. Not fit to be seen, nor yet able to work."

"Most unfortunate. They'd be sacked in any respectable household."

"Ain't no sacking here," Grimble said. "We're equals."

"Yes, that's true enough: Equals in depravity, insolence, and sloth. I'm going to join the children in the schoolroom. My breakfast will be served there in fifteen minutes. It matters not in the least who prepares it, but it will be on time and it will be edible."

"Get your own breakfast," Mrs. Grimble muttered

"The entry will be scrubbed and the common rooms dusted by nine o'clock," Amelia continued as if the harridan hadn't spoken. "If that means the three of you must do it, then you shall do it. Otherwise I will remove to Wilton Street with Tibbie and Robby this afternoon. This I promise: Once I've reported to Mr. North, he will institute an action for recovery of every groat he paid for the lease on this house. If the funds have been squandered, you'll find yourselves in Newgate."

Mouths opened to protest. Amelia smiled.

"I keep my promises," she said. "Govern your actions accordingly. This morning the children and I will be remaining at home, so the carriage won't be needed. I intend to begin a clean-up of the garden in back. Please have Mike and Mick available to render assistance."

"Tired o' gadding about? Never thought t'see the day. Y'wants Mike or Mick," Grimble snarled, "y'can fetch 'em yourself."

"More like she knows she ain't fit to see to those poor children," Hortense Grimble sniffed, eyes slitted. "Can't keep 'em from harm, an' so now she's goin' to hide here so Mr. North don't learn she's an impostor what never had charge of children in her life. Mayhap I should tell him what a poor bargain he made in her. Choused him, that's what she done. Gentlemen don't take kindly t'being choused—'specially not by females who pretend t'be what they're not."

"Wonder what we'd learn if'n we asked a few questions here an' there," Grimble threw in. "Lay you pounds to pence she's no better'n she should be, and was tired of earning her keep honestlike on her back. Bet she stole a deal of brass off them as gave her employment. Bet they'd pay t'have her back so's they could punish her good an' proper. Bet there ain't no one'd ever miss her neither."

"Remember," Amelia said, heart pounding, "I keep my promises."

Then she spun on her heel and went back into the dark corridor, not breaking into a run until she'd reached the service stairs.

Chapter Ten

According to the surgeon, Stubby Clough's arm—painful though it was—had only been bruised.

Pugs Harnette's knee, Ollie Threadwhistle's nose, St. Maure's eye, and Dauntry's jaw, the cuts they'd all suffered had been bathed and iced or bandaged. Even North's knuckles had been dusted with basilicum powder and protected with court plaster. Jitters and Pickles had seen to them once the surgeon departed, Jitters muttering like an old woman, the housekeeper silent for all her expression spoke volumes.

Then they'd been bundled off to bed like so many delinquent schoolboys, their breakfasts brought on trays by grandfatherly footmen and motherly maids who refused to smile no matter how many sallies the fellows essayed while North—infinitely guilty regarding his surprising lack of injury after such a furious battle—wandered from bedchamber to bedchamber, attempting to liven what, given his staff, was becoming a gloomy morning.

But his staff hadn't been the worst. For the first time in all the years they'd adventured together, the fellows weren't laughing and joking when there was only North to hear. Quite the reverse. St. Maure, Sinclair, and Dauntry wore the mien of stern judges. Ollie and Pugs merely appeared disillusioned, while Stubby Clough's fortitude in the face of considerable pain was a reproach strong enough to make any reasonable man suffer pangs of conscience.

When the rest had been settled, North went to his bedchamber to find his bed turned down and the draperies drawn. A tray holding a bowl of pap suitable for a doddering invalid waited on the nighttable. Jitters stood at the ready, dressing gown over his arm.

"Dammit, no!" North protested. "I will not be put to bed. I will not be fed swill, whether for the good of my soul or my body. I *will* have a rare sirloin and a tankard of ale—immediately. A pot of coffee wouldn't be amiss either. Then I'll have a bath, a shave, and some decent clothes. Once that's taken care of, I intend to seek the peace of my book room, where old Burridge and Jem had best be waiting for me."

"Sir, that isn't what Mr. Dauntry recommends."

"And Quintus Dauntry now gives the orders in this house? Tell me when and by what means that happened. I'm fascinated."

"Now, Master Valentine—"

"I am Mr. North!" North roared, then flushed at Jitters's abashed expression. Why, the old fellow was actually trembling.

"Sorry about that." North put his arm around his man's frail shoulders, and managed a contrite smile. "Didn't mean a word of it. You can call me Master Valentine anytime you want so long as there's no one else about. I'm just out of sorts. It's been a damnable few days, and an impossible evening. Be a good fellow and fetch me a decent breakfast, and I do want a bath and some fresh clothes. I've considerable business to tend to once I've been put to rights."

Jitters gulped and nodded.

A tap at the door had North back across the room on the instant. "Well?" he barked, opening it.

Stubby Clough loomed there in a borrowed nightshirt, pale as a ghost, good hand gripping the jamb, bad arm in a sling fashioned from one of Pickles's shawls, ice wrapped in a rag on top. "Anything I can do, Val?" he said.

"Yes," North sighed, "get back to bed. Don't worry—I'm not going to murder poor Jitters. Freddy's lucky he's buried across the sea, though, or I'd be performing unspeakable rites on his grave to ensure his rotting in hell for all eternity."

"Y'don't mean that." Clough padded in on bare feet and closed the door behind him. "Don't say it. Saying it's bad luck."

"The joke's worn off," North snapped. "Indeed, it wore off ages ago."

"Then if it's no longer a joke—not that it ever was one—do something serious about it."

"I intend to. Fanny's family may've disowned her when she married Freddy, but her children are rightfully their responsibility, not mine."

"And how much d'you know about them?" Clough wavered, then leaned against a chest, eyes straining to stay open. "Will they make decent guardians, or will they grudge the poor things a crust of bread and a pallet in the attics?"

"You would ask that," North sighed. "Fanny's father was a cheese-parer with more interest in his horses and dogs than his wife and children—that I know, even allowing for some self-serving exaggeration on Freddy's part. Only reason I didn't have old Burridge write Squire Fulham straight off when I got that damnable letter."

"We've been conferring, the lot of us." Clough yawned. "We want to call off the wager. Wasn't a fair one."

"What—afraid I'll win?"

"No—scared out of our wits the children'll lose, if you must know."

"Fiddlesticks. They're cozy as mice in a hayrick." North turned to Jitters with a pleading smile. "I'm wanting my breakfast, old friend," he said, "and my bath. Don't worry, I shan't run amok, but there's a lot I must see to, beginning with who this Whifler is. While there's no way he can've been behind the fracas, I danced a fine jig on his reputation last night. There won't be a door that matters open to him by the time this day's done, and he's not going to like it if he's truly come in search of a well-born wife."

Jitters nodded, then seized Clough's good arm as the poor fellow wavered again, and guided him toward North's already turned down bed. "You shouldn't be standing more than you must, sir," he reproved.

"Just a bit light-headed is all. Think Pugs snuck some laudanum in m'tipple," Clough mumbled. "Be all right'n a moment."

Between them, Jitters and North saw Clough ensconced, his arm supported by pillows, and the bed curtains drawn. By the time they were done, Clough was snoring, his lips fluttering like a butterfly's wings.

"My breakfast, please," North murmured, "and a bath in my dressing room. I don't want to wake the poor fellow. Slipping him the poppy juice was a capital idea. Otherwise he'd've insisted on bearing me company no matter what I said."

An hour later, eyes burning from lack of sleep, skin perhaps a tad tight across his cheekbones, but otherwise more or less himself with the exception of the court plaster on his knuckles, North entered his book room. Jem waited as ordered. Aaron Burridge paced like a crane seeking its supper in the shallows, sparse graying locks plastered across his pate, long neck extended.

"Be with you in a moment, Burridge," North said, then turned to Jem. "D'you still have any friends in the stews?"

Jem blanched.

"Because I'm hoping you do. Are there any old acquaintances who trust you and whom you trust, and who have a good notion of everything that happens down there? Who's come into a bit of blunt and is spending freely, for instance? A gossiper's what I want, but one who listens more than talks."

"There's Tricky Tess," Jem mumbled. "She knows most everybody. I see her sometimes, accidentallike. Always gave me half of any food she had so's I wouldn't starve when I didn't manage to steal anything for m'self. Wasn't much good at it. Got chased away most times."

"I remember. To your credit and good fortune as well as

mine, you were lamentably clumsy-fingered and remarkably innocent-faced. So Tricky Tess is a dependable woman with a heart of gold. D'you think you could find her?''

Jem shrugged. ''She works,'' he said. ''Sells flowers days an' herself at night. Least she did last time I saw her.''

North pulled out his purse and handed Jem several coins. ''Treat her to a good dinner. Plenty of ale or porter, whichever she prefers. Blue ruin if you must. I want her tongue loosened. And give her enough money so she doesn't have to work tonight. In return I want to know if there's any mumbling: Who waylaid us, and how they knew I was carrying a large sum. The attack was specific. Only my pockets were slit, and so neatly I had no notion it was being done. A master's touch.''

''That's all you want?'' Jem said as he examined the coins, then slipped them into an inside pocket.

''It's enough. Be careful. You had the self-preservational instincts of a guttersnipe in the old days, but it's been years since you lived in the stews.''

''And it's not a place I like to go back to, but if Tess's heard anything, I'll know it afore I leave.''

The door closed behind the young groom. North turned to Aaron Burridge, smiling at the look of distaste in the man's thin features.

''Don't bother telling me you don't approve, for I know you don't,'' he said. ''Jem's never been a favorite of yours, for all he's definitely one of mine. I've often wondered how I would've fared had I been cursed with his parentage and upbringing.''

''But you weren't.''

''No, I wasn't. At least you must admit he's adaptable. There's other information I need that'll have to be acquired in a more organized fashion, and you're the best one to unearth it for me. Can I offer you a glass of claret or some Madeira, or would you prefer coffee?''

''Nothing, thank you, sir.''

''For God's sake, Burridge, unbend a little,'' North snapped. ''You'll find it won't shatter you. Claret, Madeira, or coffee— which is it to be?''

The prissy old fellow was looking at him as if North were

about to order him to mount a scaffold, or else dive into a vat of boiling oil.

"Madeira, if you please, sir," Burridge managed to say on a strangled note.

Good Lord, what ailed the man? There was no telling with such a pattern-card of rectitude. If North hadn't known it to be impossible, he'd've suspected the old buzzard was suffering from a guilty conscience.

"Go sit by the fireplace," North said, heading for the drinks table. "Have you delivered Mrs. Sherbrough's allowance?"

"Yes, sir."

"And how did you find her?"

"In excellent health, as always."

"And charming, of course."

"Mrs. Sherbrough is always everything that is amiable."

"Haven't been 'round to see her much of late," North admitted, handing Burridge his Madeira and gesturing impatiently at the wing chair across from him as he sat. "Not feeling neglected, is she?"

"That would not be something we would discuss, sir." Burridge pleated himself into the chair, and set the Madeira on the candle stand beside him.

"No, I suppose not. Still, did she seemed miffed?"

"Mrs. Sherbrough was very much as always, sir."

"Not much use to me where she's concerned, are you?" North sighed. "I suppose that's to be anticipated. A man's expected to see to his own mistress, not send hirelings to do it for him. Well, that's not why I asked you to stop by. I, ah, I had a bit of a problem last night, as you no doubt gathered."

Burridge's eyes met his for the first time. "Cutpurses, I assume," he said.

"Cutpurses definitely. Perhaps something else as well. I'm not certain, but that's not the problem I mean." North shifted about, then took a generous swallow of his claret. "You're aware a distant cousin left me cursed with a pair of wards?"

"I've heard something to that effect, though I have no notion of the specifics, as you've not favored me with seeking my assistance regarding them."

"No, I haven't. Felt it was my responsibility, and then I made a wager with the fellows. I get help, and I lose. Besides, I knew what you'd say."

"You did, sir?"

"You'd've told me to pack 'em off to Hillcrest for my mother to see to. Well, you would've, wouldn't you?"

"Children are a woman's responsibility as well as her greatest joy."

"Well, in this case they're no one's joy, and they're a man's responsibility. Freddy saw to that. Hired a house for 'em and retained a governess, for I won't have my mother troubled with 'em. Pair of wild animals, if you must know."

"And the house—how did you select it?"

"A notice in one of the journals. Came staffed and cheap enough. Sort of place those with shallow pockets and a daughter to fire off lease for the Season. Perfectly respectable address. Thing of it is, Miss Sparrow took Robert and Tabitha to the park yesterday, and there was a bit of a dust-up. The lad took exception to a fellow insulting her. Stamped on his boots, and then their puppy pissed on him. Fellow knocked Robert top over tail and kicked the pup. Good thing Dauntry—former captain, sold out on his parents' insistence when he was wounded at Salamanca last year after his older brother almost died of an inflammation of the lungs before getting himself an heir—came upon them, or God knows what would've happened next."

"I see," Burridge said, clearly not seeing at all.

"The clod tracked me down at White's, demanded an apology. I, ah, well, I refused to apologize and I refused to meet him at dawn, though I did reimburse him for the boots. In the process, I took the starch out of his social pretensions."

"In other words, you ruined him."

"Oh, no," North laughed, "he ruined himself. I merely made certain those present realized it. Now I want to know who he is and where he's staying, for I suspect he's the vengeful sort, and I don't want trouble. Claims he's one Sir Reginald Whifler, has a place called Chilcomb Manor near Manchester, and was almost betrothed to the daughter of an earl. Actually said he threw her over, and that it was perfectly proper as there'd been no announcement.''

"An unsavory sort, I gather.''

"Certainly no gentleman. Trace of the manufactory about him, and a whiff of the farmyard. Not recently, but within the memory of his mother, say, or perhaps hers.''

"What sort of information do you want?''

"Anything and everything. What can be gleaned in Town I expect by tomorrow evening, the rest within the week.''

"Including the identity of the earl's daughter?''

"If she exists. My guess is she doesn't. If she does, she's well out of it.''

"And this is all you wished to see me about?''

"Other than to discuss the latest reports from Hillcrest. Fields had 'em delivered by messenger yesterday. I don't plan to spend the summer there—going to take Mrs. Sherbrough on a jaunt to make up for my lack of attention these last weeks—so he'll be contacting you regarding funds for various improvements. You're to provide whatever he requests. What else could there be?''

"What else, indeed, sir.''

Burridge drained his Madeira in a single gulp.

Amelia gazed at her employer's town house with not a little jealousy. The areaway had been swept and scrubbed. The knocker gleamed. The windows sparkled. The contrast with Milbury Place, where nothing was ever properly scrubbed or polished or swept, could not have been greater.

Once the traffic eased, she darted across the cobbled street. Then, contrary to her custom, she descended to the areaway entry employed by servants and tradesmen. There was no longer any sense pretending she came to confer with Mr. North or Mr. Tidmarsh as an almost equal. Her path, except for her initial interview with Mr. Tidmarsh, had led from formal entry to housekeeper's parlor. Why embarrass poor Bassett with again making his employer's excuses? She would never be ushered into the august presence of Mr. Valentine North, Esquire—not even on the Day of Judgment, when God Himself would be easier of access.

It was Webster who responded to her firm knock, frogged livery discarded in favor of an apron, blackened rag proclaiming she'd interrupted him polishing the plate—an unusual activity at that advanced hour. Something must have occurred on Wilton Street to upset the customary routine.

"Say now, we don't want your sort here," he said, not quite looking at her, but still managing a glimpse that confirmed she had no legitimate business at his master's home. "No, nor are there any scraps you can have, and himself already subscribes to the charities he finds worthy, so take yourself off afore—"

"Good afternoon, Webster," she said.

The first footman almost jumped. Certainly the poor man blinked—a thing he'd told her more than once he'd trained himself never to do when he could be caught at it. She smiled. He swallowed, readjusting his notions.

"Miss Sparrow?" he said.

"Indeed it is. I've come to pay a call on Mrs. Pickles, if she can see me."

"You shouldn't be coming to this door. It isn't proper."

"Why not? Certainly I've no business above, as Mr. North will always be too ill or too preoccupied to see me, and Mr. Tidmarsh isn't in London. There's no need for Bassett to tell me that again. Besides, I earn my bread just like anyone belowstairs, and have been stretching a point coming to the other door."

"Not quite the same as the rest of us. Well," he sighed, "since you're here you might as well come in. I'll see if Mrs. Pickles has a moment, but we're that busy today, what with one thing and another."

"I'm sorry, Webster," she said, heart sinking as she backed away. Apparently in descending three steps rather than climbing five she'd announced there was no longer any need for courtesy or respect. "I can return another time."

"Might be best." He gave a curt nod and shut the door in her face.

And so vanished her last refuge, and her only hope of seeking advice regarding the Grimbles' threats. As for giving notice, Mr. North had made it impossible.

Tears of frustration tangling in her lashes, she turned and mounted the areaway steps, then leaned against the railing. The sky was as blue and clear, the sun as bright, the breeze as soft as it had been moments before. How strange. There should have been thunder and lightning, and lowering clouds.

She closed her eyes against the cheerful bustle of carriages, carefully thinking of nothing. If she thought, she just might assault that gleaming front door a few feet away, have herself announced properly, and treat Mr. Valentine North to a scold not even his father would've dared give him. That mustn't happen. She might owe something to Tibbie and Robby, and at a stretch she owed something to Mr. Tidmarsh, but she owed herself something as well. The only person whose interests might be served by such a lecture would be Mr. North's. Everyone else would suffer, she most of all.

"Are you feeling faint, miss?"

She turned in the voice's direction. A beak-nosed gentleman finished descending the steps from North's front door and covered the few feet separating them. Strange, how he reminded her of some silted shore bird, head thrust forward as he sought his supper. Perhaps it was because he was slender to the point of emaciation, all angles and lines and patient watchfulness.

"Mr. North?" she said, not daring to hope.

"No, a hireling. You appear ill. Shall I summon a hackney?"

She shook her head, then sighed. "That's not necessary. I'm perfectly well, merely a trifle perplexed. Mr. North is at home?"

His eyes narrowed, regarding her with doubt as he drew back. Well, and no wonder. It was an improper question to put to a stranger, especially one in Mr. Valentine North's employ. Certainly he could have no notion who she was, or if her interest in North were of an acceptable sort.

"I apologize," she said. "That was infinitely clumsy of me. Perhaps you know if Mr. Tidmarsh has returned?"

"No, I'm afraid I have no idea. You're an employee of Mr. North's?"

"Yes, though I've yet to meet the gentleman. I have charge of his wards."

"Ah, I see. I sometimes, ah, act in the capacity of an agent for Mr. North. Might I be of some assistance?"

"If only you could," she sighed. "Unfortunately, the only people who can be of use to me are Mr. North or his secretary. No one else will do, as the responsibility is Mr. North's, and perhaps Mr. Tidmarsh's, and it's a matter I don't feel at liberty to discuss with anyone other than them."

"Very correct, though perhaps a trifle inconvenient if neither will make himself available to you. Would it relieve your mind to know I'm aware from what you've said that you're the governess of Robert and Tabitha Tyne, the orphaned children of Captain Frederick Tyne and his wife, the former Frances Fulham, that your name is Miss Abigail Sparrow, and that you reside in a house on Milbury Place?"

"I wish it did, but it doesn't."

The man stood there studying her as if she were a small fish and he was trying to decide if it would be worth the effort to gobble her up.

"I do know you've found the position difficult," he said at last, "as Mr. North has to date refused either to meet with you or to assume any personal responsibility for the children. While I don't have the information from Mr. North directly, my source is unimpeachable, and equally discreet."

"How fortunate for both you and Mr. North."

"I'm also aware of the unusual nature of the household on Milbury Place."

"My goodness, but you know a lot for a nameless stranger who acts only as an occasional agent for Mr. North. Perhaps someone should inform him of your interest in matters that do not concern you," she snapped.

She spun on her heel and made her way up the street, dodging passersby. A bony-fingered hand gripped her arm, forcing her to stop and turn.

"I am Mr. North's customary man of business," the stranger said, tone flat, "though he does employ others on occasion to act for him. I assure you that I'm entirely worthy of your confidence.''

''If you're not worthy of Mr. North's confidence, then you're not worthy of mine. Backstairs gossip is the only fashion in which you could've acquired so much information. Now, release me or I'll cause such a scene that your continuation in Mr. North's employ in *any* capacity will be highly problematic.''

He dropped her arm, frowned, then pulled out his card case.

''Well said, Miss Sparrow. You've put me on notice. In return, here's my card. If you ever find yourself in need of assistance, please feel free to call on me. That at least I can offer without compromising either your principles or mine.''

Chapter Eleven

Amelia's first impulse was to tear the creamy pasteboard in half and fling the pieces in the man's face. Fearing that would give a childish appearance, she crammed it in her reticule and stalked down the street, reviewing the cutting things she could've said if only they'd occurred to her at an opportune moment. That occupied her for the time it took to reach an area of small shops she'd noticed while taking the children on an excursion to Madame Tussaud's.

Stockings for Tibbie and caps for Robby were easy enough—the excuse she'd given Florrie for her absence. The girl was only too aware Tibbie constantly drilled holes in her heels, and Robby and caps parted company with the dependability of sun following rain.

To those essentials Amelia added a new leash for Beezle and a slate to replace the one Tibbie'd broken. Hoping no one would question the amount of time she'd spent selecting such paltry items, she was about to turn back, when she spotted a coarse woman peddling posies across the way. Inspired, she found a shop that sold packets of seeds. Now, there would be something to plant in the beds they'd begun hacking from the tired jungle behind the house.

Only a guilty conscience, Amelia admitted as she let herself in less than half an hour later, could have made her feel she'd been too long absent. She set her purchases on the chest by the stairs for one of the footmen to deliver to the nursery, noted that she'd have to remind Mrs. Grimble to change the faded flowers, then trudged up the stairs.

Her head ached. Her feet were bruised from walking on hard pavements in footwear unsuited to the exercise. Worst of all, the sense of unease she'd managed to shed while away from Milbury Place had descended on her with redoubled force when she returned. She wanted a handkerchief soaked in lavender water across her forehead, her feet up, a pot of tea, and no one to so much as speak to her for an hour. Florrie could see to Tibbie and Robby for that much longer.

Amelia removed her pelisse and bonnet, tugged on her sitting-room bell rope, then glanced out the window overlooking the derelict garden. There was no sign of Florrie, Beezle, or the children. Not surprising. Tibbie and Robby had had enough of rooting in the dirt that morning. Well, they were sure to be somewhere about the place. She'd been definite with Florrie regarding the fact that they were not to leave the house. Exploring the attics, perhaps, or else in the kitchen cadging a treat from Mrs. Chiddy, who'd taken an unaccountable liking to them over the past week.

She sank onto the chair by the window, removed her spectacles, slipped off her thin-soled boots, and propped her feet on the hassock. Goodness, but she was tired, and not just from that afternoon, or even the entire day. Tired from the endless succession of days and weeks since she'd bolted from the court, and then tumbled into this position as governess to a pair of orphans whose own mother would've been hard pressed to find anything engaging about them.

Except there was something appealing about them, an undeniable crude honesty combined with a code of honor which, if unconventional, had a certain logic to it given their history. Things had been going a bit better. Please heaven, let them continue to do so, for she couldn't take much more.

Finally, when it became obvious no one was going to answer

her bell, she struggled from her seat, put on a pair of house slippers, smoothed her hair, and descended the stairs. Beyond the echo of her footsteps and the distant clatter of carriage wheels, the house might've been a tomb. Jaws clenched, she hurried down to the kitchen for the second time that day. The stove was cold, the fire unlit. Dishes and pots were jumbled on the table, waiting to be washed.

Ignoring the fact that her feet were covered only by a pair of heelless tapestry slippers, she took the key and slipped out the door giving on the garden, went to the back gate, unlocked it, and crossed to the stable. The children's ponies were in their stalls, the carriage horses and the two hacks as well, but there was no sign of Mick Grady, Mike O'Hara, or the rat-faced fellow who called himself George Ginty and claimed to be a coachman.

She retraced her steps, not certain whether she should be furious, terrified, or both. She was just closing the garden door when she heard a thump on the floor above.

"I shall have the vapors," she muttered, tearing back up the stairs, heart pounding. "That, or a fit—I don't care which, but I shall have something for my pains."

A low moan followed by a shriek sent her into the drawing room. She might've guessed it would be Bessie, cavorting where she didn't belong. She should've known if Bessie was cavorting, then it would be William with whom she cavorted. Such a lovely word—"cavort." It covered a multitude of sins, including this highly energetic one.

"On your feet, both of you," she snapped. "Now!"

William halted in mid-buck, then collapsed on Bessie like a punctured bladder. Amelia decided she was mostly furious, but it was a fury tempered by an almost hysterical amusement. They looked so silly. And, until she'd spoken, sounded sillier. This sojourn in Town was certainly proving educational. If she didn't have a care, her cheeks would soon lose the capacity to burn.

"On your feet, I said," she repeated. "Where are the others?"

"Oh, garn—it's her," William muttered. "Shoulda knowed it was too much t'hope she'd stay gone awhile."

He managed to slip from the divan with his back still turned, fumbling with his inexpressibles. Bessie remained where she was, staring daggers.

"Hortie Grimble give us the day off oncet you left," she said. "You ain't got no right coming in here like that. Scared me half to death, you did."

"Had you been comporting yourself properly, you wouldn't've been startled. Where are the children?"

"How should I know? Ain't my lookout." At Amelia's steely glare she added, "With Florrie, I suppose."

"And where is Florrie?"

"Ain't her keeper neither. Been a mealy-mouthed gudgeon since you come here, she has. You've ruint her for havin' a bit o' fun." She yawned and stretched, then rolled over. "Go on back where you belong. I'm gonna have a nice, long nap."

"Now, Bessie," William protested. "You know Hortie said as how—"

Then Amelia was across the room, seizing Bessie's arm and pulling her to her feet. "Downstairs," she said, amazed at how calm her voice was. "Now. Both of you. That, or I'll have you arrested for public indecency."

"It wasn't public until you come in," Bessie protested. "It was real private." The girl went to the door, hips swaying, then turned. "Judgment Day's coming," she said. "Coming real soon. When it does, you'll be scrubbin' floors and hauling water, an' I'll be sleeping till noon an' giving the orders."

And then they were both gone. Amelia went to the windows overlooking Milbury Place, praying she'd see Florrie and the children. There was a boy rolling a hoop and another throwing a ball for his dog to fetch, but neither of the boys was Robby and the dog wasn't Beezle.

Amelia went back to her rooms, refusing to be truly frightened as yet. It was possible Florrie and the children had gone somewhere with Mrs. Chiddy. It was equally possible Florrie, who was a paragon only when compared to Bessie, had decided the afternoon off included her, and left the children to their own devices. Refusing to contemplate the escapades into which the children might've fallen under such circumstances, and feeling all the guilt of having entrusted them to another when she ran to Wilton Street for comfort and advice—especially as neither comfort nor advice had been forthcoming—Amelia went to where she'd earlier left her reticule, opened it, and retrieved the stranger's card.

Aaron Burridge, it said, along with an address in the City. No fulsome title. No listing of services offered, no hinting at elevated clients. Hardly the typical trade card, which customarily involved considerable puffery along with what its possessor believed to be tasteful artistic embellishment, the whole resembling an overblown ball gown. Aaron Burridge was either exceedingly modest, or so arrogant even Brummell at his most sartorially autocratic could never hope to equal him.

She returned the card to her reticule, then consulted the watch pinned on her corsage. It was only four o'clock, the sun still high. She'd give it two hours. Then? Well, then perhaps she'd look at Mr. Burridge's card again, and consider what to do next.

A careful search of nursery, schoolroom, and Florrie's cubby revealed Beezle's leash to be missing, along with Florrie's favorite bonnet and shawl, one of Tibbie's better spencers, and Robby's sole remaining cap. The rooms were neat as a pin, every toy in its place, every chair straight, every surface devoid of the litter two small children and a flibbertigibbet nursemaid inevitably produced. Amelia wasn't certain whether she should find that frightening or encouraging.

Pacing from drawing room to breakfast parlor, then dining room to back parlor and on to the drawing room again did no good, Amelia decided an hour later. Neither did consulting the clock on the parlor mantel each time she was in that room, or the one in the drawing room when she was there, and comparing them with the watch on her corsage. None of them agreed, and their hands barely moved in any case.

Attempting to read was even more futile, and when she

forced herself to retrieve some of Robby's shirts that needed mending, she quickly learned, if one was abstracted, buttons refused to be sewn in the proper places and rents became longer the more one tried to stitch them up. As for dashing to the window dry-mouthed and with her heart trying to leap from her chest each time she thought she heard the clatter of a carriage or the sound of footsteps, she was an idiot.

There was another thing she learned as the minutes dragged: Never, under any circumstances, no matter what became of her or where she went, would she want children of her own. It would be too painful, too terrifying. She didn't even like Tibbie and Robby, or at least she thought she didn't, and yet the way she was acting one would have thought they were the center of her universe. Perhaps *ton* parents such as her mother, who refused to be bothered with their offspring, had found the secret. Plenty of time to make the acquaintance of Dorothea, Charlotte, and Amelia if they survived to the age of reason. In the meantime, let those of the lower orders—who, by common consent, didn't possess the sensibilities of a lady—suffer the anxieties and the sorrows, and revel in the very few joys.

Except that, she knew, was untrue. The lower orders did suffer, and terribly, with hearts as tender and easily broken as her own.

Oh, not the Bessies of the world. Yet, did she know even that? Something had to have made Bessie what she was. There was no hope for the slut now, but once she must have regarded each dawn with a sense of wonder, and each night as the stars winked on as pure magic. Had Bessie's finer feelings been destroyed by circumstance, just as she herself appeared to have lost the capacity to be shocked on Milbury Place?

And if that were true, what had happened to Tibbie and Robby during those years in the Colonies?

Scowling, pacing furiously and thinking even more furiously, headache and sore feet forgotten, the carriages drawing to a stop made no impression on Amelia. It wasn't until Tibbie and Robby burst through the door trailed by Florrie, Mr. Sinclair, Mr. Dauntry, Mr. Harnette, and Mr. Threadwhistle, Beezle gamboling at their heels, that she realized there would be no need to climb the stairs, retrieve Mr. Burridge's card, and consider what she must do next.

She stood there, staring from the gentlemen to Florrie, unaware of the tears streaming down her cheeks as the children rushed up to her babbling of splendid teas in taverns, of rides on donkeys and sculling in boats, of Punch and Judy shows and acrobats and jugglers, and a man who swallowed swords and belched fire like a dragon, and a bear that danced for all it wasn't very happy about it. She sank to her knees, gathering the overexcited urchins to her, kissing their sticky, sun-reddened faces, and hugging them so tightly, they protested. Then Beezle yipped and started to lift his leg, and she told them to take the pup to the back garden.

As the children dashed off, Mr. Dauntry assisted her to her feet.

"From the look of you, we're in bad odor," he said. "I can't understand why. It was a harmless excursion, and they enjoyed every minute of it. So did the rest of us."

Ignoring the gentlemen, she whirled on Florrie. "I told you the children were not to set foot outside this house," she said in a trembling voice.

"These fellows're friends of Mr. North's," the girl protested. "You ain't got nothing to fear from 'em. They've ate here, and it was Quint what rescued you yesterday. They come to give Robby a new boat for one what was broke, and a doll for Tibbie so's she wouldn't go green-eyed and nasty. What with Hortie Grimble saying as how she'd give the rest the day off if we went, an' Bessie beggin' us to go an' saying what fun it would be, I didn't see no harm."

"You mustn't insist the children either be closeted here or else perpetually under your eye, y'know," Mr. Harnette said. "Quickest way to stifle 'em I can think of. You stifle 'em, and they'll break their chains in all sorts of unaccountable ways. Wouldn't ever've let 'em come to harm—not Val's wards."

"The fact remains that Tibbie and Robby are my responsibility," Amelia snapped. "I stand in place of a mother to them, and my permission is needed before anyone takes them on an outing. At the very least, common courtesy suggests I should have been informed of where they'd gone, and with whom.''

"But we left you a note. Quint wrote it out, telling you where we'd taken 'em and when we'd return, and not to worry about their supper as we'd see 'em fed. He even left you the wherewithal to hire a carriage and join us if you'd a mind to and returned from your errands early enough. Put it on that chest, where you'd be certain to see it right off.'' Mr. Harnette pointed to where Amelia's parcels still waited to be taken to the nursery. "Robby and Tibbie insisted on that, as Mrs. Grimble told the others they'd no need to stay about the place if they didn't want to. Val's tadpoles felt you deserved a treat too, which I thought was mighty handsome of them.''

In the silence that followed Mr. Harnette's words, Mr. Dauntry strode to the chest. "With your permission, Miss Sparrow?'' he said, gesturing at the parcels.

"You'll find no note,'' she said, "but certainly you may look.''

But it was there, though not where Mr. Dauntry and the others insisted he'd left it resting against the bowl of dead flowers. First he stacked the parcels on the bench Mr. Threadwhistle moved over. Then he opened the drawers, which were empty. It wasn't until Mr. Sinclair gave him a hand shifting the cumbersome thing from the wall that they found the note lying amid dust kittens and mouse droppings. Mr. Dauntry retrieved it, dusted it off, gave it a close look, then handed it to her.

"Maybe Miss Sparrow didn't see it, and knocked it off when she set down her parcels,'' Mr. Threadwhistle said.

"Couldn't have,'' Mr. Sinclair said. "Quint leaned it against that bowl so she wouldn't miss it. Didn't want her to worry, you'll remember. Neither did the children. Rough about the edges though they are, that pair's solid gold if only someone'll polish off the dross.''

Amelia turned it over. The note had been sealed with candle wax, the seal broken, then clumsily mended. She rebroke it and unfolded the note.

"Don't you need your spectacles?'' Mr. Dauntry said behind

her. "I'm certain Florrie will fetch them for you if you'll tell her where they are."

So she hadn't lost the capacity to blush. "No," Amelia said, "there's no need. I require them less and less these days. With the young ladies of whom I previously had charge, there was constant fine work. I strain my eyes far less with Tibbie and Robby."

"Ah—that explains it, then," he murmured. "I wondered."

Blushing even more furiously, Amelia read the note. It was a detailed accounting of where they were going, when they would return, and that they would see to feeding the children before bringing them back to Milbury Place, precisely as Mr. Harnette had claimed. It also explained they were taking Florrie with them for prudence's sake, and that Mrs. Grimble had given the rest of the staff the day off. There was even a postscript mentioning the inclusion of a pound, and a post-postscript in Robby's clumsy hand begging her to join them.

The money, however, was missing.

She folded the note, then looked at the group facing her. Only Mr. Dauntry didn't have the air of a prisoner awaiting judgment. Unlike yesterday, when he'd been all kindness and sympathy, he wore the black look of a gentleman not only irked, but prepared to give physical expression to his sense of injury if afforded the slightest encouragement.

"I apologize," she said, looking directly at first one, then another. "You're right. I should have had no reason for concern. In retrospect, I have none. You've given the children a treat, and I'm grateful to you all. They've been having a rather dull time of it with me, I'm afraid."

She shook her head as Florrie opened her mouth. "No, I blame you least of all," she said. "Had I been in your position, I would have done the same thing. You exercised excellent judgment in accepting Mr. North's friends' invitation. That I spent a few anxious hours is not your fault."

"Handsomely spoken," Mr. Threadwhistle murmured. "M'sister's governess was always blaming everyone and his uncle, no matter where the truth lay."

Officially ignoring the compliment, but holding it in her heart as offering redemption of a sort, Amelia turned to Florrie. "Please go find the children and take them upstairs," she said. "They need baths to calm them down as much as to clean them up, and then they need their beds. Was Beezle fed?"

"Naturally!" Mr. Harnette spluttered. "I'd never let the livestock go begging. None of us would, and if we hadn't seen to the scalawag, Robby and Tibbie would've. They're attached to the pup."

"Quint and Tony've told me what I'm to do," Florrie said, dipping the first proper curtsy Amelia had seen her perform. "I'll be seeing to the children now, and I'll make you a nice supper, Miss Sparrow, with mayhap some warm milk just afore you lay your head down. You've had that distressing of a day."

"The thing of it is," Mr. Threadwhistle said, turning to Amelia as Florrie, behaving for once like a nursemaid if one didn't count her using the gentlemen's given names, disappeared down the service stairs, "you never need worry about Robby or Tibbie when they're with us. Just want you to know that. We'd never do 'em an injury, nor would we ever permit 'em to come to harm."

"Never would, never could, never will," Mr. Harnette added for emphasis.

"That's enough, fellows," Mr. Sinclair murmured.

Then Mr. Dauntry was asking the others to wait for him outside, as he wanted to clear up the matter of the note's disappearance and the missing pound. There was a flurry of thanks and good-byes, and then she was alone with the former officer.

"All right," Mr. Dauntry said, "which one was it?"

"I don't understand. Which one was what?"

"One of the cutthroats who pass for servants in this house hid the da—blasted thing, and took the money. Which one was it?"

"I'll see to the matter."

"You can't, Miss Sparrow. You've never dealt with scum before. I, by contrast, have, and those I deal with stay dealt with. Experience of command has its uses. Now, which one was it—the slut, or one of those ferret-faced footmen?"

"It was Bessie," she sighed, collapsing on the bench.

"No, not here," he said. "Go in the drawing room and position yourself in the center of the divan. Spread your skirts, act as if you're bored, and hide those abominable slippers beneath your hem."

"That would hardly create the impression you desire."

"A lady at ease in her drawing room? That's how my mother does it when a servant's called on the carpet. Most intimidating they find it too. She's a viscountess, and knows what she's about."

"But not in this house, not in that room, and not on that divan."

"Why not? You are mistress here, according to Val."

"I caught Bessie and William on it a bit ago. In flagrante delicto."

"And survived the experience without hysterics, and can even bring yourself to speak of it afterward? You are a woman of fortitude."

"One does one's poor best," she replied, then blushed once more at his bark of laughter.

"All right," he said, "not the drawing room. Is there any other place that'd suit?"

"There's the back parlor, but it's the shabbiest of the lot."

"We'll make do. Pretend you're the daughter of a duke: head high, manner bored, nose in the air."

"A duke? Oh, dear—I don't think I could ever aspire so high."

"An earl, then. Any governess worth her salt has more airs than the most self-consequential earl's daughter, for all she rarely uses 'em on anyone but other governesses. Where's Bessie, and where's the back parlor? I don't want to keep the fellows waiting."

Valentine North prowled his book room, comparing the time suggested by his pocket watch against the hour proclaimed by the clock on the mantel. They agreed, naturally. He'd been adjusting first one and then the other to be in accord with whichever was fastest all evening.

"For pity's sake, calm yourself," St. Maure grumbled from the table where he'd returned to researching the peccadilloes of previous generations, sometimes chuckling over an obscure bit of trivia, more often exclaiming he'd never had any notion this or that famous title had its origins in a complaisant husband, a toothsome wife, and a ruler in rut. "Jem'll return when he returns."

Clough snored in North's customary chair, arm paining him far less, determined to stay until Jem returned and they knew more about that morning's attack. The others had agreed North's elderly staff had been put to far too much exertion of late. They'd also insisted they had need of a bit of peace and quiet themselves, and had departed as soon as they'd filled their stomachs with a generous nuncheon with the exception of St. Maure, who agreed to wait for Clough to surface from his laudanum-induced slumber.

"Who're you reading about now, Dab?" North said to break the silence in which only the clock ticked, pausing by the library table to peer over his friend's shoulder.

"Family named Peaseleigh. First came to prominence during Edward the Confessor's time." St. Maure glanced up, grinning. "Baron sired himself an heir and several by-blows and then, as he'd no taste for his lady wife, relinquished his title in favor of his son, shaved his head, and took to the road as a mendicant friar. Liked to travel, don't you see. New places, new faces, new, ah, curves."

"How enterprising of him."

"Very holy man, legend has it, though legend also has it the villages where he passed had a way of becoming littered with babes possessing his hooked nose and red hair nine months later."

"Infinitely enterprising."

"Famous old gossip, Stowaker," St. Maure rattled on. "Always wondered who he really was."

"No, y'haven't."

"I haven't? And here I thought I had. Ah, well, Edward

heard about Peaseleigh-the-friar, though not about his little leavings, and made the man's heir a viscount in recompense for his father's religious fervor on condition the lad follow in his father's footsteps once *he'd* gotten himself an heir.''

"Y'don't say," North muttered, bored with the topic, and only eager to fill the interminable silence. "How fascinating."

"Sank into obscurity after that. Then in Henry the Eighth's time Viscount Edwin Peaseleigh married Griselda Bottom to legitimize a couple of Henry's favorite bastards, combined the name to Peasebottom, and Henry made him an earl by way of thanks. Was reading about Griselda a bit ago, you'll remember. Doxy with yellow hair. Fellow who inherited from the first earl didn't have a drop of old Peaseleigh's blood in him. Of course, it's all gossip, but wouldn't it be amusing if it were true?''

"Very amusing." North wandered over to the drinks table and helped himself to a glass of brandy. "Want some?" he said, holding out the decanter.

St. Maure shook his head. "Don't know if you've ever run across the current holder, but a more bumptious idiot it's never been my misfortune to encounter. Got yellow hair too, what's left of it. Preternaturally attached to wagering, and abysmally poor at it. Even Pugs wins against him, and Pugs never wins against anybody.''

"No, he doesn't," North sighed, putting the decanter back. "Wish he'd give over dicing with me. Never certain what to do."

"Pugs knows the depth of his pockets, and never outruns the constable. He's convinced one day he'll win. Until then, he's content to lose."

"Still isn't right to take money from a friend who never wins any of it back."

"Stowaker claims here the Peasebottoms've spent almost three centuries trying to hush it all up," St. Maure chuckled, returning to his primary interest. "There's even a handwritten note says they've bought every set of *Origins* they could find. When they couldn't get the full set, they settled for the volumes about the Peaseleighs and Griselda. Whoever inscribed this claimed he'd been offered a thousand pounds for just those two. Turned it down, of course. Considered it a marvelous joke."

"Stubble it, Dab," North snapped. "I've no interest in hoary gossip."

"Sorry. Still, y'never know when such information might come in handy." St. Maure grinned, not the least insulted.

North snorted and resumed his pacing.

Except for the interview with Burridge and giving Jem his orders, it had been the longest, most boring day North had spent in what felt like months. He'd hated every minute of it. One wanted to be about and doing, not trapped in one's home, waiting for others to act. At least he did.

"Dammit, Jem, I hope you've been careful," he muttered, checking his watch against the mantel clock again.

Precisely ten minutes had passed since he last looked—no more, but at least it was no less. The clocks, thank heavens, were not running in reverse.

He whirled at the gentle tap on the book room door. "Come," he snapped.

It was only Bassett, inquiring whether they wanted something. North shook his head, wanting to take the old man's head off for startling him. Instead, he suggested Bassett take himself off to bed, as it had been a long day, then found himself apologizing one hundred to the minute at Bassett's look of insult.

And then, miraculously, Jem was there, hat in hand, pleading to be let in. How he contained himself then, North had no notion, for the glint in Bassett's eye proved Jem had been there all along.

"Well?" he said, crossing to the drinks table and pouring the lad a glass of the port he favored. "Learn anything?"

Stubby Clough snorted and opened his eyes as North held the glass out to the young groom. St. Maure closed the tome he'd been gobbling most of the evening, turning in his chair. All eyes were on Jem—including Bassett's. The boy belonged on the stage the way he was drawing out his moment of glory. Then he was across the room, taking the glass from North and sipping from it as if he were a member of the finest gentlemen's club in Town.

"That I did, sir," he said when one more moment of silence and North would've throttled him.

"Have a seat, Jem," North sighed. "We may be at this for a bit."

"No, sir, there's not that much to tell. Didn't find Tricky Tess for the longest time, and once I did, the only thing I learned is it sounds like the work of Whistling Willie. No one's seen him in a year or more, she said. Only one Tess knows of could pull a trick like that, for all he usually works alone. So quick with his knife, he could cut your heart out and you'd never know it, she says."

"And that's all?"

"Well, no, sir. Tess said as how I was to thank you for a fine dinner and a night to herself. Promised she'd keep her ear to the wind, but if it was Willie, she isn't likely to hear anything. He'll've gone to ground, and with pockets as full as yours was, he ain't likely to surface soon. Said Whistling Willie was never one to press his luck beyond what luck'll carry."

Chapter Twelve

Amelia struggled to waken, dry-mouthed and lead-limbed, nightmares chasing her into the daylight. And there had been nightmares, a plethora of them. If she remembered nothing else, she remembered that. Shadowy figures. Soft footsteps. Once a pup's yip, quickly muffled.

She twisted. The sheets held her trapped as securely as shackles. She didn't believe she was actually ill, though her head floated unfettered above her body, and her bed waltzed like one of the horses at Astley's Amphitheater.

"Here, head," she called, then giggled at the hoarse croak. "Down! Be a good head and return to your mistress."

Her voice sounded unnatural, the lips from which it issued not merely floating above her, but soaring far higher than that. Not like her own voice at all. Dear heaven, what was the matter with her?

She forced her eyes open, regretted it instantly. The room was too bright, the colors she glimpsed more vivid than colors had a right to be. She groped beneath the covers, trying to untangle herself. Strangely, the sheets weren't twisted, lying above and beneath her as smoothly as glass. It was her arms and legs that were at fault. No matter how sternly she commanded, while they would move on the flat, they refused to lift.

Amelia gave it up with a sigh, closed her eyes, and drifted. No nightmares now. Merely a scull in which she floated on a gently flowing river that chuckled against mossy tree roots between which clumps of cress and wild water irises grew. She was only a girl, lying on a bed of violets and daisies, carefree as the linnet singing in a branch above, her unbound hair floating like frayed embroidery silk on the breeze. No troubles. No cares. No impossible household to battle every minute of every day. No children to be seen to.

Except there were, but they could wait until the river stopped singing and the flowers faded.

It was the children who finally roused her—not their shouts or their quarreling, but that there were no shouts, no quarrels. Issuing her arms commands she only half believed would be obeyed, she managed to sit. The room tilted. With a groan she was on the floor, pulling the chamber pot from beneath the bed and, as Robby termed it, casting up her accounts. That went on for some time. When it was over, the room no longer wobbled like a top in its last revolutions.

"Florrie?" she called, but no one came.

How long she remained on her knees she had no idea, but it must have been a considerable time. Finally, still feeling ill but no longer in desperate case, she pulled herself to her feet, clinging to the bedpost. Despite her vision of brilliant light and vivid colors, the curtains remained drawn, a single band of sunshine slicing through a gap to climb covers and tumble across floor and chair like a wound. A teapot, a plate of biscuits, and a cup waited on her dressing table.

Not willing to examine that miracle too closely, she went behind the screen, rinsed her mouth, and spat into the slops jar. The tea proved tepid and bitter, but it was tea. She drank cup after cup as if she'd spent the night crawling across a wasteland. When there was none left, she tried a biscuit, then devoured the remaining six.

Still unable to think coherently, she washed, scrubbed herself dry, then donned a bombazine gown, pinned the little watch inside her corsage, as she wouldn't want it seen, and attacked her hair with a vigor that amazed her. That did the trick, for suddenly her mind was churning. In a matter of minutes she was presentable, feet encased in sturdy boots rather than the more elegant ones vanity prompted her to wear when she called on Mrs. Pickles. This time it wouldn't be North's housekeeper she'd be seeking, and she wouldn't be pleading for the favor of an interview. She'd be demanding it.

As a matter of form, she crossed the hall to the children's quarters, certain of what she'd find. That she was right gave her no satisfaction. This time they were truly gone. Not one item of clothing belonging to Robby, Tibbie, or Florrie had been left behind. There was evidence of a rapid gathering up of books and toys. Even Beezle had vanished.

The kitten, which was now an ill-tempered cat, watched Amelia through slitted eyes as she went to the schoolroom window and stared down at the garden in the center of Milbury Place. She felt nothing. Not anger. Not terror. Not even dismay or surprise. Certainly not confusion. In this house, something of the sort had been bound to happen.

And then she realized there was a cold, joyless knot at the core of her being. It had a name: determination. It was crude. It was harsh. It was implacable, and totally unladylike. And it had an impetus all its own. Her mind had never been clearer. Never had it been so focused.

She glanced around the schoolroom, suspecting she'd never see it again. Then, face expressionless, she returned to her bedchamber, donned a cap, a pelisse, gloves, and her ugliest bonnet, retrieved her reticule, made certain Mr. Burridge's card was in it along with all her funds, descended the stairs to the entry, and quitted the house.

There had been no need to question Hortense Grimble regarding the whereabouts of Bessie, William, or Charles. The sun proclaimed it was almost noon, but no lamps had been cleaned, no candles replaced, no furniture dusted, and her parcels still lay on the entryway bench, where Mr. Dauntry had put them the evening before.

Like Florrie, Beezle, and the children, the others were gone.

* * *

"What the devil?" North knew that voice. He'd known it all his life.

He glanced at Chloe. This was one time he didn't want to be interrupted, for he'd been making heavy weather of things since he arrived, the signed deed to their little nest and a generous draft on his bank in one pocket, a necklace of amethysts and diamonds he'd acquired at Rundle and Bridge that morning as a more conventional parting gift in another, and an enormous bouquet of hothouse roses clutched in a gloved hand whose palm was damp no matter how sternly he instructed it to behave.

He wanted it over and done with now that he'd finally reached a decision regarding her, blast it. That he'd come to a decision only in the small hours of the previous night, pacing the floor while consuming far too much brandy, was neither here nor there. The fire, which had never been much more than a comfortable glow in any case, was extinguished, leaving behind it an impersonal affection combined with a certain respect. He'd known that for weeks. He'd even admitted it for weeks. It was just that, what with one thing and another, he'd never found a propitious moment to inform either Chloe or himself of the change in their relationship.

Her answering smile was tentative. No surprise there. She had to know why he'd come. There was only one reason a gentleman would arrive at the home he provided his *chère amie* at the unheard of hour of noon garbed for a formal call. But he hadn't been able to bring himself to hand her the deed, let alone the necklace or the bank draft. The words that would seal their parting stuck in his throat like fish bones.

At least once he managed it, she'd realize her future was secure. She didn't have many good years left, and had to be worrying. As a usual thing, once they were over she'd've been on the streets or turning madam, for her theater contacts were primarily provincial, and long deceased.

The sound of Joseph's voice raised in protest flooded up the stairs.

"Damn!" he muttered. No, he didn't want to be interrupted until he'd completed his business, but perhaps something would happen to make it easier. "You never were a bore, y'know, Chloe. Fine characteristic in a female—never boring one."

"Why, thank you, Val," she said.

There was a loud thump. Were the old fellows actually coming to fisticuffs, Joseph defending them against intrusion, Jitters determined to have words with his employer no matter what the conventions regarding a servant seeking out his employer when that employer was closeted with his mistress?

"Maybe I should go see what's to do," North said.

And then the door was opening. Jitters quivered on the threshold, disheveled and out of breath. Behind him Joseph danced on the toes of his pumps, white wig askew, bemoaning the invasion and close to tears.

"I presume the last trumpet has sounded, and you've come to inform me I must present myself at the Throne of Judgment within the hour for my eternal fate to be decided," North drawled. "Which coat do you recommend for such a momentous occasion, Jitters—the blue or the olive? If it's to be the olive, we must change my waistcoat as well."

"Might be something akin to that," Jitters panted. "You've got to come, Master Valentine. Herself's arrived and taken up residence in the book room, and there isn't a thing any of us can do to chase her away."

"My mother's in Town?" North sprang to his feet. "Why didn't you say so to begin with?"

"No, sir—Miss Sparrow."

North froze, not even daring to breathe lest he cross the room and tear the old fellow's head from his shoulders.

"I gather something's amiss," Chloe said for him.

"Haven't none of us ever seen Miss Sparrow like this," Jitters babbled. "There's no reasoning with her, and there's no moving her. Wouldn't say aught but that she would see Mr. North, and if he was from home, he was to be fetched on the instant. Didn't even ask for Mr. Tidmarsh this time."

"Perhaps you'd best go, Val." Chloe rose, gazing at him with her brow drawn in a slight frown. "From the little you've said, Miss Sparrow is a sensible woman conscious of the conventions. She wouldn't arrive on your doorstep requesting to see you unless she had excellent reason.''

"Oh, yes, she would," North growled. "She'd arrive for any reason, or none at all, spouting any nonsense her feather-brain could invent as an excuse. That woman was put on earth to make my life intolerable—and that's only when she's dealing with Tidmarsh. I knew how it'd be. Why d'you think I invented the fellow? Forever complaining about this or that, sending me notes demanding interviews to satisfy her curiosity as to who Valentine North might be, and determine whether she can cozen him into offering for her. Well, it's not me she'll get, not this time, and not ever. It's Tidmarsh, and he'll read her such a lecture, she'll never importune me—us—whoever—again. I've lost all patience with the dratted female!''

"There's no need to work yourself into a rage. Miss Sparrow gave no reason for requesting to see Mr. North?" Chloe said, turning to Jitters. "No reason at all?"

Jitters shook his head. "Didn't request. She demanded."

Behind him, Joseph jabbered apologies as incoherent as they were desperate.

"Then let one of the fellows see her," North snapped. "Dauntry'd be best. Send her to him, or call him to her—I don't care which. He's been singing her praises ever since he rescued her in the park, and Dauntry never sings the praises of any female. Give him a chance to play hero again. Doubtless thank me for the opportunity. I, however, refuse to be imposed upon.''

The looks that met this sally had North flushing despite himself.

"Maybe no one should go," he said after giving the matter a moment's thought. "Maybe I should leave her to cool her heels until the final trumpet does sound. That'll teach her.''

"I wouldn't do that, sir," Jitters said. "There's something about Miss Sparrow says you'd best present yourself instantly without regard to your convenience, and not as Mr. Tidmarsh neither.''

"Fustian! She's a hireling—a faded nonentity who's decided

that, because she has to do with a bachelor, she can comport herself in any manner she pleases, as the fool will never know the difference. She was more circumspect in her last post—of that you may be sure. Otherwise she'd've been sacked rather than given glowing references. I've no reason to fear her, even less to cater to her crotchets."

North was grinning now, delighted by this new notion. He returned to the oversized chair he'd had delivered a few weeks earlier, leaned back, and crossed his ankles. "I do believe I'll have some coffee after all," he said more calmly. "Something by way of a nuncheon wouldn't be amiss either."

Chloe's nod to Jitters had North fuming once more. Jitters backed into the hall, dragging Joseph with him, and closed the door. Footsteps descending the stairs echoed from the hollow treads. Then there was silence.

"Well, sit, blast it, Chloe," North grumbled, watching her from beneath lowered lids. "There's no reason to lurk about like a black-visaged vulture."

She remained where she was, arms crossed, frowning at him. "Vultures don't lurk," she said at last. "They perch. North, I want you to leave."

"*What?*"

"I want you to leave now, and I don't want to see you again until you've spoken with Miss Sparrow."

"You're as mad as the rest of them," he snarled.

She shrugged, then left the drawing room and disappeared down the hall, calling, "Have my carriage summoned, Joseph. I'm going out."

She'd left the door open. After a bit he used it, deed, draft, and necklace still in his pockets, and in a worse temper than he could remember experiencing in years.

She'd realized on Milbury Place that no one would pay Abigail Sparrow the least attention, and so no matter what name she gave, it was Lady Amelia Peasebottom who had arrived at Wilton Street, and it was Lady Amelia who awaited

Mr. Valentine North's convenience. It was she who would confront him.

She'd removed her bonnet without being invited to do so, and her gloves and pelisse, and handed them to Webster as if it had been his duty to see to her outerwear all his life. Then, still slightly light-headed, she'd ordered Bassett to show her to the room where Mr. North conducted business, and to bring him to her. Then she simply waited to be obeyed.

When Bassett opened the door to Mr. Tidmarsh's office and attempted to guide her in there, she didn't move.

When Mrs. Pickles bustled up, fetched by Webster at Bassett's command, she informed the housekeeper she was waiting to be escorted to whichever room served Mr. North as an office, and would go nowhere else.

When Jitters descended to the entryway, claiming Mr. North was not at home to anyone, and had instructed him he would never be at home to her, she looked Jitters straight in the eye and said that nevertheless she had business with their employer that could not be delayed.

It had taken a bit to convince them she wouldn't be denied. When they did become convinced, the three held a conference just beyond her hearing, heads shaking. Then Mrs. Pickles had returned to whatever she'd been doing, Jitters told Webster to hail him a hackney, and Bassett led her up the great staircase at whose head North had appeared the only time she'd glimpsed him, and shown her into this glorious room, where volumes bound in mellowed leather filled bookcases that touched the ceiling.

Now, at the sound of the door opening, she turned and sighed. North had so many lines of defense, it was a wonder even his closest friends managed to be ushered into his august presence.

"What's this, hey-hey," Pericles Tidmarsh spluttered. "Come to poke and pry and inconvenience our betters, have we? And cause their staff to behave as no proper staff ever would? Come to sow discord and spread disaster wherever we turn? Ah, yes—that's what we've done! We've turned ourself into the plagues of Egypt, we have, and smeared the doorposts with blood!"

He slammed the door and tottered into the book room, garbed in a lurid gold dressing gown that reached to the floor, draped in shawls, feet encased in threadbare slippers, and sporting a nightcap from beneath which grizzled locks straggled like a mongrel's matted pelt. The spectacles on the tip of his nose were filthy and crooked. His mouth worked. More slovenly than ever, the old reprobate had nothing to recommend him beyond a pair of eyes that often saw more than one would expect or wish.

"Told you you wasn't wanted here," he shrilled, jabbing a finger at her. "Told you you'd pay a forfeit each time you came, and so you shall. Told you those brats were your lookout. Told you the household was your lookout as well. I won't be having any more of this, and neither'll Mr. North! Told you—"

She turned her back as the suffocating avalanche filled the room, ignoring it and ignoring him. When at last it ceased, she said, "My business is not with you. Fetch Mr. North, if you please."

"Your business is precisely with whom I say it is," Tidmarsh roared, loosing his high-pitched screech in his fury, "and I say you've no business here with anyone!"

"That," she said, ears ringing, "is for Mr. North to determine, not you."

She could hear him coming toward her on the slant, cane tapping on the floorboards and thudding against the carpets as he fulminated about self-important females who didn't know their places and how he was precisely the one to school them.

"The one who is irresponsible in this matter is Mr. North," she snapped, staring ahead so she wouldn't have to set eyes on the repulsive creature, "and *his* irresponsibility is of such mammoth proportions that it verges on the criminal. My patience is at an end. You will either have Mr. North informed I am here, or I shall summon the Bow Street Runners and have *them* find him for me. Don't begin to think I can't or won't, for I can and will. I suspect Mr. North would find that even less to his taste than condescending to confer with one whom he considers a vast inferior. In such an instance, I also have not the slightest doubt you would be given the sack, Mr. Tidmarsh—a highly desirable outcome, in my opinion.''

She took a deep breath, her head spinning, and waited for the next onslaught. It never came. Instead, there was the sound of the door opening, and a polite cough announcing a new presence in the room.

''What the devil're you doing here?'' Tidmarsh snarled.

''I've come to see Mr. North regarding the information he requested from me yesterday,'' Mr. Burridge's familiar voice said.

''Thank heavens—someone of sense,'' Amelia murmured.

''Well, he ain't here,'' Tidmarsh snapped. ''He don't want you now. You can wait. Got other business at the moment.''

''This is Mr. Tidmarsh, the secretary I mentioned yesterday, Mr. Burridge,'' Amelia said.

''So that's who it is. I'd wondered.''

''Yes, that's who it is,'' a very different voice said as the door closed.

She glanced over her shoulder to see if Mr. North had entered the room, but there was still only Mr. Tidmarsh. It was, however, a Mr. Tidmarsh transformed, tall and erect, his cane dangling from a hand that no longer trembled with palsy. As she watched, his hump slid down his back and landed on the floor.

''What a peahen I've been,'' she murmured. Then she rose, head high, and turned. ''Good afternoon, Mr. Burridge,'' she said, gripping the back of the chair to keep her balance. ''You'll never know how thankful I am you've arrived so opportunely, for had you not, I should have been forced to seek you out.'' Then she took a deep breath, her gaze shifting to Pericles Tidmarsh. ''Mr. Valentine North, I presume?''

''And if it is?''

''If it is, then perhaps Mr. Burridge can make you listen even if I cannot.''

''Played the game once too often, I see.'' He pulled off his nightcap. A wig came away with it, revealing dark hair that rose from his forehead in a sharp V. ''This rig-out was becoming a bore in any case. Be with you in a moment, Burridge. In the meantime, show this underbred shrew the door. Make sure she understands she's not to return. She owes me a pound, by the bye.''

He tossed the wig on a chair, followed by the spectacles. Next came a false nose and a pair of bushy gray eyebrows. He pulled out a handkerchief and scrubbed his face. Moments later, now the color of putty, the handkerchief landed on the chair. A second handkerchief removed the last streaks.

''Jitters,'' he called as he peeled off the shawls and discarded the dressing gown to reveal a gentleman in the highest style of Town elegance except for a pair of stocking feet, ''bring my boots. I know you're listening, so don't pretend you're not.''

The door inched open. Jitters peeped around it, then opened it all the way to reveal the household staff clustered behind him. North grinned, sat, held out his hand for the boots, and proceeded to pull them on. Then he rose, turned to Amelia, and bowed.

''Your servant, Miss Sparrow,'' he said, not quite looking at her. ''Now that you've satisfied your curiosity regarding my appearance, you can take yourself off to whatever sinkhole you sprang from. Give Jitters your forfeit on the way out. I have serious business which you rudely interrupted earlier, and even more serious business with old Burridge now, and have no desire to indulge hysterical females succumbing to fits of self-serving rodomontade.''

''Ah, I see,'' she said. Dear heaven, what a paradigm of the worst of the *ton,* the arrogant, puffed-up, self-consequential, heedless toad. Her father was a paragon of humility by comparison. Even Sir Reginald had been more of a gentleman, if only marginally. ''Informing you that last night I was drugged and your wards abducted is hysterical rodomontade. How fascinating. That's an application of the term I'd never envisaged when I had to write out sentences employing it correctly for my governess. You must mention your definition to Tibbie and Robby when they're found in case they ever have need of the usage. I believe it to be unique.''

Silence greeted her bitter words. She pulled several pounds from her reticule and tossed them on the floor.

"There's your forfeit, Mr. North—including interest, as I assume you have the soul of a usurer, and am amazed you haven't demanded several pounds of flesh in addition. Should you discover you wish to learn more regarding what has lately transpired at the house you leased on Milbury Place, I intend to consult Mr. Burridge about your wards' recovery as soon as he's at liberty, and will give him my new direction when I have it. It is my hope he will be more concerned about their welfare than you are, if only to keep your name from becoming a scandal in every decent household in England. Consider this my notice, effective immediately."

They were glorious words, ringing with contempt, dripping with sarcasm. Unfortunately her head, which had been stubbornly spinning, decided to take a lurch that sent her tumbling to her knees with the room dancing as her bed had earlier.

"Oh, no," she moaned, "I'm going to be sick again."

And was. Thoroughly. All over Mr. Valentine North's formerly gleaming Hessians until he prudently moved them out of her way by taking a few steps and turning his back on the noisome process. Then Mr. Burridge was at her side, holding her head and rubbing her shoulders.

She heaved wretchedly, tears streaming down her face and wishing she could die, but providence wasn't so kind. She survived, miserable and aching, but most definitely alive. And then Mr. Burridge, who didn't appear strong enough for the task, was carrying her to a sofa by the windows and telling her that she mustn't concern herself about his coat, that it wasn't becoming the least soiled. Besides, he had several others, and Jitters had already taken Mr. North's boots to be cleaned and provided him with a fresh pair. Behind them a maid was already mopping up the mess, while another set pastilles alight.

She listened listlessly as he requested Mrs. Pickles to send up a basin of water and towels. She offered no protest when he sent François to make her a pot of peppermint tea. And she was infinitely grateful when one of North's motherly housemaids arrived with the requested basin, lavender-scented soap, and soft towel, and then fussed over her as if she were a treasured daughter of the house.

Through it all, Valentine North remained by the fireplace, his back turned, his arm resting on the mantel, a booted foot on the fender. Except for a murmured conference with Jitters that she was certain had nothing to do with her or the children, the master of the house had refused to issue orders, to speak to her, even to look at her. Far from being humiliated, she found it a relief. Soon she'd have to apologize for her intemperate words. She didn't know how she'd go about it, for she'd meant every one. She still did.

"Sip it slowly. You don't want a recurrence," Mr. Burridge's voice cautioned, rousing her from her abstraction as he handed her a cup whose pungent aroma tickled her nose. "How are you feeling?"

"Still dizzy, but more myself. I must thank you for—"

"Absolutely not. The least I could do under the circumstances. It would appear you've had a lamentably difficult time attempting to see to Mr. North's wards."

"And in the end didn't see to them at all."

"Precisely right," North snapped from his place before the chimney. "You didn't see to 'em at all. I'm glad you possess suffcient honesty to admit to gross dereliction of duty, Miss Sparrow."

"Only, sir, to the extent that I was unable to convince you to listen to me regarding the nature of the house in which you insisted on lodging them, and the lamentable lack of character of the owners and staff—whom you once declared to be possessed of the highest degree of trustworthiness."

Apologize to this boor for intemperate words? Never! They hadn't been in the least intemperate. If anything, her words had been too mild. If his staff wasn't already aware of his deplorably unsteady character, it was high time someone informed them. She'd be glad to educate them further if they showed a need of it.

"Where are your glasses?"

She glanced across the room to find North scowling into the middle distance.

"As Tibbie is not yet of an age or inclination to attempt such feminine arts as fine stitchery, I found I needed them less and less and discarded them, Mr. North. Why? Was it on the basis of my wearing spectacles that you determined I was worthy to have charge of your wards? Inadequate vision appears to be a characteristic you insist your hirelings share with you, as clear vision would lead to their quitting your service on the instant. Unfortunately for you, I don't suffer from that debility."

"My God, but you've got a waspish tongue."

"Only when addressing those who deserve nothing better. I suggest you forget your self-consequence, and learn what I can tell you of your wards' abduction—unless, of course, you don't care what's befallen them, and are only too glad to be relieved of the responsibilities they represent."

Chapter Thirteen

North made a superhuman effort not to take the steps needed to reach the diminutive termagant, put his hands around her throat, and squeeze until those fiery hazel eyes dulled and the beautiful mellow tones that could turn so acrid were silenced.

"There will be no discussion until those I've sent for arrive, madam," he said, amazed his voice betrayed none of his white-hot rage. That this rage was directed primarily at himself helped not in the least in controlling it. "They should be here soon. In the interim, you will keep your no doubt thrilling tale to yourself."

Then Burridge was at North's side, encouraging him toward the far end of the book room. He shook the man's hand off, but accompanied him to the corner, where the damned rocking horse reproached him through glassy eyes.

"Miss Sparrow was drugged, and is still ill," Burridge murmured. "Yet she came the moment she was able even though, given previous experience, you would neither care nor take action. I suggest you moderate both language and attitude, Mr. North."

"She's the one who's at fault in this," North snapped, knowing his words to be untrue and yet unable to help himself.

"Keep your moralizing to yourself, or I'll have *you* shown from the house. There're other men of business in the City— ones who know their place, and keep it."

It was an interminable half hour before the door opened again, most of which he spent prowling the book room and trying not to look at little Miss Sparrow, who was dozing now that she'd finished her tea. At least her eyes were closed. Webster's unsteady steps brought North across the room at full speed. He dumped his disguise on the floor, then took the old fellow's arm and helped him to the emptied chair.

"Please get a glass of sherry, Burridge," he said. "And no, Webster, you will not fetch it. It's for you, not me." Then he turned to Jem. "Well, where are they? Why didn't they come with you? And what about Jitters?"

"Don't know where he is, sir. Still looking for Mr. St. Maure and Mr. Dauntry, I'd guess. Mr. Clough and Mr. Harnette aren't available."

"What do you mean, aren't available?"

"Gone off to a mill, sir. Left last night. Their men didn't know where it's to be, nor yet when they'll be coming back."

"The devil, you say." North gestured for Burridge, who'd come up with the sherry, to give it to Webster. "Nonsense," he said, overriding the old footman's protests. "I won't have you suffering palpitations. You'll sit there whether you like it or not, and you'll drink that sherry, and you'll catch your breath. You can tell me whatever you've learned after you've recovered yourself." Then he turned back to Jem. "And which prime practitioners of the fancy're going to be pounding each other this time? I hadn't heard news of anything of the sort taking place."

"Men didn't know, sir. And after that Mr. Clough and Mr. Harnette thought as how they might go visit a friend. No, sir," Jem rushed on before North could ask the obvious, "their men didn't know which friend, or where. Was lucky to catch 'em, as they'd been given a week's holiday and were about to leave themselves."

"I see."

Only he didn't. Stubby and Pugs never attended prizefight*

Both detested them, for all there was nothing the least lily-livered about either fellow. Rather, the reverse.

"Feeling better?" North said, turning to Webster, who was no longer breathing in shallow gasps. Webster nodded. "All right, then, what about Ollie Threadwhistle?"

"Gone off, sir," Webster managed to answer. "Yesterday. All right and proper, according to Mr. Threadwhistle's man. Sick aunt. Deathbed."

"Which aunt? Where?"

"Didn't know, sir—just that he'd be gone until the end came."

"And Mr. Sinclair?" North said, suspecting the answer.

"Mr. Sinclair accompanied him, sir, as he'd nothing better to do."

"My goodness," Miss Sparrow murmured from across the room, "it would seem your reinforcements have flown the coop, Mr. North. Shall we delay matters a month or two awaiting their convenience? I'm certain Tibbie and Robby are comfortable wherever they are. Certainly it can be no worse than the house in which they've been residing on your orders since their arrival in England."

North pretended not to hear—probably the only manner in which to deal with the viper-tongued vixen. Instead, he grabbed Burridge's arm and took him well out of the others' hearing.

"What's your opinion?" he said.

"I think it's time you made your peace with Miss Sparrow."

"That will never happen. The woman's impossible. Flowers must wilt when she passes. I'd prefer to see to this privately, but I'd counted on the fellows."

He turned at a slight sound. It was Jitters, almost as pale as Webster.

"We seem to be setting up a pesthouse." North glanced first at Miss Sparrow—who was sipping her cold tea and pretending unconcern—then at his elderly retainers. "Best get another glass of that sherry, Burridge. Bring one for Jem, as well. Mustn't play favorites. Port's his favorite tipple."

Jitters, once he'd recovered his breath, informed them he'd been able to locate Mr. Dauntry nowhere—not at Mr. St.

Maure's lodgings, not at any of his clubs, and not at any of the other venues a gentleman was likely to frequent. No one at Dauntry House knew where he was or when he might return, and no one seemed to care. Worse yet, Mr. Dauntry's valet had been absent.

Miss Sparrow's laughter raised the hair on North's neck.

With Mr. St. Maure, Jitters said, he'd had more luck. According to his valet, Mr. St. Maure had gone out about noon, claiming he had errands to run. The valet, a cooperative sort, had offered to try to intercept him, and to leave messages everywhere he knew of that St. Maure intended to go.

"I don't believe this!" North muttered, turning to Burridge. "They've decamped, every last one of them. Damn and blast— why have friends if they're never around when one needs 'em? It's almost as if they didn't want to be found."

"That is the suggestion of a Bedlamite," Miss Sparrow commented from the sofa.

"When I want your opinion, Miss Sparrow, I'll request it," North said with what he considered amazing brevity, unusual felicity of expression, and laudable calm of manner. Good Lord—what hearing the woman had! He glanced at his watch, then the clock on the mantel. Midafternoon. There were still hours of daylight. "Jem, bring the curricle around. You'll be driving Burridge.

"Jitters, have a bag packed for me. Yes, clothes for the country. Sturdy stuff. I'll be traveling light and fast, and no, you won't be accompanying me. You wouldn't be able to stand the pace, old friend. Once that's done, I have an errand for you.

"Webster, inform everyone of my impending absence if they don't already know about it, and tell François I'll be wanting an early supper before I depart."

"What, decamping as well, Mr. North?"

"Miss Sparrow," North ground out, "stubble it!" He turned at the sound of the door opening. "Thank God," he said as St. Maure strode in, "someone of sense." Then, not caring he was playing dervish, he turned back to Abigail Sparrow. "Al right, *now* you may begin your horrific recital of drugging, abduction, and all the rest."

Amelia's tale, once she had the opportunity to recount it, took little time, as she had no interest in making her own part more than it was, or dwelling on past insults. To her surprise, North made no attempt to excuse his role in what had happened, and his few questions were to the point.

No, she'd found nothing in the least out of the way in his friends taking the children on a spree the day before. They had, after all, left her a message explaining where they'd gone. Yes, Bessie had been pert when Mr. Dauntry fetched her from the kitchen. Yes, the girl had seemed more than usually malicious, and made open threats after Mr. Dauntry left. That, however, was not in the least unusual. Bessie was forever making threats, open or otherwise.

As for the incident in the park, Amelia claimed what had most struck her about the gentleman involved was his ludicrous sense of style and his petulance. No, Florrie hadn't taken French leave. The girl had waited in the carriage, tearfully apologized for what had happened, and sworn she'd never been so deceived in anyone as she had in the man who kicked Beezle and knocked Robby down. Yes, so far as she could tell, the man had been an acquaintance of Florrie's, not a chance-met beau.

"Burridge, I want you to go to the house on Milbury Place," North said as soon as she'd answered his last questions. "Break in if you have to. Take a look around the place, question anyone there, but I doubt you'll hear one word of truth in a hundred. Above all, find out if a ransom note's been delivered, though I expect that'll come here if there is to be one."

"Your pockets are so deep?" Amelia asked, startled.

"Deeper. Don't let appearances deceive you, Miss Sparrow. Not all the great fortunes or families have handles attached to 'em. There are those of us who consider our names sufficient, and've turned down numerous titles over the generations.

"I live here because it pleases me, but there's a great barn of a place on Portman Square I can open if I want. At the risk of sounding like a coxcomb, I'm a source of despair to *tonnish* mamas who want their daughters advantageously wed—one of the reasons I wouldn't meet you as myself. I've had females attempt to play tricks on me before, and have learned self-preservation.''

"It's the truth, Miss Sparrow." Mr. Burridge stood and turned to North. "Do you want me to take a constable, sir, or summon the Watch once I'm there?''

"No, that sort of thing can wait. God knows what's really occurred. It may be less than we fear. Have Jem see what he can learn in the mews. Stable boys are usually good for a scrap or two. Sprinkle a few shillings about. I'll reimburse you later."

A quick bow in Amelia's direction, and Burridge was gone. Jitters slipped back into the room and, at North's impatient gesture, took his place on one of the chairs ringing the sofa.

"You suspect the same thing I do," St. Maure said.

"It's at least a possibility. You weren't party to yesterday's larking about."

"No, I wasn't. Have you checked your housekeeper's store of laudanum?''

"Never considered it."

"Well, consider it now."

"No need, sir," Jitters said. "Mr. Clough told me he didn't have any, and so I suggested he take the phial with him. Mr. Clough was still in considerable pain when he left."

"He'll be in considerably more pain when I get my hands around his throat," North growled. "Hillcrest?''

"That's my opinion."

"No, I don't believe that's possible," Amelia threw in. "You see—"

"I told you, when I wanted your opinion, I'd ask for it." North flushed at St. Maure's shocked glance. "My apologies," he said. "I'm suffering all the guilt and apprehension you could wish, Miss Sparrow. And you're correct: It would be the most unlikely of possibilities except that I overheard two of the fellows discussing the need to get Robert and Tabitha out of London during the summer months, something I wasn't prepared to do. Quint retains his military habit of taking decisive action when he feels it's necessary." He hesitated, looking directly at Amelia for the first time. "There's someone whose intelligence I'd like to add to ours," he said. "She's unusually clever, but—"

"Sir, you can't!" Jitters broke in, horrified.

"If the lady can help fnd Tibbie and Robby," Amelia said firmly, "then I will be grateful to her for joining us."

"But you d-don't understand," Jitters stuttered.

"Oh, I think I do," she returned with a smile that included all three men.

"He doesn't mean Mrs. Pickles."

"I know Mr. North doesn't. He means someone I would never meet under less desperate circumstances."

Amelia blushed at the look of approval North threw her.

"Chloe's a clever puss," he said. "Mother was an actress, father a Captain Sharp. When her first protector abandoned her, she lived in the stews, then made her way onto the provincial stage. Her early acquaintance with the less, ah, gentlemanly gentlemen of the *ton* is extensive, as well the lengths to which they'll go when pushed. Quite a talented actress. You'd never know she wasn't a lady unless she wanted you to.

"Now, Jitters, go plead with Mrs. Sherbrough to join us. And I do mean plead. I need that canny mind of hers, and her ability to see through the murk to what lies beyond. Wait a moment. Give her these first." He pulled an official-looking document and a jewelry case from his pockets, and held them toward his man. "Then ask her to come."

"If those are what they appear to be," Amelia murmured, "I believe you should present them yourself, Mr. North— preferably in private." She smiled at his incredulous stare, then continued matter-of-factly, "You don't speak of Mrs. Sherbrough as one might expect. The obvious supposition is either your relationship was never entirely conventional, or else has altered—a conclusion fostered by that document and what I presume is a generous gift of jewelry."

"You're as bad as my old nurse," North muttered, rising to tuck the jewelry case, draft, and deed behind the mantel clock, where they wouldn't be spotted.

"Though hardly so intimidating, I'm sure," she said, unable to repress a chuckle as the corners of his lips twitched. "I'm certain no one could ever be so frightening as mine when she caught me in a folly. I'm sure yours was the same.''

''Who are you, Miss Sparrow?'' he said, eyes narrowing.

''Precisely who I appear to be: a woman who must earn her bread, and is most anxious regarding the fate of her charges,'' she returned, sobering on the instant. ''What else could I be?''

''What else, indeed.''

The time dragged. There was nothing worse than this lolling about while information was gathered so decisions could be reached and plans laid. North wanted to be out there himself taking action, any action.

Chloe arrived, dressed so conservatively in a mauve gown and burgundy spencer he'd never seen before that North almost laughed. He felt no amusement, however, when faded Miss Sparrow requested the honor of being presented to his mistress, rising the instant Bassett showed Chloe into the book room. Within moments the two females had their heads together, Miss Sparrow apparently unconcerned by the gulf of respectability that should have separated them, and going out of her way to put Chloe at ease.

''Miss Sparrow's quite a lady,'' St. Maure said from their retreat at the library table. ''You have all the luck, Val. Not half so faded as you've described her either.''

''May've been wrong about that. Only really seen her but once, and I made sure the light was poor so she wouldn't see me. Result was, I didn't see her that clearly either. Seriously,'' he said, ''what d'you think the odds are of getting Robert and Tabitha back?''

''Depends on who has 'em, and what they want. If it's only money, the chances are better than even. You wouldn't pay if they were harmed, and you'd insist on proof they weren't. If you've made some enemy who's eager to grind you in the dust?'' St. Maure shrugged and sighed. ''You do have a habit of rubbing those you consider beneath contempt the wrong way, you know.''

''Whifler?''

"The name comes to mind. There're scores of others. You aren't subtle when you take someone in dislike."

"Then you don't think it was the fellows."

"Thought it over. There's no way they'd've kept something like that from me, or even tried."

"Y'didn't know about yesterday's little escapade."

"Immaterial. Miss Sparrow did—or at least they thought she did. All on the up-and-up. This is different."

When Burridge and Jem finally returned far later than the simple errand of going to Milbury Place could account for, North was pacing the floor, shoving his hand through his hair, and ignoring the other three's attempts to reason him out of his desperation. One look at Burridge's triumphant expression and Jem's grinning phiz, and he collapsed on his chair before the dead fire.

"You've found them," he said as the others surged to their feet.

"As good as," Jem crowed.

"Where? Who? Why?"

"Hillcrest. Your friends. Why, officially? The danger of infection in Town during the summer months," Burridge said, crossing the room. "Actually, I don't believe they thought you were supervising your wards adequately. It's all in here. I stopped by my offices to see if any of the agents I'd sent to make inquiries regarding Sir Reginald had returned, and found this had just been delivered by Mr. Dauntry's man."

"I will kill them," North said, spitting the words out like bullets. "So much for your being privy to everything those nodcocks plan, Dab. Let me see that thing, Burridge."

"Don't judge them too harshly." Burridge handed the note over. "According to Dauntry's man, they were genuinely concerned for the children's welfare."

"And pigs will fly over St. Paul's at dawn," North snarled, tearing the note open. "They saw an opportunity for a glorious prank at my expense. Robert and Tabitha were merely an excuse. Well, this time they've gone too far, damn them!"

"Moderation, Val," Chloe murmured, laying a hand on his

shoulder. "Yes, it's a great relief, but there's no need to show how relieved you are by losing your temper."

"M-Mrs. Sherbrough?" Burridge's pasty features turned cherry red. "I—ah—I had no notion you were present."

"How could you, Mr. Burridge? You had far more important matters to occupy your attention. Besides, I believe I was hidden behind Miss Sparrow."

"I will not have my mother inconvenienced like this," North snapped, glancing up. "I don't care if they have included funds for shipping Miss Sparrow to Hillcrest, and took that Florrie person with them to see to the brats until her arrival. As for you, Chloe, stubble it."

"Sir!" Burridge spluttered. "I will not have you speaking in such a vulgar manner with ladies present."

"You too, Burridge. What concern is it of yours how I express myself before a pair of hirelings—just as you are, may I remind you?"

"Val, guard your tongue." There was an unaccustomed edge to St. Maure's voice. "No one here's done anything to earn such contempt. Rather, the reverse."

North watched in fascination as Burridge uncurled his fists.

"Were you about to draw my cork, Burridge?" he said with a bark of laughter. "In defense of Chloe? Or is it the faded Miss Sparrow you favor?"

"Something of the sort, Mr. North."

"There's no need to defend me, Aaron." Chloe's head was high, her features composed, her manner regal. "I'm perfectly capable of defending myself. After all, I've been doing it for years."

Then North was reeling, for the glance that passed between his mistress and his man of business was such a speaking one, it was as if the floor had opened up beneath him.

"My God," he muttered, "I can't believe this. Right beneath my nose, so to speak." Then he rose, scowling. "Am I seeing what I believe I'm seeing?" he said, cramming the letter in his pocket.

"See and believe as much as you wish, Val," his mistress returned, going to Burridge's side and slipping her hand through his arm. "Within limits, it's what's there. I've never played you false, if that's what you're wondering."

"Furthest thing from my mind. My God," North said again. "It happened because I had him start delivering your allowance just before I got that blasted letter about Freddy's sprouts. Dammit, one of you might've told me."

"Apparently we have," Burridge said, hand gripping Chloe's where it rested on his arm, "though this isn't the moment I would've chosen."

"No, you'd've waited until even I was old and gray, knowing you. So *that's* what you thought I wanted to discuss with you the other night. Good thing Chloe decided enough was enough." North scowled, shaking his head. "I'm not certain about this. I won't have you trampling on her. If you intend—"

"I've told Aaron how we were country gentry, and my stepfather raped me and then threw me out in midwinter after my mother died of consumption," Chloe said, eyes downcast after a single sharp glance at North, "and how Cadwallader Sherbrough found me starving by the roadside and married me, and forced me to fuzz the cards and entertain favored patrons abovestairs in his second-rate provincial hell."

"I see," North choked out. "You've been rather forthright, I take it."

By damn, but this sounded familiar—a scrap from a novel here, another from a farce there, the whole so twisted, it was hardly recognizable. Spain came to mind, and a ruined castle, and a duke or a prince or something.

"And I told him all about your rescuing me on your way home from a mill six months ago after I tried to cheat you at cards, only you caught me at it and realized I wasn't what I seemed."

"Well, y'weren't very good at it." North nodded at her quick frown. Only a fool wouldn't've caught the message in her eyes. "Clumsy, if you must know."

"Aaron's ever so grateful you had the man I thought was my husband investigated, and learned he had a wife and six children in Wales. Of course, I didn't know *what* to do then. Aaron understands completely about your letting me stay where you keep your mistresses, as you didn't happen to have one then. While he doesn't like my having played the part in public so no one would know, he understands that too.''

"Did have my reputation to consider, though perhaps it was a trifle unchivalrous of me to consider it quite so much,'' North admitted.

"It's terrible of me to be glad Mr. Sherbrough died not long ago, but I am,'' she declared defiantly, once more raising her eyes to meet North's in warning. "He was a monster. The wonderful thing is, Aaron blames me for none of it, and is infinitely grateful to you for rescuing me from an intolerable situation.''

"Why should he blame you? None of *that* was your fault, not any of it,'' North managed to say.

Now Chloe'd cast him as the superannuated monk in the last play they'd attended, blast her—only the monk'd been returning from a pilgrimage, not a mill, and injured innocence had masqueraded as his niece, not his convenient. North didn't dare glance at Miss Sparrow, who'd developed a choking cough. Clearly she, too, had recognized at least some of Chloe's inspiration for her convoluted past. Well, he'd realized in the beginning the woman had a highly developed sense of the ridiculous. No reason it shouldn't appear now, even if it was partly at his expense.

Then a smile he felt first in his eyes broke out over his features. "I'll be damned!'' he said.

"Blessed, rather,'' Burridge returned. "We've wanted to tell you for some time, but the moment never seemed propitious.''

"Well, this is the best one there ever could be—Chloe had that right. Been worried about her future, for things couldn't continue as they were. A double celebration, that's what we'll have,'' North said, grinning broadly now. "No need to leave for Hillcrest until tomorrow. Jem, go inform François he's to prepare the grandest dinner he's ever concocted. This betrothal will be acknowledged in style. Chloe, you're getting a fine man, even if he's something of a dry stick on occasion. Treat him honestly. As for you, Burridge—''

"I'm only too cognizant of my good fortune,'' Burridge

said. "However, Chloe is the name that devil gave her. I'd prefer you use her real one, if you're to continue calling her by her given name."

"Only with your permission," North said, beaming like a proud father, and assuming he felt very much like one. "Would you present me to your wife-to-be, Burridge? I've a great longing to meet her."

"My name's Edwina, but Aaron calls me Winnie, just as my dear parents did," Chloe said with just the right touch of shyness. "Winnie Suttersby."

North bowed deeply. "Miss Suttersby, it's my very great pleasure to make your acquaintance. Mr. Burridge is a fortunate man. I wish you both happy. And now, to ensure that state," he said, turning toward the mantel.

For no reason he could understand, Miss Sparrow was pulling his arm down with every appearance of seeking his support rather than interrupting him in mid-action, and pinching him in the process.

"Mr. North, help me walk to clear my head, please. Oh, dear—do forgive me," she jabbered. "It appears I'm not as steady on my feet as I'd thought. All this unaccustomed excitement, you know."

"Can't it wait?"

"No, I'm afraid not."

Dear Lord—was that intended to be a speaking look? Because he couldn't read it, not at all. Call it, rather, the look of eyes that had no notion how to communicate anything. He glanced at St. Maure, who nodded with what North assumed was relief.

"All right, Miss Sparrow," he said, feeling benevolent toward the entire world at that point, "a minute of my time you shall have, but no more. Then I insist—"

She was dragging him toward the window, well away from the others. He glanced back. St. Maure was sending Jem to carry word to the kitchens and beyond, then loudly marveling over the betrothal and the fellows' note with Chloe—no, Winnie, he'd have to remember that—and old Burridge, who perhaps wasn't so old or such a dry stick after all, not the way he was gazing at beautiful "Miss Suttersby." Dear God, but they smelled of April and May. How could he've missed it? And then he realized it was the first time he'd seen them together, and forgave himself. Clever, clever Chloe. So long as she was pleased with what she'd accomplished, what reason had he to complain?

"What now?" North said, turning his back on the group before the fireplace.

"Not the house where you kept her, for pity's sake, and definitely not whatever's in that jeweler's case," she murmured. "That's what you intended to give them, isn't it?"

"Why not? I bought both for her. What'll I do with them otherwise? Make a rather magnificent betrothal gift. Burridge has the lodgings of a skint."

"Heaven preserve me! Return the jewels. No gentleman would offer them to a lady unless she were his wife—or something far less. I'm sure you've spent enough over the years that Rundle and Bridge—yes, I recognized the case—will be glad to take it back in anticipation of future purchases. As for the house, sell it, or keep it for your next convenient. Do otherwise, and you'll be betraying Mrs. Sherbrough and informing poor Mr. Burridge he's been made a May game of—which I suspect he hasn't, not entirely. Please, Mr. North, consider a moment what you're about."

He stared ahead of him, mouth turning down. "Good God— I almost created a disaster, didn't I," he muttered. "Thank you for preventing me, Miss Sparrow."

"You're welcome."

"Who *are* you?" he said for the second time that day. "Other than my self-appointed guardian angel, that is?"

She shook her head, and returned to the group in the center of the room. Her very lack of reaction was an answer of sorts. That was one question for which she was prepared. He'd have to find some for which she wasn't.

Chapter Fourteen

Dinner that night was a gala affair. Champagne flowed, along with claret and one of the fine whites François favored to accompany his famous *sauté de crabe farci,* which Miss Sparrow declared to be one of the most delicious things she'd ever tasted.

That no one was dressed formally as would be expected in honor of such a magnificent dinner and joyous occasion mattered to none. Course succeeded course, the removes innumerable. Toasts were drunk to the discovery of Robert and Tabitha's whereabouts; to the happy couple and their impending nuptials; to Miss Sparrow's recovery, which was all but complete; even to North's absent Irregulars and the infamous trick they'd concocted. Through it all, North played gracious host, hardly able to believe his good fortune. No need to stumble through informing Chloe they were separating. She'd done it for him. God bless her for saving him the trouble and embarrassment, for he knew he'd never've managed it gracefully.

François had just appeared at the service door to accept their compliments following a dessert even the Prince Regent's chefs wouldn't have despised when they were interrupted by a furious pounding on North's front door.

"Chase 'em off, whoever they are. I refuse to be bothered tonight," North murmured to Bassett, then turned and poured a glass of champagne for François, and refilled the glasses of those at the table.

"I insist you join us," he said. "This has been the most glorious meal of my life, as well as one of the happiest." He raised his glass as Bassett toddled from the room. "First, to you, François: You provided us with viands suitable to a great occasion. Next, to Robert and Tabitha—and Freddy, who gave them to me, damn him—my life'll never be the same, thanks to his generosity. And third, to all those who've attempted to ensure I fulfill my responsibilities to the tadpoles: long life, joy, and prosperity. And," he added with a devilish grin intended primarily for the children's long-suffering governess, "to no more untoward surprises. I don't know about you, Miss Sparrow, but I've had my belly full of 'em the last few days."

He drained his glass, pretending the shocked expressions of the others—who'd set their champagne down while he was in mid-oration—meant nothing, then turned to face the door.

They hobbled in, filthy and bedraggled: Tony Sinclair, his arm in a makeshift sling; Ollie Threadwhistle with a bloody bandage around his head and another covering his wrist and hand; Quint Dauntry, leaning on a crude crutch and limping, his old wound from Salamanca clearly troubling him again, but either in better case than the others or more accustomed to carrying off a tatterdemalion appearance thanks to his long years in the army; Pugs Harnette, wearing what remained of his coat as a cape, his chest bound; and Stubby Clough, perhaps the most pathetic of the lot, walking with a pair of canes and wincing at every step, bandages high on one leg and low on the other. Behind them shuffled a brassy blonde, her face scratched, her shoulders hunched as if she were protecting bruised ribs.

"The delightful retainers from Milbury Place," Dauntry said without waiting to be asked as he limped to the table and gestured for Webster to get him a chair.

"Well, don't stand about," North snapped. "Sit down, blast it. You all look like you've been chewed up by some infernal stage machine. What's done is done. I'm not about to blame anyone—at least not yet. Your intentions can't be faulted."

The relief on the fellows' faces would've been laughable had they been one whit less battered.

"Who, precisely?" Miss Sparrow said, hands balled into fists. "All of them?"

Dauntry nodded, then winced as he sat. "Except the Grimbles. Bessie Scrudge and a bully named George appeared to be in charge. Given how events transpired, I suspect George has more experience of the High Toby than would be considered proper—that, or he's a damnably quick study and has friends in low places."

"George Ginty? He's the coachman," Miss Sparrow said, "or at least that's what the Grimbles claimed he was."

"Good God," North muttered.

Chloe Sherbrough—or Winnie Suttersby, or whatever Burridge wanted her to call herself—mewled and sank into her chair, covering her face with her hands. North pushed a glass of wine toward her, his eyes never leaving Dauntry's face. The name Ginty had figured more than once in Chloe's tales of Seven Dials.

"Who else?" Miss Sparrow prodded, frowning.

"The entire lot, I imagine, with the exception of Florrie. An unregenerate stews tough—some called him Charlie, some Nackett—and a pair of grooms named Mick and Mike, who started out with us but changed sides when they saw which way the wind blew. Charming pair of rogues. Said to give you their apologies and best wishes, Miss Sparrow, and to tell you there were no hard feelings."

"Dear heaven," she murmured.

"Don't forget Willie," Threadwhistle threw in, attempting a grin that failed as he rested arm and wrist on a platter he'd emptied of biscuits and turned over to protect the napery. "Whistled the whole time he was knocking us about and relieving us of fobs and such. Nightmarish fellow."

"That would probably be William. Charles was the other footman."

"Footpad, more like." Sinclair sat gingerly, then relaxed

when it appeared the chair wouldn't attack him. "They were all handy with cudgels, though it was George—Ginty, I believe you said, Miss Sparrow—had the poppers. Prime Mantons, if my eyes didn't betray me."

"Stubby got the worst of it again," Hamette said, helping Clough to the table and appearing to do more harm than good as the poor fellow grunted with every step, "though they were merely grazes, thank God, and they let Florrie see to him before they tied us up and stuffed rags in our mouths. There were several others—confrères from the stews, I presume, who wore masks and pretty much kept to the background, though one of them was rather handy with his pistols as well."

"There's a job coach below, Val." Dauntry pulled one of the glasses of champagne toward him and drained it. "I'd appreciate your paying the driver, for I assured him you would. They emptied our purses and left us tied up in a woods. Was purest chance a pair of poachers came upon us and believed our tale, for by then we resembled the most disreputable miscreants you can imagine. If I'd seen us, I'd've taken to my heels. It's been a hellish night, and a worse day. God, Val—I'm sorry."

"And Robert and Tabitha?" North said, asking the question that needed no asking.

"Gone."

"But how? Against five of you? And I assume you had a coachman at the least, and someone riding guard."

"I done it," the girl North assumed was the nursemaid sniffled from where she stood by the door. "Told Bessie about Tony an' Quint's plans acause she's always calling me a slow-top and never up for any fun. That full of myself I was, and now we've all paid for it dear. My best bonnet's ruint, even. Y'aren't gonna bring me up afore a magistrate, are you?"

"No, I'm not."

North glanced at the table on which the best napery still stretched snowy white. The festive mounds of flowers hadn't dropped a petal in the last moments. All should have become blighted on the instant. Certainly his life had.

He sank into his chair at the head of the table, and then it was all going too quickly for him to take in given the quantity of wine he'd consumed in his relief at Chloe's future being assured without his having to lift a finger.

Miss Sparrow, sending St. Maure to pay the job coachman.

Miss Sparrow, telling the fellows the rest of their tale could wait, and having Webster take the girl called Florrie to the servants' hall.

Miss Sparrow, requesting François to concoct some sort of supper for the failed conspirators, and to send someone up with fresh bandages and basins of water.

Miss Sparrow, instructing old Burridge to go by the house on Milbury Place and see what he could learn, and apologizing to Burridge and Chloe for the shambles that had become the celebration of their betrothal.

Miss Sparrow, once Burridge was gone, asking Chloe to fetch the brandy from the book room, and then telling the fellows of her betrothal to North's man of business and her invented past so they wouldn't say something untoward.

Miss Sparrow, sending word for Pickles to make sure there were enough beds to sleep everyone that night, and to have the laundry room readied for use as a communal bathing chamber by the fellows.

Recovered? The woman was a tigress faced with danger to her cubs, issuing orders as if she'd been issuing them all her life, while all he could do was stare from one face to the next, his mind numb. He didn't give a damn who she was anymore, for all he was more convinced than ever that "plain Miss Sparrow, burdened with earning her bread as other penniless unprotected women were," was as inaccurate a description of this particular governess as could be imagined.

It all happened as she ordered it: the basins and bandages, the extra beds, the supper for the fellows, the transformation of what he assumed was an ordinary laundry into some sort of Roman bath. She even thought to send Jitters around to the fellows' lodgings to collect fresh toggery as, along with everything else, the Milbury Place crew had made off with their luggage. He simply sat there and consumed cup after cup of the black coffee she'd ordered for him, and watched it all take place.

By the time she and Chloe had seen to the fellows' hurts, and Jitters to somewhat regularizing them, Burridge was back and North was infinitely thankful for the coffee.

"Nothing," Burridge said, taking his place by Chloe without a one of the fellows raising a brow. "The Grimbles were sharing a chicken they'd ordered from a cookhouse, and somewhat inebriated from the ale laced with blue ruin they were downing. Not pleased to see me, though it was almost as if I were expected. No one else was there, and no sign anyone had been. Stable was empty except for the children's ponies. They claimed to know nothing regarding the whereabouts of the others, whom they said were on a well-deserved vacation as Miss Sparrow had taken it into her head the house wasn't fine enough for her, and decamped with your wards."

"So they've not come back to Town," North managed to state.

"That's not what I said. Milbury Place is too obvious unless they've less intelligence than I give them credit for, and I don't give them much."

"No, I suppose they wouldn't at that. Make things too easy for me." North turned to Miss Sparrow. "You know them best," he said. "Is this something they could've planned unassisted? More to the point, could they've carried it out unassisted?"

"Bessie's as clever as she is conscienceless. They could manage most of it, perhaps even all. I've always suspected William and Charles had light fingers."

North and St. Maure exchanged glances.

"William. Willie? Get Jem, Webster," North said.

"But how could the incidents be connected?" St. Maure protested. "There's no way a footman at Milbury Place would know you'd won a bundle at White's."

"No? I can think of several ways in which he might."

Moments later North was satisfied the man who'd sliced his

pockets had also abducted his wards, and was a certain Whistling Willie, master cutpurse, no longer in semiretirement. Again he and St. Maure exchanged glances. North raised his brows.

"As I said earlier, there're many candidates, starting with Chuffy Binkerton if you want names," St. Maure shrugged. "No need to drag in someone you've encountered only once. Besides, it really doesn't matter who they're working with, or even if they are, except it may help us determine where Tibbie and Robby might've been taken."

"I'd still like to know more about Whifler," North grumbled. "Yes, I know, you're going to tell me I've fluff in my cockloft. Well, I don't, Dab. I've developed an uneasy prickling between my shoulders, and I'm not enjoying it. Had it just before that letter from Freddy's superior arrived, and you know what's happened since."

Burridge's polite cough had all eyes turning in his direction.

"Well?" North snapped. "What is it?"

"I stopped by my offices in case any of my agents had reported in," Burridge said, coloring slightly.

"Obviously one or more did. Well, out with it. No need to stand on ceremony."

Burridge sat taller, shoulders straight, then helped himself to some of the brandy Chloe had fetched for the fellows. North, who was about to tear whatever news he'd gotten from the scrawny rooster's throat, flinched at the pair of sharp kicks to his shins—one from St. Maure, the other improbably given him by Miss Sparrow. St. Maure winked. North glanced at the prim little governess, who first frowned, then lowered her eyes and blushed.

"Sir Reginald Whifler's poorly thought of, at least here in Town," Burridge finally said. "Pretends to wealth, but he's at low ebb. Duns everywhere, and his estate is apparently falling to ruins. According to one crony whose tongue was loosened by considerable brandy on the table and not a few pounds beneath it, he's been living on credit for years and has mortgaged everything to the hilt. Sold off the collieries that were the origin of the family fortune some years ago."

"And there you have it," North said, gaze shifting to the groom who had been waiting patiently to be dismissed. "Jem, I want you to check the clubs and the hells. See if you can locate Whifler." He tossed the young man a heavy purse. "Pay for information if you need to." Then he turned back to Burridge, who was looking disgustingly pleased with himself, as Jem slipped from the room. "So if it's Whifler, I can expect a ransom note. Certainly he wouldn't dare harm the tadpoles. Glad it's no worse. How much, do you think?"

"I'm not convinced money is what he would want, if it is he. According to that same crony—one Throckmore Binkerton, with whom I believe you're acquainted—he'd almost repaired his fortunes by insinuating himself into some elevated but primarily country circles that had no notion of his reputation. Wouldn't't've deigned to notice those who could've told them about him, you see."

"Chuffy Binkerton again, by damn." North grinned, ignoring the rest. "Wouldn't you know he'd be part of it? Knocked Miss Sparrow down right after I hired her, and tried to claim the money I'd given her was his. Summoned a constable, but she had the presence of mind to bring them all here and have me vouch for her."

"So there was some truth to Whifler's boasting at White's," Dauntry said, pouring himself a finger of brandy and passing the decanter to Sinclair.

"I don't know about that, Mr. Dauntry, but I do know he managed to come across an earl's daughter who didn't take during her only Season, and was supposedly at her last prayers. No actual dowry, but she had a legacy they'd kept so quiet, even she didn't know about it. Comfortably fixed great-aunt on the distaff side—property, consols, jewelry, and considerable more. Quite the heiress."

"Oldest story in the world," North murmured, and then quickly amended, "or almost."

"He offered for her, and her father forced her to accept Whifler so he could keep the wolf from the door by selling off his other two daughters to high bidders as he couldn't touch his eldest's inheritance. The great-aunt was apparently well aware of the earl's failings. Will was ironclad."

"Charming fellow," North murmured.

"The earl's a gamester, and either an unlucky or a very stupid one," Burridge chattered on, warming to his theme. "Then, the night before the betrothal was to be announced, Amelia Peasebottom bolted with her maid. Yes," Burridge sighed, accepting the decanter from Sinclair, "I know it's complicated, and I know it's a tawdry tale, and I heartily deplore gossip, but that's the essence of it. All sorts of sordid details regarding Whifler's character—or lack of it. He's desperate. Isn't a tradesman in Town he's patronized would give him a good name. No news from Chilcomb as yet. It's too soon, but the man I dispatched to Brighton came back with pretty much the same tale. Not knowing how events might transpire, I've been keeping a clerk on hand to receive any reports that arrive after we're closed."

"For which favor you intend to charge me an exorbitant fee," North said.

"Naturally, Mr. North. Your misfortune is invariably my good fortune, so to speak."

"Well, here's to the lady who bolted." St. Maure lifted his glass, then took a small sip. "May she've found a safe haven."

"Damned if I'll drink to her," North grumbled. "If she'd married the rotter as she was supposed to, chances are we wouldn't be in this fix now."

"Yes, I'm afraid you probably would," Burridge countered. "Between what your friends have told us and what I learned from the Grimbles—which wasn't much, and lay more in what wasn't said than what was—once you hired that house, there was no avoiding what followed. If it isn't Whifler with whom they've joined forces, it's another just like him. They were trolling for an accomplice with the trollops as bait."

"And I'm to take comfort from that?"

"No, but there are others who might."

Burridge paused as North stared in confusion at his man of business. "What the devil d'you mean by that?" he finally said.

"A general observation that includes your friends. You've been gulled, all of you. By the bye, Miss Sparrow," Burridge said, turning to the little governess, "Jem saw to bringing your belongings here the first time we went. The children's ponies as well. The hacks, team, and carriage are gone, of course. Permanently, I assume. Given all that's transpired, I forgot to mention it, for which I do apologize."

"Let's return to the main issue, if you please," North snapped. "If they're not going to demand a ransom, then what are they after?"

"Oh, you'll get a ransom note from Milbury Place. You can ignore it, for it's the principal who holds Robert and Tabitha Tyne now, of that I'm certain. And yes, there is a principal, a *ton* confederate, if you wish. That's equally clear. The only question is that confederate's identity and motive."

"Divide and conquer," Dauntry murmured. "I should've thought of that."

"I'm convinced it's Whifler," North said.

"Then the chances are you'll be required to provide a bride, but an even wealthier and younger one. Above all, one who won't flee him. In other words, entry into the highest reaches of the *ton*. He'll probably demand you frank him as well, and sponsor him at the best clubs, perhaps even hand over the wherewithal to repair the ancestral manor before he takes his bride there. It only goes back two generations, you were right about that—not the place itself, but Whifler ownership of it."

"Never!" North growled. "I do have some sense of responsibility."

"Glad to hear it."

"Perhaps," Miss Sparrow said, her face unnaturally pale, "if it is Sir Reginald who has the children, he might be willing to release them if the lady he was originally to marry were to be found, and convinced to meet him at the altar."

The scowls and chorus of incensed no's that greeted her words had her turning even paler.

"It was only a notion," she protested.

"And you accused *me* of requiring a pound of flesh? Good Lord, Miss Sparrow, you have no idea what you're proposing,"

North sighed. "I realize you mean well, and I know you're concerned about Robert and Tabitha. We all are, but that's no solution."

"I still believe finding the young lady and explaining the predicament is our best option," she said. "She cannot be entirely without conscience."

"I'm afraid it's no option at all," Burridge said. "Lady Amelia's dead. Body was found in the Ouse some miles from York. Badly decomposed, but the earl was able to identify her from some jewelry sewn in the lining of her cloak. Magnificent pieces, according to Mr. Binkerton. It's all worked out rather well for the earl, of course. As his daughter died intestate and a spinster, her fortune's now his to do with as he wishes, and he still has those other two daughters to sell off."

"Good heavens," Miss Sparrow murmured.

"Why so shocked, Miss Sparrow?" And then North's eyes narrowed. "Of course! The Countess of Pease—that's who wrote you that glowing reference. You must've known the young woman, probably left just before the tragedy. You were fond of her?"

"Not excessively. I was gotten rid of because her sisters were to make their come-outs following Lady Amelia's nuptials. I wasn't considered imposing enough to act as a dragon, you see. It was believed I'd spoil their chances."

"And Lady Amelia?"

"She could be extremely foolish on occasion, not that it matters now."

"You're not overly crushed by her death, then."

"I'll recover. It's only that the news was a surprise."

"But you must have known Sir Reginald," Burridge insisted with a deepening frown. "Why haven't you mentioned this, Miss Sparrow? You could have information your employer would find useful. To withhold it is the act of an ingrate."

"Sir Reginald was an extremely unpleasant man. I avoided him whenever possible, and am only thankful he didn't recognize me in the park," she returned stiffly.

"Made unwelcome advances to the governess while courting the daughter, did he?"

"I suppose gentlemen might consider them so. *Assaults* would be a lady's term of preference. He had a nasty habit of waylaying one. We soon learned no maid was to go about unaccompanied, though naturally the knowledge was kept from the earl and the countess. They'd've accused the victims of encouraging Sir Reginald rather than blaming the true culprit."

"Now, why doesn't that surprise me," Dauntry said, throwing her a sympathetic look.

"He wasn't liked in the village," she continued, her tone flat, "that much I can tell you, but he wasn't there long enough to run up debts such as he's left in Town and in Brighton. Of course, he may've been careful not to. I assume even the earl has his limits, for he was always careful of appearances. Sir Reginald presented an extremely fine appearance. He had his mother with him at the court, and she saw to it he did. She's an unpleasant woman, but she's the great-granddaughter of a viscount, and intended to raise the Whiflers to what she considered her level. Sir Reginald's outré garb is a new thing."

"Very glib, Miss Sparrow." Burridge leaned forward, eyes narrowed, nose twitching. "How can we be certain you're not in league with Lord Whifler? That would indeed have been an excellent game."

"I? In league with Sir Reginald Whifler?" Her laughter was too bitter to be false, North decided. "You've no idea what a ludicrous suggestion that is," she gasped, shuddering. "Believe me, Mr. Burridge: I'm not in league with that horror in pantaloons. I'll swear it on a Bible if you wish."

"Oaths are cheap. There's something here doesn't ring true."

"Good Lord, man—she formed part of the Peasebottom household for years. What doesn't ring true?" North exploded.

"I'm not certain. That's what troubles me."

"Don't be ridiculous. She tried to warn me for weeks, but I wouldn't listen."

"That, too, could've been a game intended to make you react precisely as you did—by refusing to listen, or even to meet with her."

"I'll leave if you wish, Mr. Burridge," Miss Sparrow said

rising and pushing her chair forward. "It's clear you consider me untrustworthy."

"Now see what you've done, Burridge?" North growled. "Keep your suspicions to yourself, blast you, you sanctimonious goat. They're laughable. Miss Sparrow, return to your place. If anyone should leave, it's old Burridge here, not you."

The uncomfortable silence that greeted his words disgusted North, but there was little he could do. The evening was descending from the high comedy of disembarrassed protector entertaining former mistress and fiancé at their betrothal dinner to the low farce of fiancé overplaying his hand in an effort to seem more clever than former protector in his betrothed's eyes. That Miss Sparrow was looking to Burridge for permission to regain her seat irritated North even more. Instead of making bad worse, he looked at her and waited for her to obey. When she still hesitated, North rose, went around the table, pulled her chair out, and held it. That solved part of the problem.

"The point is," he said, returning to his place, "where do we look for him?"

"Not Chilcomb or Manchester. Too easy," Sinclair responded. "He realizes we know where he lives. The man may be lacking in character, but he isn't lacking in intelligence."

"Not London," Harnette said, managing to sound entirely pleasant while throwing Burridge a look that had the man actually blanching. "Again, too easy to find him. I assume those few parts of Town we don't frequent are well known to Mr. Burridge's agents."

"They are indeed, Mr. Harnette," Burridge said with unaccustomed diffidence, wisdom superseding vainglory. "Very well known."

"Likely some place within a day of where we were accosted, but out of the way." Stubby Clough flushed as the others turned to stare at him. Clough wasn't generally known for offering opinions. "Don't think he'd want to travel far—not with that pair," he mumbled, toying with his glass. "Make things a living hell if they want to, and they don't like him."

"There I agree." North grinned. "I doubt they'll make their are and feeding easy, and they have the pup with them, I gather. That girl—Florrie—Miss Sparrow said earlier she's acquainted with Whifler. Think she knows anything?''

The others all spoke at once, creating a babel from which North gathered Florrie Whissett was a country innocent come to Town to make her fortune, and snatched by Hortense Grimble the moment she stepped off the coach. Florrie hadn't the cleverness to play a double game, they insisted. Just getting her to slip Miss Sparrow a few drops of laudanum had been a task almost beyond accomplishing. Then, they admitted with hangdog expressions, rather than just a few drops in warm milk, she'd stirred the stuff into everything on the tray for fear Miss Sparrow would reject one item or another. Florrie's confusion when scolded for not doing precisely as instructed had been pathetic, for the poor girl didn't seem to understand where she'd gone astray.

North's inquiring glance at Miss Sparrow, who had to know the nursemaid better than any of the rest, brought only a nod.

''It was a thought,'' he sighed. ''That it would be productive was too much to hope for, I suppose. I'll start out at first light.''

''*We* will start out,'' Miss Sparrow countered.

''I beg your pardon?''

''I'm going with you.''

''Out of the question.''

''Then,'' St. Maure said with a smile, ''Miss Sparrow may travel with me, or with one of the other fellows. We're all going.''

''You? If you insist. The others? In their condition? Don't be ridiculous.''

''You'll be amazed what a bath and a night's sleep in a bed rather than on the ground with stones poking in our backs and branches in our sides'll do for us,'' Dauntry said, rising. ''We're not in as bad case as we seem.''

''You'll need me when you find them, Mr. North,'' Miss Sparrow insisted. ''You're a stranger to Tibbie and Robby, and they have no reason to trust your friends. For all they know, you were all in this together to teach them some unpleasant lesson. That's the sort of action they've learned to expect from adults, including their parents. I request only that I not be forced to encounter Sir Reginald if it is he who's behind all this. There's no need for it, and I truly loathe the man. We've had our, ah, differences.''

"But your reputation," North protested.

"I have none."

Chapter Fifteen

"Riding backward is making me come all over queer again," Florrie moaned. "Another jounce an' I'll lose my lunch, and I'm shivered to death. Even your cloak isn't much good. When're we going to stop?"

"Not until sunset, I would think. Not even then if Mr. North decides we should try a new area, and wants to reach it tonight," Amelia sighed.

They'd been racketing more or less north all day, stopping to inquire for Tibbie and Robby at every farm and village and crossroads. Not even the most luxurious and best-sprung traveling carriage could make such an exercise pleasurable— not when desperation left heart in mouth, roads were in deplorable condition, and the company in the carriage left everything to be desired.

"I keep riding backward, I'm gonna be sick," Florrie repeated, eyes calculating as she stared across the footwell at Amelia. "Keep telling you I got a delicate stomach. You don't want me to be sick, do you?"

Wordlessly Amelia rose and eased to the side between the gutted lunch hampers François had packed. It was easier to cede her place than insist on a semblance of the proprieties, just as it had been to hand over her cloak. Anything to keep the girl quiet.

They changed places, bumping heads at a sudden lurch, Amelia now facing rearward. Florrie's self-satisfied smile as she settled herself had Amelia's hand itching. Any compunction the girl might've suffered regarding her part in the children's abduction had long evaporated—at least when the gentlemen weren't present to mop tears she seemed able to produce at will.

"He's got no consideration," Florrie fussed as the seat fell away and then rose to assault them. "Isn't an inch of me doesn't hurt. You should tell him to stop. Maybe he'll listen to you. Never listens to me, no matter what I say—not that I've got much chance. Don't see him one hour to the next, way he's galloping about like a squire on holiday. Don't see the others neither."

"I'll survive. So will you. Certainly I've no desire to call off the search in midafternoon. Perhaps you should consider returning to London. I'm certain Mr. North would send you back."

"What'm I supposed to do there? Grimble'd show me the door, an' they're all sobersides at Wilton Street. Not a speck of fun to any of 'em. When you said I should be the nursemaid, you wasn't doing me any favors."

"I believe my concern was more for Tibbie and Robby than for you," Amelia bit out, then held her breath for fear her honesty would truly set the girl off.

"Seems to me you owe me more'n you can pay. Mr. North too. Hundred times more work'n Bessie when I thought it'd be a hundred times less, and now look what's happened. I thought this'd be fun like when we started out the first time, but it isn't, and now Mr. North's saying as how we'll be in the country all summer. It's sinful, it is."

"If you find both Hillcrest and London unpalatable, perhaps you should consider returning to your true home."

"You got more'n one slate missing if you think that."

Florrie gripped the strap as they lurched through another series of ruts, bracing herself against Amelia's seat.

"No place a girl can go for fun, what with the neighbors watching like ferrets—*bloody hell*—and the vicar preaching at you and—*yoicks*—using your name if he catches you with your apron front to back—*God Almighty*—and the only gentleman for miles about a clutch-fisted gummer? Could bear it when I didn't know better, but now I do."

Amelia gave Florrie her profile and watched the clouds that had chased away the sun at midmorning. Her only goal was endurance. Florrie wasn't helping. Neither was the weather. The wind had risen. Rain threatened. With it would come increased misery, and Florrie would protest all the more.

The searchers had departed at dawn in three curricles and North's smaller traveling carriage, Mr. Harnette on horseback, as he detested driving almost as much as being driven, Mr. North and Jem riding as well so they could range the countryside. Hopes had been high. Tempers were unfrayed. Tibbie and Robby would leave memories of kicked shins and fits of temper wherever they passed. Finding them would be a simple matter. As the sun had leapt above the horizon, Mr. North's elderly coachman gravitating to each rut and pothole had been a minor inconvenience. Now, weary from hours of fruitless inquiries, bruised and aching, each jolt was exquisite torture.

"Wonder why they're going this way," Florrie grumbled. "Gettin' colder by the minute. We'll catch our deaths. Never know it was spring. Flowers're like to freeze their petals off."

"Because Mr. North concluded traveling this way seemed wisest," Amelia snapped. "It's in the general direction of one place the children may've been taken."

Florrie shrugged. "That's what he knows," she muttered, then squealed as they plummeted into another pothole.

The carriage creaked and swayed, complaining as it jounced back to the roadbed.

"Thought we was for it that time." Florrie grinned, amused by the near disaster.

Perhaps the girl's problem was boredom. Certainly she took on new life each time North or one of his friends came to leave word a lane had been followed until it deteriorated to a track, and then petered out entirely.

"I think Brighton'd be just the ticket."

Amelia glanced across the footwell. Florrie wore an innocent expression.

"The ticket for what?"

"For summer. Parades and gentlemen and shops and taverns and concerts and theaters and sea bathing? Much better'n the country. Robby and Tibbie'll be bored anyplace else, and they'll make my—*your*—life a misery. You should tell Mr. North. Maybe he'll listen to you."

"I don't think so."

"No, maybe he won't. Maybe I should tell him myself. Country's a harebrained scheme—just the sort a gentleman what wants to be free of his responsibilities'd have. Known lots of gentlemen like that. Sent their families to the country, and pretended what a sacrifice it was, and then went wherever they wanted for a bit of fun. I'll make him see it's his duty to send us to Brighton."

"Even if the children would prefer Hillcrest?"

"They'd never! Isn't them he should worry about anyways. It's me and you. If I tell him you want to go to Brighton, then—"

"You'll do no such thing, Florrie. I mean it. First of all, I'd prefer the country."

"No, y'wouldn't. Even if you would, won't make no difference. I ain't blind. He thinks you want Brighton, he'll send us to Brighton, and I'll see that's just what he thinks. I'm not going to the country, and that's all there is to that."

"You've concern only for your own amusement, I see, and none for poor Tibbie and Robby."

"All's well that ends well, and Brighton'd be the best ending of all. 'Sides, why should I worry about them two? What happened ain't my fault. Mr. North said so when Ollie pressed him. If he don't blame me, why should you?"

It was long past dusk when they stopped at what was little better than a hedgerow tavern. A hurried conference transformed Miss Sparrow into Ollie Threadwhistle's spinster sister, the nursemaid into her abigail. They were searching for the widowered Ollie's children, Robert and Tabitha Threadwhistle, who had run off when refused a summer in Brighton—this at the nursemaid's insistence. North became their maternal uncle, the others his friends. It was close enough to the truth, and explained the presence of an unwed lady traveling with seven bachelor gentlemen, a youthful groom, and a superannuated coachman.

He needn't have bothered with the fabrication, which he jumbled in any case. Neither the innkeeper nor his wife cared who they were or what their business might be so long as they understood that, as they would be inconveniencing those who customarily stopped by for a pint, they must pay double in advance and make do as best they could. The gentlemen could sleep in the taproom or stable, as they preferred.

North forked over the ready and make do they did, only the so-called nursemaid complaining of shared discomforts that included a greasy mutton stew and a drafty taproom. Once they'd choked down what they could of the inedible meal, Miss Sparrow and the nursemaid retired to the only bedchamber the place offered. The rest—with the exception of bandy-legged old Naysmith, who staggered off to the stable complaining of his fragile bones—gathered for a council of war. Sinclair was for angling south and west, St. Maure for returning to London and enlisting the aid of at least Burridge's agents, if not the Bow Street Runners.

"You're both wrong and you're both right." Dauntry looked from one to the other as North held his peace. "Bow Street if we have no success tomorrow, and decide that's needed. The colder the trail grows, the harder they'll be to find."

"You're forgetting it's not the children they want," Sinclair snorted. "It's blunt. Glad enough to be rid of the infantry the minute they can. They've hidden no more than a day's journey from London, or it's my hair that's green and my eyes that're red."

"Unless it's Whifler after his pound of flesh," St. Maure insisted. "Then it's not just money—Burridge had that right, whatever else he had wrong—and they could be anywhere."

"Burridge already has his people searching along the road to Chilcomb on the chance it wasn't Whifler at the Tinker's Bum," Dauntry countered. "There never was a need for us to search in this direction."

"They'll be going to the obvious places. We're not. How sure were you of Whifler?" North said, repeating the question he'd been asking Jem all day. "It's too neat—his being at a place he's known to frequent—almost as if he intended to be found."

"As sure as a guinea could make me," Jem replied, giving the same response he'd given the night before when grilled, and repeated ever since. "Told you time and again the porter wouldn't let me inside, sir—wouldn't've known Lord Whifler to see him anyway—but I hid in the shadows and heard the complaints of those'd had enough and were staggering out. Emptied more than one set of pockets last night, and them as had their pockets lightened not too pleased about it either, and suspicious into the bargain."

"But you never saw him leave."

"Told you: Wouldn't know if I had."

"So it could've been a ploy to dupe us."

Jem sighed, shrugged, and spread his hands.

"Damn and blast," North muttered, shoulders sagging as he combed his fingers through hair that already stood on end. "I've never made such a mull of anything in my life. Of all the ne'er-do-wells in England, why was it me Freddy had to choose?"

" 'Cause you haven't never been a ne'er-do-well afore, sir—not ever in your life. Not so sure as you've been one this time either."

"Stubble it, Jem. I know how I've acted in this instance, even if you don't."

Behind them, rain drummed against bolted shutters and trickled down the chimney flue, filling the taproom with the stench of wet ashes. Unless it stopped soon, they'd have heavy going on the morrow. Miss Sparrow had been done in by the time he'd called a halt. So had the fellows. So, for that matter, had he. Where he'd called a halt hadn't helped, but they'd been too deep in the country when the sun set to find a main road and search out a decent posting house. It had been this ramshackle place, or bivouacking in the mud. At this point he wasn't certain which would've been worse.

"We goin' t'be jaunting about tomorrow same's we done today?"

North turned at the petulant whine. It was the nursemaid, garbed in her shift and wrapped in a coverlet, her hair in a tumble some might've found alluring. Even he might have before he gained a clearer understanding of the strumpet's character.

"We are indeed, though I hope with more success." North placed a heavy hand on Jem's shoulder when it appeared the lad was about to rise in honor of so much pulchritude.

"And if you don't find 'em tomorrow?"

"Then we'll keep searching until we do."

"There's no need to hunt for 'em," she grumbled, sauntering over to North and letting the coverlet gape to offer a better view of her charms. "All you have t'do is stay someplace decent and let 'em come to you. Bessie can't stand them brats, and those as Bessie don't like she gets rid of quick. Always has."

"You sang that song all through dinner," North rasped, turning away in disgust as the others grinned. "It pleases my ears no more now than it did then. We're not going to Brighton to wait for 'em to be delivered to us."

"Why? There's fine lodgings in Brighton. Bessie'll have ways of knowing where we are once we stop traveling about."

Now the girl was trying to sit on his lap. North shoved her away, not caring if she tumbled to the floor. Instead, the blasted trollop landed all over St. Maure, picked herself up when he showed no interest, and perched on the table.

" 'At's where you should be sending 'em for the summer, come to that," she wheedled, "an' not to the country. Country's dull. Even Miss Sparrow says so. She wants Brighton. Says a touch of sea bathing would make up for all the rest."

"She does, does she? And no doubt sent you to inform me

of her opinion? I cut my wisdoms years ago, young woman. You're a peahen if you think differently."

"But I want to go to Brighton. Always have."

Now the girl was fluttering her lashes at him, for God's sake.

"Wouldn't any of you like to take me to Brighton?" she simpered, looking from one to the next. "I know how to keep gentlemen happy. We could see Prinny, and go to concerts, and have no end of fun. They got wonderful shops in Brighton—almost as good as London. I could do with a new best bonnet. Bessie took mine."

"I'm afraid not, Florrie," St. Maure managed to say. "We have more important matters to consider than best bonnets."

"Chasing about isn't going to do no good, not lessen you know where to look," she said, sulking, "and you don't—not the way you was scrabbling about today like a flock o' roosters what don't know what to do with a hen. I'm tired of riding in carriages."

"Nevertheless, we'll find them," Dauntry snapped, "of that you may be certain. I suggest you retreat to your pallet before Mr. North turns ugly. You're annoying him. You're annoying me as well. I'm beginning to think there's nothing to choose between you and Bessie, and you don't want me thinking that."

The girl tossed her head and stood. "I got the bed," she announced. "It's Miss Sparrow what's on the floor."

"Now, Val," Dauntry murmured, catching North's arm as he surged to his feet with a wordless roar.

"We drew lots," the nursemaid protested, backing away. "She works for her keep same as me. Ain't any reason she should have the bed any more'n there was she should ride facing forward or have a warm cloak when I ain't got one. I bruise easy an' I got a delicate stomach, an' I suffer from chills something fierce."

North was across the taproom before he drew another breath, candle in hand, storming up the narrow stairs and into the cubby filled with trunks and boxes and a narrow cot that passed for a bed, the others following him, Florrie Whissett forgotten.

Abigail Sparrow huddled beneath her cloak, only a straw tick separating her from the floor. Tendrils that appeared golden framed delicate features. Lips that were lusciously curved rather than primly pursed parted slightly to reveal even white teeth. As for the lashes that lay on her cheeks—dear God, how could he've thought her a dried-out stick?

It must have been a trick of the light, he decided as he stared down at the young woman. That, or the light was playing games now. That was more likely. Everyone knew women past first youth regained their bloom in the glow of candlelight, and avoided the sun as if it were the devil himself come to taunt them.

He set the candle on a crate, scooped her up, and laid her on the cot. Abigail Sparrow sighed and burrowed more deeply into her new nest without waking. North retrieved the candle with a sigh of his own and slipped from the room. Illusion it might have been, but the illusion had been heart-wrenchingly lovely, matching that matchless voice that had nothing to do with dried-up governesses. A pity the candlelit vision wasn't reality. He'd been finding himself admiring plucky Miss Sparrow more than was safe for a single fellow who valued his freedom—a thought he'd checked each time it arose, which had been damnably often during the past two days. If truth were told, it'd arisen in his reception room the first time he heard that glorious voice.

"We've got to stay someplace decent at least one night in four," he murmured to Tony Sinclair as they descended the stairs. "That poor woman is at the end of her strength. Start racking your brains."

The rain ceased well before morning, for all the good it did them. Naysmith could barely move after a night spent contorted in the carriage, and was sent back to London bundled between baskets of chickens and sacks of last year's turnips once they reached a main road. Mr. Sinclair—who was the best driver as well as the best horseman—assumed coachman's duties, and they slogged west and south, beginning the circle of London the gentlemen had decided on the night before, joining up with the Bath road for a bit. Jem played messenger, dashing for

Town to see if Mr. Burridge's agents had learned anything. They hadn't. Florrie was by this time riding on the box bundled in a carriage robe, preening at sitting where all the world could admire her, and complaining of the mud and the wind. *Brighton* still figured in every other sentence.

That day, and the one following, passed much as the first had. Jem's twice-daily trips to confer with Mr. Burridge were futile, as were all their inquiries. Accommodations were never worse, though never much better. Through it all Amelia retained her sense of humor and her faith that Tibbie and Robby would be found unharmed.

The fourth night, now to the south and slightly east of London, they turned in at a sprawling inn surrounded by oaks mixed with hawthorn at the end of a secluded lane. The troop was rumpled and bedraggled, the gentlemen dispirited, Florrie complaining of hunger pangs, boredom, and exhaustion. North called for the cattle to be rubbed down and baited, the carriage and curricles scrubbed, and issued orders to the landlord that saw them installed in the first private parlor Amelia had seen since they left London.

"Now, this is more like," Florrie cheered, removing the flower-decked bonnet she'd found in a village shop that afternoon while the others consumed a hurried lunch in a tavern yard. "Glad to see someone's finally got some sense. What's it called?"

Amelia ignored her, watching as efficient serving girls covered a sideboard with roast turkey, grilled trout, a baron of beef, a saddle of mutton, a brace of ducks, and so many removes, she lost count. For the first time, Jem wasn't there, instead taking his supper in the kitchen, though Florrie remained to lend a semblance of propriety. A fire burned on the hearth, more for cheer than heat. Bottles of claret were being delivered by the landlord. No, the napery wasn't finest and the glasses weren't crystal, but there was a pitcher of daffodils between a pair of open windows. Engravings of improbable scenes sprinkled with half-clad nymphs and sportive satyrs hung on opposing walls. Branches of candles rendered the parlor not only welcoming, but festive.

"Dear heaven, I shall faint from all this luxury," Amelia murmured, meaning it. "What luck, happening on this place."

"You deserve better," Valentine North said behind her, "but at least tonight you won't be dining on swill, and turning paler with each bite. Some of these out-of-the-way inns can surprise one."

"Thank you," she said, blushing as he assisted her in removing her cloak, then held out his hand for her deep-brimmed bonnet. She'd learned that claiming there was no need for him to help her in and out of his carriage or play personal servant was futile. Mr. North had become disturbingly attentive over the last days. Unfortunately, telling herself he was merely being kind to an on-the-shelf governess didn't quiet a heart that tended to flutter whenever he came near. "You know this place?"

"Ah—well—er—yes. By reputation. Heard of it, you understand. Favorite with those who want to be, ah, undisturbed, you might say. Not the sort of spot one would bring one's mother, but it's decent enough if one can get a private parlor."

"Nothing *but* private parlors," Mr. Clough blurted out from by the fire. "Not even a taproom or common dining room."

"I see." Amelia smiled, as if being brought to a gentlemen's hideaway were the most common of occurrences. "I suppose it goes by the name of the Amicable Assignation?"

"Something of the sort," North muttered, flushing in his turn as he set bonnet and cloak on a settee. "I knew the beds'd be clean and the food superior, and felt you deserved that. We could go on after we've eaten, but—"

"Oh, no—please! A clean bed sounds wonderful. Do they even provide baths?"

"If you want one. It's called the Willing Wench." Mr. Dauntry poured some claret into a glass and handed it to her, dark eyes twinkling. "Its purpose is precisely what you suspect. When a gentleman's traveling with a—ah—special friend, it can be difficult to come by decent accommodations. Places such as this are useful."

"Naturally. I wonder if there's an equivalent called the Footloose Footman to serve ladies who adhere to neither the letter nor the spirit of their marital vows."

"I wouldn't be surprised." Dauntry was now grinning openly. "No need t'look like you're about to strangle, Val. Coming here was a sterling notion. Only one other party, and they're in the opposite wing, so we shan't trouble them and they shan't trouble us. I asked while you were seeing to the cattle."

"What is this place?" Florrie demanded from the open window.

"A superior and exclusive inn." Amelia sipped the claret, which was better than anything to be had at the court, as the unusually pretty serving girls slipped from the parlor. "I doubt either of us has had the opportunity to stay in its like before, and I doubt we will again, so we'd best enjoy it while we can. Now, shall we avail ourselves of this wonderful food? I for one am famished, and it would be a crime to let it get cold."

"Isn't nothing compared to what we'd get in Brighton," Florrie carped, "and there'll be no place to go after," but it was clear even she didn't believe her words.

For once they were merry rather than morose, superior food fostering sanguine expectations of success on the morrow, or, if not then, the day after. Mr. St. Maure proved a superior raconteur, and one who knew no end of amusing tales regarding the others. Amelia forgot to be prim and correct, laughing as if she were dining in the nursery with her young cousins. Not to be outdone, she'd just launched into a tale regarding a mouse, a reticule, a postiche, and her youngest cousin—with herself rather than the boy's prissy sister as the butt—when a howl that would've woken the dead and the sound of pounding footsteps had her on her feet staring wildly at the door.

"What in God is that?" Dauntry snapped, rising and crossing the parlor as Florrie, eyes wide, slipped beneath the table. "Murder isn't generally done here that I've heard."

The door burst open just as he reached it. Two diminutive figures pelted through, hair tangled, clothes torn, cheeks tear-stained, followed by a puppy that gave a single joyful bark and began tearing around Amelia.

"Journey's end," she whispered, sinking to her knees and holding out her arms.

The children dodged past her, heading for the open window as Beezle licked her face and hands. Sinclair, with more presence of mind than the rest, snagged the ragamuffins just as they were about to climb over the sill. Robby howled, kicking and biting as Tibbie flailed with her tiny fists.

"It's us!" Sinclair roared over Tibbie's sobs and Robby's curses. "Stop it, for pity's sake. I don't want to hurt you."

And then Harnette was on his knees, forcing Robby to look him in the face.

"It's us," he said. "Blast it, Robby, you know us! We took you to the fair, remember? Just a few days ago. With Florrie, and had ever such a good time. And we were going to Hillcrest, and then—"

"What're you doing here? You're supposed to be in Brighton!"

Bessie's shriek of fury had them turning.

Behind her, neckcloth awry, bootless, and with frayed ribbons dangling from a waistcoat where once a litter of fobs suckled, stood Sir Reginald Whifler, walking stick raised like a cudgel. Just beyond him Mr. Binkerton bounced on his toes, trying to see into the parlor as he clutched a raw beefsteak to the side of his face.

Amelia sighed. That quickly ended freedom. For all their discomforts and discommodations, these last days had been the happiest of her life. So much for not being forced to encounter Sir Reginald. A shame that it should end so tawdrily.

Sir Reginald tossed his stick aside, pulled a pearl-handled lady's pistol from his pocket, and pointed it at North.

"And what do you mean to do with that silly thing?" North snorted.

"Reach an agreement. You take these blasted hellions back, or I'll shoot you where you stand."

"Oh, no—they're yours now," North returned with a shout of laughter. "Went to considerable pains to appropriate 'em. Completely unfair of me to make you waste all that effort."

"Won't go with him," Robby roared. "We want our Sparrow!"

"She's right over there." Sinclair set them on their feet and gave Tibbie's tears a swipe with his coattail. "See?" he said, pointing.

"Florrie's under the table," Tibbie blubbered. "What's she doing under the table? Not supposed to hide under tables. This is a bad place."

"You, go to your governess," Sir Reginald ordered, waving the pistol at the children, then pointing it at Amelia as Bessie crawled under the table, the better to attack Florrie. "As for you, on your feet, woman. They're your responsibility now. I don't care if he wants 'em back or not. He's got 'em. I've had my belly full. Nothing's worth the hell on earth they create."

Amelia rose, head high. She had no coal-scuttle bonnet to shield her this time, and she was tired of running, in any case.

"What the devil," Sir Reginald muttered. "My God—Lady Amelia?"

"Good evening, my lord," she said, dipping a perfect curtsy. "What a surprise to see you here."

Chapter Sixteen

North stared from the little governess to Whifler, whose complexion was sliding from gray through scarlet and cherry before reaching a satisfying purple. Except for the pup's yips, Florrie's and Bessie's screeches, and what had to be Tabitha whimpering in the background, the parlor was dead silent. Come to think of it, it wasn't silent at all.

"B-but you're dead," Whifler spluttered, mouth gaping. "You drowned. Your father told me so."

"Clearly he was mistaken."

"B-but I played inconsolable fiancé at your obsequies. Only just put off black gloves when I came to Town because it wouldn't do to court one gel while mourning another."

"How punctilious of you, for I know you never cared for me above half. Was Mrs. Whifler there as well, and equally inconsolable?"

"Who gives a damn if my mother was there! What the devil're you doing with this band of rogues? Why aren't you dead?"

"I suppose because I'm alive," Miss Sparrow sighed. "Your constantly appearing where you're least wanted is proving an inconvenience, Sir Reginald. I do wish you'd behave in a more gentlemanly manner, and stop doing it.''

"Help me get his pistol," North hissed to Dauntry, pushing Miss Sparrow—or Lady Amelia, or whoever she was—behind him. "He's likely to pull the trigger without realizing it, and I prefer farce to tragedy.''

"That's the woman who knocked me down in the street." Binkerton tugged on Whifler's sleeve. "That's her, I tell you. Stole a hundred pounds from me. North helped her do it too.''

"You're all about in your head, Binkerton." Dauntry eased in front of North and Miss Sparrow. "Neither Val nor Lady Amelia have any need to rob anyone. I'll take that little toy of yours, if I may. No brigands here, and the fellows're seeing to the infantry, so you've no need to worry about their taking French leave.''

Whifler cocked the pistol. "Stand aside," he snarled. "North's got my property, and I want it back. Fair exchange, what? My property for his. 'Course, mine's worth thousands of pounds. His'll be beggaring him for the rest of his life.''

"Don't be a fool," Binkerton pleaded. "Y'can't shoot some-one here, Reggie. And what good'll it do anyway? You got only one shot. Once you've taken it—''

"Watch me." Whifler trained his pistol on Dauntry's head. "Step away," he said.

Dauntry eased to the side, arms hanging loosely.

"You too, North. Quickly, now. Bessie, grab one of the brats. That'll be our insurance for getting away. Leave it at the first crossroads. Chuffy, get Lady Amelia.''

They'd acted in tandem before. Dauntry's shoulders bunched, his knees bending. It was all the signal North needed. Together they launched themselves at Whifler, knocking him to the far corridor wall as Dauntry forced the hand holding the pistol high above their heads, where it discharged harmlessly into the ceiling. Neither was particularly concerned that they'd sent Chuffy Binkerton tumbling. They wrenched Whifler's arms behind his back, propelled him into the parlor, slammed the door in Binkerton's face, and shoved Whifler into a chair. From below came shouts and the echo of footsteps pounding up the stairwell. Stubby Clough opened the door.

"Just an accident," he babbled, blocking the view into the parlor and preventing Binkerton from pushing his way past. "Pistol discharged when I was showing it to Whifler. Thought it was unloaded, but it wasn't. Stupid of me. Hair trigger, don't you know? Show it to you later if you wish. Bullet's lodged up there in the ceiling. Glad to pay for any damage. No, no one's in the least injured. No need for an apothecary, and certainly none for a magistrate."

Then Clough was in the corridor, closing the door behind him.

"Going to behave yourself," North snapped, "or shall we bind your arms?"

"What I want to know," Whifler panted, "is what the devil you're doing with my intended, and why the devil she's rigged out like that. Of course, given the purpose of this place, I can just imagine what you've been doing."

"What a filthy mind it has." Ollie Threadwhistle sauntered over with Tabitha perched on his shoulder. "Shall we gag it for you, Val?"

North glanced from the woman who was apparently Lady Amelia Peasebottom to Whifler, trying to remember the gossip old Burridge claimed to deplore but related with such relish. She'd bolted. That was the essence. And ended up on his doorstep, never mind how. There was only one thing to do, especially given this was the Willing Wench.

"Unnecessary. No surprise he's spouting muck under the circumstances. Game's over, fellows. Secrecy won't serve anymore. Rather, the opposite."

North grinned at his friends. Please God, let them have their wits about them. Otherwise there was no way out of this damnable mess. He threw a proprietary arm around Abigail-Amelia's shoulders, drew her tightly against him, and planted a lingering kiss on her lips. She fought him, twisting away and pinching him fiercely on the arm. He dug his fingers into her shoulder in warning.

"No need to pretend any longer, Mellie," he murmured,

inventing the pet name while his lips hovered over hers. Dear God—he was drowning, or falling from a mountain peak. No, he was soaring like an eagle. "This basket-scrambler's been making your life a misery for months, and mine into the bargain. Time to end the farce. I don't know about you, my love, but I'm heartily sick of it."

He gave her a cautioning smile, eyes hard, then turned to face Whifler. Even the Grimbles' trollops had stopped ripping clothing and scratching faces, and stood there with their mouths hanging open. Good. He had everyone's attention.

"Mellie and I've been betrothed since the year of her come-out," North lied, "so you see, Whifler, there was no way you could've been betrothed to her."

"Doesn't count, even if it's true. Didn't have her father's sanction. I do."

"Lady Amelia is of age. She has no need of her father's approval. Neither do I."

"I'm no flat. Old Peasebottom would've made the announcement before you'd completed your offer if it'd existed. Approved mine without a quibble."

"Ah, but I haven't a handle to my name, not even a trumped-up one, and of course I would never've agreed to divide Mellie's inheritance with his lordship once we were wed—not for my sake, but for hers." North's look stressed the insult. "We'd been intending to inform Lord Peasebottom of our betrothal this spring," he continued as the coxcomb glared. "Then a distant connection saddled me with his children. My mother's unwell, so I couldn't call on her for assistance. I got word to Mellie, and she came as fast as she could. Leased separate quarters for her. She took on an assumed name and passed herself off as a penniless governess, as we didn't want a breath of scandal."

Whifler went to the table and poured himself a glass of claret, then turned, sipping it as he glanced from North to Amelia, then at the others.

"If that taradiddle was true, you'd've gotten leg-shackled the day she got to Town," he sneered. "You've ruined her, doesn't matter how or why. Had your fun. Fair enough, but it ain't a reason t'play the fool. I'll have mine later. Besides, I need her pounds more'n you do.''

"You're even more of a nodcock than I thought you in the beginning," North said, hoping his laughter sounded genuine.

"I will never—"

North put his hand over Lady Amelia's mouth. "Hush, my love," he said. "Leave this buffoon to me."

"Y'don't turn her over, I'll spread the tale. Of course, I'll make it more interesting. Seven men, an earl's daughter, a hoor, and the Willing Wench should turn the trick—'specially as you kept her on Milbury Place. Hortie Grimble ain't exactly unknown."

It took four of them to drag North off Whifler. By then the children were whimpering and the pup watering one pair of boots after another.

"I'll see him in hell," North panted, shaking them off. "I mean it."

"There's no need for any of this, Mr. North."

He turned at the unexpected interruption. "My name is Val," he snapped. "There's no more reason for pretense. The games're over, Mellie."

"Indeed they are—all of them. If you think for one minute I'll permit—"

It took only two steps to reach her. He gripped her shoulders, pulled her against him, and proceeded to silence her in the most efficient manner he knew. This time there was only fury and desperation in the embrace. "I will not have you ruined because of my stupidity," he muttered when she finally stopped fighting him. "Hold your peace until we can be private."

For Amelia Peasebottom the two-day journey to Hillcrest was a nightmare.

Reginald Whifler, far from admitting defeat, had insisted he'd accompany them, intent on enlisting Mrs. North in his cause. A mother always understood where her son's interests lay, he'd informed them silkily. A single word regarding the Willing Wench, and North and his cronies could protest al' they wanted. North's mother would have the truth out of him before he drew another breath, and Lady Amelia would be his for the taking. As for North's threat to lay information against him regarding the abduction of the Tyne brats, "See, you want me to spread the tattle," Sir Reginald had sneered in the well-meaning man's face. "I was just rescuing 'em from an improper situation. Everyone'll agree."

At least Mr. Binkerton and the Milbury Place ruffians were gone when they rose the following morning. Nothing more had been said about bringing charges against either them or Sir Reginald. She supposed that was something for which to be thankful.

Now she gazed from Valentine North's carriage as they drove through the gates of Hillcrest. Gone were the threatening clouds, the sharp winds, the rain. The countryside was cloaked in the bright greens of spring. She was probably seeing the estate at its best.

"Don't worry about a thing," North said from the seat across from her. "Pugs had two days' lead, and knew to spare neither himself nor his mount. My mother's more than prepared. Tony'll be here by evening with the special license and some decent clothes for you. By this time tomorrow we'll be wed. Then let Whifler do his worst. We'll laugh in his face."

She sighed and turned her attention from what she assumed was the park. "There'll be no wedding, Mr. North. You said it yourself when Sir Reginald abducted Tibbie and Robby: If I'd married him in the beginning, none of this would've happened."

"Fustian!"

"Not that I have any more intention of marrying him—or anyone else—now than I did then. I've never permitted people to dictate to me, Mr. North, no matter how skilled and clever they are at it. I'm not about to begin now."

"Blast it, Mellie—"

"No! Now, an end to this unproductive topic. D'you think Tibbie and Robby are far behind? I'll need to see to unpacking their—"

"You will be seeing to nothing," he growled, clearly at the

end of his patience, "unless it's your own comfort. I've told you before, there's sufficient staff to see to Robert and Tabitha temporarily. Mama will have reestablished my old nurse in the children's wing. You wouldn't want to spoil Nurse's fun, would you? If more're needed later, we'll hire more."

Good. She wanted him at the end of his patience. She wanted him to despise her. She wanted his voice to turn cold and his eyes hard, just as they were now. A single kind look or soft word, and she'd lose her resolve.

"If I'm not to have charge of the children, then there's no need for me to set foot from this carriage," she said, willing her voice not to tremble.

"Be warned: If I have to drag you out by the hair and toss you over my shoulder like one of the Sabines, I will."

" 'A fellow of infinite jest,' " she murmured, turning back to the window and pretending not to hear his delighted laughter.

"One of the things I like best about you is your quick wit," he said, "though heaven knows you've not had much opportunity to indulge it of late. I promise you better in the future. Yes, I'm little more than a mummer on occasion. Pericles Tidmarsh proved that, didn't he."

They were crossing a rustic bridge. The stream they'd been lounging tumbled over a small falls into an ornamental water. Across it, on a gentle terraced rise, stood a house of no recognizable period, gray stone wings outstretched like welcoming arms, facade and portico boasting a superior Palladian makeover. "How lovely. Capability Brown?" she said, gesturing at the lake and mentioning a famous landscape designer.

"No, my great-grandfather with his wife's assistance, plus a battalion of extra workers. I'm glad it pleases you. You'll be seeing this vista every time we return."

"Then you're intending to continue my employment as the children's governess? I understood you'd rejected that notion."

She peeked at him from the corner of her eye. This time, instead of scowling or roaring, his lips twitched.

"The place is a hotchpotch, of course," he continued as if she hadn't spoken. "There're bits of the original fortified manor at the rear, mostly part of the stable block. I think you'll like the library. Lots of interesting stuff. Dab claims there're few collections its equal. As he's something of a scholar, he should know."

All too quickly North's carriage was leaving the woods, the pounding hooves behind them warning that Sir Reginald didn't mind breathing their dust so long as he kept them in sight. North had sworn the man wouldn't set foot on the threshold, but she had her doubts. Sir Reginald had a way of insinuating himself where he was least wanted, and then making it impossible to throw him out. He'd done it at the court often enough, with her father playing willing confederate.

"You'll be receiving what I've always called the royal welcome," North said as they began the final ascent. "I'll thank you to play gracious lady, and not embarrass the staff. You can knock heads with me later if you wish."

"A governess, welcomed in the feudal manner? Ridiculous."

"I want no doubts about your position here. We'll begin as I intend us to go on."

"And so much for dragging me from the carriage by my hair," she snapped, not bothering to correct him regarding nuptials that would never take place. "I suspected you wouldn't dare, and I was correct. Well, I'll stay right where I am until the butler and housekeeper have greeted you and been dismissed. In fact, I'd be much happier coming in the back way like any servant. Make my excuses however you wish."

"A glance ahead will disabuse you of that notion as no words of mine could."

"Oh, nooo," she whispered. The steps leading to the portico were lined with house servants. Gardeners, stable workers, tenants, and multitudes of children formed a small army on the terraces. In the center, framed by the portico, stood a lady leaning on a walking stick. "I thought you were joking. Even my father doesn't insist on such state when he returns to the court, and he considers himself of better lineage than the king."

"Perhaps he is, in a manner of speaking, though I doubt he's explained the reason for his opinion."

"No, he never has."

His eyes narrowed, but again he made no comment, merely saying needlessly, "We're home," as they came to a halt.

The carriage swayed, then steadied—Sir Reginald no doubt using it as a mounting block.

"One in the middle's my mother. Butler's named Pike," North rushed to say, ignoring the travel-stained face peering in at them. "First footman's Martin. Housekeeper's Mrs. Boutelle. Pugs told Mama to have Sally Pitcher serve as your abigail. The assignment's permanent if you like her. She's Bosley Pitcher's daughter. He's head groom. My mother's abigail is Martha. Cook's Mrs. Abbledore. Joshua Fields is my bailiff. Don't worry about the rest. You'll learn their names soon enough. Oh—the moppet with the flowers is Angie McPherson, the head gardener's granddaughter. You kiss her cheek, she'll think she's flown up to heaven, and old Angus'll be offered free pints at the Crowing Cock so the village can hear the tale till they're sick of it."

"Pike, Martin, Mrs. Boutelle, Mrs. Abbledore, Martha, Sally. Mr.—ah—Fields. Bosley Pitcher, Angus McPherson, Angie McPherson. That's everyone, I believe."

"You're amazing! How did you do that?"

"I pictured them in my head going about their business. Then I simply called to mind their positions in general order of precedence, and rattled them off. Mr. Fields was the only problem. He doesn't quite fit anywhere."

"They'll love you, every one of them. Best call my mother Lady Kathryn," he added as if it were a matter of no consequence. "She's the daughter of a duke."

There was nothing else to do: She had to behave.

Jem, who'd been promoted to temporary coachman so they could arrive in style rather than North handling the ribbons himself, was off the box and opening the door as soon as a pair of stable boys reached the horses' heads. He lowered the step, shoving Sir Reginald behind him as prearranged.

"Ignore them, Mellie," North ordered, leaping out and turning to hand her down. "Nobody can see 'em. Jem'll have the rotter on his way in a minute."

She remembered all the names, knelt to kiss little Angi

accepted a nosegay that was a trifle tattered from the child's loving care, and complimented Angus on his granddaughter, who was certainly the fairest flower in his gardens, while North stood at her side, beaming as she did the pretty. That it was all done in black bombazine suitable to a faded governess rather than the elegant traveling costume one would have expected of the daughter of an earl appeared not to matter in the least.

"And now, the best for last," North said, taking her arm and escorting her up the last few steps. "Mama, it's my very great honor and an infinite personal pleasure to present Lady Amelia Peasebottom, eldest child of the Earl of Pease, my soon-to-be bride, your new daughter, and Hillcrest's future mistress."

Amelia gazed into the bright silvery-gray eyes meeting hers, blushed, then swept her supposed mother-in-law-to-be a deep curtsy. "Lady Kathryn," she murmured.

"She ain't his fiancé," Sir Reginald roared directly behind them. "She's his—"

North's fist was quicker than Sir Reginald's tongue. The noxious knight crumbled at their feet, eyes dimming as he rolled down the steps.

"Dear me, what is that?" Lady Kathryn said, regarding the groaning lump of flesh with distaste.

"Merely a poisonous toadstool, Mama. Not lethal, but extremely unpleasant. I'll explain later." North gave Amelia a warning look, then turned to Jem, who was limping up the steps and rubbing his jaw. "Take Whifler to the Crowing Cock, and keep him locked up until I'm at leisure to deal with him. I don't want the fool setting foot on Hillcrest land again, understood?"

Jem nodded. "Sorry he got past me, sir," he said. "That's a trick I ain't seen since the stews. Never expected it of a gentry-cove. Your Gentleman Jackson would in no way approve, but it's effective enough, as you can see."

Dinner, which North requested be served in the smaller dining parlor at country hours, was unexceptionable. Mellie requested a tray in her suite, claiming exhaustion, and his mother, not wanting to leave the difficult girl to her own devices on her first evening at Hillcrest, had elected to join her. Fortunately the Irregulars arrived in time for him not to dine alone, a thing he detested. Now, with St. Maure ensconced in the library and Sinclair, Threadwhistle, and Dauntry playing billiards, North finally had a moment of leisure, and presented himself at his mother's door. It took a while for them to hear the scratch his mother preferred, but eventually it inched open.

"Evening, Martha. You're looking well," he said, brushing past his mother's abigail and ignoring the open boxes bearing the name of Marie Duclos's establishment and the periwinkle gown draped over Martha's arm. "How is she, Mama?"

"She? Very well, I'd imagine," his mother snapped, rising and offering her cheek, then flinging aside the rose merino whose neckline she'd been altering. "Everything that is proper. *She* had me confused at first, for I believed she was exactly what you claimed for her, but when Martin brought up these boxes a bit ago, I understood immediately. What sort of rig are you running this time?"

"Wh-what?" he stuttered.

"I cut my wisdoms years ago, Valentine. Martha, leave us. And take those—those *things* with you!"

He stared from his fuming mother to Martha's rigidly disapproving face. "Good God," he muttered, "you think just because—"

"Guard your tongue," Lady Kathryn snapped as Martha vanished into the bedchamber, closing the door behind her. "I will not permit such language in my presence. Where'd you find the clever puss—Haymarket? She's an excellent little actress—I'll grant you that. How much did you wager I wouldn't tumble to her? However much it is, you'll pay your friends triple for believing me such a peahen!"

"Oh, Lord," he sighed. "I suppose I've earned this—though not in any manner you'd understand. At least it's clear I find you in excellent health. Mama, Mellie is precisely—"

"And where was the farce to end—at the altar?" his mother forged on, ignoring him as she gathered up a length of lace an stuffed it in her workbox. "I should've known when Percival Harnette said the rest of your 'Irregulars' would be close behind you, but I didn't, the more fool I. Her manner was perfect."

She slammed the cover of her workbox and whirled to face him.

"Your 'poisonous toadstool' intended to spoil your game, didn't he? That's why you knocked him down. He was about to say she was your doxy. Of all the outrageous things you've done, this is absolutely the worst. I'm glad your father never saw you at this age, for he'd've been bitterly disillusioned. *He* always said you hadn't an ounce of malice in you. Well, either Mrs. Sherbrough—yes, I'm aware of her name, though I was informed she had raven hair, but then, actresses change that with the same insouciance they change gowns—or I will be gone from this house at dawn."

"Mama," he insisted, coming up to her, "the young lady in the rose suite is precisely who I said she was: the eldest daughter of the Earl of Pease."

"Deliver me! Valentine, all else aside, no earl's daughter would *ever* commission gowns from Marie Duclos's establishment."

"She didn't. I did."

"Nor would she permit a gentleman to provide her with gowns of any sort."

She crossed to a pair of chairs flanking the fireplace, one a lady's, one a worn leather monstrosity that had been his father's favorite.

"Sit! I'm not done with you yet," she said more mildly.

His mother, ill? Debilitated? Hardly. Oh, there were a few new wrinkles and her hair was more silver than gray, but that wasn't astonishing. It'd been more silver than gray at Christmas. Martha's reports had been exaggerations intended to make him come pelting posthaste to Hillcrest to relieve winter doldrums. No, his mother was as vigorous and fresh as the lilacs filling the cold hearth.

"The other fellows've arrived, even Tony," he said, suddenly reluctant to explain the tangle into which he'd plunged himself, dragging others with him. "Brought Jitters. Pugs and Stubby went on to Pugs's place after dinner."

"I'm perfectly aware of all that goes on here. Sit down, Valentine. I won't have you looming over me."

"They brought Freddy Tyne's brats. I saw the rest installed in the south wing as usual, and the rug-crawlers in the nursery. They were overjoyed by all the toys, and can hardly wait to meet you. Be warned: They're a pair of unregenerate scamps. You knew Freddy had died?"

"Some months ago, in the Colonies. I am *not* interested in Frederick Tyne's offspring, unregenerate or otherwise, though I'd dearly love to know how you came to be burdened with them. I would've thought his wife's family would take them in."

"Apparently not. That, or Freddy didn't want the Fulhams to have 'em. You'd best be interested in Robert and Tabitha. It all begins with them, or with Freddy and Fanny and a December storm in the Colonies."

He tried to smile, gave it up as a bad job, and went to the windows. "It's always so beautiful at this time of year," he murmured, looking out. "One tends to forget."

"And so not come except when one must—yes, I know. The country seems flat when one's very young. When one is a bit older, Town becomes tedious if one's forced to stay longer than a week or two."

He laughed. "Not quite tedious, but distinctly uncomfortable these last weeks, that I'll grant you. Freddy Tyne had best pray I live forever, or else that we end up in opposite places. Otherwise I intend to make eternity a living hell for him— unless I spend it at his feet singing his praises for making it all happen. Of course he had no intention of doing me a favor. Does an unintentional good deed carry the same merit as one that's intentional, I wonder?"

"One would hardly think so," his mother replied.

North gave her what he hoped was a reassuring grin, and took his usual place in his father's chair.

"What do you think of Mellie?" he said, cutting to the main point. "D'you like her? Forget who you think she is. You'r dead wrong—perhaps for the first time ever. The gowns were intended to irritate her. I was foxed when I ordered 'em. Thought Mellie was nothing but a faded slip of a thing named Abigail Sparrow then. She kept sending 'em back to me. Then when she did keep 'em, she never wore 'em. Can you accept sharing houseroom with her for the rest of your life?''

"My goodness," his mother murmured, "you're serious. She truly is the daughter of the Earl of Pease?''

"Without any doubt, not that it matters. I'd marry her if she were 'merely Abigail Sparrow, burdened with earning her bread like any other unfortunate,' and count myself blessed. The toadstool has a name, though: Reginald Whifler. Supposedly *Sir* Reginald Whifler. Her father intended to marry her off to the lout. That's fairly well known. Whifler recognized her instantly.''

"What in heaven's name have you been about, Val? Humphrey Peasebottom is a bombastic cipher, like all the men in his family. I've avoided the Peasebottoms for years. Certainly I'd never willingly invite one of them here.''

"She's different—not like that at all.''

"Oh, dear—this is confusing." Lady Kathryn sighed as she studied North's face in the golden light of the setting sun. "I'm having to readjust my opinions back to what they were before Anthony Sinclair brought those dreadful gowns up.''

"And?''

"I was pleasantly surprised by her. Rather unconventional, which is nothing short of a miracle, given that family. A more self-consequential lot it would be difficult to find. What you've been about, I can't imagine. No matter how I tried, all she'd say was she'd had the care of Freddy Tyne's children foisted on her, though *foisted* was hardly the word she used. She tried to convince me she belonged in servants' quarters. Naturally I paid no attention. Then she pleaded for a carriage to take her to Bristol.''

"She's being difficult.''

"Apparently. She also insisted you weren't betrothed, never would be, and I should inform the vicar there's no need to come in the morning.''

"I see. I've made a mull of everything, haven't I."

"Whatever everything is. Yes, I suspect you have."

"But she's not ill?"

"No, merely in extremely poor spirits, and exhausted. Don't lose heart. If she weren't a young woman of obviously strong character, one might almost say she's on the verge of a decline. When did it happen, Val?"

"It? What 'it'?"

"When a devoted son returns after several months' absence, barely acknowledges his mother while seeing to the comfort of a young lady, and then the next time he's in his mother's presence inquires repeatedly after the health of the young lady in whose company he was less than two hours earlier without giving a thought to his mother's well-being or lack of it, I would think the 'it' is as plain as the nose on your rather handsome face, Val," his mother said with a burble of laughter. "The dreadful stuff that came out of her hair when we washed it aside—coal-scuttle bonnets are fine and well if one's determined to hide one's face, but she appears to've taken the term literally—I found her lovely and charming. Her hair's guinea gold and curls naturally, in case you wondered. Only her eyes trouble me. You appear to have robbed them of their sparkle."

"Damn," he said, not bothering to apologize.

"I believe the term you young men use is 'planted a facer.' When did she plant you a facer, Val? And why didn't you bring Freddy Tyne's children to me when they arrived in England, for heaven's sake, rather than attempting to see to them yourself?"

"Didn't want you burdened with them. Martha wrote you hadn't been well." It was easier to admit to that than explain the other, especially to his mother. "Then the fellows and I made a wager, and one thing led to another."

"One of those 'anothers' being Abigail Sparrow, I take it, who was in reality Amelia Peasebottom, though you weren't aware of that at the time. Come now, Val, if I'm to be the least use to you, I must know the whole. Otherwise you might as well shrug your shoulders, and I'll summon a carriage to take the young lady to Bristol, as I'll not permit you to send her back to her father now that you've done with her."

"Done with her? Good Lord, Mama! I'll never be done with her, not if I can help it." He glanced at his father's drinks table, another of the bits his mother had moved into her new quarters over eleven years earlier in a fit of sentimentality. As always, it held several decanters along with her favorite cordials. "Would you mind?" he said, pointing.

"Not at all, if it will loosen your tongue."

"It was her voice." He rose and went to pour himself a glass of brandy. Admitting the first part was far easier with his back turned. "I'd advertised for a governess. Mellie turned up on my doorstep, coal-scuttle bonnet, spectacles, black bombazine, and all, just as I'd given up hope of finding someone to take charge of Freddy's droolers. What little I saw of her face would've turned a blind man's stomach, what with all the odd things she'd done to it to hide her identity should she encounter someone who knew her, so it wasn't that. Medusa, I called her then."

Haltingly, he explained about Pericles Tidmarsh, his fear of being entrapped, all the justifications that seemed so rational at the time and now struck him as sheerest lunacy. Then, before launching into the tale of the last few days, he explained what little he knew of Mellie's bolt from Bottomsley Court.

He began pacing the room as the rest of it came out, hesitantly at first, and then in a flood that amazed him. Oh, he stumbled over parts of it, such as the nature of the house on Milbury Place and precisely how he happened to know of the Willing Wench. Chloe Sherbrough's presence had to be given some sort of explanation, for as a normal thing he'd never've entertained Burridge in his home, certainly not to celebrate the pompous old fellow's betrothal. The rest was easy enough if he was willing to appear a complete cloth-head.

He fetched up at the windows as he came to the end of it— Whifler's threats, and his following them to Hillcrest.

The sitting room was almost dark by then. The sun, after lingering on the horizon to cast long shadows across lake and lawns, had set at last, merely a glow lingering behind the trees. A door opened. Someone—Martha, no doubt—bustled about lighting lamps.

"And that's the lot," he said.

At first he couldn't identify the choked sound behind him. Then he realized it was laughter, suppressed at first, then breaking free in a silver torrent.

"Dear heaven," his mother gasped, "I wish your father had lived to hear this. Well, there's no question: Our first task will be to disembarrass ourselves of Lord Whifler. Then you'll have an opportunity to court the poor girl properly."

"I did my best on the way here. Fellows helped by keeping to themselves and seeing to Freddy's droolers. Even guarded us from Whifler."

"Do better. Unless your young lady will meet you joyfully at the altar, my dear, I can't countenance a wedding. I have considerable respect for the determination she's shown, for all she'd doesn't appear to've planned well beyond her dash to London. This tale could've had a far worse ending."

Chapter Seventeen

Hillcrest wasn't just beautiful. It wasn't even just a wealthy and productive estate, though it was that too. It was a happy, even a lighthearted one. The families here suffered their private sorrows as well as shared their more public joys. That was an inescapable part of the human condition. But they suffered those sorrows and celebrated those joys well fed and decently garbed, treated with affection and respect, and with an answering love for the fields in which they labored and the family that held such power over their lives. Both land and people were in excellent heart.

The contrast with the court's surly tenants and shutter-eyed household, its eroded lands and stunted crops, couldn't have been greater. Amelia didn't need a formal tour to know that. She had only to gaze out the window as she was now, or help herself to a sip of tea and a nibble of one of the biscuits brought by Sally when she'd stirred just after dawn.

Hillcrest was a secure refuge in an insecure world, the twin of Mrs. Pickles's cozy parlor on Wilton Street. The problem, Amelia realized with a sigh as she watched North run down the steps and spring into the saddle of a rawboned gray gelding being held by Jem, was that for her the refuge was as ephemeral as a conjurer's trick created with veils and colored smoke.

He was riding down the drive now, the sun striking his back. Then he disappeared into the woods, a lay figure of no meaning in the reality of Lady Amelia Peasebottom, late of Bottomsley Court, and even more recently Milbury Place, London.

She couldn't help wondering where he was bound so early, then smiled. Given his garb—a shirt open at the neck, buckskin breeches, a leather jerkin, a workman's cap—he was doubtless visiting the fields, perhaps even planning to join in the work. The notion of her father doing such a thing was preposterous. For the earl, Bottomsley was only a source of revenue from which every last sou must be wrung, the setting in which he played *grand seigneur.* Hillcrest and its people clearly meant far more to its owner.

No, North was hardly the careless absentee landlord or irresponsible man-about-town he portrayed with such skill. Life might be a game to him, but there was a serious core no matter how he tried to hide it. Never had she so misjudged a man, but then, never had a man given her such a false impression of himself. She wasn't, she decided, entirely to blame.

At least his insistence that they wed wasn't the masterstroke to play the great man before his friends that she'd deemed it. It sprang from an honorableness masked by schoolboy pranks, and a refusal to turn life into a grim game of knights and pawns in which the knights invariably triumphed and the pawns lost. North saw to the pawns. His offer—if it could be called that— had been duty ridden, and completely in earnest.

Strange—that one could learn so much of a man just by seeing his home.

One might even have called the journey to Hillcrest a strange form of courtship. He'd taken her for walks once they'd stopped for the night when he must've wanted nothing but a quick meal and his bed. He'd joined her in endless rounds of backgammon while his friends entertained Tibbie and Robby and kept Sir Reginald at bay, or in hours of conversation that revealed a strong intelligence and a keen sensitivity to those in less favorable circumstances than himself. That he'd done it to salvage the pride of a woman gowned in black bombazine was almost beyond belief. Such a man didn't deserve the curse of a wife for whom he felt no affection, no matter how highly she'd learned to esteem him.

"My lady?"

She turned at the soft voice.

"Will you be having your wash-up now, my lady? Breakfast'll be between the time himself gets back and when he goes out again, which'll be about an hour from now. Your hair's not done, nor have you chosen a gown."

Sally had been busy. The bedchamber was spotless, even to a clumsy nosegay of wildflowers beside her bed and a more elegant arrangement of hothouse roses on the mantel.

"Did you do these for me?" Amelia said, going to the nighttable and bending to breathe in the spicy aromas of spring. "They're lovely. Thank you."

"Oh, no, m'lady," the girl giggled. "Them's from himself. Went out and picked 'em when the dew was still on 'em, he did, from his favorite place, and brought 'em back afore going to the fields like he does first morning he's home. Mr. North don't know nothing about flowers. Just stuck 'em in a jug, but he said you'd like 'em as they was, an' not to pretty 'em up. Wanted you to have a bit of the best of Hillcrest by you when you woke, only I told him you was up and about already. Mr. McPherson brung the others on account of your kissing Angie. Fair gloried him, that did."

Tears welled in Amelia's eyes as she touched the sparkling petals.

North was playing the role of besotted suitor to perfection. Another game. Dear heaven, would she never be done with them? And then she realized that no, she wouldn't. For the rest of her life she'd be forced to give the illusion of being heart-whole when she was the reverse. She'd find this favorite place of his before she left, and leave her heart there, where at least it might sense his presence on occasion, for all he'd never be aware it lingered there in honor of him. And, when she dared, she'd imagine him there gathering flowers for the woman he loved, and wish him well with a brave smile.

"You got to decide what you're going to wear this morning, my lady," Sally chattered on. "There's lots to choose from. Real busy last night, Lady Kathryn and Martha and me were. And my sisters, too, and my ma come up from the cottage. Made a regular party of it, willing hands and light hearts meaning merry work. This one with the stripes is my favorite on account of I worked on it myself. Took the littlest stitches I ever took in my life too. Can't hardly see 'em."

Amelia glanced behind her. Sally was holding up a square-necked gown of creamy gingham striped in deep rose, three rows of matching ribbon at the hem.

"This is ever so much prettier than those things Mr. Sinclair brought from London, and there's a spencer bit darker'n the stripes, and a sunshade too, and a fichu for the neck, and a straw bonnet with them same ribbons, only wider. You'd look a fair treat in that," she cajoled. "Lady Kathryn said not to take insult, as they're new. Ordered 'em up for this summer when Miss Christina and Miss Georgiana come with their families."

"Good heavens! But I can't—"

"Lady Kathryn knew as how you didn't have nothing but those dreadful black things even a scullery maid'd be ashamed of, my lady, and those two dresses what aren't very nice for all they're fancy as peacocks trimmed in ostrich feathers and come from a London shop. There's always people stopping by afternoons, and her ladyship knew you'd want to look your best for Mr. North's sake even if you don't care for yourself."

Amelia blinked back her tears, regarding the country girl with amazement. Where had Sally been when she'd had charge of Tibbie and Robby? Where had the girl been the night she escaped from the court while the rest of the world slept?

"The gown you've chosen is fine," she managed to say. "No, it's better than that. It's absolutely elegant, Sally. Oh, dear."

She dashed across the room and hugged her while the girl laughed and protested the gown would be beyond rescue from crushing if she didn't stop.

"Thank you," she gulped, releasing Sally at last, "and please thank Lady Kathryn for me, and your mother, and—oh, dear, you'd best make me a list of all who helped, for I must thank each of them personally. No one's ever done me such a kindness before.''

And then, not caring if her eyes were red for weeks, Lady Amelia Peasebottom indulged in a bout of tears she kept telling Sally were tears of joy and gratitude. She'd permit herself this one morning, she decided, and build what happy memories she could, but she'd be gone where he'd never find her before the clock struck noon.

North glanced up from Joshua Fields's plowing and planting records as the door to the family breakfast parlor opened. A single glance had him on his feet as much from astonishment as from courtesy.

He'd expected her to clean up well if his mother had a hand in the matter, but this was beyond belief. A handsome woman had been within the realm of the possible, one of character and presence whose features, while they'd never launch a thousand ships, would at least not cause his gorge to rise when he faced her across the breakfast cups. He hadn't expected a vision of loveliness who put the fairest angel to shame.

"My God, what possessed you?" he blurted out. "I thought the best of you was your voice," then stumbled out a clumsy apology that had him flushing like a bumpkin.

"Who would've hired me like this?" she said as she closed the door. Far from appearing put out by his candor, he could've sworn she was relieved by it. "Especially as a governess. Would you?"

"No, I'd've had another notion entirely. A highly improper one, if you must know, or else one that was terrifyingly proper."

"Households requiring a governess generally have gentlemen present. Even the most retiring governess is glimpsed on occasion, whether her mistress wishes her to be or not. Bombazine and spectacles seemed wise." She went to the sideboard and peeped beneath the lids, examining the usual assortment offered in the morning when he was home. "Certainly no agency would have represented my customary self—not that I'm more than passable. It's the contrast that startles you.''

"But your hair. I've never seen such a travesty as you perpetrated on yourself.''

"You haven't? How interesting.''

She turned to face him, still garbed as he had been for his early ride. Beside her daintiness, he was a clod. He'd thought she'd appear in her usual black, blast it, not some stylish confection of claret stripes, and had wanted the contrast between them to seem less. No matter what he did, it rebounded on him. And she hadn't even mentioned his flowers, drat it. Well, her eyes were red. Perhaps she suffered from rose fever. There was so much they didn't know about each other. The morning he'd planned so carefully was galloping from bad to worse.

"I seem to remember a Mr. Pericles Tidmarsh,'' she said after a clash of eyes that would've done credit to a pair of master swordsmen.

"That was different.''

"In what manner? Because you're a gentleman?''

"No, blast it! Because—because—''

"Because you're a gentleman, and everything a gentleman does bears the stamp of reason while anything a woman does is silly? I've heard that song before, and find it as unconvincing now as I did in the past, Mr. North.''

"What a tongue it has,'' he muttered.

The best that could be said of her at the moment was she didn't simper or pose, and spoke her mind with a clarity that would send any poor fellow accustomed to the usual fawning schoolroom misses reeling. All over bristles, and that was the least of it. What ailed her, for pity's sake? It was as if she were trying to give him a disgust of her.

"And it's not likely to change,'' she snapped.

"What the devil did you do to your hair?'' he said, returning to a point on which he felt more secure. Good Lord, she was as bad as his mother when displeased.

She swept him with a glance that would've done any governess proud.

"I dulled it with a mixture of watercolor pigment, coal dust, and coffee, and pulled it back. This style and color would've been most unsuitable to a governess. Sally may not have London training, but she's the best and most willing abigail I've ever seen, as well as a delightful and charming child. The principal credit goes to her, and to Lady Kathryn and Martha for beginning her training in anticipation of the day you'd present Hillcrest with its new mistress. I'm merely a chance beneficiary of their foresight.''

''I can see there will be certain points on which we'll never agree,'' he chuckled as he came over to the sideboard. ''You're a diamond of the first water.'' She was shy of him in this new guise—that was it. ''Let's call a truce. I've no desire to spend the morning brangling. Here, let me fill a plate for you. Would you prefer coffee or tea? Or would you care for chocolate? I'll be glad to ring for some. Unless I'm mightily mistaken, Martin is hovering behind the service door. Is there anything you want that's not here? He'll bring it on the instant.''

''I'm partial to larks' tongues in currant sauce,'' she said, piling her plate with everything in sight. ''They must be presented on grilled toast made from corn grown in Cornwall, and lightly roasted before it's milled. This must be followed by a syllabub from the cream of white cows born when the moon's full. Otherwise I'll go into a decline. See to it, Mr. North.''

Then she turned and grinned at him so sunnily that he burst into laughter.

''Minx,'' he murmured. ''I can see even at dawn my life will never be dull.''

''Possibly.''

He managed to reach the table before she did, and held out the chair closest to his. ''My mother doesn't appear until noon, though she's up with the sun like the rest of us. The fellows never try to adjust to country hours, so I'm afraid I've only myself to offer for your entertainment until then,'' he apologized.

''Sally tells me it's your custom to inspect the fields the morning of your return. I've no desire to interfere. Perhaps you have a carriage in which I can tour the grounds?''

"No," he said, scowling at her too-innocent expression, her too-deep interest in the food she was steadily consuming.

"Whyever not?"

"You've been known to bolt. This is one time and place you won't be permitted the option. And no, I won't listen to reason. While generally the most accommodating of fellows, you'll find there are moments when I'm intransigence itself. Bosley and Jem've been warned you're not to gad about on your own, so don't try cutting a wheedle at the stables. You'll only be escorted back to the house. I shouldn't care to see you put out of countenance—or them either. They deserve better from you."

"So I'm to be held prisoner here? Then there's nothing to choose between Hillcrest and the court. I've merely exchanged a careless jailer for a more astute one."

He regarded her steadily. At last she averted her eyes.

"I didn't mean that," she said on a choked note, pushing her half-emptied plate away as if she'd lost her appetite. "Hillcrest is lovely, and Lady Kathryn has been all that's kind and welcoming. So has everyone I've met. You're to be envied, though I realize it's you who set the tone, and that it probably extends back through many generations."

"And still you intend to bolt. That's why you asked for a carriage."

She seemed to be having an argument with herself, eyes downcast, lower lip caught between even white teeth. Expression after expression he wished he could read flitted across her features. He held his breath. At last she raised her gaze to his, her eyes clear and candid, though the pain in their depths caught at his heart.

"No, I truly would love to tour at least the park, and see this favorite place of yours where you gathered flowers this morning," she said. "I haven't thanked you for them, have I? Well, I do. They were lovely, and a delightful surprise. How could you have known I prefer the most unprepossessing daisy to the grandest rose?"

"I watched what you admired on our walks the last two days."

"Why would you do that?" she said, then flushed at his derisive glance.

"You'll like the spot," he continued as if she hadn't asked her foolish question. "It's at the top of a hill—the one this place is named for. Most people think the name comes from the knoll where the house stands, but it doesn't. There's a grand old oak at the crest beneath which, by tradition, we Norths ask the ladies we love if they'll join us here for the rest of their lives. No betrothal's official until the offer's made and accepted there, and sealed with a kiss that can last as long as one wants."

"Good heavens, I didn't realize North gentlemen fancied hareems."

He stared at her in confusion, then broke into laughter. "Oh, no—no hareems. We choose only once, and so take care to choose extremely well. Now, if you'll permit me, I'll excuse myself. I smell of the stables, and as I'm not riding out again this morning, I'd best change into more conventional gear. If my mother saw me like this, she'd comb my hair with a stool."

He'd said more than enough for Amelia to know why Sally Pitcher insisted on rearranging her hair so it would show to advantage beneath the chip straw bonnet with the burgundy ribbons, artfully coaxing a few curls to frame her face as if by accident. She understood why the girl giggled as she created the sauciest of offset bows rather than tying a simple one beneath her chin. Her fichu had to be just so, the spencer open at the neck to reveal a touch of rosy lining. On and on it went.

Amelia drew the line at darkening her lashes with soot, insisting on such a warm day the stuff would smudge, and refused the shawl her temporary abigail tried to drape at her elbows.

No doting mother about to lead a cherished daughter into Almack's assembly rooms had ever fussed over that daughter's appearance with such devotion. The tradition of the oak on the hill's crest would be known to all. News of their destination had traveled through the household. If Amelia had doubts, the sight of Sally flying down the corridor to Lady Kathryn's apartments, her triumphant cry of "They're off, your lady-ship!" set them to rest.

Maids and footmen lurked everywhere, curtsying and bowing and wishing her good morning, and smiling as if they were flowers and she the sun. Tibbie and Robby waited at the mouth of the long gallery where North had told her he and his sisters had often played when the weather was inclement. The children were scrubbed and combed, their eyes like platters, nurse and nursemaids beaming behind them.

She knelt and held out her arms, but they hung back as if they feared her.

"It's really I," she said, trying a smile that trembled at the edges. "Don't let the gown fool you. It's not mine."

"You're not our Sparrow anymore," Tibbie said, then stuck her thumb in her mouth, a solecism she hadn't committed since just before she and Robby hid in the coal cellar. "You're Lady Amelia Peasebottom. Nurse said so. And you *look* like a Lady Amelia. You don't look like a sparrow at all."

"I'll always be your Sparrow, even if I must be Lady Amelia to others," she said, still holding her arms out. "How is Beezle? Do you like your new schoolroom?"

They came to her then, pushed by North's old nurse, but they treated her as if she were a porcelain shepherdess rather than a sturdy poppet of straw and leather. Robby's little bow, Tibbie's bob, kisses that barely touched her cheek broke her heart.

"I haven't changed in the least inside," she whispered, hug-ging and kissing them soundly without a thought to rumpling her spencer or creasing her gown, but it was clear they didn't believe her.

"You look like Mama. You smell like her too." The way Robby said it, it was the strongest indictment he could issue.

And then the mites were backing away as if she were royalty. She sighed as they turned tail and dashed back toward the nursery quarters.

Even Jitters managed to put himself in her path, giving her an avuncular smile as he passed her on the stairs. Dear heaven, what an ordeal. Pike waited in the grand entryway to usher her out, Martin hovering by the doors leading to the state apartments. Kitchen staff clustered near the service doors.

And then she was on the first of the broad terraces leading to the drive in front of the house. Heaven alone knew where North had been, but he was taking her arm and leading her down the sweeping steps. Dark green riding coat, striped green and gold waistcoat, a single exquisite gold fob, dark unmentionables—he was dressed as if he were about to set off for Hyde Park except for the lack of walking stick, hat, and gloves. Had his mother or Jitters made the same fuss over him that Sally had over her? What pains he'd gone to, and all for naught.

She glanced up at the impressive facade. It couldn't be Mr. St. Maure, Mr. Sinclair, Mr. Threadwhistle, and Mr. Dauntry peeking from an upper window, the draperies pulled aside—it couldn't! Even as she watched, the draperies fell into place.

"Will they follow us, do you think?" she said without thinking.

"No, thank heavens. That's another of Hillcrest's traditions. We Norths stumble through this part of our lives as best we can without advisers, and without witnesses should we turn ourselves into clunches. It happens, on occasion. My grandmother claimed my grandfather was paying little attention to where he knelt, and put his knee in a cowblake where no cowblake was supposed to be. Could've been worse, I suppose. As least it was dry. I do know my father handed my mother a peony that was inhabited. Bee-stung lips, indeed! He admitted as much when I was a lad, and I happened on them when she was twitting him about it. We're rather graceless about certain things, we Norths, when all's said and done."

"It almost sounds as if you pride yourself on the failing."

"If it is one. My father always claimed it made for delightful tales to tell one's children around a winter fire. My sisters and I agreed. Even the most serious things need a touch of humor, or they become tedious," he said, looking directly into her eyes, "and some of those serious things must never be touched with tedium or they turn grim. Grim is something I've avoided all my life. I intend to continue avoiding it."

He turned her onto a walk that led around the house. "Stable block," he said, pointing. "Very old, some of it, but always kept in excellent repair. Carriage house, paddocks—all convenient, but at sufficient distance that we're not troubled with unwanted aromas or sounds. Dairy over there, has its own spring. Poultry houses and dovecotes and the usual barns and sties behind, with stabling for plow horses and such. Kitchen gardens that way, cutting this, forcing houses down there. Orchards're over that rise. Beyond them's storage for ice in a cave my grandfather had enlarged. Folly up there, built by my grandfather. There's another across the lake my mother designed. Down that track's what amounts to a reasonable-sized village—tenant cottages and so forth, and the bake house. Shrubberies and aviary down that walk with fish ponds beyond, then the grape arbors. Smokehouse that way. It's at a considerable distance from both the barns and stables. Horses're terrified of smoke."

"I know." She opened her sunshade, managing to disengage his hand. "It maddens them. They can injure themselves trying to kick their way out of a stall if they think the stable's on fire."

She might as well not have bothered. The hand was back the moment she'd angled the thing to suit her.

Each fence, each doorway and window held its observers.

"Wave," North said, following his own command. "Yes, it's quite a gauntlet you're running, but it's well meant. They've seen you only the once last night, and are wishing us both well. Besides, you'll get used to it."

"No, I won't," she murmured.

"Ah—contrary porridge for breakfast, I see. At least that's what Nurse used to call it. I'll have to inquire about those larks' tongues."

To her, his chuckle sounded more determined than good-humored. Then the walk curved through a cutting garden sheltered behind high walls. Even there they weren't safe, for Angus McPherson was leaning on a spade and pulling off his cap as a phalanx of workers respectfully tugged forelocks.

"Just a moment," she said, attempting to pull free. "I wan

to thank your head gardener. He sent up a beautiful arrangement of hothouse roses this morning.''

Keeping her firmly at his side, North strolled her over to the old man. Even then he didn't set her free, staying at her side and smiling down at her as if she were the most precious thing in his world while she thanked the gardener for his kindness, and extolled the beauty of his flowers.

Once they were out of sight beyond the walls following a path through a spinney, she wrenched her arm free and turned to face him.

"There is absolutely no need for all this pretense," she snapped, a catch in her voice.

"It must have been a superior form of contrary porridge," he murmured. "It's made you as difficult as an east wind. Come, let's not fly at each other like a pair of schoolchildren. If you'd rather not take my arm, then don't. Mind the roots, though, and where you step. There are rabbit holes through here."

"There weren't any in the cutting garden."

"No, there weren't. Hasn't it occurred to you that I like having you on my arm?"

"No, it hasn't."

"Well, I do. I enjoyed it before we reached the Willing Wench, and I enjoyed it on our evening walks when we were coming here, and I enjoy it now. Is that so strange?"

"Surpassingly so."

He kept his peace for a while after that, leading the way through the woods along a path that twisted and climbed. They passed a stream tumbling over mossy rocks, then twined through stands of beech and hemlock, breaking at last into a flower-dappled meadow that continued to rise, at its crest a giant oak whose rough bark was black with age, its branches sweeping the ground like the train of a ball gown.

"The wind *is* from the east," he murmured, glancing at her from the corner of his eye. "I should have known. We Norths never have any luck when the wind's from that quarter."

She pretended not to hear him rather than correct him about the wind's direction, which was decidedly from the south.

Instead, "How perfectly lovely," she said. "I can understand why this would be your favorite spot at Hillcrest."

"It's well enough most of the time, but I believe today it's at its best. Requires just the right lady to set it off, you see. Otherwise it can be rather dull. One can see much of the estate from the crest. Shall we go the rest of the way?"

"Please," she said, knowing she should claim exhaustion from a walk that wouldn't've tired a child in leading strings, but loath to let go of that moment and the place she'd carry in her heart for the rest of her life.

They took their time about it, picking flowers she collected in the bonnet she'd removed to let the breeze cool her head, he creating another nosegay such as the one he'd brought her that morning. He even tucked a few flowers in her hair. They laughed and chattered as if they'd been given a reprieve in this place that seemed at the very top of the world and yet completely isolated from it, luxuriating in the bright sunshine and the songs of the birds. And yet, inevitably, they drew toward the oak.

When he tucked her hand in his arm as they covered the last few feet, she made no demur. Then they were beneath the tree, and he was turning her to look over distant rolling hills that were a violet dream on the horizon, more woods feathering their crests. She could tell he was gazing at her. She met his eyes, knowing this was what she'd dreaded, and not knowing how she'd survive the next minutes, or all the minutes and hours and days and years that would follow.

"You know why I've brought you here," he said.

She nodded.

"Lady Amelia—Mellie—will you do me the very great honor, grant me the infinite joy of—oh, dammit, it gets all tangled up no matter how much I've rehearsed it. I am definitely not one for pretty speeches. Mellie, please, will you marry me?"

"Why?"

"Because," he said after a moment's thought, "it's right."

Then he dropped the nosegay he'd been crushing in his other hand, and turned her around on the crest of that windswept hill beneath the ancient oak where North gentlemen sought the hands of their beloveds, and kissed her. She answered his kiss. She couldn't help it. And right then, as a lark soared high above them, she laid her heart at his feet, only she didn't tell him.

Instead, once he'd done and was looking at her with every appearance of hope in his eyes, she said, "I think not." And then, because she couldn't bear to refuse him entirely, she said, "At least, not yet."

"Why?"

"Because it's *not* right. We barely know one another."

"I know all of you I need to know, though not all I want to."

"You know almost nothing of me," she said, trying to keep the sorrow from her voice, "except things that are hardly to my credit. You've made your offer here, as North gentlemen do. I've said we should wait a bit, as I must. I'm sorry if that's not the answer you expected, but it's the only one I can give you."

She turned, gazing out over the flowery meadow and the distant hills. "I'll never forget this place," she said, not adding that she'd never forget him either. "Can we go back now?"

On the way down the slope she pretended she'd dropped a handkerchief, and went alone to retrieve a few of the flowers he'd picked, intending to press them, while he waited at the edge of the wood. Their trip to the house was silent, he abstracted, she barely managing not to burst into the tears which, if she shed them, would make her the happiest of women and he the most miserable of men—only they wouldn't, for if he was miserable, then she'd be miserable too.

They passed through the cutting garden, which was deserted. No one watched from stable or paddock or dairy. Word had traveled ahead of them in that inexplicable fashion unpleasant news has of swiftly reaching every cranny while good news languishes undelivered. And then they were rounding the house and striding toward the lowest of the terraces. A carriage whose doors bore an all too familiar crest was being walked in the drive. Sir Reginald strode up, grinning like the self-satisfied monster he was.

"Pleased with my little surprise, Lady Amelia?" he gloated,

ignoring North. ''Such a happy occasion, our being reunited. Thought the earl should share it—especially as he's insisting you've been dead for months. Think of the palpitations he must've suffered when Chuffy told him we'd been cozened, and you're very much alive.''

Chapter Eighteen

Whifler stood there, preening like a peacock, almost as if it were he who owned Hillcrest, and not North. That, or as if he owned Mellie.

"Damn," North murmured, drawing her aside. "I'd hoped to avoid this for you. Go to your apartments, or, better yet, my mother's. Martha'll know what to do."

"I must face his lordship soon or late."

"You call your father that? I begin to understand. Well, perhaps you must, but not here, and certainly not now. Later, after we're wed, will be soon enough." She didn't contradict him regarding the latter event. Good—she was learning some sense. "There's a door around the side. Take the service stairs to your right, go down to the kitchens, and ask to be escorted because you'll never find your way alone from there." He plucked the daisies from her hair and tossed them on the drive, then ran his fingers down her cheek. "There's nothing to fear, Mellie. Off with you now, and no arguments. I'll send for you if you're needed, but you won't be."

She gave him a smile that wrenched his heart, and then hurried back the way they'd come.

"Here now, where's Lady Amelia going?"

North clenched his fists, then turned to face the popinjay from Manchester. "Be glad I'm not drawing your cork again. I gave orders you weren't—"

"I gave orders too." Whifler pulled a pistol from behind his coattails. "Did you think that toy at the Willing Wench was the only one I've got? Don't worry, it's not cocked. Was earlier though. Your groom found that persuasive. So did your butler. Now, let's go see my future father-in-law, shall we?"

"Put it away. You're likely to hurt yourself—not that that would be any great sorrow to me." North ran up the series of steps without waiting to see if he was obeyed or followed. If necessary, he'd get the popper from Whifler later.

Pike babbled mortified apologies as soon as he opened the door.

"Don't think a thing of it." North took the time to put an arm around Pike's shoulders and give him a reassuring smile. "Much rather have the louts inside than you injured. Where's the earl, and who's with him?"

"State drawing room, sir," Pike said. "Her ladyship, Mr. St. Maure, Mr. Sinclair, Mr. Threadwhistle, and Mr. Dauntry."

"Not Chuffy Binkerton? Fattish fellow, nose like a turnip, face like raw dough?"

"No, sir—only those I've mentioned."

"Chuffy toddled back to Town," Whifler said behind them. "Told him he wouldn't be needed once I had the earl. Doesn't care for the country, so he was just as glad to go."

"Mr. St. Maure detoured by the library, sir," Pike continued as if the rotter hadn't spoken, "before joining the others."

"He did, did he?"

"Yes, sir. Asked me to inform you of that with reference to a conversation you had at dinner yesterday regarding family histories. And Martin, Christopher, James, and Wells are also present. That seemed wisest until you arrived, sir."

"Good thinking, Pike. Thank you. I won't forget this."

"Just so your young lady's safe, sir, and isn't importuned beyond what she can bear. Quite taken with her, all of us are, sir."

"So am I," North murmured with a genuine smile. "Pro

foundly and permanently. I hope soon you'll all be able to wish
me happy. No, I'll let myself in if you don't mind. I'll be
sending Martin and the others out. Do me the favor of taking
yourselves off to the servants' hall. I'd rather this be private.''

Then he squared his shoulders, took a deep breath, crossed
the reception area, and opened the door to the first of the state
apartments, Whifler hard on his heels. He slammed the door
in the fellow's face and held it closed. After a moment the
jerks and tugs ceased.

The fellows were ranged around his mother, who held court
in the chair they'd always called ''the throne,'' and had once
been graced by Queen Elizabeth's elevated rump. A pasty-
faced, heavyjowled walrus with a few strands of yellow hair
lined up across his pate raised a quizzing glass. It was obvious
where Whifler got his sense of style. A brocaded waistcoat at
this hour? In the country? Especially an orange and blue one
embroidered with purple nymphs and pearls? Good Lord—
what a jackass.

''Well, what d'you want?'' he snapped after a quick glance
at St. Maure, who was seated at a table slightly apart from the
others, apparently so engrossed in the tome before him that he
didn't notice North's presence. ''I haven't got all day.''

''We've been granted such an honor,'' Lady Kathryn fluttered. ''Valentine, dear, you'll never believe who this is.''

''Yes, I will. Pike's already informed me of our singular
honor.''

''Such barbarism, Valentine. Where are your manners?''

''In this instance, on holiday. Breaking into my home at
pistol point is not what I consider good manners. Why should
I accord better than I receive? Ah, Martin?'' North raised his
brows and nodded at the door. The four footmen filed out,
expressions blank.

''Young people these days,'' his mother apologized with a
wave of her hand, turning to the earl. ''One must forgive them
everything however, wouldn't you agree, your lordship? They
are, after all, our future as well as our deepest joy. Do have a
seat, Val. No need for you to lurk like a great gawk.''

''Told Reggie it was a fool's errand but he would insist the earl shrugged, still wielding his quizzing glass. "When Reggie insists on something, I ain't got the energy to go against him. Dreadful energetic fellow, Reggie, what? Always rushing here and there. Insisting I rush too, which ain't to my liking. Never was one for rushing. Totty-headed notion, coming here, but he insisted on that too, or at least his friend did. Gone now, thank heavens. Dreadful fellow. Puffs like a grampus, Reggie's friend does. Think he wears a corset. Shouldn't need a corset at his age."

"How fatiguing for you," Lady Kathryn murmured. "Such fortitude you've shown, coming all this way. You humble me, for I'm certain I wouldn't't've been able to support the journey, certainly not in the company of a dreadful fellow who puffs."

"Y'wouldn't't've liked it, Mrs. North. Y'wouldn't't've liked it a bit," the earl said, puffing not a little himself. "Most annoying."

What in heaven's name was his mother about? She sounded almost as feather-brained as the earl, who clearly had no idea he was being played for a fool by an expert.

"Well, what's your business?" he said, throwing his mother a warning glance and remaining near the door in case Whifler decided to join them. "My guests and I want to try my trout stream, and I haven't got all day."

The earl dithered with his quizzing glass, pretending to examine the room. He helped himself to a pinch of snuff, making a messy business of it. No mirrors for that one. He removed a speck of lint from his cuff, resettled his fobs, and smoothed his waistcoat over his considerable paunch.

"Understand from Reggie you've got someone claiming t'be my daughter here," he said finally, eyeing North.

"But you told me your daughter is deceased, your lordship," Lady Kathryn gasped with perhaps a trace too much drama. "You said the young woman Valentine brought with him must be an impostor. Were you perhaps misinformed? Is it possible she is indeed alive? Oh, what a joyous moment for you!"

"Won't know until I see her. Where is she? You're keeping her deuced secret. Back from her walk, since North's here."

"Oh, but I wouldn't dream of bringing an impostor into your presence. Much too painful, your lordship."

Lady Kathryn gave the earl a smile, head bobbing like a bird's.

"Why, if it were Val and I'd thought him dead, and then someone told me he wasn't dead at all after I'd gone into mourning, and then produced him only it wasn't he, I'd suffer such seizures and palpitations. Do you suffer from seizures and palpitations, your lordship? Your complexion is turning rather ruddy," she chattered, barely pausing to draw breath. "Perhaps a glass of milk? Valentine, do order some milk for his lordship. I've always found warm milk particularly soothing, and I suspect his lordship wants soothing just now. Of course you're not in mourning, your lordship, so perhaps you weren't totally overset by your daughter's death? How odd that would be in a father—not to be overset by a beloved daughter's death. Why, it's only been a matter of some weeks, has it not? I'd've thought you'd be in deepest mourning."

Good Lord, what a fiddlestick! His mother belonged on the stage. The fellows were choking. They'd never survive this with straight faces, any of them.

"Wasn't a particularly comfortable daughter," Peasebottom rumbled, complexion further deepening. "Got a much better pair at home. Lookers too. Your son wants a wife, I can provide him a better one, what? Eldest always had an odd kick to her gallop. Besides, if it is her, she's promised to Reggie Whifler. Couldn't have her going back on her word, now, could I? Set a bad example for the others."

"Oh, was there an announcement? I must have missed the notice."

"Ah, not quite. She died—ah, disappeared—ah, was abducted—ah—met with an unfortunate accident before anything official—"

"She bolted rather than marry Whifler," North snapped, tiring of the game. He ignored the murmur in the reception area. Whatever it was, someone would see to it. "My assumption is you purposely confused a thieving maid with your daughter when the opportunity offered. Certainly the tale I heard was that according to you, Mellie and her abigail ran off together—which, as it happens, they didn't. Must've been a mixed sorrow identifying the woman with jewels sewn in her cloak as Mellie. On the one hand, you'd lost a daughter, but on the other, you'd gained a fortune."

The earl, after looking from one accusing face to the next, shrugged. "Supposition, all of it. But let's say there's a scrap of truth in there somewhere. Pockets to let. What would any reasonable man do, given the opportunity? Didn't do me any good alive. Much better to me dead, what? Twist it any way you will, she's gone."

"Then you'll be delighted that I'm prepared to relieve you of her permanently."

"Can't have that. Already said so. Promised her to Reggie. Besides, she drowned in the Ouse."

"Failing my acceptability as a candidate for Lady Amelia's hand, there's always the option of ceding her the inheritance from her great-aunt that became hers legally upon her majority. No need to invoke Whifler."

"Can't. Spent most of my half already."

"Your half?" Lady Kathryn frowned, then turned to North. "But I don't understand, Val. What can his lordship mean? I thought an inheritance belonged to the one who inherited it."

"Not if one keeps the legacy secret from one's daughter while striking a bargain with a crony to divide it once they're wed. Not if one's father then declares one dead to get his hands on all of it, and intends to claim one is an impostor if one should happen to turn up alive, just as Mellie has."

"Wouldn't matter one way or the other. Fathers have rights. Ain't her anyway."

"Oh, yes, it is, your lordship."

"Damn," North breathed.

Mellie stood framed in the doorway, hanging leachlike on Whifler's arm like an inane miss whose father had just landed her a fat trout. What the devil was she doing here? And then he had it. Oh, yes, he had it. Well, he wouldn't let her get away with it—not that the earl would either, or he'd learned less about the venal fool in the last minutes than he thought he had.

North glanced at his mother, then at the fellows. Their expressions were blank. Now anything could happen, dammit. Then he saw Whifler was reaching behind him.

"No, you don't!" he growled, grabbing Whifler's arm and forcing it in front of him as he tore the man away from Mellie, then relieved him of his pistol, and a smaller one tucked in his waistcoat. "Arms aren't allowed in the drawing room at Hillcrest, whatever the custom is at—what d'you call it again, Coxcomb Manor?"

"Chilcomb, damn you, *Chilcomb.*"

"Ollie, take care of these, will you?"

North held out the unmatched pistols. Threadwhistle unloaded them while the rest watched, mesmerized. Once he'd resumed them to Whifler, the earl shook himself, struggled from his chair, lumbered over, and inspected Mellie through his quizzing glass.

"That ain't my daughter," he said. "No, it ain't her. Amelia's—ah—taller, and she ain't so scrawny. Never saw this female in my life. Won't do you any good to claim she is, Reggie, because it's me the courts'll attend to, not you."

"You see?" North said, managing to smile despite clenched fists. "Your way won't work, Mellie. The earl won't turn over a penny for you to divide with Whifler so you can run away to wherever it is you intend to run next. Mine, however, will."

She shook her head. "Ah, no," she said, "yours won't work at all, Mr North."

Her dignity as she turned to her father amazed him.

"Question me, your lordship," she said. "Ask me anything."

"Won't prove a thing. Reggie coached you, or these fellows."

"I contracted the measles when I was four."

"Apothecary in the village could've told anyone that."

"No, he couldn't. The current apothecary is Jonas Whidby. Mr. Curzon was apothecary when I was four and died when I was seven, but he couldn't've told anyone either. It was Dr. Mayhew who attended me. He has four daughters, Mary, Jane,

Anne, and Cecelia. He carries peppermints in his waistcoat pocket. His wife died when I was ten, and—''

''Don't mean a thing,'' the earl insisted, regaining his seat. ''Common knowledge, all of it. Besides, who cares whether a chit was seen by an apothecary or a doctor? Not I, that's certain. Never cared for her above half. No sense of family or position. Good riddance, far's I'm concerned. Might as well be on your way, Reggie. There's nothing for you here.''

''My head was shaved,'' Mellie persisted. ''Before that my hair was straight, but it grew back in curls.''

''Don't give a da—fig what your hair was like, afore or after. Y'aren't going to trick me into saying you're someone you're not, so y'might as well take yourself off.''

North realized he'd never known what rage was. Irritation, yes. Even anger. Never this thing that made him want to tear a fellow human limb from limb and grind him into the dirt, and then do it again. He didn't dare move for fear he'd start.

''Mrs. North,'' the earl went on as if he'd said nothing untoward, ''I could do with a spot of nuncheon if you'd order it up. Nothing but slops at the inn. Then I'll join your son and his friends in a bit of fishing, tell 'em about the girls I got left. Pretty things, know their duty. Not like the dead one at all. Amiable pusses. Let him have one of those if the settlements're generous enough and my wants're seen to.''

That broke the spell. He could see again. North glanced at Mellie. He wanted to drag her into his arms and reassure her none of it made a speck of difference, that she could count on him even when she could count on no one else. Instead, he took her arm and guided her to stand beside the throne.

''I wonder what the *ton* will think when they learn your father was unable to recognize you after a separation of only a few months,'' he said in as offhand a manner as he could manage, clasping her icy hands in his. ''Especially when they learn of the disposition of your great-aunt's legacy, and how your father first intended to divide it with Whifler, and then appropriated the whole.''

''Don't matter what anyone says or thinks,'' Peasebotto insisted. ''If I say that gel ain't my daughter, there's not m you can do. How about that nuncheon, Mrs. North? Don't like to be kept waiting."

"Here now, this is interesting," St. Maure broke in. "Are you aware of your famous antecedents, my lord? Panderers and thieves, every last one of 'em, just like you. Y'see," he continued as Peasebottom turned ashen, mouth opening and closing like a beached fish's, "Viscount Edwin Peaseleigh did old Henry VIII the favor of marrying a yellow-haired trollop named Griselda Bottom to legitimize a couple of his favorite bastards. Combined their names to Peasebottom, and Harry made him an earl by way of thanks. That's how you got your title. There's not a drop of Peaseleigh's blood in you—just a king's and a whore's, and there's serious doubt about the king's. Seems Griselda had a habit of sneaking out to meet her pimp. It's all right here."

Whiffler stared from St. Maure to Mellie, his eyes like saucers.

"I'll dine out on this for months," he murmured. "Years, by God. And be invited everywhere. This is even better'n marrying the chit."

The earl stumbled from his chair with a roar. St. Maure closed *Extracts of the Origins of the Great Families* and rose, clasping the heavy volume in his arms like a breastplate. Dauntry and Sinclair stepped in front of him, blocking the earl.

"You see, my dear?" North declared. "Sometimes having a gossip-prone grandfather can be useful—not that I believed it until today."

"W-where'd you get that damnable thing?" his lordship spluttered. "Give it to me, b-blast you! Let me by. You ain't got a right to it. Thought I'd bought 'em all up. Paid enough for the last one, dammit, but they keep surfacing like corpses out of a bog. Nothing but a passel of lies. Written by a scandalmonger who didn't get things right. Didn't even use his own name, which proves it's all lies and inventions."

"Who is the young lady beside my mother?" North snapped. "Perhaps you should take another look. She might suddenly become familiar."

"I'll pay you for it," Peasebottom wheedled, lumbering from

one side to the other like a hog trying to reach a bucket of swill. "Fifty pounds."

North grabbed Peasebottom's arm and hauled him in front of his daughter. "Who is she?" he snarled.

"Don't know. Never saw her before in my life. A hundred pounds."

"Please don't do this," Mellie begged.

"Who is she?"

"Five hundred pounds. A thousand."

"No sale. Who is she?"

"My daughter, dammit! Amelia Caroline Regina Peasebottom. Born in ninety-one. Give me that cursed book."

"I'll have it in writing, along with your blessing on our nuptials. Tony, Quint, take him to the library and see he writes it out, including Mellie's pseudonym of Abigail Sparrow, that she was in my employ when I was unaware of her identity, and that he signs and dates it. He's to recant the identification of the abigail. Witness the thing. Then show him the door. Dab, he doesn't get *Extracts* until Ollie's satisfied all's right and tight, with no room for him to wiggle out of it like the slimy eel he is."

"Here now, I didn't say anything about any document," Peasebottom protested. "Out of the question."

"That's the price. Your choice. What's it to be?"

The earl glanced from the book to his daughter and shrugged.

"Mellie will inform you of her solicitor's name and direction within the week," North continued. "You'll provide him a complete accounting of her inheritance, including every jewel, every property, and all funds. In their entirety," he stressed.

"But I can't. I told you, I already used my half."

"Then unuse it. There are ways. I'm sure you're experienced in them."

"But it'd beggar me!"

"I'm afraid that prospect doesn't concern me."

"I'll be more than content with the half that's left," Mellie said, sinking into the chair Dauntry'd brought her. "I wouldn't accept even that if I could avoid it."

"No, y'won't," North snapped. "You'll receive every sh

ling that's yours by law. The old sod should be grateful y'don't sue him for fraud. He's getting off light.''

''I have a mother and two sisters who are innocent in this.''

''Your sisters? Possibly. Your mother? I doubt it.''

''What's left,'' she insisted, ''or I'll marry Sir Reginald as originally planned.''

''Now, that's a clever, dutiful puss,'' Peasebottom beamed. ''Knew a daughter of mine couldn't be without a sense of family.''

''Marry her?'' Whifler squeaked. ''I wouldn't marry her now if the fortune were intact and I was to get all of it. When my mother learns your history, Peasebottom, she'll faint dead away. Has pride, my mother does. Great-granddaughter of a viscount. Doesn't want any scandal attached to our name. Reason she chose Lady Amelia—not a murmur about her anywhere before this. I've had a lucky escape, that's what I've had.''

North gauged Mellie's determined expression and shrugged. She was running true to form. ''Have it your way,'' he said, ''but you're a fool. He deserves to be taught a lesson. This won't teach him anything. I assume the estate's entailed. Whoever inherits it and the title has my sympathy.''

He strode to the door and opened it. Pike hadn't followed instructions. The footmen were lined up by the service door, too far to have caught more than a word in twenty, but close enough were they needed. He gestured for them to come back.

''Out, all of you,'' he said, turning to those in the drawing room. ''I'd like to be private with Mellie and my mother. Martin will see you to the earl's carriage, Whifler. A word of caution: Should news of today's occurrences, or the events in Town, or in Yorkshire, or anywhere else including the Willing Wench, find its way into *ton* drawing rooms—or any other location, no matter of what sort or in what part of society—I will personally extract your teeth, every last one of 'em. Slowly. One by one. And then break your jaw in so many places, you'll never be able to speak again. I hope I've made myself clear?''

''But what do I get?'' Whifler bleated. ''Sending Chuffy for ⌐he earl didn't come cheap. Then there's my shot at the inn, ⌐d those brats of yours cost me a pretty penny, in addition to which they made my life a misery, and their damned dog ruined three pairs of my boots and two walking sticks.''

"You keep your teeth—if you're lucky.''

Whifler's eyes narrowed. "Clear as a pikestaff you intend to marry her. Shouldn't think you'd want word of—that's right," he gulped, "y'said y'didn't. Well then, I'll dine out on Peasebottom's origins. There's one copy of that book, there's got to be dozens—unless you want to pay for my silence?''

"That well's run dry," North snapped, advancing on the toad as he unbuttoned his coat and started to remove it. "When I said anything relating to Lady Amelia, I meant anything *and* everything. That her father happens to benefit doesn't please me, but there's nothing I can do about it. How fond are you of your teeth, Whifler? I wouldn't mind beginning their extraction immediately in proof that I'm a man of my word.''

Whifler scuttled backward, mouth working, turned tail, and dashed for the front door. Martin reached it just before him and opened it wide. North laughed as the rotter tore through and stumbled down the steps to the drive, coattails flapping.

"The earl will join you in a moment," he called.

Then he sighed, watching as the fellows escorted Peasebottom up the stairs to the library on the floor above. Just like that it was over. Interesting, how vermin crumbled when confronted with resolution. Only a villain whose personal history wouldn't bear close examination would've been so effectively cowed by "Stowaker's" gossip.

He stepped back into the drawing room and closed the door to be confronted with resolution himself—by Mellie, who was rising from where she'd knelt in front of his mother.

"You will summon a carriage for me, please, Mr. North," she said.

"Why?''

"Because, given his love of his teeth, Sir Reginald will never utter a word against me. There's no more need for rescue, or pretending to a nonexistent inclination. It was kindly meant. For that you have my gratitude, as well as for ensuring I'll never be penniless. My thanks for your efforts.''

"You're bolting again. There's no need for that. You sa'

you wanted time, that we should learn more of each other. I don't agree, but you can have all the time you want. Stay. You're safe here, and my mother's an excellent chaperon. Besides, what am I to do about Robert and Tabitha?''

"Lady Kathryn is far more capable of advising you where they're concerned than I am. Her son bears a strong resemblance to Robby."

"But—"

"Lady Kathryn tells me a stage stops at the inn shortly after sunset.''

"No, dammit—at least you'll wait here. No, you won't do that either. You'll listen to reason, and you'll listen to it immediately," he barked.

"Valentine," his mother said, "leave well enough alone."

"But—"

"I believe you'd be wise to pass the rest of the day here, however, Amelia. You're likely to encounter the earl—I refuse to call him your father, for a more unnatural parent I've never seen—or Sir Reginald in the village. Without my son there, you might find yourself importuned in a manner you wouldn't care for. There's only so much Val can do to safeguard you. Prudence dictates you agree to his suggestion."

"I'm cognizant of Mr. North's many kindnesses." Mellie eased toward the door, eyes blank. "However, I feel that for his peace of mind as well as my own, it would be best if I make an immediate departure. Nobility should be stretched only so far."

"Naturally you must despise Hillcrest after the scene that took place in this room, and be eager to see the last of both it and us, and I'm certain even Val will admit he treated you shabbily in the beginning. Pericles Tidmarsh, indeed! No one will come bothering you if you agree to wait here—not even Val."

She stood there, looking from him to his mother. He nodded, not trusting his voice. She swept them a deep curtsy, murmuring, "Nevertheless, it's best if I depart as soon as possible. Lady Kathryn, Mr. North, again, my gratitude for your hospitality. If you will bid farewell to your friends for me, Mr. North, and to Tibbie and Robby?''

"But where will you go?"

"Bath, Bristol, Brighton. Timbuktu. It doesn't matter."

And then she was gone.

"Damn," he muttered, staring at the closed door. "Damn, damn, damn!"

"Was there ever such a nodcock?" his mother sighed. "Don't you realize there's something you've never admitted, even though it's written plain on your face every time you look at her? It's a detail a lady needs to hear. At least this one does. I suspect you'd fare better if you put it into words instead of merely demonstrating it every second of the day. Robert and Tabitha Tyne aren't the only ones who've learned mistrust in the interest of self-preservation."

Chapter Nineteen

The reception area was empty. She crossed it, ignoring the echo of her footsteps, and climbed the great staircase to the next floor, the walls staring down at her in reproof. The corridors were silent and untenanted. It was as if she were in a place from which all living things had been banished, or else fled at the sight of her.

Amelia went to the suite assigned her, wandering the rooms, gazing from the windows. Memorizing, just as she'd memorized his face that morning on the hill from which the estate took its name—not that there was the least hope of forgetting those deep blue eyes or the dark hair that plunged in a sharp V, or the fine laughter creases at the corners of his eyes and mouth.

It was well past noon. The early bustle had died. Woods and ornamental water lay somnolent beneath the bright sun. Distant voices lacked reality. She could smell lilacs, even with the windows barely cracked. She closed her eyes, drinking in the scents, the song of a robin that traveled clearly from a tree by the lake, a horse's nicker, the lowing of a cow. Time, for the moment, had ceased. So had the ability to feel except for sensing the vacuum she'd built about her, one unspoken word at a time, a fortress that kept her in as much as it kept others out.

Finally she opened her eyes, retrieved the spencer and sun shade, discarded the faded wildflowers, and dusted out the bonnet. Delaying her departure wasn't making matters easier. It was making them worse—the reason she'd refused North's offer of shelter until it was time for her to board the stage. If she lingered, she might never have sufficient fortitude to get in the carriage that would take her to the village.

She allowed herself one last look in the tall bedchamber pier glass, then ordered herself into the dressing room as she unfastened the striped gingham gown's tabs. Thinking wasn't permitted. She wouldn't dare think for hours, perhaps days. Certainly not until she was on the stage, her fare paid, with no possibility of glimpsing Hillcrest or its owner. She smoothed the lovely gown, then laid it on a bench where either Martha or Sally would find it later. The alterations had been few. Lady Kathryn could still get some use from it unless the memories it fostered gave her a distaste of it.

Slipping into the bombazine and fastening it was a matter of moments. She exchanged the elegant jean half boots she'd been wearing for the sturdy black things that belonged to Abigail Sparrow. Removing the pins from her hair, dipping a brush in the ewer on the washstand, and then attacking it vigorously to suppress the curls took little time. She pulled the long, golden tresses back, skinning them against her skull, and pinned them in their usual knot. Then she took down her portmanteau, tossed in the things that belonged to her previous life, and paused, puzzling.

What to do with the watch that had been her first downfall? There was no question now whose portrait it held, or to whom it belonged. Clamping her lips, she placed it in the center of the dressing table, crushing the temptation to take this one bit of Hillcrest with her. Like everything else, she had no right to it.

Then she donned her coal-scuttle bonnet, her pelisse, and her gloves, slipped her old black reticule over her wrist, picked up her portmanteau, and took one last glance around the bedchamber. The wildflowers on the nighttable still straggled in their little jug just as North had crammed them at dawn. Angus

McPherson's more elegant roses perfumed the room. She forced back tears, willing the pain and desolation to subside so she could put one foot in front of the other and leave this room before it spat her out.

She had no notion how long she stood there, but at last she was moving through the sitting room and out into the corridor, a great hollow where once there had been heart and mind and soul. Sally waited at the head of the stairs, white-faced, lips trembling.

"Can I help you with that, your ladyship?" She held out her hand for the portmanteau.

Amelia shook her head. "No, I'd best see to it myself. Please thank everyone belowstairs for me."

"You're truly leaving?"

"I'm afraid so."

"There's not a one of us wants you to go."

"It can't be helped, Sally. It's all been a silly misunderstanding, you see." She tried to smile, but couldn't quite manage it. "Midsummer madness, one might call it, though it's barely spring as yet. I've left Lady Kathryn's gown in the dressing room, and something else I believe belongs to her on the dressing table." She took several guineas from the reticule and pressed them on the girl. "Please divide this among everyone as is customary. One day Mr. North will bring the bride he loves to Hillcrest. Greet her with love and kindness for my sake, as well as for his."

Then, head high, one hand gripping the balustrade, the other her portmanteau, she carefully descended the stairs, not wanting an unlucky stumble either to end her life right then or, worse yet, make it impossible for her to quit Hillcrest.

The choked words "Bless you, my lady. I'll pray for you" followed her down the broad steps.

"Do that, Sally," she whispered. "I'll need every prayer I can get."

At last she reached the foot of the stairs. This time the reception area wasn't empty. Jitters stood beside a cloak bag and small trunk. Wordlessly he took her portmanteau and put it with the other luggage.

"I understood there would be a carriage waiting for me," she said.

"It will be ordered when your business at Hillcrest is concluded, my lady."

"Whose are those?" She pointed to the trunk and cloak bag.

"Mr. North's, my lady. If you will follow me, please?"

"No, I won't follow you. Why are you so formal with me? We're old friends, I thought."

"If you have a friend in this house at the moment, I cannot think who it is unless it might be Lady Kathryn or Mr. North. They're more tolerant of folly and ingratitude than we simpler folk. And yes, were they to learn I've been so honest with you, I'd probably be sacked for impertinence, for all I've been Mr. North's man since he inherited, and before that his father's. This way, if you please."

"Jitters, I've acted in the best interests of others."

"The common opinion is that you've played us all for fools, your ladyship, and used both Mr. North and his mother without regard for their feelings or merits. When Mrs. Pickles hears of this, she'll be greatly disillusioned. She believed you a true lady. Of course, I suppose it's entirely proper for the daughter of an earl to treat a mere gentleman in any manner she chooses. Rank has its privileges."

"You don't understand," she pleaded, white-faced.

"No, I don't—but then, neither I nor any others here or on Wilton Street have served among those with elevated handles to their names, and so have no notion what is considered acceptable in such circles."

"But Sally came—"

"Sally Pitcher is very young, my lady, and far too impressionable. She confused a lovely face with a beautiful soul. The others were not so easily taken in. Mr. North offered you his heart and his hand. You spurned both."

"No, Jitters," she sighed, "he forced the protection of his name on me when Sir Reginald recognized me at the Willing Wench. There was no offer made or accepted, and I could never impose on his generosity by permitting such a sacrifice, no matter what the circumstances. Mr. North deserves a wife he can love and respect, not one thrust upon him by mischance. Were I to be so lacking in conscience as to wed him, Mrs. Pickles would have far greater reason to despise me.''

Jitters studied her for a moment, frowning. "So that's the way of it,'' he muttered. "Now I understand. The other made no sense. You might consider the possibility that just as we misjudged the situation, so have you.''

"That possibility doesn't exist. I'm merely a burden Mr. North is attempting to shoulder out of a misplaced sense of responsibility. I honor him for the intent, but will never countenance the travesty. I couldn't bear to see him become a martyr to what he considers his duty.''

The elderly valet shook his head, turned, and went toward the back of the house, opened a hidden door, and waited. After a moment she followed. They descended some steps into what appeared to be an older part of the house, the ceilings lower, the walls darker. The journey through the warren of empty rooms and silent corridors seemed endless.

"Where are you taking me?" she said finally.

"The estate offices. Mr. North has some business to see to before, well, before.''

"Before what?''

"That is what he wishes to discuss with you. I'm not playing him false by telling you that much. Pride's a poor companion though. Keep that in mind.'' And then he stopped before a dark wooden door with nothing to set it apart from the others they'd passed. Jitters opened it without knocking. "Lady Amelia, sir,'' he said.

The room was plain, whitewashed where it wasn't paneled, heavy beams supporting the plain ceiling. A clerk's desk stood to one side of an exterior door. Banks of cabinets and bookcases containing what had to be centuries of estate records flanked a blackened stone fireplace whose thick oak mantel held tankards and a pair of lamps. On the other side of the outer door a massive worktable had been placed before a window opening on a cobbled courtyard. Stable block and paddocks stood lifeless in the distance. Beyond them a hill of lilacs formed a living curtain that shimmered like watered silk in the afternoon sun.

North glanced up from the sheaf of papers he'd been going over with his bailiff. "Thank you Jitters," he said. "Have the traveling carriage brought up in half an hour. That should give us enough time. Take a seat, if you please, my lady." He gestured at the chairs ranged before the worktable.

She sat as the door closed behind the elderly valet. This was the heart of Hillcrest, the most personal and yet impersonal room on the entire estate. Why did he want her there? For convenience? Because it was a room he wouldn't have to enter every day?

It didn't matter. Half an hour, and she'd be gone. She could endure that much. Just so must a soldier lie in the surgeon's tent counting the last moments he had two arms or two legs, only it wasn't an arm or a leg she'd be leaving there. It was what remained of her battered heart. They said the wounded felt pain in a limb long after it was cut off. Hearts, she suspected, would prove the same.

"That's it, then, Fields," North continued as if she weren't there—an entirely different person from the one she'd known, not a laugh or a prank or a joke in him. "New thatch for the Parmenter and Crofton cottages, a rebuilt chimney for the Mowbrys, and the far paddock to be repaired and extended. And the nursery and schoolroom quarters to be brought up to snuff, of course. Consult with my mother, do whatever she says is necessary or desirable. Beyond that, everything as we discussed at Christmas. The refurbishing of my apartments and the ladies' sitting room can wait another year or two. No hurry about that now."

The bailiff put the sheaf of papers between a pair of covers and set them aside on the worktable. "Then if there's nothing else, Mr. North?" he said.

"No, that's everything. You're in charge. Contact me through Burridge. He'll know where to find me."

Fields gave her a curt nod and a muttered "My lady," and was gone.

"You're in traveling clothes," she said as soon as the door closed.

"As it happens. I see you've turned yourself back into Abigail Sparrow. I suppose that was to be expected, but I'd be grateful if you'd remove that abomination on your head. Calling it a bonnet gives it far too much dignity," he said with a grin that didn't reach his eyes. "Call it a scuttle, and be done with it."

She sat unmoving, hands tightly folded. After a moment he rose and turned to stare out the window. Somewhere a sparrow chirped, a commonplace sound that had no reality in this gulf of silence they were creating. It seemed hardly possible that just hours before they'd climbed the hill to the old oak, gathered flowers, stood beneath its generous branches, even laughed.

"You've been paid for a year's employment," he said. "My mother tells me replacing a governess on moment's notice is difficult, not to say impossible. I'm going to have to ask you to stay until one is found."

She shuddered at the thought of the phantom who would greet her in every room, on every hill and path. "I can't. Some other arrangement must be made."

"I'm afraid not, especially as I don't want my mother burdened with constantly seeing to them. She fulfilled her duties in that regard with my sisters and me. Once is enough to have one's nights interrupted by childhood illnesses and infant nightmares."

"If it's the money," she said, untying the strings of her reticule and pulling out her purse, "I won't need half what you paid me, and will be glad to sign a note for the total at any rate of interest you consider appropriate. I should be able to repay you in a month or two at most."

"I don't give a damn about the money. You're welcome to every penny I have with the exception of what it would take to keep my mother comfortably housed." He sighed and turned, regarding her through eyes she couldn't read, his hands gripping the chair's back. "There's the matter of your safety until your father accepts he can no longer force you to anything you don't wish."

"He's gone. I assume you have the paper he signed? Well then, there's nothing over which to be concerned."

"There's more than enough, believe me. The notion of relinquishing your inheritance is so contrary to the earl's view of how the world should be ordered that he hasn't even begun to grasp it yet. My grandfather's book was a ruse to get him out of the house, nothing more—the first time I've been glad the blasted thing exists. The old gentleman had a devilish sense of humor, and enjoyed bringing the self-important up short. It's all true, the stuff in those books, but there were times when I heartily wished it weren't widely suspected he was the author. Made my life a misery on occasion."

"I see," she said.

He looked at her strangely, mouth thinning, almost as if he were recalling something. "Full circle," he muttered, then shrugged, dismissing whatever it was as unimportant.

"The point is," he said, "by now his lordship is certain to have come up with some plot to do away with you, at worst, or retain what's rightly yours, at best. Whifler's more or less dealt with. Where your father's concerned, you're making it impossible for me to accomplish as much. You need the protection of my name and the forces I can marshal to stand at your back and bring him to reason. I'll do what I can, but it won't be as much as I'd like, or consider necessary for peace of mind. I wish you'd reconsider for your own sake, if not for mine."

"I can't, though I appreciate your concern. I believe it's exaggerated, however. The earl would never dare act openly against me, glad though he was to seize an opportunity when it offered itself at the cost of a few misspoken words and a blind eye."

"You think not? I disagree, but if you refuse, there's not much I can do about it. If you insist on leaving today"—he continued strolling over to the clerk's desk and consulting a ledger on it—"I'm afraid it will have to be in my company. There's no one else I trust to see to your safety anywhere but at Hillcrest, not even Tony or Quint. Sally and Jitters will go with us for propriety's sake. My mother's seeing to that right now. We'll give it out you're a recently widowed connection of some sort. Of course, you could delay your departure until tomorrow.''

He dipped a pen in the well, made some notations, continued to study it with his back to her, running his finger down long columns of figures. ''My mother's offered to take you to Brighton if you refuse to remain here,'' he said, ''or else to stay with one of my sisters, but that shouldn't be necessary. I'd form part of those bargains as well, so I doubt they'd be any more to your liking. To Hillcrest as a haven you can have no objection, and I have sufficient staff here to ensure you're protected. It's only my presence you find contrary to your taste, and I'll be ridding you of it within the hour, so long as you stay.''

''But where will you go?''

He set the pen in the pewter standish, capped the inkwell, and closed the ledger, each movement precise, almost mechanical.

''Bath, Brighton, Bristol. Timbuktu was mentioned, I believe. One place will be much the same as another. As I don't care, why should you?''

''You can't leave,'' she whispered. ''There are too many who depend on you.''

''Fields will see to things. In the meantime you'll be safe.''

He was by the fireplace now. She turned to watch as he inspected the empty grate, almost as if he expected to find coals burning there.

''I like the thought of you at Hillcrest, even if I can't be here,'' he said. ''Then in a year, when people have forgotten the murmurs about the earl's daughter who bolted rather than wed Whifler, and your father's been brought to heel, my mother will take you to London for the Season. We've already discussed it.''

''You have? How officious. And unnecessary.''

She was flushing, whether from mortification or fury, she wasn't certain. That a man could be so unfeeling was no surprise, but she'd thought better of Lady Kathryn. They hadn't said much. There hadn't been time, but she'd suspected her ladyship understood why she could never become Hillcrest's next mistress, how impossible it would be for her to become mistress elsewhere.

North turned to examine her, mouth twisting. He almost looked bitter. Well, he was probably insulted. She'd heard it took some gentlemen that way when they were refused—even when they wanted to be.

"With any luck, you'll meet someone more in keeping with your idea of what the husband of an earl's daughter should be," he said, turning away again and straightening the lamps and tankards on the mantel. "Or, if there's no one there who meets your standards, you can remain a wealthy spinster. Wherever I have a home, its doors will always be open to you."

She felt as if she were falling into the abyss of words they'd created.

"It's not like that at all," she protested.

He turned again, a tankard dangling from his hand as he stared at her, his expression inscrutable. "No? Then how is it?"

"I can't stay here. And you must."

"But I'm not. I owe you that much, at least."

"You owe me nothing, Mr. North."

"I owe you everything—Robert and Tabitha's safety and well-being, and their improved manners, among others—but I don't believe I'm thinking of debts at the moment. I can't be comfortable unless I know you are, so I suppose one might say it's my own comfort and convenience I'm considering."

"Will you stop being so noble? I despise martyrs," she snapped. "That's why I went to London—because I refused to be turned into one." She'd thought she wanted his voice to be cold and his eyes hard? Well, she had her wish now, for all the good it was doing her. Each word was a dagger, each glance a small death.

"Then why be one now?" He returned the tankard to the mantel with the same care he'd shown earlier with inkwell and pen, adjusted the angle of another. "You are, you know, insisting on going off like this. I doubt you've even considered where you'll go, or what you'll do there, or how you'll liv once you arrive. As you won't accept heart and hand, at least accept my assistance."

"You never offered those," she protested. "You merely insisted on a marriage of great inconvenience to you and great convenience to me."

"What the devil d'you think I did on the hill this morning? What d'you think I was doing the entire time we journeyed here?" He slammed the next tankard down. She could hear his teeth grinding from halfway across the room. "Dammit, Mellie, a man can take only so much." He stalked over to her, shoulders squared, fists clenched. "Will you stay, or will you leave? The first decent posting house is some hours distant, and time is passing."

"I'm of no use to anyone at Hillcrest, as you won't permit me to have charge of Tibbie and Robby—only now you will, won't you. You just said you would."

"Yes, you can have charge of Freddy's droolers if that pleases you."

"But I still don't understand why you want me here. It shouldn't matter to you where I am."

"It does, however. It matters terribly."

"Then I believe I might better stay." She reached up with trembling hands to untie the bonnet ribbons. "I don't want to be a bother, and it seems I have been."

"All right, then. Good. That's settled. My mother will be glad of the company."

"But only if you do."

"We've already agreed I can't remain if you do. I make you uncomfortable."

"Yes, you do. Very uncomfortable. More uncomfortable than anyone's ever made me."

"Well then, you see?"

"No, I don't see—except I think I do now, and Jitters was right, and what's more, I have no more interest in business arrangements than I have in martyrdom."

"Business arrangements! Jitters? What the devil are you talking about?"

"You forced the protection of your name on me at the Willing

Wench—and a more misnamed inn I've never heard mention of, for I was anything but willing, let me tell you. Now you're attempting it again in a different guise. Well, I won't have it." She dropped the bonnet on the floor and rose. "Why do you want me to stay? For my own safety? To relieve you of an obligation? To see to Tibbie and Robby? To keep your mother company while you go off to Timbuktu? To salve your conscience? Why?"

"Because without you Hillcrest will be a wasteland, blast it. Because the sun will never shine here again if you leave."

"Why?"

"Why? Because nothing can survive without sunshine, Mellie, not even I. If I try it, I fall into the dismals and can't cut so much as a single caper. Y'wouldn't have such a dreadful fate befall me, would you? I've got to know it at least shines on Hillcrest."

"But why should my departure cause such havoc?"

He stared at her, looking as if he'd dearly love to throw something, then went to the window and leaned against the sill, looking toward the lilac-covered hill.

"Because I love you, dammit," he muttered, his back turned. "Satisfied?"

"I'm sorry—I couldn't quite hear you."

"Because I love you," he shouted. "I love you more than life itself—and don't ask me the why of that, for you're the most difficult, contrary female it's ever been my misfortune to encounter."

He turned to her then, haloed by the sun, his features almost invisible.

"I don't give a damn about duty and honor, or your reputation, or any of the rest of that nonsense," he said more calmly. "I want to marry *you.* I want *you* to be my wife. That's what I've wanted for longer than I can tell, though it's been a long time and I've fought it every step of the way. You terrified me. I terrified myself, deuce take it. Why d'you think I refused to see you? Why d'you think I wanted no more of Chloe? Go knows when I started, but I suspect it was that first day y came to Wilton Street. You do have the most wonderful voice, you know.''

He was across the room, gripping her shoulders with hands that shook, or else it was she who was trembling, or perhaps it was both. She could see his eyes now. They weren't cold or hard. They pleaded as she'd never seen eyes plead before.

''Please, Mellie? I know I'm no great prize. I have a dreadful temper when I'm crossed or happen on an injustice. I doubt I'll ever stop playing pranks. Lord knows, my father never did. It's in the blood, just like my grandfather's damnable book. That was a prank on the grand scale. He spent his whole life at it, or almost. You'd be saddled with the fellows, and I'd insist on their being able to stay whenever they wish or need to. Quint, in particular, has a devil of a time of it at home. He's not wanted now that his elder brother's produced an heir, but his father made him sell out after Salamanca for fear that'd never happen, and now he has nothing. And then there're Tabitha and Robert, and any we might have of our own. At least the house is big enough to hold us all.''

She was barely able to see him through her tears, and she definitely hadn't lost her heart for all she'd given it away, for the drafted thing was pounding so fiercely, she thought it would knock her across the room. ''Do we have to be on the hill for me to say yes, or may I say it here?'' she gulped.

''Good God—my mother was right. She said showing you every way I could would never be enough. Oh, Lord, Mellie, I'm sorry. I thought you understood, dammit. There'd've been other ways to ensure your reputation.''

And then she was in his arms, clinging to him and spilling every tear she hadn't permitted herself and forgetting the ones she had.

While they settled essentials privately in Hillcrest's unromantic estate offices—though they would always argue about who tumbled top over tail first, for she insisted it couldn't't've happened that first day when he was Pericles Tidmarsh and she was Abigail Sparrow—his grinning face and merry waves told the tale as North dragged Amelia into the sunshine moments later, bustled her across the cobbled courtyard and past the cutting garden, up the path and through the woods to the crest of the hill. They ran the same gauntlet they had that morning, though she claimed later it was worse because of the cheering and the pelting with flowers old Angus McPherson insisted he never grudged. Good news at Hillcrest had a habit of traveling even more quickly than bad.

Valentine North and Amelia Peasebottom were married a month later surrounded by the Irregulars, who declared themselves equally delighted and dismayed by this first feminine breach of their masculine company. Tibbie served as flower girl, a decorated Beezle romping at her heels. North's two sisters arrived to act as Amelia's attendants, bringing their families with them. Robby bore the ring to the altar with solemn pride and many a peep at Lady Kathryn for nods of encouragement. It was, all declared, a perfect wedding, for the sun shone on it, the breezes were light, and no one was there from Bottomsley Court to mar the day's joy.

At Amelia's insistence, there was no bride journey. Instead, they passed the summer at Hillcrest, taking Robby and Tibbie on picnics and fishing, visiting in the neighborhood, and entertaining North's band of friends whenever they stopped by. When summer slid into fall, a tutor arrived. Skilled in cricket as well as Latin, conversant with riding as well as mathematics, Mr. Acres soon convinced Robby there were practical uses for a knowledge of angles and sums and the ways in which the great Caesar had planned his battles. Amelia continued Tibbie's instruction until just after Boxing Day, when she informed North a governess would soon be essential, as she'd be presenting him with their first child in May, and would have little time for Tibbie for a while. Lady Kathryn's and North's joy on hearing the news was unbounded.

Old Burridge, whatever his faults, was efficient. A solicitor the earl couldn't ignore arrived at Bottomsley Court a week after his return from Hillcrest. Shortly thereafter, Amelia came into delayed possession of her shrunken inheritance. She retained the jewels out of affection for her great-aunt. Knowing the old lady would've approved, she set aside the rest to be divided between Robby and Tibbie upon their majorities, as North's children would never lack for anything.

Chloe Sherbrough—in her guise of Edwina Suttersby—wed Aaron Burridge within days of her former protector's quitting London to search for his wards. She made North's man of business a passable wife, not straying from her vows that he knew, not outrunning the constable, and never presuming on her former relationship with North. Social intercourse didn't exist between the two couples, however, and Burridge became more formal than ever in his dealings with his employer. It was as if, whatever he claimed publicly when Robby and Tibbie disappeared, the man realized Chloe's tale of woe had more of theatrics than reality to it.

The Grimbles sold the house on Milbury Place and departed for the Colonies, taking Bessie and Florrie with them. Sir Reginald Whifler never did find another lady to accept him, and upon his mother's death got what he could for Chilcomb Manor and sailed to join his former co-conspirators. Word eventually reached Burridge, who had the man watched on North's orders, that he'd opened a gaming house and married Bessie Scrudge. The rest of the Milbury Place band disappeared into the stews from which they'd sprung, never to be found.

And North's Irregulars? As would be expected, Lady Amelia's was only the first of many breaches, though they remained the most devoted of friends, ever ready to come to each other's assistance—or to play a prank or cut a caper—when the occasion arose.

ABOUT THE AUTHOR

Monique Ellis lives in Arizona with her husband, Jim, a gifted artist and popular watercolor instructor. The author of five other Zebra Regency novels as well as four anthologized novellas, she is currently working on her fifth novella, *The Year Father Christmas Came Calling,* to be included in Zebra's 1998 Christmas anthology. To answer the obvious questions: Yes, North's Irregulars will have further adventures; yes, characters from the Fortescue series will appear in future books; and yes, two characters from *Three Nights in a Country Inn* in Zebra's *A Winter Wedding* anthology (January 1998) will appear in her Christmas tale.

Monique loves to hear from readers, and can be reached at P.O. Box 24398, Tempe AZ 85285-4398. Please include a stamped, self-addressed envelope if you wish a response.